The Least Likely Bride

JANE
FEATHER

WHEELER
PUBLISHING, INC.
ROCKLAND, MA

★ AN AMERICAN COMPANY ★

Published in Large Print by arrangement with Bantam Books, a division of Random House, Inc. in the United States and Canada.

Wheeler Large Print Book Series.

Set in 16 pt Plantin.

Library of Congress Cataloging-in-Publication Data

Feather, Jane.
　The least likely bride / Jane Feather.
　　p. (large print) cm.(Wheeler large print book series)
　ISBN 1-56895-877-3 (hardcover)
　1. Pirates—Fiction. 2. Large type books. I. Title. II. Series

[PS3556.E22 L24 2000b]
813'.54—dc21

00-026762
CIP

Preface to The Brides Trilogy

LONDON, MAY 11, 1641

Phoebe swiped one hand across her eyes as she felt for her handkerchief with the other. The handkerchief was nowhere to be found, but that didn't surprise her. She'd lost more handkerchiefs in her thirteen years than she'd had hot dinners. With a vigorous and efficacious sniff, she crept around the hedge of clipped laurel out of sight of the clacking, laughing crowd of wedding guests. The high-pitched cacophony of their merrymaking mingled oddly with the persistent, raucous screams of a mob in full cry gusting across the river from Tower Hill.

She glanced over her shoulder at the graceful half-timbered house that was her home. It stood on a slight rise on the south bank of the river Thames, commanding a view over London and the surrounding countryside. Windows winked in the afternoon sunlight and she could hear the plaintive plucking of a harp persistent beneath the surge and ebb of the party.

No one was looking for her. Why should they? She was of no interest to anyone. Diana had banished her from her presence after the accident. Phoebe cringed at the memory. She could never understand how it happened that her body seemed to get away from her, to have a life of its own, creating a wake of chaos and destruction that followed her wherever she went.

But she was safe for a while. Her step quickened as she made for the old boathouse, her own private sanctuary. When her father had moved the mansion's water gate so that it faced the water steps at Wapping, the old boathouse had fallen into disrepair. Now it nestled in a tangle of tall reeds at the water's edge, its roof sagging, its timbers bared to the bone by the damp salt air and the wind.

But it was the one place where Phoebe could lick her wounds in private. She wasn't sure whether anyone else in the household knew it still existed, but as she approached she saw that the door was not firmly closed.

Her first reaction was anger. Someone had been trespassing in the one place she could call her own. Her second was a swift pattering of fear. The world was full of beasts, both human and animal, and anyone could have penetrated this clearly deserted structure. Anyone or anything could be lying in wait within. She hesitated, staring at the dark crack between door and frame, almost as if the tiny crack could open to reveal the dim, dusty interior for her from a safe distance. Then her anger reasserted itself. The boathouse belonged to *her*. And if anyone was in there, she would send them off.

She turned into the rushes, looking for a thick piece of driftwood, and found an old spar, rusty nails sticking out in a most satisfactory fashion.

Thus armed, she approached the boathouse, her heart still pattering but her face set. She kicked the door open, flooding the dark mildewed corners with light.

"Who are you?" she demanded of the occupant, who, startled, blinked but didn't move from her perch on a rickety three-legged stool by the unglazed window where the light fell on the page of her book.

Phoebe entered the shed, dropping her weapon. "Oh," she said. "I know who you are. You're Lord Granville's daughter. What are you doing here? Why aren't you at the wedding? I thought you were supposed to carry my sister's train."

The dark-haired girl carefully closed her book over her finger. "Yes, I'm Olivia," she said after a minute. "And I d-didn't want to b-be in the wedding. My father said I didn't have to b-be if I d-didn't want to." She let out a slow breath at the end of this little speech, which had clearly cost her some effort.

Phoebe looked at the girl curiously. She was younger than Phoebe, although she was as tall, and enviably slim to the eyes of one who constantly lamented her own intractable roundness. "This is my special place," Phoebe said, but without rancor, sitting on a fallen beam and drawing a wrapped packet from her pocket. "And I don't blame you for not wanting to be in the wedding. I was supposed to attend my sister, but I knocked over the perfume bottle and then trod on Diana's flounce."

She unwrapped the packet, taking a bite of

the gingerbread it contained before holding out the offering to Olivia, who shook her head.

"Diana cursed me up hill and down dale and said she never wanted to lay eyes on me again," Phoebe continued. "Which she probably won't, since she's going to be in Yorkshire, miles and miles away from here. And I have to say, if I never lay eyes on her again, I won't be sorry." She looked defiantly upward as if braving heavenly wrath with such an undutiful statement.

"I d-don't like her," Olivia confided.

"I wouldn't like her for a stepmother either.... She'll be absolutely horrible! Oh, I'm sorry. I always say the wrong thing," Phoebe exclaimed crossly. "I always say whatever comes into my head."

"It's the t-truth, anyway," the other girl muttered. She opened up her book again and began to read.

Phoebe frowned. Her stepniece, as she supposed Olivia now was, was not the friendliest of creatures. "Do you always stammer?"

Olivia blushed crimson. "I c-can't help it."

"No, of course you can't," Phoebe said hastily. "I was just curious." In the absence of a response from her companion, she moved on to the second piece of gingerbread, idly brushing at a collection of tiny grease spots that seemed to have gathered upon her pink silk gown. A gown specially made for her sister's wedding. It was supposed to complement Diana's pearl-encrusted ivory damask, but somehow on Phoebe the effect didn't quite work, as Diana had pointed out with her usual asperity.

There was a sudden whirlwind rush from the door that banged shut, enclosing the girls in semidarkness again. "God's bones, but if this isn't the peskiest wedding!" a voice declared vigorously. The newcomer leaned against the closed door. She was breathing fast and dashed a hand across her brow to wipe away the dew of perspiration. Her bright green eyes fell upon the boathouse's other occupants.

"I didn't think anyone knew this place was here. I slept here last night. It was the only way I could get away from those pawing beasts. And now they're at it again. I came here for some peace and quiet."

"It's my special place," Phoebe said, standing up. "And you're trespassing." The newcomer didn't look in the least like a wedding guest. Her hair was a tangled mass of bright red curls that didn't look as if it had seen a brush in a month. Her face looked dirty in the gloom, although it was hard to tell among the freckles what was dirt and what wasn't. Her dress was made of dull, coarse holland, the hem dipping in the middle, the perfunctory ruffles on the sleeves torn and grubby.

"Oh-ho, no I'm not," the girl crowed, perching on the upturned holey hull of an abandoned rowboat. "I'm invited to the wedding. Or at least," she added with scrupulous honesty, "my father is. And where Jack goes, I go. No choice."

"I know who you are." Olivia looked up from her book for the first time since the girl had burst in upon them. "You're m-my father's half b-br-brother's n-natural child."

"Portia," the girl said cheerfully. "Jack Worth's bastard. And so you must be Olivia. Jack was talking about you. And I suppose, if you live here, you're the bride's sister. Phoebe, isn't it?"

Phoebe sat down again. "You seem to know a great deal about us."

Portia shrugged. "I keep my ears open...and my eyes. Close either one of 'em for half a second and the devils'll get you."

"What devils?"

"Men," Portia declared. "You wouldn't think it to look at me, would you?" She chuckled. "Scrawny as a scarecrow. But they'll take anything they can get, so long as it's free."

"I loathe men!" The fierce and perfectly clear statement came from Olivia.

"Me too," Portia agreed, then continued with all the loftiness of her fourteen years, "But you're a little young, duckie, to have made such a decision. How old are you?"

"Eleven."

"Oh, you'll change your mind," Portia said knowledgeably.

"I won't. I'm n-never going to m-marry." Olivia's brown eyes threw daggers beneath their thick black eyebrows.

"Neither am I," Phoebe said. "Now that my father has managed to make such a splendid match for Diana, he'll leave me alone, I'm sure."

"Why don't you want to marry?" Portia asked with interest. "It's your destiny to marry. There's nothing else for someone as well born as you to do."

Phoebe shook her head. "No one would want to marry me. Nothing ever fits me, and I'm always dropping things, and saying just what comes into my head. Diana and my father say I'm a liability. I can't do anything right. So I'm going to be a poet and do good works instead."

"Of course someone will want to marry you," Portia stated. "You're lovely and curvy and womanly. I'm the one no one's going to marry. Look at me." She stood up and gestured to herself with a flourish. "I'm straight up and down like a ruler. I'm a bastard. I have no money, no property. I'm a hopeless prospect." She sat down again, smiling cheerfully as if the prophecy were not in the least disheartening.

Phoebe considered. "I see what you mean," she said. "It would be difficult for you to find a husband. So what will you do?"

"I'd like to be a soldier. I wish I'd been born a boy. I'm sure I was supposed to be, but something went wrong."

"I'm going to b-be a scholar," Olivia declared. "I'm g-going to ask my father to g-get me a t-tutor when I'm older, and I want to live in Oxford and study there."

"Women don't study at the university," Phoebe pointed out.

"I shall," Olivia stated stubbornly.

"Lord, a soldier, a poet, and a scholar!

What a trio of female misfits!" Portia went into a peal of laughter.

Phoebe laughed with her, feeling a delicious and hitherto unknown warmth in her belly. She wanted to sing, get to her feet and dance with her companions. Even Olivia was smiling, the defensive fierceness momentarily gone from her eyes.

"We must have a pact to support each other if we're ever tempted to fall by the wayside and become ordinary." Portia jumped to her feet. "Olivia, have you some scissors in that little bag?"

Olivia opened the drawstrings of the little lace-trimmed bag she wore at her waist. She took out a tiny pair of scissors, handing them to Portia, who very carefully cut three red curls from the unruly halo surrounding her freckled face.

"Now, Phoebe, let me have three of those pretty fair locks, and then three of Olivia's black ones." She suited action to words, the little scissors snipping away. "Now watch."

As the other two gazed, wide-eyed with curiosity, Portia's long, thin fingers with their grubby broken nails nimbly braided the different strands into three tricolored rings. "There, we have one each. Mine is the one with the red on the outside, Phoebe's has the fair, and Olivia's the black." She handed them over. "Now, whenever you feel like forgetting your ambition, just look at your ring....Oh, and we must mingle blood." Her green eyes, slanted slightly like a cat's, glinted with enthusiasm and fun.

She turned her wrist up and nicked the skin, squeezing out a drop of blood. "Now you, Phoebe." She held out the scissors.

Phoebe shook her fair head. "I can't. But you do it." Closing her eyes tightly, she extended her arm, wrist uppermost. Portia nicked the skin, then turned to Olivia, who was already extending her wrist.

"There. Now we rub our wrists together to mingle the blood. That way we cement our vow to support each other through thick and thin."

It was clear to Olivia that Portia was playing a game, and yet Olivia, as her skin touched the others', felt a strange tremor of connection that seemed much more serious than mere play. But she was not a fanciful child and sternly dismissed such whimsy.

"If one of us is ever in trouble, then we can send our ring to one of the others and be sure of getting help," Phoebe said enthusiastically.

"That's very silly and romantical," Olivia declared with a scorn that she knew sprang from her own fancy.

"What's wrong with being romantic?" Portia said with a shrug, and Phoebe gave her a quick grateful smile.

"Scholars aren't romantic," Olivia said. She frowned fiercely, her black eyebrows almost meeting over her deep-set dark eyes. Then she sighed. "I'd b-better go back to the wedding." She slipped her braided ring into the little bag at her waist. With a little reflective gesture, as if to give herself courage, she touched her wrist, thinly smeared with their shared blood, then went to the door.

As she opened it, the clamor from the city across the river swelled into the dim seclusion of the boathouse. Olivia shivered at the wild savagery of the sound. "C-Can you hear what they're saying?"

"They're yelling, 'His head is off, his head is off,' " Portia said knowledgeably. "They've just executed the earl of Strafford."

"But why?" Phoebe asked.

"Lord, don't you know anything?" Portia was genuinely shocked at this ignorance. "Strafford was the king's closest advisor and Parliament defied the king and impeached the earl and now they've just beheaded him."

Olivia felt her scalp contract as the bloody, brutal screech of mob triumph tore into the soft May air and the smoke of bonfires lit in jubilation for a man's violent death rose thick and choking from the city and its surroundings.

"Jack says there's going to be civil war," Portia continued, referring to her father with her customary informality. "He's usually right about such things...not about much else, though," she added.

"There c-couldn't be civil war!" Olivia was horrified.

"We'll see." Portia shrugged.

"Well, I wish it would come now and save me having to go back to the wedding," Phoebe said glumly. "Are you going to come, Portia?"

Portia shook her head, gesturing brusquely

to the door. "Go back to the party. There's no place for me there."

Phoebe hesitated, then followed Olivia, the ring clutched tightly in her palm.

Portia remained in the dimness with the cobwebs for company. She leaned over and picked up the piece of gingerbread that Phoebe had forgotten about in the events of the last half hour. Slowly and with great pleasure, she began to nibble at it, making it last as long as possible, while the shadows lengthened and the shouts from the city and the merrymaking from the house gradually faded with the sunset.

Prologue

THE ISLE OF WIGHT, JUNE 1648

IT WAS THE DARK HOUR before dawn. Rain fell in a ceaseless torrent upon the sodden clifftops and smashed straight as stair rods onto the churning, white-flecked sea beneath. Great waves rose in the Channel and surged around St. Catherine's Point to curl and break upon the jagged rocks in a thundering, relentless roll, sending white spray into the darkness.

There were no stars. No moon. Only an occasional flash of lightning to illuminate the island crouching like a whale at the entrance to the Solent, its downs and valleys black with rain. The melancholy sound of the bell buoy off the rocky point pierced the rushing wind, bringing warning to the ships battling the summer storm in the seething Channel. Warning and a welcome sense of security.

A small boat plunged into the troughs, the men at the oars grim-faced as they fought to keep the fragile craft upright. They approached the bell buoy, the boat vanishing into the waves, then bobbing up like a piece of driftwood. From the stern, one of the men hurled a rope around the buoy and hauled the boat hand over hand until it was touching the rocking buoy and the rhythmic sound of the bell was deafening amid the roar of the water and the wind and the ceaseless battering of the rain.

No one spoke; the words would have been torn from them anyway, but they had no need of speech. The oarsmen shipped their oars while the man in the stern held the boat fast to the buoy and one of his companions swiftly, deftly, with hands of experience, wrapped thick cloth around the bell's tongue, silencing the dull clang of its warning.

Then they sprang loose from the buoy and the small craft headed back to the beach. As they pulled against wind and tide, one of the men raised a hand, pointing to the clifftop. A light flickered, then flared strongly into the wind, a beacon throwing its deadly message into the storm-wracked night.

Willing hands waded into the surf to pull them ashore, hauling the boat up the small sandy beach. The men shivered in their soaked clothes and drank deep of the flasks thrust at them. There were maybe twenty men on the beach, dark-clad, shifting figures, blending into the darkness of the cliffs as they huddled with their backs to the rocks, their eyes straining across the surging sea, watching for their prey.

There was a sudden brighter flare from the clifftop and they moved forward as one.

And she came out of the darkness, white sails torn and flapping from her spars, the strained rigging creaking like old bones. She came heading for the light that promised a safe haven, and with a dreadful grinding and splitting she met the rocks of St. Catherine's Point.

Screams rose to do battle with the wind. Figures flew like so many remnants of cloth from the steep, yawing sides of the ship, plunging down into the boiling cauldron of the sea. The vessel cracked like an eggshell and the watchers on the beach raced into the foam, eyes glittering, voices raised in skirls of triumph. Desperate men, women, children, drowning in the maelstrom around the sinking ship, called to them, but they slashed with cutlasses, hammered with broken spars, finishing by hand what the sea would not do for them.

They dragged chests, boxes, bodies to the beach. They plundered the bodies, cutting off rings and ripping away fine garments, prancing around the beach in a mad and murderous dance of greed.

Above them on the clifftop a man stood close to the firelight of the treacherous beacon, his cloak pulled tight against the lashing rain. He gazed out at the doomed ship and smiled as he listened to the murderous mayhem in the foam as his men did their work. They had snared a fat pigeon on the rocks this storm-wracked night.

He turned and doused the fire. All was darkness again, only the sounds of the madness on the beach competing with the wind and the rain and the sea.

Out beyond the point, another ship wrestled with the storm. She carried no sail and her master stood at the wheel, holding her into the wind. His slender frame was deceptive, belying the hard bunched muscles, the strength in the long, slim hands, that fought the storm that would tear his ship from him, while he listened for the warning bell off St. Catherine's Point.

"The beacon's gone, sir," the helmsman shouted in his ear against the tempest's roar.

The master looked up at the clifftop where the betraying flare had shown, and now they could hear the screams that were not the screams of gulls in the wild night, and under a great flash of lightning, the stark outline of the vessel on the rocks sprang out, for a second hideously illuminated.

And still there was no sound of the bell off St. Catherine's Point.

A strange and heavy silence fell over the ship, its men for an instant falling still in their fight with the storm. To a man they had all sailed these waters from boyhood, and they knew their hazards. And they knew that the worst danger of all came from the shore.

"May God have mercy on their souls," the helmsman muttered, crossing himself involuntarily.

"She looks like a merchantman," the master returned, his voice cold and distant. "There'll be rich pickings. They chose a good night."

"Aye," the helmsman muttered again, his scalp crawling as the screams of the dying were lost in the crash of the waves that pounded the broken-backed vessel to so many shards and splinters.

One

THE SUN SHONE hot and bright upon the now quiet waters of the English Channel. Olivia Granville strolled the narrow cliff path above St. Catherine's Point, for the moment oblivious of her surroundings, of the fresh beauty of the rain-washed morning after the night's storm. She bit deep into her apple, frowning over the tricky construction of the Greek text she held in her hand.

The grass was wet beneath her sandaled feet and long enough in places to brush against her calves, dampening her muslin gown. A red admiral was a flash of color across the white page of her book, and a bee droned among the fragrant heads of the sea pinks.

Olivia glanced up, for a moment allowing her attention to wander from her text. The sea stretched blue and smooth as bathwater to the Dorset coastline faintly visible on the horizon. It was hard now to imagine the ferocity of the storm that had wrecked the ship she could see far below on the rocks. Men swarmed antlike over her at the work of salvage. The talk in the house this morning had been all of the wreck, of how it was believed that the ship had been deliberately lured to its death by the smugglers and wreckers who had become very active on the island during the past winter.

Olivia drew a deep breath of the salt-and-seaweed-laden air. The sixth winter of the civil war had been an interminable one. A year ago it had seemed it was all but over. King Charles had surrendered to Parliament and was held in London at the palace of Hampton Court, while negotiations for a permanent end to the war took place. But then the king had reneged on his parole, had broken all tentative agreements, and had escaped from Hampton Court.

He had fled to the Isle of Wight, a royalist stronghold, and had put himself under the protection of the island's governor, Colonel Hammond. The colonel had proved no royalist friend to the king, instead following his duty to Parliament, holding the king an informal prisoner in Carisbrooke Castle. As a result, the protracted negotiations with Parliament had perforce moved to the island.

Olivia's father, the marquis of Granville, was a leading Parliamentarian and one of the foremost negotiators, so at the end of the preceding year he had moved his oldest daughter, his nine-month-old son, and his once again pregnant fourth wife to the island. His two younger daughters had been left at their own request in the quiet Oxfordshire house where they had lived for the preceding three years under the care of their adored governess.

On the island, Lord Granville had acquired

a long, low, thatch-roofed house in the village of Chale, just a few miles beyond the great stone walls of the royal prison at Carisbrooke Castle. The house was cramped and drafty in winter, but at least it was outside the castle. For Olivia and her father's wife—who was also her own dearest friend, Phoebe—such accommodations were infinitely preferable to life in a military compound. The king continued to hold court in the castle's great hall, and an attempt was made to disguise the true nature of his situation, but nothing could disguise the military nature of his surroundings.

Olivia had spent her first sixteen years in her father's massive fortress on the Yorkshire border, and during the early years of the civil war she had grown accustomed to a life lived for all intents and purposes under siege; but when the war had moved south, so had Lord Granville.

She had grown soft, Olivia thought now, with a half smile, stretching under the sun's warmth. Her northern resilience had been eroded by the south's mild climate and gentle vistas. She was accustomed to deep snow and bitter cold, and the damp drizzle of a southern winter offered no challenges to the soul. It brought a dank chill that seeped into your bones, and the northeast wind blowing off the sea was a vicious thing indeed, but it grew monotonous rather than menacing.

But here now was summer. And it was as if the winter had never been. Here were brilliant skies and the wonderful expanse of the sea. She had never before known the sea. There were moors and mountain ranges in her native Yorkshire, and winding rivers in the Thames valley that she had called home for the past three years, but nothing to compare with this wondrous sense of expansion, this vast vista where sea met sky and promised only infinity.

Olivia threw her apple core far out across the headland and felt her soul lift, her spirit dance. There were sails out there, pretty white sails on lively craft. Below her, gulls wheeled and drifted on the currents of warm air, and Olivia envied them their wonderful freedom, the ability to give themselves to the current without purpose or necessity, but for the sheer joy of it.

She laughed aloud suddenly and took a step closer to the edge of the cliff. She stepped into a patch of undergrowth. She stepped into nothing.

THERE WAS PAIN, a confused morass of pain against which no one hurt stood out, distinguishable. There was a murmur of voices, one in particular, a quiet voice that accompanied cool hands upon her body, turning, lifting, anointing. A pair of gray eyes penetrated the dream tangle where all was confusion and fear. There was a drink of gall and wormwood that brought a muddled skein of terrifying images in the world of nightmares, things she could put no name to that writhed around her like Medusa's serpents.

She fought the bitter drink, knocking away the hands that held the cup to her lips. The quiet voice said, "Just one more, Olivia," and her flailing hands were held in a clasp, cool and firm, and her head rested in the crook of an arm.

With a little moan, she surrendered to a strength and a will much greater than her own, and the foul liquid slipped between her parted lips so that she swallowed in a choking gasp of distaste.

And this time she sank into a dark pool, and the green waters closed over her head. The hurt receded and now there were no nightmares, only the deep, restful sleep of healing.

OLIVIA OPENED HER EYES. What she saw made no sense, so she closed them again. After a minute, she opened them once more. Nothing had changed.

She lay very still, hearing her own breathing. There was no other sound. Her body was filled with a delicious languor, and she had no desire to move. As she took inventory, she was aware of a stiff soreness at the back of one thigh, a certain tenderness here and there, but as she ran her hands languidly over her body, everything seemed to be where it was supposed to be.

Except that she was naked.

She remembered standing on the cliff path, throwing her apple core across the headland. Then there were dreams, nightmares, voices, hands. But they had been part of the dreams, not real.

Her eyes closed and the deep pool took her again.

When next she swam to the surface, she could sense movement around her. Men were talking in hurried whispers; a chair scraped; a door opened and closed. Her breathing quickened with the atmosphere of urgency around her, but she kept her eyes tight shut, instinctively reluctant to draw attention to herself until she could regain a sense of herself in whatever this place was.

In the renewed quiet, she opened her eyes. She was lying on her back in a bed that was not a bed. Or at least it resembled no bed she had slept in before. Tentatively she moved her legs and encountered wooden sides. They were not high, but it felt as if she was lying in a box. She looked up at a ceiling of oak planking. An unlit lantern hung from a chain. But there was no need for lamplight, because great slabs of sunlight slanted into the room from latticed windows a few feet from the foot of the bed.

But the wall wasn't straight. It was paneled in some glowing wood and curved. The windows were set into the curves, and they stood open, soft sea scents wafting in on a gentle breeze.

Olivia turned her head on the pillow. She turned it tentatively because it hurt a little to do so. The pillow beneath her cheek was crisp and smelled of the flatiron and fresh morning air.

She looked into a chamber, a paneled room with latticed windows and rich Turkey carpets on the shining oak floor. There was an oval table and a sideboard, several carved chairs. But it was not a regularly shaped room. It had no corners. And it seemed to be moving. Very gently, but definitely. Rocking like a cradle.

Olivia's eyes closed once more.

When she next awoke, the sun still shone, the chamber still rocked gently. She was looking into the room as she had been when she'd fallen asleep. And this time she was not alone.

A man stood at the oval table, bent over some papers, working with something in his hand. He seemed to Olivia to be cast in gold; a shining aura surrounded him. Then she understood that he was standing in the sunlight from the window and the bright rays glinted off his hair. Hair the color of golden guineas.

He was completely absorbed in whatever he was doing. He held himself very still, only his hands moving. He seemed detached, centered on himself and his work. It was a quality Olivia recognized because it was her own. She knew what it was to lose oneself in the world of the mind.

She wondered whether to speak, but it seemed impolite to disturb his concentration, so she lay watching him through half-closed eyes, deep in the languid warmth of her peculiar bed. Her body was still sore, and the back of her head felt bruised. Other disparate aches and pains lingered with the slight

11

muzziness in her head. She felt remote, contented, the terrors of the nightmare world vanquished. And she was aware of the strangest connection between herself and the man at the table. It was puzzling but only vaguely so. Mostly it made her feel happy.

And then he spoke. He didn't raise his head or look up from his work, but he said in the harmonious voice she remembered from the dreams, "So, Sleeping Beauty returns to the world."

The question didn't so much break the silence as slide into it. "Who are you?" she asked. Of all the questions that came to mind, it seemed the only one of any importance.

He looked up then. His hand fell idly to the papers on the table as he regarded her, with a half smile on his lips. "I was expecting you to brush your brow and say, 'Where am I?' Or words to that effect."

When she didn't immediately reply, he came around the table and perched on the edge facing her, stretching his legs, crossing them at the ankle. The sun was behind him and his golden head was ablaze. He laughed, a light, merry sound. His teeth flashed white against the deep bronze of his complexion, and laugh lines crinkled at the corners of his deep-set gray eyes. "Don't you wonder where you are, Lady Olivia?"

She wondered if he was mocking her. She sat up, clutching the sheet to her chin. Only as she did so did she realize anew that she was naked. The sheet, crisp and fresh and clean, was all that lay between her bare skin and this man, who sat there so insouciant, laughing at her.

"How do you know my name?"

He shook his head. "No prescience, I'm afraid. 'Olivia' was sewn into all your undergarments. A common enough practice, I believe, in large households with busy laundresses. I had to undress you to tend to you, you understand." There was a glimmer of secret amusement in his eyes that made Olivia's skin prickle. Then he leaned sideways to a small table and picked up a book. It was the book she had been reading when she had stepped into thin air.

He flipped it open to the title page. "Olivia Granville." He held it for her so she could see where she herself had inscribed her name. "Aeschylus...not what I would call light reading." He raised an interrogative eyebrow, the smile still playing about his mouth. "So, Lord Granville's daughter is a Greek scholar?"

"You know my father?" Olivia rested her head on her drawn-up knees. She had the feeling that there should be some sense of urgency about this conversation, but somehow she could find none. She still felt remote, detached.

"I know of him. Who on the island doesn't know of the marquis of Granville? Such a conscientious jailer of His Sovereign Majesty." An ironic note entered his voice, and the smile was less pleasant.

Olivia flushed. It seemed she was in the company of a Royalist sympathizer. "My

13

father negotiates with the king for Parliament," she said stiffly. "He is no jailer."

"No?" Both eyebrows lifted, then he laughed again. "On politics, we shall agree to differ, Olivia.... Oh, by the bye, this was in the pocket of your gown. I put it in the book for safekeeping." He reached over and handed her a small ring of braided hair. "I would have put it on your finger, but I was afraid it might become unraveled and I assumed it had some special value."

Olivia took the ring. "Yes, it does." She held it tightly in her hand and it seemed to impart some greater sense of reality. The ring belonged to another world, to people who still seemed remote, but it helped her to feel grounded again. She waited for him to ask for an explanation, but he didn't, merely continued to perch on the table, lightly drumming his fingers on the highly polished surface.

"And what of your name?" she demanded, still stung by his tone when he'd spoken of her father, and yet still inexorably drawn to him as if with reins of silk.

"I am the master of *Wind Dancer*. You may call me Anthony, if it pleases you."

He made it sound as if he'd plucked the name from the air and didn't mind whether it was his or not. "Wind Dancer?" Olivia queried, seizing on this as one question that might bring enlightenment.

"My ship. You are aboard her and I'm afraid you'll have to remain so for a few more days." He picked up a piece of paper and a quill

14

from the table beside him, rising in leisurely fashion from the edge of the table. "It was not what I had intended, but we were obliged to set sail this morning, so I can't return you home until we return to safe haven."

As he moved away from the table, Olivia saw how tall he was, his head almost brushing the ceiling of the cabin. He was very lean, the ruffled sleeves of his white shirt rolled up to his elbows revealing strong brown forearms. His manner was relaxed, casual almost to the point of carelessness, but Olivia felt the power contained in the long, spare frame. A sense that he did nothing without purpose for all his air of easy indifference.

It had been his hands on her body. His were the cool, competent hands that had touched her so intimately, had lifted her, anointed her, held her head for the bitter draft that had brought her sleep. Her skin prickled again and a soft flush crept up her neck at memories she would rather not have.

He continued to talk casually from somewhere behind her, and she was glad not to have to look at him as the memories of his attentions rose with stark clarity.

"The cliffs on this side of the island can be hazardous. There are deep clefts and gullies that are concealed beneath the undergrowth. One false step and you can slip to the undercliff and beyond. I imagine you were so deep in your Greek that you didn't notice where the cliff gave way. But you were fortunate. You slid into a cleft and it delivered you neatly at the feet of one of my watchmen on the under-cliff."

Olivia pushed her hair away from her face. "When?"

"Three days ago." He began to whistle softly between his teeth as he stood behind her.

Three days! She had lain here for three days! "But...but Phoebe...everyone...they will be frantic!" Olivia exclaimed. "Did you send word?"

"No. There are certain difficulties," he said, sounding quite unconcerned about them. "But we will find a way to return you as soon as possible."

Her father was not at home. He had gone again to war. The Scots were threatening to cross the Border in defense of the imprisoned King Charles, and there were renewed Royalist uprisings across the land. Sporadic and ill-thought-out as they were, they nevertheless posed a serious threat to Parliament's ultimate victory. But if Lord Granville away at the wars was unaware of his daughter's disappearance, Phoebe would be beside herself with worry.

"I must go home," Olivia said, her desperation wildly at odds with her companion's apparent calm indifference to her situation. "You must put me ashore at once."

"Believe me, if I could, I would," the master of *Wind Dancer* said, and continued to whistle softly from somewhere behind her.

"Where are my c-clothes?" Olivia demanded with a rush of anger. "I want my c-clothes!"

16

she insisted, swiveling around to glare at him, too angry now to care that the stammer that had plagued her since childhood had escaped the rein she had finally and so painstakingly managed to put upon it.

He frowned down at the paper in his hand almost as if he hadn't heard her, then said coolly, "Adam is doing what he can with them. You fell a long way and they're much the worse for wear. But I have hopes of a miracle. Adam works wonders with the needle."

He looked up, the frown still between his fair brows, then he nodded and smiled, tossing the paper and quill onto a stool beside the bed.

Olivia stared at the paper. "That's...that's... that's my *back*!" she exclaimed. It was an ink sketch of her bare back, curved as she'd rested her head against her knees. It was her nape, the dark hair falling forward over her shoulders; her shoulder blades sharply delineated; the line of her spine; the indentation of her waist and the flare of her hips; the beginning of the cleft at the base of her spine.

It was all there in just a few deft strokes of the quill.

Outraged, she stared up at him, at a loss for words.

"Yes, I'm rather pleased with it," he replied. "The lines are particularly graceful, I think."

"How...how c-could you? You c-can't go around drawing people's backs...their bare backs...without asking!" She found her voice finally in a stumbling cascade of anger as she belatedly fell back against the pillows.

17

"It was irresistible," he said. "You have a beautiful back." He smiled at her with all the indolent benignity of a tabby cat.

Olivia stared at him, clutching the sheet to her chin. "Go away." She flapped her hands at him like a desperate child shooing away an importunate duckling.

He did not do so, however, but perched again on the edge of the table, long legs stretched out before him, hands thrust deep into the pockets of his britches. His thick gold hair was caught at his nape with a black velvet ribbon, and his throat rose strong and brown from the open collar of his shirt. There was a glimmer of amusement in the gray eyes, a flicker of the fine mouth that showed her crooked white teeth.

"I don't think this maidenly outrage really suits you," he said. "It was only your back and you forget perhaps that I have been tending you for three days."

Olivia felt the color mount again to her cheeks. "It is ungentlemanly to remind me."

He threw back his head and laughed. "I have been called many things in my time, Olivia, but not even my most partisan friend would call me a gentleman."

Olivia sank deeper into the feather bed that enclosed her. "Then what are you?"

"Apart from a reasonably skilled physician, a man who lives off the sea," he responded, folding his arms as he regarded her with that same secret amusement. But there was a hint of speculation now in his regard.

"A fisherman?" Even as she asked, she

knew it couldn't be so. Nothing so mundane as fishing could capture the interest of this man.

"I go after a more challenging catch than fish," he told her. He touched his fingertips to his mouth in a reflective gesture, before saying slowly, "I believe there are things about such a life that would speak to you too, Olivia. Will Lord Granville's Greek scholar of a daughter allow herself to be entranced for a few days?"

Olivia heard the challenge beneath the musical cadence of his voice. And she knew it was not lightly spoken for all the smile and the little ripple of amusement. "I don't know what you mean," she said.

"Oh, but I think you do, Olivia." He looked at her keenly. "Maybe you don't feel it as yet, or perhaps you don't yet understand it. It may seem strange to you at first, but I promise that if you will allow yourself, you'll come to see and understand many things that Lord Granville's daughter would never see and understand in the ordinary course of events. Things that will show you much that you do not yet know about yourself."

He came over to the bed and bent over her. His fingers brushed her cheek in a fleeting caress, and there was a light in his eyes like the glow of a fire. "I know these things about you, because I know them about myself," he said.

Olivia looked back into his eyes and that strange sense of connection returned. She knew nothing of this man and yet she felt as if she had been waiting to know him for a long time...as if this moment in the sun-filled cabin was always going to happen. Her scalp lifted with premonition and her palms were suddenly clammy. And yet despite the tingle of danger, she felt elation. As heady as it was confusing.

"Yes, you do see it," he said quietly. "You feel it too..." His tone changed suddenly, became brisk at a sharp knock on the door. "*Enter.*"

A grizzled man, short and squat, with powerful shoulders and corded arms, came into the cabin. He glanced incuriously at Olivia and gave her a nod. "The *Doña Elena* is in sight, sir. And the wind's backing to the southwest."

"I'll be up directly. Oh, and, Adam, our guest was wondering about her clothes," the master of *Wind Dancer* said, stretching in the sunlight.

"I'll be done soon enough," the older man said. "But there's other things to fuss with at present."

"True enough." Adam departed, and his master strolled to the door, saying cheerfully over his shoulder, "I must go to work, Olivia. Don't be alarmed by what you may hear in the next hour or so. There's nothing to be afraid of." With that he left, closing the door behind him.

Olivia sat up slowly in the now empty cabin. She looked around more carefully this time, noticing the richness of the furnishings. There was nothing ostentatious in the large space, but everything looked to be of the best. The sun glinted off the bright windowpanes and accentuated the glow of beeswax on the furniture, the floor, and the paneled bulwarks. There were shelves lined with books set into the bulwarks, silver handles to the cupboards below them.

The man had given her a first name, but it seemed he had plucked it from the air as a matter of convenience. Simply so that she would have some way of addressing him. He was no gentleman, or so he said, yet everything about him bespoke privilege and authority. He was master of a ship. His voice was pleasant and harmonious, no rough edges, and his hands, so long and fine, were not those of a laborer or a man who had come up from the ranks of plain seamen.

So what was he? Who was he? A man quite out of her ken, that much she understood.

Olivia pushed aside the covers and sat up, pulling the quilted coverlet around her. She stood up, and nearly fell down again as the motion of the floor beneath her took her by surprise. Her knees were alarmingly like butter and her head spun a little as she took a tentative step towards the table. Three days on her sickbed, sedated with that bitter medicine, was bound to have an effect.

She kneeled upon a cushioned seat below the window and looked out. Sun-dappled sea to all sides. And far away, almost on the horizon, was another ship; a garishly painted craft of crimson and purple and gold, with great white sails bellying in the wind. She could hear feet and voices on the deck above and the master's voice rising above the chatter, calling orders.

Olivia turned back to the cabin. The quilt was a cumbersome covering and without conscious intent she opened one of the cupboards in the bulwark. It contained plates and glass and silverware. Another yielded a pile of lavender-strewn linen. She rifled through it. Shirts, nightshirts, kerchiefs. Something here would do.

She shook out a nightshirt. The master of the ship was a tall man, and the garment would almost serve her as a gown. It was a matter of a minute to pull it over her head and tie the silk ribbons at the lace collar. The sleeves were far too long and wide, and she rolled them up to her elbows. The hem of the nightshirt brushed her ankles and billowed around her in what seemed like acres of material. But even this makeshift dress made her feel much less vulnerable. She turned back to the pile of linen in the cupboard and selected a crimson kerchief. It made a passable sash and brought the voluminous folds somewhat under control.

There was a small mirror set into the bulwark above a marble-topped washstand, and Olivia peered at her reflection. She was even paler than usual and her black eyes seemed exceptionally large, with bruised shadows beneath. Her nose, the long Granville nose, always a prominent feature, struck her as particularly so today.

She took an ivory comb from the wash-stand and pulled it through her hair. The black ringlets were hopelessly tangled, resisting all her efforts at tidying. Her hair needed to be washed; it was dull and lifeless, the lank hair of a bedridden invalid.

Olivia found that she resented her appearance. So pale and wan and slightly grubby, she thought, as if she'd just crawled out from beneath a damp stone. Her skin was still sore in places, and when she explored the tight ache at the back of her thigh, she found a thick bandage.

Her fingers touched it lightly and that flush crept over her skin again. He had bandaged her hurts. He had cleansed her, attended to her most intimate needs. She could feel his hands upon her now, almost as vividly as if the memory were reality. He called himself a physician, but Olivia had never met a physician quite like the master of *Wind Dancer*.

And what had he been offering her just before he'd left her? Something he had said he knew she wanted. He talked in riddles and yet his words struck a chord somewhere deep inside her, a chord she could as yet put no name to.

Riddles must be solved. With a swift movement, Olivia tossed aside the comb, caught the thick, tangled mass of her hair, and tugged it behind her head. She used another of his linen kerchiefs, a blue one this time, to bind the curls tightly away from her face, and gazed again at her reflection. Her pale countenance stood out in stark relief against the bright scarf. She bit her lips, hoping to put some color into them, and pinched her cheeks with the same aim. It didn't help.

She turned away from the mirror, nibbling her thumbnail. He had talked of showing her things that Lord Granville's daughter would never see in the ordinary course of events. More riddles.

And why did she still feel this strange detachment, not from this craft as it skipped over the sea, not from the warmth of the sun on her face and the vibrant awareness of her body, but from who and what she had been before she stepped into thin air?

She conjured Phoebe in her mind's eye. Phoebe would look at her anxiously from her round blue eyes, her hair as always escaping from its pins. Phoebe would be frantic with worry. Phoebe would think Olivia was dead.

She opened the hand that still held the ring, pressed into her palm. If she could send it to Phoebe, then Phoebe would know that there was nothing to worry about. She glanced out of the window again, at the bright water. She'd need a homing pigeon to send that message, and she didn't make a habit of carrying such birds around with her.

And yet, for some reason, Olivia's concern for her friend's anxiety seemed distanced, separate from the self that stood in this cabin, going God only knew where. She could do nothing to allay Phoebe's fears, and her concern seemed to slip away from her like water

24

on oiled hide. Her overwhelming sensation as she stood in the sunlight, inhaling the sweet scents of the sea, was of elation. Of promise. Of expectation.

Two

"My lady, Lord Charles is crying." The nurse-maid spoke softly, almost hesitantly, in the doorway to the gallery where the marchioness of Granville was pacing from one end to the other, pausing at each open window to stare down into the sun-dappled drowsy garden.

Phoebe put a hand to her breast as the baby's thin wail instantly set the milk flowing. "Give him to me." She took the infant, nuzzling his round cheek. "Is he teething? His cheek is so red."

"I believe so, my lady. I've rubbed a little oil of cloves on the gum to ease the soreness."

Phoebe nodded. She sat on a broad padded window seat and unlaced her bodice as the baby dived hungrily, still wailing, towards the source of nourishment.

"Is Nicholas still asleep?"

"Aye, my lady. I'll bring him to you as soon as he wakens from his nap."

"He played hard this morning," Phoebe observed with a fond maternal smile.

"He's a right little devil, that one...such a bundle of energy," the nursemaid declared in a tone that implied only approbation. She curtsied and turned to leave the gallery.

"There's no message as yet from Lord Granville?" Phoebe asked the question although she knew she would have been informed the instant such a message arrived.

"Not as yet, my lady. Sergeant Crampton thinks his lordship is at Westminster, but he's sent another messenger to Maidstone in case his lordship is with Lord Fairfax."

Phoebe sighed and the baby dropped the nipple with an indignant wail.

"Try not to worry, m'lady. It's bad for the milk," the nursemaid said anxiously. "It'll make it thin and maybe even cause it to dry up."

Phoebe tried to force herself to be calm as she settled the infant to the breast again. "Giles has no news from the search parties on the island?" Again she asked a question to which she knew the answer. Giles Crampton, her husband's trusted lieutenant since the beginning of the war, would have reported any information immediately.

"Not as yet, madam." The nursemaid curtsied again and left.

But someone must have seen Olivia. Phoebe stroked the baby's head as he sucked, trying to calm him even through her own agitation. How could she possibly just disappear off the face of the earth? She hadn't taken a horse, so she couldn't have gone too far. And besides, the island was so small. Surely she couldn't have been abducted?

But that was her main fear. A few years ago, way back at the beginning of this interminable war, an attempt had been made to abduct Olivia and hold her for ransom. The abductor had taken the wrong girl...or, it might be said with the benefit of hindsight, the right girl, since Portia, Lord Granville's niece, was now her onetime abductor's ecstatically happy wife.

With Cato away, Phoebe felt responsible. She knew he wouldn't hold her so, but Olivia was her husband's daughter as well as her own dearest friend, and in Lord Granville's absence, Lady Granville was supposedly his locum in the household. But Cato never objected to Olivia's roaming unattended. The island was safe. It was occupied by Parliament's forces, whose presence was everywhere, the inhabitants were peaceful although for the most part staunchly Royalist; and the king's imprisonment in Carisbrooke Castle was being conducted with the utmost grace and civility.

So where was Olivia? If she'd been hurt, someone would have found her. She'd have found some way to send a message home.

Phoebe moved the child to her other breast and leaned her head against the window frame, looking down into the garden. The scent of wallflowers rose thick and sweet from the bed planted beneath the window; a small fountain played musically in the center of the pond set in the middle of the lawns. It was a soothing and peaceful scene that didn't lend itself to thoughts of violent abductions, hideous injuries.

She concentrated all her thoughts on Olivia, with whom she'd lived for close on six years. She knew Olivia almost as well as she knew herself. They were bound by ties that transcended mere friendship. Phoebe closed her eyes and pictured Olivia, with her penetrating black eyes, the little frown of concentration that had almost permanent residence between her thick black eyebrows, the full bow of her mouth. She allowed Olivia's presence to fill her mind so that she could almost feel her beside her.

The baby had fallen asleep, allowing the nipple to slide from his rosebud mouth. Phoebe cradled his head in the palm of her hand as she slipped her free hand into the pocket of her gown. Her fingers closed over the little ring of braided hair that she carried always. Portia had taken locks of their hair and made three rings at the very beginning of their friendship when they'd all sworn they would never succumb to marriage and the ordinary lot of women. Two of them had succumbed to marriage, but definitely not to the ordinarily submissive role of married women. Only Olivia remained with her oath completely inviolate. And knowing Olivia, she would probably remain so, Phoebe thought.

Portia had braided the rings as a joke, making them mingle their blood in a vow of eternal friendship. Phoebe knew that Olivia, like herself, always carried her ring. Portia probably didn't; it was a little too sentimental and whimsical for the soldierly Portia. But as she held the ring, Phoebe knew that if any harm had come to Olivia, she would know it in her bones. And the knowledge just wasn't there.

So just what was Olivia up to?

OLIVIA LEFT THE CABIN, barefoot, in her borrowed raiment. She had to clutch the wall of the narrow corridor once or twice when the vessel broke into a particularly exuberant dance across the waves and her still rather wobbly legs threatened to give way.

A ladderlike staircase was at the far end of the corridor. Sunshine puddled onto the floor at the foot of the steps, pouring from an open hatchway where Olivia could see a wedge of blue sky and the corner of a white sail.

She scrambled up the steps and emerged blinking onto the sun-soaked deck under the vivid blue brightness of the morning. The decking was smooth and warm beneath her bare soles, and the wind caught her makeshift gown, pressing it to her body one minute, sending it billowing like a tent the next.

Olivia looked around at the orderly bustle of men laughing and singing as they handled blocks and tackle, shinnied into the rigging, spliced rope. No one seemed to notice her as she stood at the head of the companionway, wondering where to go.

Then she heard a familiar voice calling out an order, and she looked behind her to see the master of the ship on the high quarterdeck, standing behind the helmsman at the wheel.

The golden head was thrown back as he looked up at the sails, feet apart, legs braced on the moving deck, hands clasped behind his back, eyes narrowed against the sun. His tones were calm and unhurried, but his posture, his expression, were both taut and alert.

Olivia hesitated for a moment, then made her way to the ladder leading to the quarterdeck. She climbed slowly, needing to catch her breath at every step, but despite slightly shaky legs she felt as free and light as one of the seagulls wheeling and diving overhead.

"Well, what a resourceful creature you've turned out to be," Anthony observed as she stepped onto the dazzling white decking. His eyes crinkled, a smile gleamed as he took in her costume.

"Do you mind?" Olivia grabbed the rail as a gust of wind filled the big mainsail and the ship heeled sharply.

"Not in the least. It's an ingenious use of a garment for which I myself have no use at all," he responded with a careless gesture.

Abruptly Olivia wondered where he'd been sleeping while she'd been occupying his bed. A slight flush warmed her cheeks and she turned her studied attention to the landscape.

"You don't mind my coming up here?" She

shaded her eyes to look out across the expanse of water, welcoming the breeze that cooled her cheeks.

He shook his head. "Not if you feel strong enough. But don't forget that you've spent three days on your back."

"I feel perfectly strong," Olivia asserted, reflecting that it was not entirely true.

Anthony didn't believe her; she was still far too wan for robust health, and he knew better than anyone how much essence of feverfew, wormwood, and poppy juice he'd poured down her resistant throat in the last few days.

"I only look so pale and limp because I've just left my bed," Olivia said, reading his shrewdly assessing gaze correctly. "I need to bathe and wash my hair. I feel grubby."

He nodded with a little accepting shrug. "That can be arranged later. We might even be able to find you some fresh water."

"Hot water?" she asked eagerly.

"That might present more of a problem. But if you speak really nicely to Adam, it could be forthcoming."

"Galleon on the port bow," a voice sang out from way above Olivia's head. She looked up into the rigging and made out a tiny figure standing on a ledge way at the top of the mizzenmast.

"Ah, good!" the master of *Wind Dancer* said with obvious satisfaction. "Now we'll wear ship, Jethro."

"Aye, sir." The helmsman began to turn the wheel.

Anthony kept his eyes on the mainsail now, whistling softly between his teeth, then he said crisply, "Olivia, hold the rail, we're ready to go about."

"Go about where?" Olivia looked puzzled. Where was there to go?

He only laughed. "I forgot you're a landlubber. Just hold the rail as the great boom swings over."

Olivia did as he said, and clung tightly to the railing as he called a series of incomprehensible orders that took men swarming into the rigging, loosening shrouds as the frigate swung into the wind. The massive boom hung in the air for a moment, the mainsail empty of wind, then as the helmsman put the wheel hard over, the wind caught the sail and the boom swung to starboard with a thump. The sails filled once more and *Wind Dancer* skipped along on her new tack.

Now Olivia could see that the painted ship she'd noticed from the cabin was much closer, sailing straight towards them, it seemed.

She waited until everything had settled down again and the ship's master was once more serenely looking up at the sails, hands still clasped at his back.

"What is that?" She pointed to the painted ship.

"Ah, now that is the *Doña Elena*." He looked down at her and his eyes were alight with pure mischief. "We've been waiting for her to venture forth from her cozy harbor for several days."

"Why...why have you been waiting for her?"

"Because I am going to catch her." He took a telescoped spyglass from the pocket of his britches, opened it, and examined the painted ship. "Have you ever seen a Spanish galleon before?"

Olivia shook her head.

"Here, take a look." He handed her the glass.

Olivia put it to her eye and the garish vessel sprang into her vision. "Why are you going to c-catch her?" She flushed with annoyance at the slight stammer. "I wish I c-could stop that!" *C* was the hardest consonant for her, and despite all her best efforts she still sometimes stumbled. "It's only when I'm excited or upset or cross," she added disconsolately.

Anthony said cheerfully, "I find it appealing."

Olivia looked astounded. "You do?"

He laughed down at her. "Yes, I do. Now, guess why I want to catch the galleon. I told you I live off the sea, remember?"

Olivia slowly lowered the glass. She looked at him in dawning comprehension. This was certainly no gentleman. "That's *piracy*."

"Yes, indeed it is." Now unsmiling, Anthony regarded her. He knew the kind of response he wanted from her. But would she give it to him? During the days he'd tended her through the fevered concussion, he thought that he had recognized in Olivia the flicker of true individuality that was the bedrock of his own personality.

But did she have the courage to blow that

independent spark into full flame? Would she throw background and caution to the wind and give in to adventure?

It seemed important to him to find out. He waited, watching her face.

Olivia frowned at him, speculation in her dark eyes. "But...but it's dangerous."

"Therein lies the appeal."

"Does it?" Olivia wondered, the murmur little more than a softly spoken reflection of her own thoughts. Was danger appealing? A little tremor lifted the fine hairs on her nape, and she glanced quickly up at the pirate. He smiled slowly at her and she found herself returning the conspiratorial smile.

She looked again through the glass. The galleon seemed much bigger than *Wind Dancer*, its four great sails billowing. And now she could see banks of oars along the side, rhythmically sweeping the sea. "She's going very fast," she said consideringly, pursing her lips. "Is she faster than your ship? C-can you c-calculate her speed?"

The little stumble of excitement had given Anthony his answer, and he hid a smile of satisfaction.

"She's more cumbersome than *Wind Dancer*. She responds much more slowly to the helm. Of course, under full sail and with the slaves at full sweep, she could outrun us."

"Slaves?"

"Galley slaves. You see the oars?"

Olivia nodded, still looking through the glass.

"You'll smell them soon enough." His mouth curled in disgust and the amusement vanished from his eye. "They're kept permanently chained to the oars. They hose them down periodically."

"How barbarous!" Olivia's voice quivered with indignation. "Shall you set them free when you've taken the ship?"

Anthony laughed silently. "You have no doubts that we'll succeed in this little venture, then?"

Olivia looked up at him again, her eyes agleam. "No, indeed not. I assume you've planned every move with the greatest c-care. You will have taken into account things like wind and tide and the speed of the oars. Things of that nature."

"Yes, of course," he agreed gravely. "All things of that nature have been accounted for."

"I would like to know how to make such calculations," she said thoughtfully. "Mathematics is a favorite subject of mine."

"More so than Greek philosophy?"

Olivia gave the matter some thought. "Sometimes I prefer one, and sometimes the other. It depends if a particular aspect captures my interest."

"I can see how that would be." He looked out over the rail, the secret amusement in his eyes deepening.

"What of the galleon's c-cargo?" Olivia asked, dismissing scholarship for the moment. "Is it very rich, do you know?"

"Very," he agreed as solemnly as before. "I select my catches with some care. She's carrying gold doubloons and silks from the Indies. I feel sure I can put them to better use than can her Spanish masters."

"And will you set free the slaves?" she pressed.

"If you wish it."

"I do." Olivia nodded vigorously. "That seems to me an object much to be desired."

"Then we will augment piracy with a little philanthropy," Anthony stated. He turned to the helmsman at the wheel behind him. "Jethro, I think it's time we took her wind."

The man licked a finger and held it up to the wind. "Oh, aye, sir. Come up on the starboard bow, then, shall us?"

"That's my idea." Anthony took the wheel from the helmsman.

"What is it that you're going to do?" Olivia came to stand beside him.

"You see the direction of the wind. It's coming from her right, from the starboard side. If we come up alongside her on that side, we'll steal her wind and her sails will flatten. She'll have only the oars to keep her under way. And while she's helpless, we shall board her."

"That sounds like a good plan," Olivia said consideringly. "Do you have guns?"

"A battery on either side. But we'll get really close before we run 'em out. The more confused they are about our intentions, the better." He glanced up at the sun and said with a curve of his mouth, "Perfect timing, though

36

I say it myself." He made a minute adjustment to the wheel.

"What do you mean? How's it perfect timing?"

"The Spaniards enjoy their midday meal," he replied, and his smile took a cynical twist. "A heavy dinner where the wine flows free invites a long siesta. We'll catch them with their bellies full and their heads muddled."

Olivia abruptly realized that she was famished. "Do you not eat at midday on *Wind Dancer*?" she asked involuntarily.

"Oh, are you hungry?" He glanced down at her. "I forgot you've had nothing solid to eat for three days. We will dine in style when the engagement is over. The cookstoves are out at present."

They were gaining on the galleon now, and Olivia became aware of a different atmosphere on *Wind Dancer*. The men in the waist of the ship were no longer laughing and singing. They were moving silently into positions against the rails, standing shoulder to shoulder, tense and purposeful. And now Olivia could see the line of guns and the gun ports that for the moment remained closed.

As they came closer to the galleon, she saw how the other ship's sails began to flap. "Oh, yes, you *are* stealing her wind!" she cried softly.

Then a voice hailed them across the narrowing stretch of water. A stout man in flounced petticoat britches, his coat smothered in gold braid and silver buttons, had emerged from the companionway onto the galleon's poop deck. Olivia couldn't understand the language but the tone was unmistakable. The Spanish captain was livid as his sails flapped uselessly. He waved a soiled table napkin as if it might do the work of his empty sails as he bellowed through a megaphone.

And then Olivia smelled it. A vile cesspit stench that reminded her of rotting meat and the unmentionable filth of the kennel. She covered her mouth, choking, her hunger vanished.

Anthony pulled a handkerchief from his pocket and handed it to her, advising grimly, "Cover your mouth and nose."

The frigate was almost alongside the galleon, and Anthony called, "Starboard guns...nets... let's waste no time, gentlemen."

And things happened very fast. There was a great rattling as the guns rolled forward into the ports, and boarding nets flew through the air, grappling irons hooking onto the side of the galleon.

The Spaniard was screaming and hopping from foot to foot on the poop deck. Olivia could now hear the violent creaking of the oars under frantic arms, the vile crack of a whip, the ugly groans and cries as scarred backs were lacerated anew. Men on the galleon raced to throw off the boarding nets, but even as they did so, the pirate's men were swarming across the now narrow gap.

"Starboard guns...*fire!*"

The deck beneath Olivia's feet shook under the booming cannonade, and she would have lost her footing had Anthony not thrown out an arm and clasped her tightly against him as he swung the wheel, bringing *Wind Dancer* impossibly close to the galleon. So close it seemed she must ram the other ship. The sound of splintering wood filled the hot summer air as the frigate's guns tore into the galleon's side.

Olivia looked up at him and he laughed down at her and she realized she was not frightened, only filled with a wild elation.

Then Jethro, the helmsman, appeared as if on command and took the helm, and Anthony drew his sword. With a swift movement, he bent and took Olivia's chin on the palm of his hand and kissed her mouth. "Piracy seems to suit Lord Granville's daughter."

Before she could answer, he was gone, swinging himself over the rail, across the stretched netting, to leap into the midst of the thronged Spaniards on the opposite deck.

Olivia, wonderingly, touched her mouth where he'd kissed her. A man had never kissed her on the lips before. She clasped her arms around her body with a little shiver. But it was of excitement, not fear. She looked at Jethro and saw that his countenance was utterly calm, utterly confident. He swung the frigate's head into the wind so that her sails emptied and she came to a stop, bobbing gently alongside the Spanish vessel.

Olivia looked into the anarchic maelstrom

on the galleon's deck and saw Anthony's bright head. It seemed to be everywhere, and his sword flashed like the archangel's blade at the gates of the Garden of Eden.

"Will it be all right?" The question spoke itself.

"Aye, never you fear, lady. The master's never lost a fight yet." Jethro spoke with stolid calm.

And in truth it seemed that the chaos was dying down, the shouts and screams fading, no longer competing with the squalling gulls. Anthony leaped onto the galleon's poop deck where the Spanish captain and three other grandees in braided coats and high plumed hats had materialized.

Olivia watched as the pirate swept his victims a flourishing bow, his sword cutting a swath through the air. She caught herself throwing a calculating glance over the side at the bridge of netting. It had looked easy enough, although the water seemed a long way down.

What in the world was she thinking? But reason seemed to have abandoned her. Mad though it was, Lord Granville's daughter wasn't going to miss out on any aspect of this adventure. Olivia chuckled to herself as, with a little unconscious toss of her head, she gathered the folds of her makeshift gown into her hands, lifting it well clear of her bare feet. She swung over the rail.

"You can do it in three steps. But expect it to move beneath you."

At the pirate's cool tones calling to her from the opposite deck, Olivia looked up. There was both challenge and invitation in his steady gaze. She nodded, biting her lip with concentration, released the rail, and sprang forward. The netting bridge bounced beneath her and she gave a cry, half alarm, half exhilaration, and then she'd reached the galleon in safety, the wind whipping her hair from beneath the blue scarf. She tumbled over the rail to the deck and climbed up to the poop deck.

"Gentlemen, may I present the lady Olivia." Anthony introduced her with another bow and a flourish of his sword. "She will take your swords, if you'd be good enough to disarm yourselves." He smiled politely. "A simple precaution, but one I'm sure you'll understand."

"This is *piracy*!" spat the captain in thick accents.

"Precisely," Anthony agreed. "Piracy on the high seas. Your swords, gentlemen, if you please."

"I will not dishonor myself to a common pirate!" one of the other three spluttered. "I will die on my sword rather than surrender it to a thief."

"Then pray do so, sir. It is one of your three options." The smile that flickered over his lips was one of polite indifference. "You may surrender your swords to Lady Olivia; you may die upon them if you so wish; or I will remove your swordbelts myself. And your britches with them." His sword flashed suddenly, its point coming to rest against the captain's considerable paunch.

The man jumped back with a squawk. The sword followed. Three quick cuts and the captain's swordbelt clattered to the deck.

"If you would be so kind, Lady Olivia," Anthony murmured. His sword point danced as deftly as a needle, and the buttons on the man's britches flew to the four winds. He grabbed at his britches as they began to slide, and stood helplessly, glowering, swearing.

The other three stared in loathing and fear at their smiling tormentor.

Olivia picked up the captain's heavy sword and placed it carefully on the deck some distance from its owner.

Anthony raised an eyebrow at his remaining victims, and his sword point leaped forward jauntily. A second sword fell to the deck; a second man stood helplessly clutching his britches lest they fall to his ankles.

Olivia picked up the fallen sword and put it with the other. Laughter bubbled within her but she tried to emulate Anthony's cool composure. He stood now leaning against the rail, his sword point resting between his feet as he regarded the two remaining Spaniards.

With an oath, one of them unbuckled his swordbelt, and his companion slowly did the same. Anthony leaned forward and took them. "My thanks, gentlemen. Now, if you would all be so good as to accompany my man to your cabins while we complete our business, we shall leave you in peace all the sooner." He gestured to the stairs down to the companionway, and Olivia saw a grinning sailor waiting with sword and cutlass.

The man gave the Spaniards an elaborate mock bow. "Thisaway, gennelmen, if'n ye please."

Olivia, her lip curled, watched them stumble away. Now the amusement was over, she was once more violently aware of the stench coming from the bowels of the galleon. It made her want to retch.

"What preposterous creatures," she declared. "So pompous in their braid and finery, with their great fat bellies full of food, living off the slave labor of those poor starved, tortured wretches down there."

Anthony sheathed his sword and came over to her. He had blood on his cheek, and he took from her his handkerchief that she still held, and dabbed at the cut.

"On that subject, should we hand the ship and her masters over to the slaves and let them do what they will with them? Or should we put the masters aboard one of their longboats to fend for themselves? Their fate is in your hands."

Olivia considered. "Perhaps the slaves would murder them if they had the chance?" she muttered. "Do you think that's likely?"

"Highly likely."

"That seems like divine retribution," she said savagely.

"You don't think maybe that losing their

cargo, their slaves, and their galleon would be punishment enough?" he suggested. "The freed slaves would have the galleon and we could leave them some doubloons so that they could go where they wished." He raised an interrogative eyebrow.

"I don't think you're nearly bloodthirsty enough for a pirate," Olivia observed. "But perhaps we should let them go their separate ways."

"So be it." He turned and leaned over the rail, calling down an order, and in minutes came the ring of steel on steel, a steady rhythmic hammering, as men set to work breaking the slaves' manacles.

Olivia hung over the rail, watching the activity. Anthony's men were bringing things up from the depths of the galleon, boxes and crates and bundles. They moved them across to *Wind Dancer* in a smooth operation that looked as if it had been performed many times. The galleon's crew were assembled in the waist of the ship, and a few of the pirate's crew were disarming them, moving cheerfully among them, chatting and whistling as if they were at a tea party.

"What about the holes in the ship's side? Will it not sink?"

"Not if its new owners know anything about patching," Anthony said carelessly. "They're less than a day's sail from Brest."

"Brest?" Olivia tried to picture the French coast. How far from the Isle of Wight was Brest? She thought it was beyond the Gulf of Saint-

Malo. How long would it take to sail back home?

Home. It was a concept so distant and so unreal, it seemed that it existed in another life. Suddenly she felt very tired as the surge of excitement ebbed. She glanced at the netting bridge with a tremor of apprehension. It looked very unstable now and very, very high above the churning blue-green water.

"Too tired to make it alone this time?" Anthony spoke at her side, and she looked up quickly to catch that little flicker of a smile in his eye.

"How do you know?"

"I make it my business to know what might be troubling the members of my crew," he said. "Particularly my newest and most inexperienced member."

"I thought I was very good at disarming villains," Olivia protested, forgetting her fatigue for a minute.

"Oh, you were. A natural," he assured her. "A pirate to the manner born. Only pirates, you see, think of their victims as the villains."

"And I just fell into that way of thinking," Olivia said in tones of wonderment. "Isn't that amazing?"

"Oh, I knew it all along," he replied airily. "Come, let me take you back. I can see that you're thinking longingly of your bed."

It was perfectly true, although Olivia still didn't know how he could so accurately pinpoint her uppermost thought. He took her elbow and walked her down to the rail in the main body of the ship.

Olivia regarded the netting doubtfully, her heart beating uncomfortably fast. The distance seemed to expand and contract before her eyes, and it astonished her now that she had leaped across it as nimbly as a monkey a mere half hour earlier.

And then as she hesitated, despising herself for her apprehension, Anthony swung her into his arms, holding her securely against him. "This won't take a second," he said, and with that cheerful whistle between his teeth he leaped across the gap, his feet just once touching the netting bridge.

"There, now you may seek your bed, and when you awake, we will be on our way and we shall dine on...on...oh, whatever Adam has planned for us." He held her against him for a moment, and she could feel the steady beat of his heart against her breast.

Then he set her on her feet and swiftly pulled away the blue scarf that had come loose around her hair and was threatening to blow off into the wind. He tied it around her neck. "I'd hate to lose it, it's one of my favorites." He put his hands at her waist and stepped back, surveying her crimson sash. "That one is growing on me." He left her then and Olivia knew he would be smiling.

Thoughts of bed were now irresistible. She was too exhausted for hunger, too exhausted even to consider the unreality of her present circumstances. She left the quarterdeck and climbed down the companionway, her legs so heavy it was hard to lift them. The cabin was sun-splashed and peaceful, and without a second's hesitation, Olivia fell onto the bed, dragging the quilted coverlet over her.

" 'Tis mad y'are. Mad as a March hare." Adam glowered at his master. He had served this man since the man was a mere babe new delivered from his mother's womb, and he knew when *Wind Dancer*'s master had mischief afoot. He could read it in the angle of his head, in the devilment in his eye.

Adam knew exactly where the devilment came from, and he didn't hold with women on board ship. They were unlucky. He stood at his master's side as the enriched *Wind Dancer* skipped true to her name on a freshening breeze.

"What's troubling you, Adam?" Anthony didn't take his eyes off the horizon, but he sounded amused, as always reading his friend and servant's mind with uncanny accuracy. "She'll not betray us," he said.

"I don't know as 'ow you can know that," Adam grumbled. "Look at who 'er father is."

"The marquis of Granville. Parliament's man." Anthony shrugged. "But let us not visit the sins of the father onto the daughter, Adam. Not without cause."

"Oh, y'are impossible. There's no talkin' to you." Adam glowered up at him. "An' there she was, bold as brass, watchin' you take the *Doña Elena*—"

"She did her part, if you recall." Anthony

47

interrupted him before Adam could lose himself in his argument.

" 'Twas a disgrace," Adam declared. " 'Er bein' who she is."

"This is no ordinary woman," Anthony said with conviction. He looked down at Adam and the gray eyes now were serious, intent, his mouth set. "Trust me, Adam. Olivia Granville is no ordinary woman."

"I suppose that's another o' your instincts," Adam muttered.

"And are they not always right?" Anthony raised a quizzical eyebrow.

"Aye, but there's always a first time," Adam muttered without too much assurance. Anthony's mother had had the same uncanny ability to understand people on a level they didn't understand themselves.

Anthony shook his head. "Not this time."

"Well, if y'are thinkin' of beddin' her, I hope you'll remember she's no village doxy. An 'ighborn lady, she is. And you'd do well to remember that!"

"I will, Adam. I will." Anthony laughed. "There'll be no irate papa beating down my door." He looked down at his man's creased expression, teasing, "There never has been as yet."

"Aye, well only the Lord knows why not. An out-an-out rake is what y'are," Adam declared roundly.

"Nonsense," Anthony scoffed. "I take my pleasure when it's offered like any other red-blooded male."

Adam sniffed at this and Anthony kept his counsel. It wasn't so much that he intended to bed Olivia Granville as that it was inevitable. And he knew that on some level she knew it too.

What he didn't know was what it would mean in the greater scheme of things. The riches liberated from the Spanish galleon would go a long way to swelling the coffers of the Royalist insurgents and their Scots backers as they broke the uneasy truce that had been in place since the king's imprisonment, and brought war once more to the English countryside in one last attempt to secure the king's sovereignty.

In this enterprise, Cato Granville was the enemy. At the moment, he was not at Carisbrooke Castle, but he would be back. The renewed fighting by the king's supporters and the news of his undercover negotiations with the Scots would harden His Majesty's jailers. They would try to move him off the island and back to London. Before that happened, Anthony intended that King Charles would take safe passage to France on *Wind Dancer*.

Just where Olivia Granville would fit into his planning remained to be seen.

"You got any idea what was on that ship the wreckers brought down the other night?" Adam inquired. "Mighty rich pickin's, I'd guess. You think you got the word out all right?"

Anthony's face was wiped clean of humor.

"Oh, yes, the word's out, Adam. However rich the pickings, the goods have no value if they can't sell 'em. If whoever controls them knows there's a discreet buyer, he'll make contact. I don't know what we'll get, but I'll lay odds it's good. The ship was a merchantman."

He gave a harsh laugh and Olivia would not have recognized this man. His eyes were gray iron, his mouth twisted. There was no vestige of the softness or amusement she had come to expect. "Why not let someone else do the work for a change?" he said.

The setting sun was throwing a great palette of colors across the western sky, and the lively water beneath *Wind Dancer*'s bow was pink and gold. The good rich smells of cooking came now from the rekindled fires in the galley. The hardness left Anthony's countenance as quickly as it had come. He was remembering his promise to the newest member of his pirate crew.

"What d'you have for our dinner, Adam?"

"A leg o' mutton on the spit," the older man said begrudgingly. "An' what ye took from the Spaniards' table. A fine show o' pastries and some of that there manchega cheese."

"Then we'll dine in an hour. My Sleeping Beauty should be awake by now." He nodded at Adam and left the quarterdeck.

Adam shook his head. His master was so many different men, and it astonished Adam how he was able to keep them all separate, each in its own compartment. It had much to do with his growing, Adam knew, but it still chilled him even through the deep love he felt for the man he'd nurtured and served since Anthony had entered the world on that demon-ridden night twenty-eight years earlier.

Three

Olivia awoke refreshed from a dreamless nap and was for a moment disoriented, then she heard the cry of a seagull and smelled the fresh salt tang on the air and remembered. She smiled slowly at the renewed prickle of excitement that crept over her skin. Fatigue had caused her to question the magic that now embraced her. But she was no longer tired and this strange new world was filled with wonder. Lord Granville's daughter was the aider and abettor of pirates. Of course, one could say that she'd been kidnapped by a pirate and was held captive on his ship on the high seas. One could say that. And it would be the perfect truth. Except that she had no desire to be anywhere else, and it seemed she had acquired a shockingly keen desire for further adventuring. Her appetite for piracy had merely been whetted by the encounter with the Spanish galleon.

She had more in common with Portia than she'd realized, Olivia thought with a soft chuckle. Her father's illegitimate niece had a penchant for soldiering and had been married on a battlefield in britches with a sword at her hip. Olivia was beginning to see the appeal in such wildly unconventional behavior. Hitherto she'd simply assumed that Portia was unique, a law unto herself. What Portia did had no relevance to what ordinary people did. But maybe not. Or maybe her uniqueness was rubbing off on her friends. Or maybe Olivia herself was not ordinary either, she just hadn't known it until now.

Grinning to herself, Olivia pushed aside the coverlet and sat up, sniffing hungrily. The most wonderful scents of roasting meat were coming from somewhere, setting her juices running. She glanced curiously around the cabin, wondering what it could tell her of *Wind Dancer*'s master.

Not for a moment did it occur to her that she might be invading his privacy as she began to explore. There were charts on the table, with a sextant and compasses. She peered at the calculations written in the same bold hand that had drawn the lines of her back. The calculations fascinated her mathematician's mind, although to understand them would take some study.

She examined the books on the shelves set into the bulwarks. An interesting assortment. Poetry, philosophy, some of her own favorite classical texts. The ship's master had an intellectual mind, it seemed. She looked at the chess-board set out on a small table under the window. It looked as if he was in the middle of a game, unless it was a chess problem he was working on.

Olivia bent over the pieces, frowning. She moved the white bishop to king four, and stood frowning at the board. Then she gave a little nod of satisfaction. She'd been right. It was inevitable that white would now mate in two moves. Not a particularly difficult problem, she thought.

Humming to herself, Olivia turned back to the chart table. Idly she opened a drawer beneath the tabletop. There were papers, a thick pile of them, facedown in the drawer. She took them out and laid them on the table. They were drawings, pencil sketches. It seemed the master of *Wind Dancer* was a draftsman who found objects for his talent wherever he looked. These seemed to be entirely of his crew.

She gazed fascinated at the series of sketches. Some of the faces she recognized from the time she'd spent above decks. Jethro, the helmsman, appeared several times. In some of the draw-ings, men were working on the ship, sewing sails, splicing rope, climbing rigging. In some they were playing, dancing, laughing, lis-tening to one of their fellows strumming a lute, his back against the mast. And then there were three or four where naked men stood beneath a pump on the deck, the water glis-tening on their skins, laughter in their eyes.

Olivia had spent far too much time among

the texts and illustrations of ancient Greece and Rome to be embarrassed by depictions of male nudity. But it seemed to her that this artist had no small talent for anatomy. The human form obviously intrigued him, judging by the number of small sketches of a hand, a foot, an ankle, the turn of a thigh. But the faces too were full of life, depicted in just a few lines, and yet an entire moment was captured in the tilt of a head, the slant of an eye.

"In general, when my work is not in plain sight, it's not for anyone's eyes but mine."

Olivia hadn't heard the door open. She looked up with a gasp, the drawings fluttering to the table, one or two sliding to the floor.

The master of *Wind Dancer* stood in the cabin doorway, and his expression had lost its habitual amusement. A deep frown corrugated his brow and his eyes were annoyed.

"I beg your pardon, I didn't mean to pry," Olivia said, flushing. "The drawer wasn't locked or anything."

"No, because my people don't make a habit of invading my privacy," he said curtly. He was carrying two wooden buckets from which steam curled upward.

He came into the cabin, kicking the door closed behind him, and set the pails down. "You wished to wash your hair, so I've brought you hot water."

"Thank you." Olivia pushed her hands through her hair. She was embarrassed at being caught prying and didn't know how to put it right. "I…I'm truly sorry for looking in your drawers. I…I just had this overpowering urge to find out about you…things about you. It didn't feel like spying."

He regarded her still with an air of displeasure. "You could ask me anything you wish, or did that not occur to you?"

"You weren't here." She shrugged and offered an apologetic smile. "And when I have asked you questions, you haven't exactly been forthc-coming."

"So you simply followed an impulse."

Olivia nodded, a puzzled little frown drawing her thick black brows together. "I seem to be doing it rather a lot at the moment, like jumping onto that galleon. I wouldn't have said I was impulsive. Phoebe's the impulsive one of the three of us."

"Three of you?" He raised an interrogative eyebrow.

"Phoebe, Portia, and me. We're all related to one another but in rather roundabout ways. We're best friends," she added, reflecting that Anthony couldn't possibly be interested in the ramifications of their complicated threesome. Simple friendship was easy enough to understand.

It seemed she was right, because he didn't press for more detail. He turned to open a cupboard in the bulwark. "So, do you like my drawings?"

"They're very accomplished," Olivia said hesitantly, still embarrassed.

"And the subjects?" he inquired, turning with

an armful of towels. "What do you think of my subject matter?"

He was definitely mocking her now; there was no disguising the slight sardonic tilt to his mouth, the ironic gleam in his eye.

"I've noticed that anatomy is a frequent favorite with artists and draftsmen," Olivia said, meeting his gaze, refusing to be put out of countenance. "I'm very familiar with the Renaissance artists, and I don't expect to see fig leaves, if that's what you mean."

He laughed, and the unpleasantness left his expression. "Of course, scholars are inclined to be less squeamish about naked truths than those who sit at home and sew fine seams."

"I c-can't sew," Olivia confided.

"Oddly enough, I didn't imagine you could." He set the towels on the table and reached beneath the bed, pulling out a round wooden tub. "There's not enough hot fresh water for you to bathe properly, but if you kneel here, I'll wash your hair for you. Then I must dress the wound at the back of your leg."

Olivia hesitated. "Why's my leg bandaged?"

"It was the worst of your hurts." He knelt beside the tub, crooking a finger at her. "It's a long gash that had picked up a quantity of dirt and pieces of gravel on your slide down the cliff. I was obliged to stitch it, which is why it probably feels rather tight."

Olivia touched the bandage through the folds of the nightshirt. It was very high up on her thigh. "I can manage to tend to myself now," she said. "And I c-can wash my own hair."

"You need to be careful of the bruise on the back of your head. It'll be easier if I do it, because I know where it is," he responded calmly. "Besides, Adam will be bringing dinner soon and I for one am very sharp-set. So come."

He unwrapped a cake of soap from one of the towels. "Verbena," he told her. "I'll lay odds you thought a pirate's soap was made of pig's fat and woodash."

Olivia couldn't help laughing. "I suppose I did. But I don't think you're a proper pirate. You're not bloodthirsty enough and you laugh too much. Pirates have black curling beards and they carry cutlasses in their teeth. Oh, and they drink a lot of rum," she added.

"I for one prefer a decent claret and a good cognac," Anthony said solemnly, shaking out a towel. "And I am a passable coiffeur, not to mention lady's maid, so let's get on with it, shall we?"

There seemed nothing for it. Olivia knelt beside the tub, the folds of the nightshirt billowing around her. Anthony draped a towel around her shoulders and scooped her hair off her neck, tossing it forward as she bent her head.

The hot water felt wonderful, but not as wonderful as his fingers moving gently across her scalp, cleverly avoiding the soreness that she had felt when she'd turned her head on the pillow. The scent of verbena filled the cabin, and the hot water washed through the thick black fall of her hair. Olivia's eyelids drooped and she drifted in the warm scented hinter-land behind her eyes.

"There, that should do it." The sound of his voice was shocking in the silence. Olivia lifted her head hurriedly and water dripped down the back of her neck, soaking the collar of her makeshift gown.

"That wasn't very clever," Anthony observed, gathering her hair between his hands and wringing it out over the tub. He wrapped a towel turban-style around her head. "You'd better change that...that...what would you call what you're wearing?" He regarded her quizzi-cally.

"Your nightshirt," Olivia responded, standing up slowly. "Maybe Adam's finished my c-clothes now."

"He's busy cooking, but I have dozens of nightshirts. My aunt embroiders them for me. She has the strangest notions about me." He opened the cupboard in the bulwark.

"You have an aunt?" Olivia exclaimed. "Pirates can't have aunts."

"Well, as far as I know, I wasn't the result of immaculate conception, so this particular pirate does have one.... Ah, this one should do. As I recall, it has some particularly exquisite lacework on the sleeves." He shook out another of the voluminous garments.

"And an emerald sash, I think, since we're dressing for dinner." He selected a rich green silk cravat. "You won't need one for your hair this evening."

"No," Olivia agreed faintly. She was still

trying to equate embroidering aunts with *Wind Dancer*'s master. "Where does your aunt live?"

"Not far away," he responded casually and uninformatively, tossing the fresh nightshirt and sash onto the bed. He opened another cupboard and took out a wooden casket. Then he turned back to Olivia with a speculative air. "Do you wish to lie on the bed while I dress your leg? Or would you rather stand? I can manage either way."

Again Olivia felt the bandage. "I'm sure I can do it myself."

"No." He shook his head. "I am something of a physician, Olivia, as I told you. There's no need to be shy."

"How c-can you say that? It's one thing when I'm not really c-conscious, but it's different now."

"I don't see why. I'm wearing my physician's hat. I grant you it would be different...very different...if I were not. But I promise you I have no trouble separating any, shall we say, masculine responses to your body, from the purely practical and medicinal."

"Would you have...would you have a masculine response, then?" Olivia blurted the question, astonished at herself, but only on some distant plane.

Anthony smiled slowly. "Oh, yes," he said softly. "Most definitely. But as I said, that's not the point at this moment."

He set the casket on the table and flipped open the lid. Then he hooked a stool over with

59

his foot and sat down, reaching for Olivia's hands. He drew her towards him and with his hands at her waist turned her so her back was to him.

"Now, why don't you lift your skirts as high as you feel comfortable. I just need to be able to unfasten the bandage."

"But it's right at the top of my leg," Olivia protested faintly, gathering her skirts in both hands and lifting them slowly. The breeze from the window was cool against the backs of her legs. "Is that high enough?"

"Just a little higher."

"But...but you'll see my bottom!"

"And it's quite the prettiest little bottom," he said, laughing. "No...no, don't run away. I beg your pardon, but it was irresistible. I promise I won't see anything I shouldn't, but I do need to get at the pin."

"Oh!" Olivia said in mingled disgust and resignation. She hauled her skirt up as a freshening gust of evening breeze blew cold into the cabin, raising goose bumps on her skin. Or at least, they could have been caused by the cold air, but then again, maybe not.

Anthony unfastened the pin that held the bandage closed and unwound it. His fingers brushed against her skin, reminding her vividly of the strange dream time, but now she was in full possession of her senses, and vibrantly aware. He touched the inside of her thigh and she jumped as if stung.

"Be still," he said calmly, steadying her with his hands on her hips. "I can't do this without touching you. I'm going to clean the wound now, and then dress it with salve and rebandage it. It's healing nicely and tomorrow I should be able to take out the stitches."

Olivia gritted her teeth and tried to pretend she was somewhere else, doing something quite other than standing here holding up her skirts for the intimate attentions of a male stranger.

But it was over at last. He wound the bandage once more tightly around her thigh and refastened the pin. "There, you can let your skirts down now."

Olivia let the material slip back to her ankles and stepped away from his knees. She pulled the towel off her head, and her wet hair fell to the soaked clinging collar of the nightshirt. She shivered.

"Why don't you wash and change now?" Anthony suggested. "There's plenty of hot water left in the other pail. Just leave a little for me when you're finished." He strolled to the chart table as he spoke, adding cheerfully, "Piracy is devilishly dirty work."

Olivia eyed the tub, the curl of steam from the pail. She ran a hand inside the sodden collar of her makeshift gown. She looked at the fresh clean raiment, the brilliant emerald sash. "I'll be about fifteen minutes," she said.

"Take your time." He was bending over the chart table, the sextant in his hand.

"I'll call when I'm finished," she offered.

"Oh, I expect I'll know when you're finished," he observed amiably.

Olivia swallowed. "Are you staying in here, then?"

"Of course. But I'll keep my back to you. I give you my word of honor." There was a laugh in his voice.

"Honor?" Olivia exclaimed. "You're not a man of honor. You're a pirate and a thief, and you draw people's naked bodies when they're not aware of it, and I'm sure you've killed people as well. You're not a gentleman. How c-could you possibly talk of honor?"

"But have you never heard of honor among thieves, Olivia?" he inquired without turning from the chart table. The laugh remained in his voice. "I promise you, you'll see only my back. But do, I beg you, make haste. Otherwise the water will be cold by the time it's my turn, and I'm in sore need of soap and fresh clothes."

Olivia hesitated, then approached the tub with a sense of helpless resignation. If he did turn around, what did it matter? He'd see nothing he hadn't already seen. But then he'd had on his physician's hat, she reminded herself. Whatever hat he was wearing now, it had crowned no physician's head.

She poured hot water into the tub and drew the nightshirt over her head. She looked quickly over to him, but he was still studiously working on the charts, humming to himself.

Hastily she dipped a piece of towel in the hot water, rubbed soap on it, and sponged her body. It felt so wonderful that she almost forgot that she wasn't alone. Then she heard a movement behind her and grabbed up a towel to cover herself, an indignant exclamation on her lips. But he'd gone in what seemed like a straight line to the chessboard beneath the window, and he still had his back to her.

"I see you've completed the problem," he observed casually. "It wasn't a particularly challenging one, I found."

"Then why didn't you finish it yourself?" she demanded, drying herself as quickly as she could.

"I was about to, but I was called away," he replied with an airy wave of his hand. He selected several pieces from the wooden box that stood beside the board and placed them on the squares. "Let's see how you do with this one."

Olivia drew the clean nightshirt over her head. Her sigh of relief was audible and Anthony raised his head and looked at her. His eyes held his secret smile. He came over to her and cupped her face in both hands, then he ran his fingers through the mass of damp black curls framing her face, combing and fluffing out her hair. "I told you I was a passable coiffeur."

He laughed and lightly ran the pad of his thumb over her mouth. "You have such a beautiful complexion. Like thick cream. And your eyes are magnificent. Black and soft as velvet."

Olivia stared at him. It was the first she'd heard of this. "Are you...are you making love to me?"

"Not yet." He laughed again and pinched her nose. "I never make love when I'm hungry."

Olivia stepped away from him, regarding him rather in the manner of a Christian facing the lions. "I think you are a rake," she pronounced. "And I will not let you make love to me."

"No?" He raised an eyebrow. "Well, it's an academic question at present." He turned from her and pulled his shirt over his head. His back was tanned to a deep burnished gold. It was long and slim and tapered.

Olivia felt a curious little tug in the base of her belly. She dragged her eyes away and picked up the emerald sash, tying it around her waist. She heard the clink of his belt buckle and involuntarily looked towards him again.

He tossed his belt to the floor and with one smooth movement pushed his britches off his hips and stepped out of them.

Olivia's jaw dropped.

"You did say you were accustomed to the male form," he said. "Without the fig leaves."

Yes! On paper or cast in bronze. Olivia tried to speak but her throat felt stuffed with cotton. He was bending over the tub, splashing his face. His buttocks, smooth and flat, were as tanned as his back, his thighs dusted with fair curls, the hard muscles rippling in thigh and calf as he braced himself. And she could see between his thighs the dark shadow of his sex.

"The human body is the greatest wonder of creation," Anthony remarked in the tone of one instructing a pupil. "In all its manifestations, thin, fat, long, short. Every line, every curve, is beautiful." He turned as he spoke, sponging his torso with the soaped towel that Olivia had used.

Olivia knew a challenge when she heard one. She refused to look away and indeed she couldn't have dragged her eyes from this perfect example of the human form if she'd wanted to.

Every inch of him had been touched with the sun. Fair hair clustered around his nipples, cloaked his sex. He stood naked before her, alone in this cabin, and yet she realized with a shock of what could only be dismay that he was not aroused.

Her reaction, instead of the requisite maidenly horror at the sight of this naked man, was one of confused disappointment. Did he not find her in the least appealing? He hadn't behaved as if that was the case, but maybe she was too inexperienced to understand. She felt herself blush even as her eyes drank him in.

"Would you prefer to dine on deck?" he asked as casually as if they were in some drawing room. "It's a beautiful night and your hair will dry in the breeze." He turned away from her again, to Olivia's profound relief. She found his back view much less disturbing. "Could you find me a clean shirt from the cupboard?"

She still couldn't find her tongue but shirts were a different matter and a welcome distraction. He had wrapped a towel around his loins when she turned back to him with the garment.

"My thanks." He thrust his arms into it and left it open as he went to another cupboard for a clean pair of britches.

"So, the deck or the cabin?" He cast aside the towel and stepped into the britches. Olivia noticed that he wore no undergarments. Men usually wore drawers beneath their britches. That much she did know from the washing lines around the washhouse.

He buttoned the shirt, leaving it open at the neck, and thrust the tail into the waistband of his britches. He bent to pick up his belt and fastened it at his hip again, adjusting the set of the short dagger in its sheath.

"On deck." Olivia finally managed to speak, now that the world had returned to more orderly proportions.

"Good." He went to the door and called for Adam, who appeared almost immediately, as if he'd been waiting outside the door.

"Dinner'll be ruined," he grumbled. "What took ye so long?"

"We'll dine on the quarterdeck," Anthony said, ignoring the complaining question. "Get young Ned to clean up the cabin while we're above...oh, and we'll drink that '38 claret, Adam."

"Oh, aye," Adam muttered, entering the cabin. "It's celebratin', are we?"

"We have cause for celebration," Anthony responded.

"Oh, aye?" Adam repeated with a skeptical eyebrow. He glanced rather pointedly at Olivia. "You'll not be needin' yer clothes, I see."

"I borrowed these," Olivia said with an attempt at dignity. "But when I leave the ship, I'll need my own c-clothes."

"And when'll that be? I ask meself," Adam muttered, taking a bottle and two glasses from a cupboard. " 'Ere, you want to take these up." He thrust bottle and glasses at Anthony, who took them meekly.

"Come, Olivia."

"When *will* it be?" she asked, going past him through the door, holding up her voluminous skirts as she stepped over the high threshold.

"When will what be?" He followed her, leaving the door open to the sounds of Adam banging around in the cupboards, collecting plates and cutlery.

"When I leave *Wind Dancer*," she said impatiently. "When you stop kidnapping me."

"Oh, is that what I'm doing?" he said as they climbed the companionway and emerged on deck. "You tumble down the cliff and fall unconscious at the feet of one of my watchmen. We succor you and minister to your wounds, and that's called kidnapping."

"You knew who I was; you could have sent word and someone would have fetched me." The real world was intruding again without her agreement, forcing the magic of wonderland into retreat.

"Ah, but you see I have no visiting cards.

Pirates in general don't pay calls on the local gentry," Anthony explained solemnly. His gray eyes gleamed with amusement, vanquishing her unwitting edge of antagonism.

"Oh, you're absurd!" Olivia declared, climbing up to the high quarterdeck. "You kidnapped me and took me off to the high seas and my family will all think I'm dead, and even if I ever do get back to them, my reputation will be ruined.

"Not that that will matter," she added. "Since I never intend to get married, and only potential husbands worry about such things."

Anthony listened to this stream of words as he uncorked the bottle and poured the rich ruby wine into the two glasses whose long stems he held between the fingers of his free hand. He took the scent of the wine with a critical frown, then nodded and passed a glass to Olivia.

"I trust a vow of celibacy doesn't also involve a vow of chastity. The two are not synonymous." He regarded her over the lip of his glass.

Olivia took a larger gulp of wine than she'd intended, and choked. Anthony solicitously thumped her back.

"Take it easy. It's too fine a wine to quaff like small beer."

"Oh...oh, I didn't!" Olivia protested. "It went down the wrong way."

"Ah, I see." He nodded and leaned back against the rail, looking up at the star-filled sky. "What a beautiful night."

It seemed he'd dropped the topic of chastity, and Olivia took a more moderate sip of her wine. The sky was deepest blue with a crescent moon low on the horizon and the broad diffused swath of the Milky Way directly above them. The helmsman stood at the wheel, and *Wind Dancer*, once more true to her name, seemed to be playing in the wind over the swelling sea. "Do you navigate by the stars?"

"A less disturbing topic, eh?"

"Do you use the stars to navigate by?" she repeated determinedly.

"After dinner I'll show you how," he said, drawing her to the rail beside him, out of the way of Adam and two other sailors, who clambered onto the deck with a table and chairs and a basket of plates and cutlery.

Adam threw a snowy cloth over the table, lit an oil lamp, and set out two places. "There y'are, then. I'll bring the meat."

"My lady Olivia..." Anthony drew back a chair for her with a punctilious bow.

Olivia couldn't resist a little curtsy, laughing inwardly at the thought of her bare feet and her strange gown. The master of *Wind Dancer* seemed to know exactly how to change her mood. With a word, a gesture, a smile, he drew from her whatever response he wished. And while part of her resented such manipulation, another part of her was entranced.

Adam set down on the table a platter of sliced roast mutton studded with slivers of garlic and sprigs of rosemary, a bowl of potatoes baked in their skins in the embers of the fire, and a salad of field greens and mushrooms.

"Oh," Olivia said. "I don't think I have ever been so hungry."

"Well, eat slowly," Anthony cautioned. "Your belly's had almost nothing in it for three days. You don't wish to be sick."

"I couldn't possibly be sick," Olivia said, spearing a slice of mutton on the tip of her knife. "It smells so wonderful. Adam, you're a genius."

For once, the elderly man's expression softened and his mouth took a slight curve. "The master's right," he said gruffly. "Your belly's shrunk, so go easy."

Olivia shook her head in vigorous denial and took a large bite of meat. It tasted as wonderful as it smelled. She ate a potato smothered in butter and wiped the grease from her chin with the back of her hand, too hungry to worry about the niceties of the napkin on her lap.

Anthony refilled their glasses and watched her. There was something undeniably sensual about her robust enjoyment of her dinner. He thought of the blithely exuberant way she'd hurled herself across the netting between *Wind Dancer* and *Doña Elena* that morning to join in the fray. It was as if Olivia Granville, separated from all that had protected and enclosed her, had discovered a new self. Would she bring that same robust enjoyment to bed? he wondered.

A smile touched his lips as he thought of her declaration that she would remain unwed. It was an absurd intention for a young woman of her family background. And yet, as he examined her countenance, took in the firmness of her mouth, the set of her chin, he thought that maybe she would manage it. He was certain Olivia Granville thought for herself.

"What are you looking at?" Olivia asked, suddenly aware of his scrutiny.

"Oh, I was just enjoying your enjoyment," he said carelessly, leaning back in his chair, lifting his glass to his lips. "Rarely have I seen a gently bred maiden devour her dinner with such gluttony."

Olivia flushed. "Was I being greedy?"

"No." He shook his head and leaned over to put another potato on her plate. "I'm just wondering what else you devour with such enthusiasm."

Olivia put a slab of butter on the potato and watched it melt. "Books," she said. "I devour books."

"Yes, I had gathered that."

"You have a considerable library in your cabin. Where did you go to school?" Olivia was rather pleased with the sly question that she thought would give her some clue to the pirate's background.

Anthony merely smiled. "I'm self-taught."

Olivia looked over at him. "I don't believe you."

He shrugged. "That is as you please." He reached over to refill her glass. "Do you wish me to show you how to navigate by the stars?"

This was too interesting a prospect for further probing. Olivia nodded eagerly.

"Come here then." He stood up with his glass and went to stand behind the helmsman at the wheel. He slipped one arm around Olivia's waist and drew her backwards, so she stood with her back against him. "Now, you see the North Star?"

Olivia tried to follow the lesson, but for once the sharpness of her mind seemed blunted. She was aware only of the body at her back, the warmth of his arm at her waist, the wine-scented breath rustling against her cheek as he pointed out the constellations. The stars all seemed to merge and she felt stupid as she struggled to grasp concepts that would ordinarily have been perfectly simple for her.

The hand at her waist moved upward against her breast, and she drew a swift breath. But he said nothing, merely continued calmly with the lesson, his hand pressing against the soft swell of her breast.

"You interested in puddin'?"

"Oh, yes," Olivia said almost jumping away from the encircling arm. "What is it?"

"Rhubarb pie." Adam set a pie dish on the table with a jug of thick cream. "Lord, you 'ad an appetite on you," he muttered, surveying the wreckage of the table.

"It was very good." Olivia sat down and reached for the pie knife. Her heart was beating too quickly and she thought her voice sounded a little squeaky as she asked as casually as she could, "Are you going to have some pie, Anthony?"

He came back to the table. "Funny, but I'd have thought the fascinations of astronomy would have held your attention rather longer. But then, no one makes a rhubarb pie to rival Adam's."

Olivia put a large slice of pie on her plate and made no response. She felt as if she'd been cut loose from everything that had made sense of her life hitherto. And she didn't know what to make of any of it. The only thing she did know was that her blood was racing, and despite the confusion, she felt more alive than she'd ever felt before.

Four

"So what does the message say?" The questioner put a spill to his pipe, and the acrid smell of strong tobacco filled the taproom.

"Jest that if'n we're interested in sellin' what we culled, then 'e'll be 'ere in the Anchor at the end o' the week."

"And how does he know there was any culling?" The questioner was young, dark haired, swarthy of complexion. He was dressed in a suit of turquoise silk and wore his hair in the Cavalier style, tumbling to his shoulders in elaborate curls, glistening with pomade. He drew on his pipe in the smoke-wreathed room and surveyed his interlocutor through cold green eyes.

The man shrugged. "Doubt it's a secret, sir. Message come the mornin' after. Thought you'd want to know."

"Of course I want to know!" There was a snarl to the well-bred voice. "We need customers, you dolt! But how do we know it's not a trap?"

The other man shrugged and lit his own pipe of rather more noxious tobacco. "Dunno, sir. Reckon that's your business. Ours is to cull."

The young man was silent in the face of this truth. "There's been no one sniffing around? No awkward questions?"

"No, sir. 'Twas pitch black that night an' the storm was strong. Ship could 'ave gone aground on 'er own. But the whole island reckons 'twas a wreckin' job," he added. "Jest can't prove it."

"And whoever's buying knows it was a wrecking job," the young man mused. "And he knew whom to contact? Who brought the message?"

"Didn't 'ave no name, sir. An' he was all swaddled in a cloak, with the 'ood pulled down. 'Twas an 'ot night too," the man added reflectively. "But 'e was an island man. Spoke like an island man."

"Mmm. Landlord, bring me a pint of porter," the young man bellowed suddenly across the counter.

74

"Right y'are, sir." The host of the Anchor, who had been listening to a conversation that held no secrets for him, slapped an overfull tankard on the counter before the customer. "I was expectin' me casks, sir," he said in an unconvincing whine. "Any sign of when I might be gettin' 'em?"

"You'll get them when I have them," the other snapped, taking up the tankard. He drank deeply and stared up at the blackened ceiling rafters, watching the smoke curl from his pipe. He'd been expecting a delivery from the French coast for over a week, and it was hard now not to believe that something had happened to the boat. Her captain had always been reliable in the past, but the smuggling trade was far from a certain business. Which was why those who needed a more assured income and could banish moral scruple augmented their smuggling with wrecking. Godfrey, Lord Channing, had never been troubled with moral scruple.

He had customers for his smuggled goods, like George of the Anchor here, who had already paid well for the overdue consignment. If it didn't arrive, he'd be facing an ugly situation. These were not patient men. He looked at the landlord with new eyes and didn't like what he saw. The man had the face of a prizefighter overly fond of his drink, with a roughly broken nose, bloodshot eyes, and a complexion crimson with broken veins. His hands, busy with an ale keg, were massive.

Godfrey felt a faint tremor of alarm. If his

75

unsatisfied customers on the island joined forces with their grievances, life could become most unpleasant.

But there was hope. If this interest in the profits of the wreck was genuine and not a trap, then he had a way out. Even after the wreckers themselves had taken their commission, there would still be a decent profit left for the brain behind the muscle.

"So, ye'll be comin' to meet wi' him, then, sir?" the landlord asked.

Godfrey didn't deign a response.

"I'll be able to point 'im out to ye, sir," the landlord continued. He shot a sly look at Godfrey. "Anythin' I can do to 'elp, like."

Godfrey was not taken in by this generous offer. He slammed his empty tankard and still-smoldering pipe on the counter and stood up, regarding the landlord with distaste. He snapped, "I can take care of my own business."

The landlord touched his forelock, radiating mockery. "Then I can expect me cognac soon, honored sir?"

"Damn your insolence! You'll get your cognac." Godfrey threw a coin on the counter. The door slammed on his departure.

A man who'd been sitting in the inglenook rose to his feet and left in Godfrey's wake. He limped badly, leaning heavily on a stick. Yet despite his obvious disability, he caught up with Godfrey before he had mounted his horse.

"A word with you, Lord Channing," he said softly.

Godfrey spun around. "How do you know my name?"

The man who had addressed him regarded him with a malicious smile, his small brown eyes glittering. His countenance bore the deep lines of one who has known pain. At first Godfrey thought he was an old man.

"I made it my business to know," the man responded, and his voice was that of a much younger man than his appearance indicated. "Wrecking and smuggling are not the best ways in which to improve one's fortunes," he observed conversationally.

Godfrey's heart raced. *Was he about to be arrested?* He stared at his interlocutor.

"Don't worry, I'll not blab," the man said with an unpleasant chuckle. "But I think I might be able to offer you a surer route to fortune."

"I don't understand."

"Not yet, no. But let us walk a little and I'll explain."

Godfrey looped the rein again around the tethering post. There was something almost mesmerizing about the stranger, something in the eyes that drew him in. This too was a man not given to moral scruple.

"Forgive the slowness of my gait," the man said, limping into the lane.

"What happened to you?"

"A duel," Brian Morse replied, his voice low and grim. "I have a plan that will serve both our purposes, my lord, if you'll give me a hearing."

In the Anchor, the remaining customer mused, "Reckon that smugglin' boat of 'is has gone astray." He stared hopefully into his now empty tankard. "Reckon it's our friend what took it, don't you, George?" He pushed his tankard around in a circle.

"You want another, you pay for it, Silas," the landlord declared.

With a grimace Silas dug into his pocket for a farthing. He placed it on the counter with the air of one donating his life's blood.

The landlord scooped it up, then picked up the tankard and refilled it from the keg, filling one for himself at the same time. "Aye," he said, wiping foam from his mouth after a long draft. "Reckon it *is* our friend. But it'll take more than that young lordling"—he gestured contemptuously to the door from which Godfrey had left—"to outwit *'im*!"

"You know what I think..." the customer said, staring fixedly at the bottles behind the counter. "You want to know what I think?"

"I might if you'd up and say it."

"I think, George, that you'd do best to switch yer orders to our friend, 'stead of that clothes'orse."

"Aye, mebbe," the landlord replied. "But answer me this, Silas. Is it better fer a man to deal wi' a greedy fool, or wi' a man as dangerous clever as our friend? That's what I asks meself."

"You wouldn't want to get on the wrong side of our friend," Silas agreed, nodding solemnly. "An' a man can always outwit a fool."

"Aye, an' put the frighteners on 'im too. Can't do that wi' our friend, I reckon."

"No." Silas shook his head vigorously. "An' any road, our friend ain't in the smugglin' business so much these days, is 'e? Used to be there wasn't a boat went over to France from the island wi'out 'is say-so, but he's other fish to fry these days, I reckon."

He gazed down into his tankard before pronouncing, "O' course, if'n a man wanted a cask of cognac an' a morsel o' that Valenciennes lace fer 'is woman, our friend could get it fer 'im, that's fer sure. But 'tis not 'is regular trade, like." He looked up thoughtfully. "D'ye reckon our friend's tried 'is hand at wreckin' an' all? Pays better than smugglin'."

"Aye, could be, but there's no tellin'. Powerful close-mouthed, 'is men are," George declared. He tapped the side of his nose and winked. "Howsomever, what d'ye wager it's our friend what's after that young lordling's culling? He's such a clever 'un, it'd be like 'im to let someone else do the work fer 'im."

"Could be," agreed Silas.

The two men drank to this consensus and lapsed into contemplative silence.

"WHY DON'T YOU go below now? You can barely keep your eyes open." The pirate leaned back in his chair, a glass of cognac cupped in his hands, regarding Olivia with a slight smile.

Olivia stifled a yawn. It was true, she was very sleepy. The remains of dinner had been cleared away, and while Anthony sat savoring his cognac, she had been drifting in a half sleep to the music of the wind in the rigging and the motion of the ship on the gentle swell of the night sea.

"It's such a perfect night," she said, looking up at the sky. "You never see stars like this on land."

"No, you don't."

"When will we get back to the island?"

"If the wind holds fair, we'll sight land by noon tomorrow."

"And will it hold fair?"

He shrugged and smiled. "That's hard to say. The wind is a fickle mistress." He called softly to the helmsman. "What do you think, Jethro? Will the wind hold fair for us?"

"Might drop towards dawn."

"What am I to say at home?" Olivia cupped her chin on her elbow-propped hands. "How am I to explain things?"

"Why don't we cross that bridge when we reach it?" Anthony leaned over and brushed the curve of her cheek with a fingertip. "Are you so anxious to break free of entrancement, Olivia?"

She shook her head. "No, but this is just a dream and I must wake up sometime."

"Yes, you must. But not before noon tomorrow."

"I suppose there wouldn't be much point

waking up yet, since I'm still kidnapped," Olivia observed gravely.

"Precisely so…. Go to bed now."

Olivia pushed back her chair and rose reluctantly. "I would like to sleep under the stars."

"You would be cold."

"Even with blankets?"

"Even with blankets."

Olivia continued to hesitate, looking at him as he sat at his ease swirling the cognac around the crystal. He returned her gaze, that smile deep in his eyes, and something else that she couldn't read. It was a promise of some kind. She was aware of a quiver in her belly, a strange tightening in her thighs.

She turned to the steps leading down to the main deck. "Good night."

But he didn't return her farewell.

The cabin had been cleaned and tidied, the lantern above the bed lit, throwing a soft golden glow over the polished wood and the rich colors in the Turkey rugs. The windows had been closed and damask curtains drawn across them.

Olivia pulled back the curtains and flung open the windows again. It was too fresh and beautiful a night to shut out. She turned back to the cabin. There was clean linen on the bed; the covers were turned down invitingly. She fingered the emerald sash at her waist, then untied it, folded it carefully, and replaced it in the cupboard in the bulwark. She began to untie the ribbons at the neck of the nightshirt when her eye fell on the chessboard.

Anthony had set up another chess problem, she remembered now. She went over to look at it, twisting the silken ribbons around her fingers as she gazed down at the pieces in frowning concentration. It was definitely not as immediately solvable as the previous one.

A deep yawn took her by surprise, and Olivia lost interest in the problem. In the morning, when her mind was fresh, she'd solve it in a minute. A problem she *couldn't* solve in a minute was what she was to sleep in. Her makeshift gown felt too much like a gown now to do double duty, and besides, she would need it in the morning.

She'd slept naked ever since she'd arrived on *Wind Dancer,* and Olivia, on reflection, could see no reason to do any different tonight. She pulled the nightshirt over her head, folded it as carefully as she had folded the sash, and put it away, then she climbed over the wooden sides and into the bed. The sheets were cool and crisp and the bed was wonderfully familiar.

She turned onto her side and closed her eyes only to realize that the lantern was still lit. But what did it matter? She was too tired to be bothered by such a soft glow, and it would go out in its own time when the oil was burned...

When she awoke, it was to a pale darkness. And she was not alone in the bed. Something heavy was holding her down into the deep feather mattress. Olivia investigated and found that it was an arm across her waist. And it was another leg that was tangled with her own.

As she lay, rigid with shock, she could hear her bedmate's deep, even breathing. She investigated further. He was as naked as she was.

"Did I wake you?" the pirate asked sleepily.

"You're in my bed!"

"Actually it's my bed."

Even through the tendrils of sleep, Olivia could hear the laugh in his voice.

"But I'm sleeping in it," she objected, wondering why she wasn't screaming her maidenly outrage. Maybe it was the magic again, but she was utterly aware in every fiber of her body of the powerful physical presence beside her. This was not entrancement, it was reality, and the reality held only fascination.

"It's been my bed for three nights...or is it four?" she murmured.

"This would be the fourth," he said, his breath rustling against the back of her neck. The arm around her waist moved so that his hand flattened on her belly.

Olivia's stomach contracted involuntarily. She tried to push his hand away with as much success as an ant trying to move a mountain. But then, she didn't seem to be pushing with true conviction. "You didn't sleep in it before," she protested.

"In the opinion of your physician, you were too ill for a bedmate," he responded solemnly. "The medical opinion has now changed."

The hand on her belly remained still and warm and curiously unthreatening. Olivia felt his other hand now on her back, moving up between her shoulder blades, clasping her neck firmly, pushing up into her hair, cupping her scalp. It felt wonderful and strangely familiar, as if sometime he'd touched her in this way before.

"Let yourself go," he instructed softly. "Just lie still and feel."

He pressed his lips into the groove at the back of her neck, and the hand on her stomach moved upward to cup her breasts. Her nipples hardened as if she'd been dipped in cold water. Olivia felt herself slipping back into the dreamworld of the past days, where her mind was adrift and her body merely a sensate shape floating in feathers.

Fingers caressed the curve of her hips, danced down her thighs, played in the little hollows behind her knees. She could feel the length of him against her back, and she could picture his body as vividly as if she were facing him. The small nipples so different from her own, like little buttons in the broad expanse of his chest, the indentation of his navel in the concave stomach, the darker line of hair drawing her eye down to his sex.

But what had once been quiescent was now rampant. Olivia could feel the hard length of his penis pressing into the crease of her thighs. Jubilation...wicked, outrageous, delicious...throbbed in the secret places of her body.

And then she stiffened, straightening her legs. "I'm not going to marry," Olivia said. "Never. I'm never going to marry."

"A laudable determination," the pirate

84

murmured into her hair as his flattened hand slid between her thighs. "One that I share." He caressed the inside of her unbandaged thigh until she relaxed once more, her body softening against him.

"But we can't do this if we're not going to marry," Olivia protested.

"Celibacy is not the same as chastity," Anthony reminded her, touching his tongue to her ear, nibbling her earlobe. "We had this discussion once."

"But...but I might c-conceive," Olivia murmured, wondering why it should be that such considerations seemed to have lost all urgency. "Then we would have to marry."

"I'll make sure that doesn't happen," he said, and he was laughing, she could hear it in his voice. "You're still an innocent despite all your learning. Intellectual experience is no substitute for reality, my flower."

Olivia made no reply. She was incapable of reply.

Anthony turned her onto her back. She saw his face in the pale starlight from the still-open window. He bent to kiss her mouth and she gave a tiny sigh against his lips.

They were wonderfully pliant lips, soft and yet muscular. His tongue pressed for entrance and her own lips parted. He tasted of wine and cognac and the salt spray from the waves that lifted *Wind Dancer* and the wind that filled her sails.

She sucked on his tongue with sudden greed, and he held her face, probing deeper into her mouth. The length of his body was hard against her own softness. She put her hands in his hair. No longer confined in the black ribbon, the locks, gold as guineas, fell to his shoulders. His face was a wedge of light in the moon's glimmer from the window as she pushed the hair away and in her turn held his face.

"I am dreaming you," Olivia said.

"No, no dream." And he parted her thighs with his knee.

Olivia felt her body open, a liquid rush filling her loins with an anticipation of delight. His hands slid beneath her bottom, lifting her. The stab of penetration shocked her for a second and then there was only this wonderful liquid fullness and her body closed around him. She raked her hands through the golden fall of his hair, caught his mouth with her teeth, lifted her hips to meet the steady thrusts of his body.

"You are miraculous," Anthony said.

"You are a dream," Olivia replied. "But it was a dream I was always going to have."

"And I," he replied. He withdrew to the very edge of her body.

"Am I supposed to feel like this?" Olivia ran her hands from his buttocks along his hard muscular thighs as he held himself above her. "In the interests of intellectual inquiry?"

"I believe so." He moved slowly, burying himself within her again. Then he touched her. The hard little nub that Olivia had never known she possessed. He brushed it. Touched it. Rubbed it. And he moved within her.

Olivia was no longer Olivia. She dissolved into myriad parts. She was lost in the Milky Way. She thought she cried. She clung to the body that was her only connection to reality. She clung and she was held, tight, warm, safe, until she came to herself.

Anthony gathered her against him. He had known, known from the first moment she'd been delivered to his waterside doorstep, that Olivia Granville was going to govern his life in some impenetrable, unfathomable fashion.

Five

SHE RAN, the deserted corridor stretching ahead of her, impossibly long. She would never get to the end before he caught her. She could hear him behind her, his step almost leisured compared with her own racing feet. He called, softly taunting, "Run, little rabbit, run." Her breath came in gasps, hurting her chest, her throat was dry with fear and despair. He would catch her as he always did, just by the last window before the massive ironbound door that led into the family rooms of the castle.

She was almost abreast of the window when the footsteps behind speeded up. He grabbed her around the waist, swinging her into the air. She kicked, her short stockinged legs flailing. He laughed and held her well away from him so that her struggles were as effective as a fly's in a spider's web. "You haven't wished your brother good morning, little rabbit," he taunted. "Such discourtesy. Anyone would think you weren't pleased to see me this fine morning."

He set her on the thick stone windowsill that put her on his level. She stared into his hateful face and shook with helpless terror. He held her wrists clipped at her back, and she knew that if she opened her mouth to cry out, he would shove his handkerchief into it as a gag and she would feel as if she were suffocating. "Let's see what we have here," he murmured, almost crooning as he pushed his free hand under her skirt. ...

Olivia pushed herself upward through the slimy black tendrils of loathsome memory, thrusting herself towards the bright sane sunburst of waking reality. Her eyes flew open. Her heart was racing, her breath coming in labored gasps as if she were still running for her life.

She sat up, hugging her knees, shivering as the sweat dried on her skin. She was alone in the cabin but the pillow beside her own still bore the impression of Anthony's head. Sun poured through the open windows and slowly her panic receded, her heart slowed, her breathing became normal. But she couldn't shake the horror, or the latent terror of what had been no nightmare but a re-creation of long-buried reality.

A jug of water stood inside a basin on the marble-topped dresser, and Olivia pushed aside the sheet and stood up. She ached from top to toe as if she'd just lost a wrestling match. The water in the jug was hot. The verbena soap was in the soap dish, with fresh towels folded beside it.

Olivia poured water into the basin and washed. As she sponged between her legs, she shuddered, knowing now what had unlocked the dreadful memory. After the night's loving with Anthony, she felt the same stretched soreness that had tormented her after her stepbrother had walked off, whistling, leaving her quivering on the windowsill.

Every time, it had been the same during that hideous year when Brian Morse had lived at Castle Granville. Every time that he'd hurt her, ravaged her with his hard probing hands, he had whispered with soft yet utterly convincing menace that if she ever told a soul, he would kill her. And then he'd walked off, whistling, leaving her on the windowsill like a discarded doll.

How old had she been? Eight or nine, she thought. And she'd been so certain he would fulfill his threat that she had simply refused to allow herself to remember what had happened.

Olivia felt sick. It was an old familiar nausea. She rested her hands on the dresser, waiting for it to pass. Her nakedness troubled her as it had not done before, and she turned from the basin, one hand massaging her throat. She had put her makeshift gown back in the cupboard before she'd gone to bed last night.

Feverishly she flung open the cupboard door and pulled out the nightshirt. Only when she had it on did she feel safe again. She went to the window and looked out at the sea. It no longer stretched smooth and unbroken; there was land ahead. The humpbacked shape of the Isle of Wight. They were nearly home. Anthony had said that if the wind was fair they should see the island by noon today.

Olivia turned back from the window, her arms wrapped around her body as if she were cold, although the sun was warm as it fell across the oak floor where she stood barefoot. All the joy seemed to have been leached from her soul. She felt tarnished, violated, somehow unworthy. And it was as old and familiar a feeling as the vile memories that would not now be put back in their box.

Her eye fell on the chessboard. In an attempt to distract herself from the tormenting tempest of emotion, Olivia examined the problem she hadn't been able to solve the previous evening. And once again, as so often before, the mental gymnastics soothed her, took her out of herself.

"Solved it yet?"

Olivia spun around at Anthony's light tones. Her heart began to race again and she was unaware that she was staring at him as if at a monster, her face milk white, her eyes big black holes in her ashen countenance.

"What is it?" He came forward, the smile on his face fading; his voice lost its customary light amusement. "Has something happened?"

90

"No," Olivia said, shaking her head. Her hands lifted as if to ward him off, and she forced them to her sides. "The problem," she said vaguely. "I was just absorbed." She turned again to the board but her back prickled as he came up behind her.

He bent and kissed her nape and she bit back a cry.

"Olivia, what is it?" He put his hands on her shoulders and she stiffened with revulsion, holding herself rigid as she stared fixedly at the chessboard.

Maybe if she didn't move, didn't speak, he would go away.

Anthony looked down at her bent head. What could have happened? He'd awoken holding her, her body curled softly against him. He had been filled with the most wonderful sense of completion, his mind drowsily revisiting the wonders of the night. She'd been fast asleep when reluctantly he'd left her...three hours ago...

So what had happened? He could feel her revulsion, feel the power of her will as she tried to drive him away from her.

"White rook to bishop three. Black queen's bishop's pawn to knight three," she stated dully without moving the pieces.

"Yes," he said, letting his hands fall from her. "Exactly right." Her relief as he released her was palpable, but she didn't raise her eyes from the board.

"How soon before we get home?"

"We'll reach our anchorage after dark," he

replied. His hands lifted again to hold her shoulders and once again fell to his sides. "Will you not tell me what's the matter?"

"Nothing's the matter," Olivia said, moving chess pieces at random, still unable to look at him. "Will my clothes be ready, do you think?"

"Adam was putting the finishing touches a while ago. You slept through breakfast but I came to tell you that we do eat at midday if we're not otherwise occupied. The table is set on the quarterdeck."

The words were warm, reminding her of the boarding of the *Doña Elena*...of that exhilaration...of what it had led to...of how hungry she had been. But she could summon no answering warmth. "Thank you."

Anthony waited a moment, then said, "Will you come, then?"

"Yes...yes, in a minute."

Again he hesitated, and the silence stretched, taut as a lute string. He left the cabin, going on deck with a deep frown on his brow. He felt that somehow he had offended. But that was ridiculous.

They had been so in tune, body and soul, each complementing the other. He had felt it and he knew she had too. From the first moment she'd fetched up at his doorstep, he'd felt it. And suddenly it was as if that connection had been abruptly severed.

Was she regretting their loving? Regretting that she was no longer a maid? Was she frightened by the consequences of what had happened and blaming him? It would not be an unusual response, and yet Anthony would have sworn Olivia would not respond in predictable ways.

He climbed to the quarterdeck and stood behind Jethro, looking up at the sails, then across to the hump of the island. The green of its downs, the creamy white of its cliffs, were now faintly visible. He called an order and men swarmed up the rigging, loosening the sheets of the great white topsail, furling it on the yards as it collapsed.

Olivia stood on the lower deck watching the operation. It was all so smooth and neat, each move clearly ordered. It reminded her of finding the solution to a chess problem or working out a particularly satisfying mathematical formula.

The table was laid on the quarterdeck as it had been for their supper, and as she climbed the ladder Anthony left his position at the wheel and came over to her. His face was grave, the light in his eye extinguished.

Olivia sat down at the table. There were boiled eggs in a bowl, wheaten bread and a crock of butter, a jar of honey, a pink ham, a jug of ale. Despite her inner torment she was hungry.

Anthony sat down opposite her. He tilted his face to the sun and the breeze, closing his eyes briefly.

"Why did they bring down that sail?" She tried to keep her voice calm, ordinarily interested, as if there was no reason for there to be constraint between them.

"The tops'l is the first sail to be visible

from land," he told her in neutral tones. "I don't want to draw attention to our approach." He picked up the jug and leaned forward to fill her tankard. His eyes lifted, met hers, and Olivia turned from the puzzled question in his gaze.

She took a boiled egg and tapped it on the edge of the table to crack the shell. "Do you want to approach secretly because you're a pirate or because of the war?" she asked, trying for his own neutral tones.

Anthony shrugged. "Either or neither."

"But you're for the king," she insisted. "You talked of my father as the king's jailer."

He regarded her through narrowed eyes. "I have no time for this war. The country has been soaked in blood for close on seven years, brother against brother, father against son. And for what? The dueling ambitions of a king and a Cromwell." He gave a short, rather ugly laugh. "I'm a pirate, a smuggler, a mercenary. I sell my ship and talents to the highest bidder."

His bitter tone and the cynical statement chilled her to the marrow. She said almost desperately, "How am I to go home?" Her fingers shook as she peeled the egg and it slipped to the table. She picked it up again, flushing.

"What is it?" he asked quietly, and his eyes were once more soft, the bitterness gone from his expression.

Olivia just shook her head. How could she speak of something that she had held locked inside her for so long? And how to speak of it to the man who had forced the vileness back into her life, now as vivid in memory as it had been in reality during that dreadful year of her childhood?

"If you don't wish to draw attention to yourself, how am I to go home?" she repeated, removing the last shard of shell from the egg.

Anthony carved ham. Hurt warred with anger, and anger won because for as long as he could remember, he had protected himself from the hurt of rejection. If this was the way she wanted it to be, then he wouldn't fight for her confidence. He had more important things to concern him. Olivia Granville could come and go in his life and leave barely a trace. So, for once he'd been mistaken. His instincts had been awry. As Adam had said, there was always a first time. He would let the little innocent go back to her calm, privileged life. She'd suffer no untoward consequences, he'd made sure of that.

"May I offer you a slice of ham?" he asked coldly.

"Thank you."

He laid a slice on her plate, then said in the same cool tone, "One of the crew who has family on the island will take you ashore, where you'll be met and driven home. The story you will tell will not be far from the truth. You lost your footing on the cliff and fell to the underpath. The farmer, Jake Barker, found you, took you back to his cottage, where they tended you. Mistress Barker has some experience of physicking. She has more children than I've ever been able to count."

A smile flickered in his eyes for a bare instant. Then it was gone and he was continuing in the same cold tone. "You will say that you had no recollection of who you were for several days. When you regained your senses, they drove you home. You will, of course, be suitably grateful to the Barkers for their care and attention, and will, I trust, ensure that Lord Granville rewards them."

It was as if he were giving her a lesson in noblesse oblige because she couldn't be trusted to recognize such obligations herself. Olivia flinched at the frigid tones but she could do nothing to change this atmosphere. She couldn't begin to frame the words. Her skin seemed to have shrunk on her skeleton and become too small for her.

"My father is not at home." But they would have sent for him, she thought. As soon as she had disappeared, Phoebe would have sent for him, so he could be there now. And however difficult it was going to be to face him and to deceive him, nothing could be worse than being with the pirate now.

Olivia had no knowledge of *this* man. The master of *Wind Dancer* was once again transformed. She couldn't imagine this man laughing. Showing tenderness. His face had changed, the skin drawn tight over his cheekbones and around his jaw. That golden hair, caught once more in the ribbon at his neck, threw his face into harsh relief under the bright sun. There was no softness in this man. No laughter.

"Well, I trust you or his wife will honor his obligations in his absence." Anthony lifted his tankard to his lips.

His tone was so insulting, Olivia wanted to dash the contents of her own tankard into his cold, sardonic face. She pushed back her chair and stood up. "Excuse me." She stalked off the quarterdeck, her head high, her cheeks flushed with anger.

Anthony gazed out over the railing towards the island. It was taking greater shape now, and he thought he could distinguish the vicious rocks of the Needles at its farthest western point. They were approaching the maelstrom around St. Catherine's Point, but on a brilliant summer day there was no threat from those hidden rocks.

He had an appointment in the Anchor with the brain behind the wreckers. He took a slow sip from his tankard. Was it a brain or just a vicious, greedy man who had struck lucky?

A cynical smile touched his lips. If the man was a greedy fool, then he'd be easy to outwit. A sharp brain...that was another matter.

Olivia no longer interested him. She had failed him. Or he had failed her. It had ceased to matter. Interludes, however pleasant, could not be allowed to influence decisions.

"I've finished the dress. Not quite up to me usual standard." Adam interrupted his master's reverie, holding up Olivia's gown. He gave a disdainful flick at the work he didn't consider satisfactory. "Not much else t' do wi' it, though."

"I'm sure Lady Olivia will be suitably grateful," Anthony said distantly.

"Oh, so that's the way it is." Adam regarded Anthony with a knowing eye. "So what 'appened, then? Thought all was sweetness an' light wi' the lady."

"Take her her clothes, Adam."

There was a weariness to the instruction that Adam recognized. Recognized and hated to hear. He hesitated. "What's amiss?"

"I wish I knew." Anthony stared across at the island. Then he shrugged. "What does it matter? I thought...but I was wrong." He gave a short laugh. "There's always a first time, isn't that right, Adam?"

"If'n you say so."

"I thought that was what *you* said," Anthony declared savagely. But he made the declaration to empty air. Adam was already climbing down the ladder to the main deck.

Olivia stood over the chart table. She puzzled over the notations Anthony had made beside the charts, trying to make sense of them. They related to the sextant and the compasses, that much she knew. The island was there on the charts, as were other bodies of land that didn't mean anything to her. And the water was in different shades of blue marked with numbers. She lost herself in the puzzle. It was safe, clean, numbing. When the door opened, she was so absorbed she didn't notice immediately.

"Did what I could wi' yer clothes."

Olivia turned from the chart table, saying

with as much warmth as she could muster, "Oh, I'm sure they're perfect, Adam."

"Doubt ye'll think that when you look at 'em." He laid her gown and petticoats on the bed.

Olivia went over to look at them. "They do seem rather short," she said doubtfully.

"By the time ye'd finished yer tumblin', there wasn't much left to work wi'."

Olivia heard his disappointment and picked up the sadly reduced garments. "No, of c-course not. You've done wonders, Adam. At least I'll be able to go home looking halfway decent." She gave him a brilliant smile.

Adam nodded. He didn't like that smile. The girl was at some edge and it wouldn't take much to push her over. She hadn't been on that brink before. Probably explained Anthony's dark expression. The master of *Wind Dancer* hadn't looked like that in quite some time.

"Well, put 'em on an' see 'ow they do," he said, turning to one of the bulkhead cup-boards.

"How long before we land, Adam?"

"Bless ye, we don't land." He turned back with the shoes she had been wearing at the time of her fall. "These'll still do, but the stockin's were in shreds. Reckon ye'll 'ave to manage wi'out."

"That doesn't matter," Olivia said impatiently, taking them from him. "Why won't we land?"

Adam regarded her in silence. He didn't know how much Anthony had told her of the chine where *Wind Dancer* had safe haven, and he wasn't about to blurt out their secrets.

Of course, Anthony had said that she would be taken ashore, Olivia remembered. "Is there a cove, then?" she pressed.

"Not fer me to say." He gave her a nod and left.

Olivia, once more alone, knelt on the window seat watching as the island grew clearer. She would never see the pirate again once she'd left *Wind Dancer*. It was as it must be. As she wanted it to be. As she needed it to be.

She got off the window seat and went to the bed to examine her mended clothes. They would do. Once out of the pirate's night-shirt, clothed in her own garments, she would feel like herself again. This thing that had happened between herself and the pirate would cease to exist.

And then she began to shiver. Once before she had tried to make a thing that had happened cease to exist.

She threw off the nightshirt and scrambled into her clothes. Gown and petticoat ended at midcalf, but Adam's needle was skilled and the rents were almost invisible. She thrust her bare feet into her shoes. They felt strange, unnatural almost, after the time she'd spent barefoot...so carefree, so lost in entrance-ment.

She went to the window again, kneeling up to watch their approach to the island as it grew more and more distinct. She recognized St. Catherine's Point. She often walked along the cliff path to the headland above the point. Just a few days ago, before the wreck, she and Phoebe had taken a picnic up St. Catherine's Hill. It had been a steep climb to the top of the down from where they could look out across the Channel to the Dorset coast.

Would she tell Phoebe the truth of what had happened? It was almost impossible to imagine keeping anything from the woman who had been her dearest friend for so long. Someone who shared her life in its most intimate details.

The door opened behind her and Anthony came in. "I have to close the windows and draw the curtains." His voice was cool and neutral. "And I'm afraid you must stay in here. Our destination is secret. No one who is not of this ship can be aware of it."

He was almost accusing her of treachery. Anger was a much easier emotion to indulge than the wretchedness of a revulsion she could not explain.

"I know it must be somewhere above the cliff path where I fell," she retorted. "It's insulting to imagine I would betray your anchorage to anyone."

He shrugged indifferently and leaned over her to pull the windows closed.

Immediately Olivia slid off the window seat, ducking beneath his arm as she moved away from him. It was as if she could not bear to be near him; a muscle twitched in Anthony's cheek and his eyelid flickered, but Olivia was not looking at him and saw nothing.

He drew the curtains across and the light was

immediately muted. "We will reach our anchorage just after dark."

He struck flint on tinder and lit the oil lamp above the bed. "I need to remove the stitches from your leg. I would leave them for your own physician, but the farmer's family who have been caring for you these last days would not have had the skill to stitch the wound themselves or the coin to pay a physician. There would be questions."

"It seems illogical that you trust me enough to lie about what happened on this ship, and yet you insist upon hiding your anchorage from me."

Anthony had taken the wooden casket from the cupboard. He said in a tone of near indifference, "I trust your instincts for self-preservation. I can't imagine that you would risk the scandal that would result from the truth of your disappearance, however careless you say you are of your reputation. But if you do so choose, then what you know will do me no harm, as long as you do not also know how to find me and my ship."

Olivia thought now that even if she could explain why things had changed between them, it would make no difference. This man had no forgiveness, no compassion, no understanding in his eyes. She had offended him and that was sufficient. But how could she have been so mistaken in him? And yet in all honesty she knew that he must also be feeling that way about her. She had shown him a person who didn't exist, one who could embrace entrancement and yield to passion. So she had deceived him.

"Come." He opened the box and took out a pair of thin scissors. "This will take no time."

Olivia raised her skirt and petticoat and this time there was no suppressed excitement, no sense of a dangerous lust. It was a matter-of-fact business that, as he had said, took no time at all.

He closed the casket with a snap. "Adam will stay with you to ensure that you're not tempted to draw back the curtains."

"I need no jailer," Olivia protested. "I will not look if you do not wish it."

He paused at the door. "If you will not give me *your* confidence, how should you expect me to give you mine?"

She had no answer and turned from him with a shake of her head.

Adam came in with a large basket of mending. He sat stolidly on the window seat and began to sew. After a minute Olivia returned to her cogitations over the charts.

Wind Dancer crept along the coastline, tucked beneath the cliff in the deep channel known only to island mariners. In the shadow of evening she passed St. Catherine's Point. As the sun dipped well below the horizon she slid past small deserted coves under minimal sail. And then she vanished into the cliff.

Olivia felt the cessation of motion. She heard the rattle of the anchor chains. Adam had refilled the oil lamp several times during the hours they'd been immured in the cabin. He had offered no conversation and Olivia herself had been disinclined for any. She had lost herself in the charts until they were as easy to read for her as for any experienced mariner.

"Reckon we'd best get ready to go on deck." Adam broke the long silence, laying aside his needlework.

Olivia followed him on deck. It was very dark and she could see only the faintest sliver of sky and the smallest pinprick of a star. Almost as if they were in some kind of a cave. The night air was warm and felt enclosed. Very different from the brisk freshness of the open sea. But it was still sweet, and she could detect scents of sea pinks, the warm grass of the clifftop, honeysuckle and clover. They may not have landed, but land was not far distant.

"Are you ready?" The master of *Wind Dancer* spoke at her shoulder and she turned her head, meeting the steady gaze of those deepset gray eyes.

A wash of sadness, of remorse, of longing for what might have been surged over her. "Forgive me," she said involuntarily.

"For what?"

It was so cold, so unforgiving. Wordlessly she just shook her head.

"Can you climb over the rail?"

"Yes."

"The boat's waiting below. I'm afraid they're going to have to cover your eyes until you're put ashore."

Olivia made no response. What could it

possibly matter now what they did? She went to the rail and looked down in the darkness to the small single-masted bobbing boat. "Should I go now?" Her voice was without inflection.

"Yes." He offered her no help as she swung over the rail and lowered herself into the boat. She looked up at him. His face was pale in the darkness, his eyes glittering like gray ice. Then he took the kerchief from around his neck, balled it tightly, and tossed it down into the boat. One of the crew picked it up.

The linen was warm over her eyes. The scent of him was so powerful her stomach dropped. She inhaled in the soft darkness and there was a space, a clear space where entrancement was so strong, so clear, that the horror of the past was no longer there. She could feel his body against hers, his hardness against her softness. His lips. She felt faint, dizzy, and clung to the edge of the thwart.

"You all right, miss?"

The concerned voice brought her back. "Yes, thank you. Will we soon be there?"

"In a while."

Olivia listened to the soft plash of the oars as they rowed away from *Wind Dancer*. The wind was suddenly fresher and she heard the crew hoisting sail. She had no sense of direction, or even of time after a while. Someone began to hum softly and was joined by another. It was a sweet melody. And then the humming stopped. Sand grabbed the bow of the dinghy and there was a jarring stop.

"May I take this off now?" Olivia put her hands to the blindfold.

"Aye, miss."

She untied it and blinked into the half-darkness. She had no idea where they were, except that it was a small cove. The sea was black; cliffs rose high on three sides. But she could see the sky again and the mass of stars. Of *Wind Dancer* there was no sign, but that was hardly surprising. She'd been in the sailing dinghy for quite some time.

The men jumped out of the boat, hauling it up onto the beach. They were solicitous as they helped her out onto the sand. "It's a bit of a climb up the path, miss."

"That's all right, I c-can manage," she said, smiling at the man who had spoken. He looked so anxious.

"Ye want us to wait fer ye, Mike?"

"Nay, I'll spend t'night at 'ome." The man called Mike started off across the beach towards a thin white line in the cliff. "This way, miss. The cart'll be waitin' at the top."

Olivia followed, stuffing Anthony's kerchief into the pocket of her gown.

ANTHONY SURVEYED HIS IMAGE in the mirror in his cabin. He adjusted the curling mustache now gracing his lip and with a frown took a dark pencil to his eyebrows.

"What d'you think, Adam? Will it do?" He spoke in the broad accents of the island people.

"Aye." Adam spoke gruffly and handed

106

him a sailor's knit cap. "That's it wi' the girl, then, is it?"

Anthony didn't reply. He busied himself tucking his hair under the cap, pulling the brim low. "I think I look sufficiently villainous," he observed. "The blackened teeth are a nice touch, don't you think?"

"Thought you said she was different."

"Damn your eyes, Adam! I don't wish to discuss it!"

"Touched ye on the raw, then?" Adam was unperturbed by his master's roughness. He'd nursed him from the moment of his birth, changed his breechclouts, fed him milk from a dropper, kept him safe through the dreadful flight from Bohemia after the Battle of the White Mountain. Kept him safe and delivered him to his father's family in their grand mansion on the Strand in London.

And seen the infant repudiated by those who had duty to protect him...

"Adam, devil take you, man. You're falling asleep! Give me a hand with this rouge. I need to redden my nose, give myself some broken veins."

Adam took the pot of rouge that was thrust under his nose. "You want to turn yourself into a clown?"

"No, just a man who likes his drink. Hurry now. You have a defter hand than I with this stuff."

Adam did as he was bid and his hand was certainly artistic. When he'd finished, Anthony's mottled countenance shone like a rosy apple.

"Who're you takin' to watch yer back?"

"Sam...but I expect no trouble. The man has goods to sell. I have coin to pay. Why should there be trouble?"

"Unless it's a trap."

"They'll not be after me. The wreck was not mine."

"There's other things that are," Adam said dourly, screwing the lid back onto the pot of rouge.

"I know what I'm doing, Adam."

"Oh, aye. 'Tis a dangerous game yer playin', I'll tell ye that fer nothin'."

Anthony turned slowly. "I made a promise to Ellen, Adam, and I'll not renege. My father betrayed her; I'll not do so."

"Much good it'll do Ellen if ye find yerself swingin' off the 'angin' tree."

"I will not."

"Your father didn't think 'e would either," Adam said somberly. "And he didn't think 'e was betrayin' Ellen neither...not at the beginnin'. Went off full o' high thoughts. We stood together on the deck of the *Isabelle*, as sure an' certain of duty and righteousness as you stand there, an' look where it all ended."

"My father fought for religion, for ideals." Anthony gave a short laugh. "He was a crusader. And he betrayed the woman who loved him, first for those ideals, and then for..." His voice faded, then came back strongly.

"But I fight for self-interest, Adam. It's a much easier master, one who doesn't force hard choices on a man. I watch my own back and

108

I make my own decisions. I don't march to anyone's drum but my own." He lightly touched the elderly man's shoulder and smiled as he turned to leave. "Therein lies my security."

"If'n ye says so," Adam said to the closed door. He sat down heavily on the seat below the window. The curtains were drawn back again, the windows open. The air was still, laden with the night scents of the cliffs that concealed the chine where *Wind Dancer* had her safe anchorage.

Twenty-eight years ago, Anthony's father, Sir Edward Caxton, had set sail from Dover in the company of a group of eager, like-minded ideological young men to volunteer for King Frederick of Bohemia's Protestant army in its struggle against the Catholic Emperor Ferdinand. Adam had accompanied Sir Edward as his body-servant. Their ideals had died a bloody death in the massacre of White Mountain.

Anthony's father had escaped the battlefield, but he hadn't escaped the vengeance of the emperor. Ferdinand's agents had found him and had slaughtered him as he defended the door to his bedchamber, where his mistress was laboring to deliver their child.

They had watched her labor, watched her give birth, before they had cut her throat and left her and the blood-streaked child lying between her legs, the cord that attached him to his mother still pulsing. They had not expected the child to live.

But then they hadn't known that Adam was there, hidden behind the window curtains. There was no way he could have been of help to either Sir Edward or the lady Elizabeth, but he took the child, cleansed his mouth and nostrils and breathed life into him. And he succored him and carried him back to London to his grandparents.

His grandparents had repudiated him. His father's rejection of family duty in pursuit of ideals, and the child's illegitimate birth, were cause enough. They had turned Adam and the child from their door, threatening to set the dogs upon them. Adam had gone to the only person he knew who might take in Edward Caxton's bastard.

Ellen Leyland, the daughter of a country squire, had loved Edward Caxton. He had loved her after his fashion, but had left her to follow the bugle call of religious zeal. And in the glories of war he had forgotten her, turned instead to the illicit pleasures to be found in the bed of Lady Elizabeth of Bohemia.

Ellen had taken her late lover's child as her own. In the tiny Hampshire fishing hamlet of Keyhaven, she had ruthlessly taught Anthony his letters, mathematics, introduced him to the philosophers; set him on his own path of learning. And with Adam's help she had encouraged him to find his way among the smugglers, the fishermen, the men who made their living from the sea however it was to be made.

Anthony had always known his history,

known that he was rejected by his father's family, known that he had no legitimate place in the world, and he had learned the bitter lessons of survival. Just as he had learned what it was to be loved by Adam and by Ellen, whom he called aunt to all who might ask.

He had proved competent at survival, Adam reflected as he stood up, wincing at the creak in his knees. Competent but unorthodox. There were many who loved Anthony Caxton, and there were those who would gladly see him hang.

Six

THE CART WITH A STURDY COB between the traces was waiting at the head of the path. A lad of about twelve held the reins and jumped down from his perch as Olivia, following Mike, climbed the last steep stretch of the path to emerge on the clifftop.

"All well, Billy?" Mike called softly, crossing the springy turf towards him.

"Aye. Pa says as 'ow yer to come 'ome tonight and drink wi' him." The lad regarded Olivia curiously from beneath an unruly thatch of black hair. "If 'tis all right wi' the master."

"Oh, aye. He'll not be lookin' fer me back till the mornin'," Mike responded easily. He turned to Olivia, offering her his hand. "Let me 'elp ye up, miss. 'Tis probably a mite dirty," he added with an apologetic smile. "Cart was used to take the chickens to market this mornin'."

"I don't mind a few chicken feathers," Olivia said, taking the proffered hand and climbing into the cart. It was fortunate she didn't mind, since the floor was thick with feathers and there was a strong odor of livestock. "Smells more like pig to me," she observed.

"Oh, aye. Ma's piglets went off t' market this mornin'," the lad said, brushing at the seat with his sleeve. "Got a good price she did fer 'em, an' all."

Mike swung himself into the cart beside Olivia. " 'Tis not far, miss," he offered.

"You're taking me home?"

"Aye. Master says we're to deliver ye to the door. He says we're to say nowt. Ye'll do the talkin'." He gave her a rather anxious look as he said this.

"Yes, that's right," Olivia reassured him. "I know just what to say."

"That's good, then. I'm not much fer words meself." His relief was clear.

The lad clicked his tongue and the cob moved off slowly across the cliff and onto a narrow lane. Olivia had no idea where they'd landed or in what direction they were headed. The blindfold had disoriented her, and after five days of the gentle motion of the sea, the land felt hard, unyielding to her body as the cart jolted along the lane. She looked for the North Star but the clouds had come in from the sea and the sky was dark.

It wasn't long, however, before they began to pass cottages along the way. "There's the inn, miss." Mike pointed ahead to the faint glimmer of a light some half mile away.

"The coaching inn in Chale?"

"Aye, miss. Reckon we'll find Lord Granville's place just past on the left."

"You turn left at the crossroads," Olivia said. Now she was so close to home, she couldn't seem to think straight. Would her father be there? It would be so much easier if she had time to collect her thoughts, talk with Phoebe, before she had to face him.

She would have to tell Phoebe the truth, Olivia knew that now. It was not something she could keep to herself. But she would not, *could* not, tell Phoebe of what she had remembered.

Gales of laughter erupted from the open door of the coaching inn as they passed, and Mike glanced longingly towards the convivial light. Then they had passed and the lane was dark once more. At the crossroads, Billy turned the cob to the left. The hedgerows were high, the lane very narrow, but they reached the stone gateway leading to Lord Granville's house in a very few minutes. The gates were locked for the night and Mike jumped down and pulled the bell.

The gatekeeper appeared at the door of his cottage, holding his lantern high. "Who goes there?"

"It's me, Peter." Olivia leaned over the side of the cart so that he could see her clearly. "Open the gate."

"Well, I'll be blowed," the man muttered at the unmistakable voice. He raised his lantern higher, illuminating the speaker. "Well, I'll be blowed," he said again, louder this time, and ran to unlock the gates. He swung them open and Billy trotted the cob smartly through, giving the man a cheeky wave as he did so.

"Should us go to the front door, then?" Billy inquired as the lights of the house came into view.

"Of course, you dolt!" Mike said, cuffing him lightly. "Who d'ye think we got 'ere?"

"Dunno. No one told me," Billy muttered. "Jest 'miss' is all I 'eard."

"Yeah, well that's all ye need to know," Mike stated, heedless of the contradiction.

"The front door is fine," Olivia said hastily, although in her present state of stockingless dishabille she thought the kitchen door might be a more suitable point of entrance.

Billy halted the cob at the front door. There were lights in the windows but the thatch-roofed mansion had a rather desolate air, as if everyday life had been suspended. Mike jumped down and politely offered Olivia his hand.

She stepped to the gravel and stood for a second, hesitating. The prodigal returned was not an easy part to play. Then she lifted her chin and marched to the door. She raised the knocker and banged it with imperious firmness.

There were footsteps, the sound of the bolts being drawn back, then the door swung open. Bisset, the butler, stood outlined by the lamplight from the hall behind him. He stared at Olivia as if at some spirit.

"Yes, Bisset, it's me." Olivia stepped past him into the hall. "Where is Lady Granville?"

But she had no need to ask the question; Phoebe was coming down the stairs, her step impetuous, as she called, "Who is it? Who's there, Bisset?"

"It's me," Olivia said, running to the stairs, needing now only the comfort of her friend's arms, the security of home.

"Oh, Olivia! Where have you been? I've been frantic!" Phoebe wrapped her in her arms, tears of relief pouring down her cheeks. "What *happened* to you?"

Olivia clung to her. "Is my father back?"

"No, not yet." Phoebe drew back slightly to look into Olivia's eyes. "Where on earth have you been?"

Olivia remembered Mike and Billy. She remembered bitterly the pirate's injunction that she reward them for their trouble, as if she didn't know how to behave to those who served her.

"I'll explain later, Phoebe, but I must show my gratitude to these people. They've been so kind to me." She gestured to Mike, who had withdrawn from the doorway and stood hesitating in the shadows just beyond the shaft of lamplight.

Phoebe understood what was required immediately. She didn't need reminders any more than Olivia of the lady of the manor's obligations. She controlled her impatience with difficulty and went to the door. "Please, do come in for a minute."

Bisset had the air of one whose breath had been knocked from his body, but he stepped aside to allow the reluctant Mike entrance to the hall.

Mike made a jerky bow. "Mike Barker, madam."

Phoebe gave him a friendly welcoming nod and turned back to Olivia. She took the key to Cato's strongbox from her pocket as she made for her husband's study, Olivia on her heels.

"What should they have?" Phoebe asked as she opened the strongbox. "Since I don't know what's going on, how can I—"

"Five guineas." Olivia interrupted Phoebe. She could hear the impatience rising in her friend's voice and knew that Phoebe would not be able to restrain herself for much longer.

Phoebe handed five gold coins to Olivia, who took them without a word and returned to the hall.

"Mike, please thank your family for everything they've done for me. I know my father will be so grateful when he returns. But please give this to your mother. It will help pay for the medicines."

"Oh, aye," Mike muttered, staring at the

winking riches on his palm. It seemed a generous sum for telling a tale and the loan of a cart. However, the master always paid for the favors he asked, and there were a great many mouths to feed at the family hearth. Mike slipped the coins into his pocket.

The lad Billy had ventured to the open door and now gazed wide-eyed at the square hall with its oak floor and gleaming brass and pewter. A massive fireplace stood in one wall, the grate filled with a jug of fragrant stocks and marigolds instead of winter logs. A wide staircase with an elaborately carved banister curved upward at the rear. Billy saw that the newel posts were carved into the shape of lions' heads. His family's entire farmhouse could fit into this one apartment, and yet there was no sign that this room, if such it could be called, served any useful domestic purpose. It was just wasted space. What it was to be rich, he thought with some disapproval mingled with envy.

He caught the eagle-eyed stare from the black-clad figure of the man who'd opened the door. Did the man think he was looking for something to steal? Billy put his thumb to his nose and grinned at the man's thunderstruck expression.

"That'll do, our Billy!" Mike turned sharply. He hadn't seen the exchange but he knew his little brother. "We'll be off now, miss." He gave Olivia a nod, touched his forelock to Phoebe, and hastened away, sweeping Billy before him.

Phoebe turned to Olivia. For a moment concern took precedence over her desperate need to know what had happened. "You look exhausted," she said.

"That's hardly surprising." Olivia offered a tired smile.

Phoebe spoke briskly to the butler. "Bisset, ask Mistress Bisset to prepare a sack posset and have it brought to Lady Olivia's bedchamber. And then send someone to find Sergeant Crampton. He will need to know that Lady Olivia is returned safely."

Bisset contented himself with a bow and turned to the kitchen regions, his step for once a little less measured. He was most anxious to get Mistress Bisset's impression of this extraordinary business. Lady Olivia had looked like a scarecrow, half dressed it had seemed to the scandalized butler. And yet apart from looking rather heavy eyed, she showed no obvious ill effects from whatever had happened to her.

As Bisset departed, Phoebe took Olivia's hand and almost dragged her abovestairs.

In Olivia's bedchamber she closed the door and stood with her back to it, regarding her friend gravely. "Now, for God's sake, Olivia, tell me what happened!"

Olivia sat on the bed and looked with a degree of surprise at her bare legs and stockingless feet. She'd forgotten in the flurry of return to this ordinary environment how disreputable she must look. "I was hurt. I fell off the c-cliff and for some time I didn't know who

118

I was. I hurt my head." She touched the back of her head where there was still a residual tenderness. "Mike's father found me and took me to his farm, and his wife nursed me until I remembered who I was...am."

"Why don't I believe you?" Phoebe demanded.

Olivia sighed. "Because it's not all true." She met her friend's somewhat outraged gaze with an almost apologetic smile.

"I was trying it out on you," Olivia continued. "It has to satisfy my father and Giles. You need to help me perfect the details."

"*Were* you hurt?" First things first, Phoebe thought.

"Yes, that's all true about falling off the cliff and losing consciousness and being ill. Except that I always knew who I was, just not what was happening. It was the drink...it made me c-confused..."

"Drink? A drug? Someone drugged you?" Horrified, Phoebe pressed her hands to her mouth.

"It was purely medicinal," Olivia said slowly. "It made me very confused, though, and most of the time I didn't know whether I was asleep or awake. But once he decided I didn't need it anymore, he stopped giving it to me."

"*He? Who?*" Phoebe flung her hands in the air in utter frustration. "Olivia, would you *please* start from the beginning before I go crazy." She pushed herself away from the door and came over to the bed. She stood looking down at Olivia and felt a stab of fear, as strong as

119

any she had felt during the dreadful days of Olivia's disappearance. There was something badly wrong. It was as if the Olivia she knew had returned only in body. The spirit, the person, had been changed in some as yet indefinable way.

"What happened to you?" It was an anguished whisper.

Olivia looked up. "I'm not entirely sure myself. I feel like a changeling."

"You seem like one," Phoebe returned. "And you aren't answering me."

"Do you believe in enchantment, Phoebe?"

"No, I believe in medicines and physic, birth and death, sunrise and sunset," Phoebe said bluntly. "There's no room there for enchantment, superstition...don't you remember what happened to Meg?"

Meg, the healer, their friend from the years they had spent in Oxford, had been taken up for a witch after the death of a child she had physicked. The memory of that dreadful day was indelible for both Olivia and Phoebe.

"I'm not talking about witchcraft," Olivia said. "But you do believe in...in passion, in...in...attraction, the mystery of attraction?"

Phoebe did not immediately reply. She sat on the cedar chest at the foot of the bed. How could she not believe in those things? She herself had been conquered by love and lust, that devastating, unpredictable, mortifying pair. Against all reason, all logic, totally out of the blue, she had fallen in love and lust one winter morning with the marquis of Granville. And her life had been governed by them ever since.

"You met someone?" she asked, resigned now to hearing this story in a roundabout fashion. "Someone who attracted you...someone who...? Oh, Olivia, for pity's sake, what are we talking about here? Just get to the point."

"I'm trying," Olivia said. For some reason she was finding it difficult to talk directly about Anthony. She had the feeling that anything she said would come out wrong, would either not do him justice or would make her seem like a passion-crazed loon. She wasn't at all sure why she needed to do him justice, but...but it seemed that she did.

"I don't know his surname. He wouldn't give it to me."

"Why not?" Phoebe asked sharply.

"Because he...well, he doesn't live within the law," Olivia replied. Then she shook her head dismissively. "It doesn't matter. I'll never see him again."

"It most certainly *does* matter!" Phoebe exclaimed. "You haven't told me anything that makes sense yet."

Of the three of them—herself, Portia, and Olivia—Olivia had always seemed the one least likely to succumb to the sensual temptations of the human condition. Those temptations had felled Olivia's two friends while Olivia herself had found all she sought in scholarship.

Until now, it would seem, Phoebe thought—

always assuming she was somehow grasping the right end of the stick.

Olivia kicked off her sandals and flexed her bare feet. She couldn't blame Phoebe for being irritable. She wasn't making much sense to herself. The reason why she would never see Anthony again had nothing whatsoever to do with his illegal activities. But maybe that was the issue she could focus on to explain things to Phoebe.

"Rufus was an outlaw when he and Portia first met," Phoebe pointed out. "That didn't stop either of them."

It was true that Rufus Decatur, Earl of Rothbury, hadn't always been a pillar of respectability.

"Portia wasn't my father's daughter," Olivia said quietly. Portia and her wastrel father had always lived outside the rigid confines of society. It wasn't until his death that she had come under Lord Granville's protection.

Phoebe took Olivia's point but she brushed it aside, demanding, "Tell me the whole, *now*!"

Olivia told her everything, except what Brian had done to her...of what she had allowed him to do to her. That was a private shame, one never to be revealed.

"And so, after he'd finished his piracy, he sailed the ship back to its anchorage and had me brought home," she ended with a little shrug.

Phoebe listened in frowning astonishment. Olivia had always been so vociferous, so certain that she would never yield to the wiles of man. And yet she'd fallen into this passion seemingly without a murmur of protest.

"Maybe the drugs affected you," Phoebe suggested. "It can happen with some of the more powerful simples. Do you know what he gave you?"

Olivia shook her head. She found that she didn't care for Phoebe's explanation for her entrancement. It negated so much of what she had actually felt, and perversely she didn't want that to happen. Even while she was trying to forget it, while she shrank in revulsion from what it had thrown in her face, she seemed still to want to keep some of the golden aura of that adventure.

There was a knock at the door, and Mistress Bisset entered with the posset. She set it on the table and regarded Olivia gravely. "Should we send for the physician, Lady Granville? Lady Olivia looks right peaky."

"No, she had a bad bump on the head, but I can take care of it myself, thank you," Phoebe replied.

The housekeeper hesitated, but Lady Granville's skills as a herbalist were well known. Her ladyship might not be adept at the running of a household, but no one denied her other talents.

"Very well, m'lady."

"That will be all, then, Mistress Bisset," Phoebe prompted when the lady still remained, her curiosity evident.

"Yes, madam." The housekeeper curtsied and left.

Olivia couldn't help a half smile. "A year ago you could never have routed Mistress Bisset like that. She never took any notice of you."

"No," Phoebe agreed, momentarily distracted from Olivia's situation. "And she calls me Lady Granville now instead of just Lady Phoebe. I think I've acquired a deal of gravitas since the boys were born."

That made Olivia laugh, for a moment banishing her melancholy. But it was a short moment. Then she said seriously, "My father mustn't know anything of this, Phoebe."

"Good God, no!" Phoebe exclaimed. "It wouldn't do him any good at all!" She eyed Olivia seriously. "Do you want to see this man again?"

"No!" Olivia shook her head vigorously. "It was…it was almost a fantasy, a dream. It's over, Phoebe, and I don't want to think about it anymore. The most important thing now is to manage to keep it from my father."

Phoebe hesitated. Something about the denial didn't quite ring true. But Olivia was exhausted and mustn't be pressed further. Phoebe handed her the sack posset. "You need to sleep, Olivia. We'll talk more in the morning."

"Yes." Olivia returned Phoebe's hug with sudden urgency. She wanted everything to be the way it used to be, and for a moment as they embraced she could almost imagine that it could be.

Phoebe went out and Olivia sat on the bed, sipping the sack posset. It was nursery comfort. She set the empty cup down and stood up to undress herself. As she took off the ruined dress she felt the bulge in the pocket. She took out the pirate's kerchief and almost without thinking pushed it beneath her pillow, then she fell into bed and sought oblivion.

GODFREY, LORD CHANNING, entered the taproom of the Anchor in the little village of Niton, just above Puckaster Cove. He peered through the blue wreaths of pipe smoke at the taproom's inhabitants and could see only locals nursing tankards, puffing pipes, for the most part in a silence that could have been morose, except that the island folk were not in general gregarious and spoke only when they had something they considered worth saying. This Friday evening it appeared that no one had anything of moment to impart.

Godfrey approached the bar counter. He leaned back against it on his elbows with the appearance of a man taking his ease and surveyed the room again. Was one of these taciturn villagers the man who would buy his culling? They all looked unlikely, not a man among them with the wherewithal to be a customer for Godfrey's ill-gotten gains.

"Yes, sir?" The landlord spoke behind him and Godfrey jumped. He turned to front the bar counter.

George regarded him with a malicious eye. "What can I get ye, sir?"

"Who's the man I've come to see?"

"Don't know as yet," the landlord said. "What can I get ye?"

"Porter." Seemingly he had no choice but to play the man's game.

The landlord reached for the leather flagon and filled a tankard. "Threepence."

"Since when?" Godfrey demanded. "It's always a penny three farthings."

"Price 'as gone up, sir. Supplies is short," the landlord said meaningfully.

"You don't order porter from me," Godfrey snapped.

The landlord shrugged indifferently. "Supplies is powerful short when it comes to cognac."

With difficulty Godfrey controlled a surge of rage. The man's insolence was intolerable and yet Godfrey knew he had no suitable comeback. "I'm waiting for the ship," he said, burying his nose in his tankard.

"A bit overdue, is it, then?"

"You know damn well it is!" His knuckles whitened around the tankard. The man knew he was desperate, knew he could needle him all he wanted. But Godfrey could see a way out now, a permanent solution to his financial needs. And then, oh, and then the landlord of the Anchor and his ilk would watch their manners.

"Then per'aps I should be lookin' to place me orders elsewhere, sir," the landlord said. "But I'd need me earnest money back, o' course."

Godfrey ignored this. Deliberately he turned

away again and resumed his examination of the taproom's inhabitants. He was damned if he was going to ask for George's help again.

"The one ye wants is sittin' in the corner, by the inglenook." George finally spoke into the studied silence. "Been waitin' fer ye close on an hour, I'd say."

Godfrey shrugged with apparent indifference. He knew he'd have to pay for the information; George would have his price. But if tonight's business went well, the price would be easy to find. He looked closely at the man George had indicated and was immediately disappointed. A villainous-looking customer in the rough garb of a fisherman with a lank, greasy mustache and a raddled countenance.

"Over there?" he demanded incredulously, finally stung into a response. The man didn't look as if he had the price of his drink.

"Aye."

"What's his name? I'll pay for his name."

" 'Tis not one he gives to all who asks," the landlord replied.

Godfrey pushed himself away from the counter, took up his tankard, and approached his would-be customer.

"Can I buy you another?" he offered.

The man looked up. His eyes were bloodshot and he grinned, revealing foully blackened teeth. "Lord bless ye, sir. That's kind o' you. I'll 'ave a drop o' brandy. Jest tell George to make sure it's from the special cask. None of that thin piss he passes off to those what don't know any better. You an' me does, o' course."

He leered and offered a conspiratorial wink.

Godfrey shuddered but held his tongue. He could only guess what George would charge him for a drop of the best. However, with every appearance of good cheer, he called over to the counter, "Two cognacs, George. The best."

"Well, sit ye down, sir." The man gestured to a stool. "Can't do business on yer feet."

Godfrey hooked the stool over with his foot and sat down. The sawdust on the floor at his feet was clotted with spilled ale and other things that Godfrey didn't want to consider. A mangy hound chewed a marrow bone and growled at him, hackles raised, when he inched his stool away from something particularly noxious-looking and came a little too close to the bone for the beast's liking.

The landlord gave the animal a kick as he put the two pewter cups of cognac on the table between the two men. The hound sloped off, the bone gripped in his jaws.

"That'll be a shillin' apiece, sir."

"That's daylight robbery!" Godfrey couldn't contain himself.

" 'Tis in short supply, sir." The landlord sung his tune again.

"Here, George." Godfrey's companion dug in his pocket and tossed a pair of silver coins on the table. "But we'll 'ave a free fill-up fer that."

The landlord scooped up the coins and grinned. It was a genial grin, not an expression Godfrey had ever seen on his face.

"Right y'are, my friend."

The other man nodded and tasted the cognac. It met with his approval and he gave another nod. The landlord returned to his counter.

"Now, young sir, to business. What d'ye 'ave?"

Godfrey took a gulp of cognac, trying to think what it was about this unsavory character that was so unsettling. There was the most unlikely air of authority about him, and even though he sat slumped in his torn and grimy jerkin, he gave the impression of being completely in charge of the proceedings.

"Silks...some of them painted," he said, tapping a finger on the stained table. "Velvets and lace from the Low Countries."

"Silk and salt water don't mix. As I understand it, they came from a wreck." Something flickered in the deep-set gray eyes. Something cold and unpleasant.

"They were in chests," Godfrey said, despising the defensive note and yet unable to prevent it. "Protected."

The other man nodded. "An' pulled out in double quick time, I daresay." Again there was that flicker in his eye and a note in his voice that sounded almost sardonic.

Once again Godfrey controlled his rage. For the moment, he was powerless, obliged to take what insults this disgusting, low-bred creature tossed at him. But that *would* change. "It's the business," he said coldly. "One you know yourself, I imagine."

His companion made no reply. He drank again from his cognac and glanced towards the bar counter, raising a hand at George, who nodded and came over with the brandy bottle to refill the cups.

When he'd departed, Godfrey's companion asked coolly, "So, what else beside stuff? D'ye have tea? Silver? Glassware? China? She was a merchantman, wasn't she?"

"Aye." Godfrey's eyes sharpened. "Very rich. We had great good fortune."

"That ye did," the other man murmured. "Pity 'tis that what's good fortune for some should be the devil's own luck fer others."

It was almost too much. Godfrey half rose from his stool at this taunt. Then he sat back and shrugged. "I'm willing to share my good fortune, otherwise you wouldn't be here."

"True enough, true enough, young sir," the man said, his tone suddenly placatory, almost wheedling, so that Godfrey began to feel confused and as if he stood on shifting sands.

"So, I'd best take a look at the spoils," the man continued. "I don't buy sight unseen."

"How much are you interested in buying?" Godfrey forgot confusion. His heart beat faster as he saw salvation.

The other man shrugged. "Depends what I see. I buys what I likes. If ye've goods that please me, then I might take the lot. As I say, it depends."

"The full consignment..." Godfrey fought to conceal his jubilation. He said decisively,

"For the full consignment I'll be asking a thousand."

The other man merely raised an eyebrow. "If 'tis worth it, then I'll pay it."

Godfrey considered. Now he was unsure. How could this miserable-looking man have the means? Fear prickled his spine. Was it a trap?

"Don't worry, my young lordling, ye'll not be betrayed by me." The voice was soft, indolent, and the eyes were suddenly clear and to Godfrey's astonishment youthful.

And once again came the sense that all was not as it seemed. "When do you wish to look at the consignment?" he asked, forcing himself to speak firmly and steadily.

"Tomorrow, at midnight. Meet me in Puckaster Cove." The man stood up, pushing aside his stool. He stood for a minute, hands thrust deep into the pockets of his patched britches, looking down on Godfrey. "I'll wait no more than a quarter hour. Come alone. Ye'll find me alone."

"How can I trust you?" Godfrey demanded.

The man shrugged. "Same way as I can trust you, I reckon." Then he turned and strode from the inn.

Godfrey watched him go. He seemed to stoop but it did little to disguise his height and nothing to conceal the lithe, supple strength in his slender frame. *Who was he? What was he?* Not what he seemed, that was for sure.

Godfrey's expression darkened. He hated mysteries and this one was a dangerous puzzle.

If he didn't know with whom he was dealing, if he underestimated him, it could bring utter ruin. He must control his impatience and tread carefully. He looked up and caught the landlord's eye. Mine host was regarding Godfrey with an unholy gleam, as if he was reading his thoughts.

Deliberately Godfrey spat his indifference to the landlord's challenge into the hearth before stalking from the inn. His horse was stabled at the rear. He retrieved it and rode back to Carisbrooke Castle, his mind in a ferment. That little glimpse at the man behind the unpromising exterior had convinced him that whoever his unpleasant and insolent customer was, he would be able to come up with the required funds. That was really all that mattered.

The guards at the gatehouse challenged him as he rode up the ramp to the arched entrance to the castle. They opened the gates and let him in and he went straight to his quarters in the governor's mansion. His room lay beyond the guarded chamber in the north curtain wall that now housed the king.

The king's three escape attempts had exhausted the patience of both the governor, Colonel Hammond, and Parliament. His Majesty had been moved from his commodious quarters in the Constable's Lodgings to a more secure and easily guarded location. He continued, however, to conduct daily audiences in the great hall adjoining his previous bedchamber.

Godfrey, Lord Channing, was one of the governor's equerries. A post that, while it brought little in the way of financial recompense, was prestigious, provided comfortable room and board for himself, and maintenance for his horses—a great drain on any nobleman's purse.

Such considerations for the impoverished scion of a proud, ancient, but penniless family were not to be derided. They were not, however, sufficient for a young man of Godfrey's personal ambitions. He was heavily in debt. The lifestyle he believed was due his family name and position was a hugely expensive one. Clothes alone cost him a small fortune, and while smuggling and wrecking offered some remedy for his financial ills, the trade and his own desperation put him at the mercy of men like the landlord of the Anchor and potential customers like the villain he'd had to placate this evening.

When he entered his chamber, he was still seething over the insolence he'd had to endure.

"You look as if you lost a sixpence and found a groat," Brian Morse observed. He was sitting at the table in front of the fireplace, a sheet of parchment in front of him. He moved the candle so that it illuminated Godfrey's face. "Did your business not prosper?"

Godfrey shrugged and filled a pewter goblet with wine from the leather flagon on the table. He noticed sourly that in his absence the flagon had become very light. Brian Morse had obviously had a thirst on him. "The man's a villain," he observed.

Brian chuckled softly. "Aren't we all, my friend? Aren't we all?" He drank from his own goblet. "I've been composing a letter for your potential father-in-law." He indicated the parchment on the table. "You need the right words to get his attention. And when you meet my little sister, you'll need to have something to offer her. A knowledge of the Greek poets might help...a talent for chess...a delight in Pythagorus's theorems." He raised an inquiring eyebrow.

Godfrey sat down on a stool beside the fire, stretching his booted feet to the fender. "I'm a man of action," he stated with a touch of complacency. "I have no scholarship...no time for it."

"Well, you'd best cultivate some," Brian said harshly. "Because I assure you, this particular little prize won't fall to a man who rejoices in a lack of learning."

Godfrey frowned. "If there's one thing I detest, it's a prating woman scholar."

"This one is very rich, and quite tasty too, as I recall." Brian's thin lips flickered in a reminiscent smile. "Her nose is somewhat long—the Granville nose always is—and she has the devil's own stammer. But a man can get used to anything with the right incentives."

Godfrey regarded him sardonically in the candlelight. "And of course, once I'm wed to the heiress, I'll be keeping you too in high style."

"Well, you wouldn't expect me to offer my help for nothing," Brian said, clicking his tongue reprovingly. "This will suit me very well.

I'm in need of a modest income, and in addition I have a private score to settle. Seeing Cato's daughter married to a man of your...your unformed morality, shall we call it, will do just that."

Brian got to his feet, pushing himself up against the edge of the table. He reached for his cane. "Read the letter, make changes if you wish, but keep to my gist. Believe me, I know the Granvilles very well. Write it in your hand and have it delivered."

Godfrey said sharply, "My family, my lineage, are all worthy of a Granville."

"Oh, yes, dear boy, no doubt about it. But you, my friend, are not." Brian laughed and limped to the door. "I'll see myself out. I'll not show my face in the castle again. I'd hate to run into my adopted father. He thinks me dead and buried in Rotterdam. You'll find me in Ventnor, putting up at the Gull. I'll plot your campaign from there."

Godfrey was too angry to bid his guest farewell. For two pins he would have told Brian Morse to go to the devil. But the man had offered a seductive pact, and one couldn't always choose one's partners.

ADAM TOOK ONE LOOK at Anthony's face as the master climbed from the dinghy onto the deck of *Wind Dancer* and decided to hold his tongue. Anthony was in a foul mood. It was not his habit to take his moods out on his men, but they all recognized the wisdom of steering

135

clear of the master when his eyes were as cold and distant as they were this evening.

"Brandy, Adam," he said shortly as he brushed past him on his way to the companionway.

"You want food?"

"No."

Adam shrugged and went to find the bottle.

Anthony entered his cabin and stood for a minute in the pale wash of moonlight from the open window. He drew in a breath and thought he could scent Olivia.

Stupid! Sentimental nonsense! He snatched off the knit cap and threw it onto the window seat.

He went to the mirror and with a grimace peeled off the mustache. The pain made his eyes water but banished sentimentality. He dipped a cloth in water and then in the saucer of salt Adam had laid ready and cleaned the black off his teeth. He was starting to look like himself again. Soap and water took off the rouge.

He was throwing off his unsavory garments when Adam came in with a flask of brandy. "Sam says ye've a meetin' fixed fer tomorrow, then?"

"Aye. I'll be taking Sam and one other to watch my back. Although I don't think the bastard will try anything tomorrow; he needs me too much. He's desperate as a starving rat, for all he tried to hide it." He poured cognac into a glass and drained it, then refilled the glass.

136

"Left a bad taste in yer mouth, did 'e?"

"Foul as a cesspit. I need to know who he is."

"Reckon George at the Anchor'll know?"

"I doubt it. The man's desperate and a villain but not, I think, stupid." Anthony paused, his eyes narrowing. "Dangerous yes, stupid no," he mused. "He'd not broadcast his identity across the island. I'd lay odds he's something to do with the castle. There was something of the courtier about him." Anthony's lip curled.

"Then ye'll run into him," Adam said matter-of-factly, picking up the discarded clothing, "when you go off to play courtier yerself."

"Even more inducement to show myself in the king's presence chamber at tomorrow's little soiree," Anthony declared. "Leave me now, Adam. I'm in a vile humor."

Adam made no reply, but left immediately.

Anthony sat on the window seat and looked out at the sliver of moon on the narrow black water of the chine. *Damn the woman!*

Seven

"IT'S SO NEAT," Phoebe said with undisguised admiration, looking up from her minute inspection of Anthony's handiwork. "Just three stitches and the wound's closed to the thinnest line. You'll have a scar, but only a faint one. I wonder what thread he used. Did he say?" Her herbalist's curiosity was aroused.

"No, and I didn't ask either." Olivia rolled away from Phoebe, turning onto her back. She lay with her arm over her eyes, struggling to control the surge of emotion as memory, rich, lushly sensual, flooded every pore and cell of her body.

Phoebe regarded her with a worried frown. "You said you didn't want to see him again."

"I don't. It was a magic interlude, Phoebe. It was only supposed to last until I had to come home. The spell is broken."

"Somehow I don't think so," Phoebe observed dryly.

Olivia sat up, her dark eyes burning. "I'm confused, Phoebe. I don't know how or why it happened, but I *do* know that it will never happen again. C-could we not talk about it anymore?"

The slam of the front door, violent and hasty, reverberated through the house. Olivia said, "My father."

"Yes." Phoebe was already halfway to the bedchamber door.

"I need time, Phoebe," Olivia said urgently. "Don't let him come up. Tell him...tell him I'm getting dressed and I'll c-come down to him."

"I'll get him to see the children first." Phoebe hurried out. She ran down the stairs, lifting her skirts clear of her feet. Cato's imperative voice seemed to fill the house.

"Cato...my lord." Phoebe tripped on the last step in her haste and tumbled into her husband's waiting arms. He'd anticipated a misstep the moment he'd seen the speed of her arrival.

"Olivia is safe and well," she said when she could regain her breath.

"So Giles tells me." He gestured to the burly figure of the sergeant standing behind him. "I'll go to her at once. Is she abovestairs?"

"She's getting dressed to come down to you. I believe she's bathing; you can't see her immediately," Phoebe prevaricated. "She really is all right, Cato," she said when he looked dismayed.

"I suppose I must wait, then," he said. Some of the worry was smoothed from his face as he looked at his wife. He tilted her face and kissed her mouth.

"And you, my ragged robin. Are you well?" he asked, drawing back from her but still holding her face.

"All the better for seeing you, sir," she responded, her eyes aglow. "And Charles is

139

grown so big since you left, you won't recognize him."

"I've been gone but two weeks," Cato protested.

"Oh, but he eats so much!"

Cato's mind returned to what was uppermost. "Do you think Olivia will be well enough to accompany me on a visit to these Barkers? Giles has discovered their whereabouts."

"If she doesn't ride," Phoebe said, thinking of the wound in Olivia's thigh. "I expect it would be all right."

Cato frowned. "It seems strange to me that Olivia could not remember where they lived."

"A blow to the head can cause much confusion," Phoebe said. "When she remembered who she was, I don't believe anything else mattered, except to get home. She could only think of one thing at a time. It's quite common with such injuries."

Cato considered this, noticing absently that Phoebe's hair was springing loose from its pins as usual and the lace collar of her gown was tucked into the neck. He straightened the collar without conscious thought. "Has she been seen by the physician?"

Phoebe put her chin up. "I believe I have all the necessary skills, sir. Or do you not think so?"

"I wouldn't dare to dispute it," he said, throwing up his hands in laughing disclaimer.

"Will you not see the children now? While Olivia is dressing?"

"Is the baby awake?"

"If he isn't now, he soon will be. I'll fetch them straightway."

Cato, smiling, watched her hasten back up the stairs. Babies were still mysteries to him. He was beginning to feel comfortable with Nicholas, who at fourteen months walked quite steadily and had a few words, but the baby, Charles, Cato's fifth child, who had been born soon after their move to the island, still alarmed him with his fragility. The mothers of his other children had never attempted to interest him in the daily progress of their infant offspring. Phoebe, however, was a very different character, unique in her way of viewing the world. She had made it clear from the first that he was to be a deeply involved parent whether he liked it or not. Cato found that on the whole he liked it.

"We'll be goin' to the Barkers, then, shall us, m'lord?"

"In a short while, Giles. When I've talked with Lady Olivia. There's no hurry, I believe." Cato raised an eyebrow.

"No...no, sir." Giles sounded disconsolate. He couldn't abide wasting time.

"Have you dined, my lord?" Bisset had been hovering at the rear of the hall and now moved forward.

"No, we have ridden since dawn. But just bring me bread and cheese in my study...and ale, if you please." The butler bowed and Cato went into his sanctum. A small pile of sealed documents sat on his desk, awaiting his return. He picked them up and ran his eye over

141

them. The writing on most he recognized. A missive from Cromwell, another from Governor Hammond, another from the governor of Yarmouth Castle. The last, however, was addressed in a hand he didn't know. He turned it over. The wax seal bore the imprint of a coat of arms that was also unfamiliar. He reached for his paper knife just as the door opened.

"Here we are, my lord." Phoebe came in carrying on her hip a fat rosy baby sucking a dimpled fist. A toddler in short coats held her free hand. Little Earl Grafton regarded his father solemnly for a moment as if deciding his next move, then dropped his mother's hand and advanced with a gleeful little chuckle, reaching up his arms.

Cato lifted him and swung him through the air. The child shrieked with delight and presented his cheek for his father's kiss.

"Charles was wide-awake and, like his brother, is in great good humor." Phoebe nuzzled the top of the baby's head. "Greet your papa, little one."

Cato set down his son and heir and took the infant as he was clearly supposed to do. The baby wobbled in his arms and it took him a minute before he felt he was holding him in a natural fashion.

Phoebe watched attentively. She was determined that Cato should learn how to manage his babies and bit her tongue on anxious words of advice.

"Olivia says she will be down shortly."

Cato nodded. The infant was gripping his father's finger, and Cato was astonished at the strength and determination of the grip. He reached behind him on the desk and gave Nicholas his great seal. The child sat down under its weight and began examining it intently.

Phoebe smiled and glanced curiously at the missives on the table. "Anything of importance, do you think?"

"I haven't opened them as yet. There's one in a hand I don't recognize." He tried to pull his finger free, but Charles only clung tighter.

"Was the fighting bad?"

"More of a nuisance than anything. The king's supporters won't give up easily. I'm afraid there'll be another attempt to rescue His Majesty from the island."

He looked over the baby's head and smiled slightly. "It means I'm going to be needed here to work closely with Colonel Hammond. All the king's supporters on the island must come under suspicion. So if you've a mind to, you and Olivia may join the court, such as it is, in the castle. The colonel and his lady have issued a most cordial invitation for this evening. It might provide you with some amusement."

Phoebe's nose wrinkled. She had neither the time nor the inclination for the trivialities of court life and knew that Olivia despised the games as heartily as she did.

"There's to be a poet there, I believe," Cato added, seeing her expression. He was well aware of her disinclination for formal gatherings. "You might find him amusing, although in all honesty I don't believe Mr. Johnson is a very good poet. But you could talk meter and the various merits of prose and rhyme with him." His smile was somewhat cajoling.

Such a diversion might serve to take Olivia's mind off her melancholy, Phoebe reflected, if only as an irritant. "Yes, of course. One evening wouldn't be too much of a hardship."

Cato laughed. "You are too obliging, madam wife." He handed the baby back to her. "After I've seen Olivia, we'll visit the Barkers and I can express my gratitude in proper form, then we can put this unfortunate business behind us."

If only it were that simple. Olivia had a long way to go, whatever she might say, before she could put her encounter with the pirate behind her. Phoebe reached down a hand to pull Nicholas to his feet. He showed some reluctance to yield up the seal, and Cato gently took it from him, giving him instead a blunted quill pen that Nicholas regarded with immediate favor.

Phoebe said, "I'll talk to Olivia about going to the castle. Make sure she feels up to it."

Cato turned back to his letters as the door closed behind his wife and sons. He slit the wafer with the unfamiliar seal and opened the sheet.

Godfrey, Lord Channing, equerry to Colonel Hammond, presents his compliments to Lord

144

Granville. His position as equerry has given him some information about His Majesty that he thinks Lord Granville would be interested to hear. Lord Channing most earnestly begs the favor of an interview at a time and place convenient for his lordship.

It was signed with several flourishes in the style of the old court.

Cato frowned, trying to remember if he'd ever met the man. The renewed fighting had kept the marquis from Carisbrooke Castle in recent weeks, so it was possible he hadn't encountered a new equerry. The name was familiar, though. The Channings were an old and well-respected lineage, with estates in Wiltshire, Cato thought. But why, if the man had information relating to the king, didn't he report it directly to Governor Hammond? An intriguing question and one certainly worth pursuing.

There was a knock at the door and Cato laid the letter down on the desk. He went swiftly to open the door.

He regarded his daughter with close concern. Always pale, she looked almost ghostly today. So wan and fragile. He put an arm around her, drawing her against his chest, gently stroking her hair. "My poor child, what a dreadful time you've had. Come and sit down." He drew out a chair for her, then perched on the desk, examining her anxiously.

"Can you tell me what happened? Or will it tire you too much?"

"No, no, of course not." Olivia offered a hesitant smile before embarking on the story she had perfected with Phoebe.

"Phoebe said you wish me to accompany you when you visit them," she said at the end of her recital.

"I think, if you can manage it, it would be a courtesy," Cato said.

"They are simple folk," Olivia said. "They're not free with their words." She could only hope that they had been well enough briefed by Anthony to say no more than the minimum.

"But generous with their spirit," Cato said. "How lucky for us all that they found you." He shook his head, his eyes still searching Olivia's pale countenance. "I've been out of my mind with worry since I received Phoebe's message."

"I'm so sorry," Olivia said inadequately.

"My dear, a crumbling cliff is hardly your fault." He leaned over and lightly brushed her cheek with a fingertip, then turned as the door opened to admit Bisset with a tray of food and ale.

Glad to escape her father's close scrutiny for a moment, Olivia began to rearrange a vase of yellow roses on the mantelshelf as behind her Bisset bustled to lay out his lord's meal. She didn't want to visit the Barkers; it was too close a reminder, too soon. They knew Anthony. She remembered his smile as he'd told her that Mike's mother had so many children he'd never been able to count them all. He must have spent much time with them. They would know him well.

But if she was there, then she could deflect any awkward questions, make sure that the incident from her father's point of view was closed once and for all.

"When do you wish to leave, sir?" she asked as Bisset left.

"When I've eaten this. It'll not take many minutes; it's hardly elegant fare, but I missed my dinner." Cato broke bread, cut cheese. "Phoebe says you shouldn't ride, so I'll tell Giles to harness a pony to the trap." He took a swallow of ale.

"I'll fetch my hat and cloak and be down in ten minutes."

Cato nodded with his mouth full and Olivia left him to his makeshift dinner. She went up to her bedchamber, hurrying past the open door to the nursery as she heard Phoebe's voice talking to one of the nursemaids. She didn't want to discuss this upcoming visit with Phoebe. Not just yet.

Holding her straw hat, she wandered to the window in her bedchamber. It looked over the garden and out over the sea towards the Needles. The sun was climbing high, setting the clear blue water sparkling. And yet it was not such a magnificent blue as the open sea.

The Barkers must know *Wind Dancer*'s anchorage. Mike served on the ship.

Suddenly Olivia felt as she had when she'd tied the pirate's cravat around her eyes. When they'd parted with such icy unforgiveness and despite it all she'd been overpowered for a moment by the physical consciousness of him, of what they had shared. Suddenly she could smell and feel him, hear him, see the glow in his eye, the curve of his mouth. Her gut twisted as, just as suddenly, she shrank from the power of the physical memory.

The wound in her leg throbbed.

THE BARKERS' FARMHOUSE was isolated, set well back from the lane down a cattle track. The nearest human habitation was a scattering of cottages in a small hamlet that they had passed some ten minutes before they turned up the track to the Barkers' door.

Olivia, sitting beside Giles, who was driving the pony trap, reflected that such isolation would suit a pirate who wished to come and go freely and in secret. She glanced over at Cato, who was riding beside the trap.

He caught her eye and asked anxiously, "Not too tired?"

"No, not in the least, sir. It's pleasant to be out in the fresh air."

He smiled, reassured, and Olivia returned to her thoughts.

The farmyard was bustling. Children tumbled with chickens and a litter of puppies on the straw-covered dirt. Two yellow dogs raced to the trap, barking frantically.

"Quiet! Get off!" A woman emerged from the house and chased the dogs off with a broomstick. They ran yelping into the barn.

"Goodwife Barker?" Cato inquired pleasantly, for the moment remaining on horseback.

"Aye, sir." She regarded him warily before her gaze took in the trap, its driver and passenger.

Olivia took matters into her own hands and jumped down from the cart. She advanced on the lady, holding out her hand. "Goodwife Barker, this is my father, Lord Granville. He has come to thank you himself for your kindness to me."

Comprehension was immediate. "No need fer that," the woman said, taking Olivia's proffered hand. She was a woman of ample girth, and her bright intelligent eyes were like shiny currants in her round face. " 'Twas only what any Christian body would have done."

Cato dismounted. "I stand in your debt, goodwife."

"That ye don't, sir. Ye've more than paid yer debts," she replied, dropping him a curtsy. "I'd not looked fer payment, but I'll not say it came amiss." She nodded at Giles, who remained in the pony trap. "Good day to ye, sir."

"Good day, goodwife."

"D'ye care for a glass of elderflower wine, my lord?" There was no air of subservience about Goodwife Barker as she offered the hospitality of her farmhouse to the marquis of Granville.

"My thanks." Cato accepted with a smile, well aware that a refusal would cause grave offense.

"The lass knows the way," she said casually, gesturing that Olivia should precede her.

A large square kitchen occupied the entire ground floor of the farmhouse. The cooking fire was built high, pots on trivets simmered merrily, and the rich smell of baking came from the bread oven set into the bricks of the fireplace. The room was as hot as the oven itself. There seemed to be children everywhere, crawling babies, tottering toddlers, and several older girls who were busy at domestic tasks.

"You have a large family, goodwife," Cato observed, stepping carefully over an infant who seemed to have fallen asleep where she sat on the floor.

"Oh, aye. My man, Goodman Barker, likes to think he has enough of his own to manage the farm and the fishing without hired help," she said placidly, taking a flagon from the dresser.

"Is he here? I'd like to meet him. To thank him myself." Cato perched on the corner of the massive pine table. The perch was a trifle floury but it seemed safer than remaining on his feet when he might tread on a soft body.

"Bless ye, no, m'lord. He's out from sunup to sundown, rain or shine. He'll be bringin' in the crab pots about now. Like 'e was doin' when he found your daughter on the undercliff." She set two pewter cups on the table and filled them with wine. She handed one to Olivia, saying blandly, "This'll put strength in you, dearie."

Olivia took it with a smile of thanks. Mike's mother had the situation well in hand, and there was nothing here to arouse Lord Granville's suspicions.

Something tugged at Olivia's knees. A determined baby was trying to pull himself up on her skirt. She set her cup on the table again and bent to gave him her hands. He hauled himself to his feet with a squeal of delight. She knelt on the stone-flagged floor still holding his hands to steady him, and then she saw something that sent a shiver down her spine.

A small boy was playing with a wooden ship a few feet away from her. It looked to Olivia's eye to be an exact replica of *Wind Dancer*. The baby tugged at her hands, clearly demanding that she help him walk, so she obliged, guiding his shaky steps over to where his brother was playing.

She could hear Cato questioning the farmer's wife pleasantly about the farm and her husband's fishing. Neither of them were taking any notice of her.

"What's that you have?" she asked, sitting down on the floor beside the child with the ship, taking the baby onto her lap.

" 'Tis a frigate," the boy informed her with a note of scorn for her ignorance. "I'm puttin' up the tops'l now." He pulled on the fine strings that served as shrouds and hauled up the topsail. "See?"

"Who made her for you? One of your brothers?"

"Our Mike," he said. " 'E sails in a ship like this."

"Oh." Olivia nodded. "Does your ship have a name?"

"I calls 'er *Dancer*."

"That's a splendid name. Where does she sail to?"

" 'Cross the sea to France, mostly."

"Does she have an anchorage on the island?"

"Aye." The boy began to turn the wheel. "I'm goin' to sail 'er on the duck pond in a minute."

"Is that where she has her anchorage?"

"In a duck pond?" The child burst into exaggerated gusts of laughter. "Y'are daft, you are."

"Well, I don't know much about ships," Olivia said. "Can I come and watch you sail her?"

"If you like." He scrambled to his feet.

Olivia set the baby on the floor and followed the child out of the kitchen and across the farmyard to the duck pond. He squatted at the edge, bottom lip caught between his teeth as he very gently pushed his pretty toy onto the green water.

A soft breeze filled the sails and little *Wind Dancer* skipped a little until an indifferent duck blocked her path.

The boy waded in, holding up the legs of his britches, gave the duck a careless smack on the beak, and set his ship going again.

"So where does she have her anchorage?" Olivia asked as he came back to her.

"In a chine," he said.

A chine. Of course. The island cliffs were studded with these deep gorges known as chines. Narrow tongues of water that disappeared into the cliff and in many cases were not visible from the sea, or from the cliff above. She'd heard that smugglers used them to unload their goods in secrecy. And now she remembered the enclosed feel to the air, the thin sliver of sky that was all she'd been able to see from the deck of *Wind Dancer* when they'd dropped anchor. The pirate's frigate had its own secluded harbor in a chine. A chine somewhere below where she'd slipped off the cliff.

"When Pa doesn't need our Mike, 'e sends a message to the master that 'e can go on *Dancer*. Sometimes the master sends a message to our Mike. Sometimes he's gone fer a month or more, our Mike," the child added, taking up a stick and poking his little ship loose from some pond weed.

Olivia had some familiarity with the minds of children and understood that this boy had invested his toy with all the realities of the big ship.

"How do they send messages?" she heard herself ask.

"Leaves 'em up on Catherine's Down. At the oratory, I 'eard 'em say. There's a flag." The little ship keeled over under a gust of wind, and the child lost interest in the conversation. He waded once more into the pond to rescue his vessel.

He seemed to have forgotten Olivia. But he

was clearly a case of little pitchers having big ears, Olivia reflected. In such a large family in such a small house, it was hardly surprising a bright child would hear things he shouldn't, things whose importance he didn't understand.

Olivia returned to the farmhouse, where Cato had finished his wine and was preparing to take his leave. Olivia came in, momentarily blinded by the dimness after the bright sunshine. "That's a fine wooden ship Mike made," she observed. "I was watching his brother sail her on the duck pond."

"Aye, he's good with 'is 'ands, is our Mike," the goodwife responded, her eyes suddenly sharp as they rested on Olivia, standing in the doorway.

"Does he help his father with the fishing?" Cato inquired.

"Off an' on. But mostly 'e hires 'imself out as an extra hand on the big fishin' boats that go out from Ventnor." She moved towards the door. Her guests were ready to leave and she had her own work to do.

Cato walked back out into the farmyard and Olivia followed. The boy was still playing with his ship in the duck pond. Olivia climbed back into the trap as Cato mounted his horse. "Thank you again for all your kindness, good-wife."

" 'Twas nothin', miss." The goodwife didn't smile and her eyes darted to where her son was playing.

"It's all right," Olivia said quietly. "No one has anything to fear from me."

The goodwife looked as if she was about to say something, but then Cato was offering his own renewed thanks and she was obliged to turn to the marquis.

They left the farm and very little was said on the return to Chale. Olivia responded to her father's occasional remarks, but her own thoughts absorbed her.

So *Wind Dancer* had an anchorage in a chine. There would be no path from the clifftop down to the chine. It was how they were kept hidden. Olivia knew that much about the island. The chines drove in from the sea, and the clifftop, while it might be eroding in part—hence her own fall—would offer no direct access to the gash in the cliff at sea level.

And she knew how to get a message to Anthony.

"Did Phoebe talk to you about attending the king at the castle this evening?" Cato inquired as he helped her out of the trap at the front door. "I would like you to be presented. It can be done another time, of course, if you're too tired. But we need not stay for long."

"Phoebe mentioned it. Of course I will accompany you both." She smiled. It was an effort but it seemed to satisfy Cato. "I understand you've promised her a poet, sir."

"I fear he has not her talent," Cato said. "But he's about all that's available at present."

"Phoebe will take any poet on offer," Olivia said with perfect truth.

Cato laughed and turned to Giles with a question. Olivia went into the house.

So she knew how to contact the master of Wind

Dancer. Had she wanted to know that? Had she tried to discover it?

Of course she hadn't. The man she'd last seen, the man who'd bidden her such a coldly indifferent farewell, who'd refused to hear her hesitant and inarticulate apology, was not a man she would wish to see again, and he'd made it clear he had no wish to see her again. She simply possessed a piece of useless information. Its only satisfaction lay in the knowledge that the master of *Wind Dancer* would not wish her to possess it.

Eight

"THAT GOWN SUITS YOU so wonderfully well," Phoebe observed when Olivia came into the parlor that evening in a gown of orange silk edged in black lace that set off her dark hair and pale coloring to perfection. Phoebe was always slightly envious of Olivia's unerring dress sense. Olivia never seemed to give her clothes or appearance any thought, but she always knew exactly what suited her. Phoebe, whose own taste was somewhat haphazard, relied heavily on her friend's advice in such matters.

Olivia managed a wan smile at the compliment. The gown had been a present from her father on her seventeenth birthday, but she'd had little opportunity to wear it in the intervening eighteen months. A soiree at Carisbrooke Castle and an audience with the king, prisoner though he was, seemed a suitable occasion.

"Are you sure you wish to go out tonight?" Cato asked. She didn't look at all well to him. "An early night might be a better idea."

"No, sir. I'm looking forward to meeting the king," Olivia assured him. It was hardly the truth but she couldn't bear to spend an evening alone with her melancholy.

"Diversion is good medicine, my lord," Phoebe said. She'd tried herself earlier to persuade Olivia to stay at home but without success. "We need not stay above an hour, need we?"

He shook his head. "No. Let us go, then."

A team of fast horses was harnessed to the light coach that Cato kept for Phoebe's use. His wife was not a comfortable horsewoman. Fortunately the roads were dry enough for coach travel in the summer months, and distances around the island short enough to make coach travel a perfectly reasonable alternative to horseback.

It was a seven-mile drive to Carisbrooke and, with the swift team, took them little more than an hour. Olivia felt the first stirrings of interest as they drove up the ramp and under the gatehouse. She had not seen the inside of the castle in the months they'd been on the island, although its great curtain walls high on the hill outside Newport were visible from many

157

of the hilly downs where she and Phoebe walked.

They descended from the carriage under the arched gatehouse and were escorted into the main courtyard. The governor's residence was an Elizabethan country house set in the middle of a fortress. The castle keep rose up on a great mound behind it, and there were soldiers everywhere, but it bore little resemblance to her father's castle in Yorkshire, Olivia thought. This was much softer in feel, even though its bulwarks and curtain walls made it impregnable and its site dominated the island.

They crossed the courtyard to the door to the great hall, and Colonel Hammond came immediately to greet them. Behind him hurried a lady in a gown of an unfortunately bright yellow that seemed to give a greenish tinge to her sallow complexion. She had an angular face and a very pointed nose, and her thin smile revealed a near toothless mouth.

Cato introduced his wife and daughter to the governor and his lady. Mistress Hammond's scrutiny was sharp and not particularly benign.

"We are so glad to welcome you, Lady Granville. Your husband is much in our company, but we have missed yours." There was no mistaking the reproof.

Phoebe bridled immediately. "I have been very busy with my work and my children, madam."

"Ah, a devoted mother. How nice." The lady

turned her attention to Olivia. "Lady Olivia, I trust we can find you some amusing companionship this evening. You must find it very tedious, isolated in that house in...in Chale, is it? So far from our little society here."

"On the c-contrary, madam." Olivia smiled. "I spend most of my time in the society of the great philosophers. I find nothing else can quite match their stimulation."

Cato's sigh was inaudible. His wife and his daughter would make short work of Mistress Hammond if given half a chance. Phoebe was already readying herself for a return to the offensive.

"I would present Lady Granville and Lady Olivia to His Majesty, Mistress Hammond," he said smoothly. "Would you be good enough...?" He bowed to the lady, ignoring Phoebe's indignant stare at being handed over in such cavalier fashion.

"But of course." Lady Hammond's attitude visibly improved at this request for patronage. "Come this way, Lady Granville... Lady Olivia. I will see if the king will receive you." She sailed away through the crowd, waving people from her path with a flourish of her fan.

"Self-important, toothless old bat," Phoebe muttered. "She'll trip over her own self-consequence one of these days."

Olivia grinned. She was beginning to feel better.

King Charles was seated before the fireplace,

where despite the warmth of the summer evening a fire had been kindled. His head rested on the high carved back of his chair and he held a chalice of wine in his hands as he listened with the appearance of patient good humor to the man who was addressing him.

The alacrity with which he acknowledged Mistress Hammond, however, was telling.

"Ah, madam, such pleasant company we're enjoying." He turned his heavy-lidded gaze on the two young women with the governor's lady. "May I have the pleasure...?"

Mistress Hammond made the introductions. Olivia and Phoebe made their curtsies. The king looked tired but his smile was exceptionally sweet.

"In happier times, I counted Lord Granville as my most loyal servant," he said with a sigh. "But matters have run out of hand. Tell me how you find this island. It has a pleasant aspect, I believe. I was used to ride out regularly, but..." He sighed again. In the early days of the king's imprisonment, Colonel Hammond had granted him considerable freedom, but after his ill-fated escape attempts, such privileges had been revoked.

"Very pleasant, Sire," Phoebe said, prepared to do her duty.

Olivia heard nothing. She was gazing at a man across the room—a man who stood head and shoulders above the crowd. The pirate was dressed in bronze silk; his golden hair flowed loose and curling to his shoulders. A black pearl nestled in the crisp ruffles at his neck.

The crowd parted around him and now she could see him clearly. His swordbelt was of finely tooled leather and the hilt of the sword itself studded with precious stones. It was not the sword he had used to take the *Doña Elena*. Olivia's heart jumped at the rush of memory. She gazed at him, unable to tear her eyes from him.

What could he be doing here?

He moved his hand in conversation and she saw the great onyx ring on his signet finger. Those long, slender hands, so deft with a quill, so strong on the wheel of his ship, so cool and clever on her bare skin.

Oh God, how could this be happening? The color rushed to her cheeks and then ebbed. Her skin prickled as if she'd been stung by a swarm of gnats.

A sharp pain in her ankle yanked her back to reality. She was in the king's presence and couldn't ignore His Sovereign Majesty as if he were of no more importance than a groom.

"My stepdaughter, Lady Olivia, finds the island peace most conducive to her studies, Your Majesty," Phoebe said, surreptitiously kicking Olivia's ankle again. Olivia was thrumming like a plucked lute and she was looking as if she'd lost her wits.

"Studies, Lady Olivia?" The king looked languid. "What is it that you study?"

"Uh...uh..."

The king laughed, not unkindly. "Your stepmother is partial, I can see. The rigors of academic study are not for young ladies. They prefer lighter pursuits, I know well."

Olivia was stung into speech. "Of c-course, Sire. I am, like all women, feeble of brain. The complexities of analytical thought are beyond my sex."

"Well, it is certainly true that women cannot grasp the finer points of logic and discourse," the king responded. His eyes wandered as he spoke, and it was clear he had lost interest in his present company.

Phoebe and Olivia curtsied and withdrew.

"What is it?" Phoebe demanded.

"The retiring room...I need the retiring room...most urgently." Olivia plunged into the noisy, odorous crowd.

Olivia had no idea what she was doing as she wove her way between bodies whose perfume fought against sweat and candle grease. The heat from the fire made her head spin. She could hear Anthony's laugh. It seemed to draw her across the room. Everything about him as he stood in the thronged great hall in his elegant clothes bespoke the careless, humorous ease that had so bewitched her on the high seas.

And now she could barely remember the anger and the hurt of their parting. As she pushed her way towards him he turned his head slightly and looked directly at her. His gray eyes were bright as the summer sea, glinting with merriment, and fleetingly she wondered how she could have turned from him with such fear and repulsion when she'd left his bed.

Anthony had seen her the minute she'd

walked into the great hall. He had rather hoped to avoid an encounter that he had guessed would nevertheless be inevitable on some occasion. What more natural than that the daughter of Lord Granville would attend the governor's social events? And here she was now in that stunning orange gown, and he must find some way of dealing with her.

She was coming towards him with definite purpose, and he had to stop her in her tracks. She could not come up to him, acknowledge him in public, in this hall full of enemies, spies, gossips. It had been too much to hope that she would ignore him, he supposed. Although after the way she had rejected him after their loving, it was not a ridiculous hope.

This evening was his own first formal visit to the presence chamber. He needed personal access to the king now that his plans for rescue were in place, and he could only get that access by frequenting the court. His role was simple. A nobody, a country squire with delusions of grandeur. A flirtatious fop who never had an intelligent thought. There were many of them hanging around the imprisoned king, basking in reflected glory. It was a part Anthony could play to perfection. The king had been warned to expect such an approach, and Anthony was now awaiting a summons to be presented to His Majesty.

And Olivia Granville was about to complicate matters rather dramatically.

He turned all his attention to the lady

standing beside him, offering with a lazy but inviting smile, "May I replenish your cup of canary, madam?"

"Why, thank you, sir. I do seem to have finished this one already. So absorbed in your conversation, I didn't notice." She simpered, quite unable to gather her thoughts beneath the power of those warm, merry eyes and that crooked smile.

Anthony took the cup from her, his fingers brushing hers lightly as he did so. The lady quivered. Anthony turned away the instant before Olivia reached him.

Olivia re-collected herself. She must tread very carefully, follow his lead, learn the steps of deception. Whatever he was, whoever he was here in the great hall of the governor's mansion in the presence of the king, he was not the pirate master of *Wind Dancer*.

She glanced around and saw that Phoebe, still standing where she'd left her, was watching her with a puzzled expression. Olivia didn't appear to be heading for the stairs leading to the retiring room. Olivia threw her a tiny reassuring smile.

Anthony was exchanging the empty cup for a full one at a sideboard standing against the fireside wall. He was separated from her by a trio of deeply conferring men.

Olivia stepped around the trio. As Anthony turned to go back to his previous companion, she glanced around as if looking for someone in the throng, stepped blindly sideways, and knocked into the pirate.

The cup he held spilled its contents over her gown. "Oh, look what's happened!" she exclaimed, giving him a fairly convincing glare. "It'll stain, I know it will."

"Oh, mercy me! Pray forgive me, madam." He set the cup on the sideboard behind him, tutting and chattering all the while. "Such clumsiness. How *could* I have done such a thing?"

He whipped out a handkerchief from his pocket and flourished it. "Let me dry it for you...oh, I cannot believe I could have been so clumsy...so unlike me. I pride myself on...oh, and such a beautiful gown...such elegance...I am mortified, madam. Absolutely mortified." He dabbed at her gown with the handkerchief. "We must hope that as it's white wine it won't stain."

Olivia listened incredulously to this stream of words, the sighs and the tittering laugh that accompanied them. He didn't sound in the least like himself; even his voice was pitched higher.

"Pray don't concern yourself, sir," she said, twitching her skirts free of his hold as he continued to dab ineffectually at the damp patch.

"Oh, but I must concern myself. I do so trust that it's not ruined," he lamented. "To spoil such a bewitching gown would be nothing short of criminal."

"*Please* do not blame yourself, sir," Olivia said in some desperation. If she'd known her ploy would have turned him into this blathering jackass, she would never have used it.

He straightened at last and for a second he

met her eyes. The noisy crowd around them seemed to recede, leaving them standing alone, locked together.

Then Anthony bowed with an elaborate flourish. "Edward Caxton at your service, madam," he said. "I have never been so mortified. How may I make amends?"

Olivia's eyes flickered. So in the king's presence Anthony had become Edward.

"Pray...pray tell me how I may make amends," he insisted. "If you could but slip out of the gown, I could try to...oh, but, of course, how could we manage such a thing here?"

Olivia shook her head and murmured, "Stop it!"

"I protest, madam, you cut me to the quick," he responded solemnly, placing his hand over his heart. "To refuse to allow me to do what I can to pay for my clumsiness."

Olivia didn't know whether she wanted to laugh or scream. "Believe me, sir, it is *nothing*."

"Ah, how kind of you to say so." He sighed heavily. "But how well I know that such denials so often mean quite the reverse. I recall such an instance just the other morning." He regarded her with a fatuous smile on his lips and a pointedly sardonic gleam in his eye.

Olivia opened her fan with a flick of her wrist. Her voice was cool and even. "Are you often in the king's presence chamber, Mr. Caxton?"

"When I have business," he answered, with the same smile and the same look in his eye.

Business? But of course, a mercenary's business. Olivia recalled his cynical statement that he sold his services to the highest bidder. Was the king the highest bidder here?

"And your business requires you to play the idiot?" she asked softly from behind her fan.

The gleam in his eye intensified. "Madam, I must protest. 'Tis too unkind of you," he murmured. "But I can bear such arrows when they fly from the quiver of such a beautiful lady."

"Olivia...Olivia, is all well? Does your head ache? I saw you stumble." Phoebe was suddenly beside her. She regarded Olivia's unknown companion with a faint hauteur.

Anthony offered another vapid smile and once again began his lament. "So doltish of me... I fear it was all my fault. Such clumsiness. I was—"

"Phoebe, allow me to present Mr. Edward Caxton," Olivia interrupted firmly. "Mr. C-Caxton, Lady Granville."

Anthony bowed so low his head almost touched his knees. "Lady Granville, I am delighted. I wish only that we could have met in happier circumstances." He gestured sorrowfully to Olivia's gown.

Phoebe curtsied automatically but she looked inquiringly at Olivia. Something was going on here. Olivia was so obviously on edge and Phoebe could see no reason why this Mr. Caxton with his asinine smile should cause that. He was undeniably attractive with his commanding figure and golden hair, but

Olivia did not suffer fools gladly, and this one bore all the marks of a prize nitwit.

Of course, being forced to be in his company could easily explain Olivia's agitation, Phoebe reasoned. She'd been on an urgent visit to the retiring room and had been interrupted by this buffoon. Rescue was required.

"I'm looking for a poet to enliven things a little. My husband promised me there would be one, but I don't seem to have found him yet. I don't suppose you would happen to know if there's a poet around, sir?"

Anthony inclined his head and gave her a bewildered smile. "I beg your pardon, dear lady?"

"Phoebe is a considerable poet herself," Olivia explained coolly. "My father enticed her here with the promise of a poet to talk to. Though not a good one, he said."

"A poor poet is better than no poet at all," Phoebe declared, looking around them as if the man she sought would be carrying some identifying mark. "That man over there. The one in the rusty black coat and lank hair. He looks rather distrait and otherworldly. Could that be him?"

Anthony followed the direction of her gesturing fan. "I believe you're looking at Lord Buxton, madam. He's more interested in cattle breeding than poetry. Indeed, I should be surprised to find he can pen his own name." He simpered at his own witticism.

"You seem very knowledgeable, sir. Are you acquainted with most people in the hall?" Olivia inquired, plying her fan languidly.

"I see no poet, madam," Anthony responded with another irritating little laugh.

"I shall ask my husband to find me the poet at once," Phoebe stated. "Will you come, Olivia? I'm sure Mr. Caxton will excuse you." She gave the gentleman in question a cold stare.

"I *must* visit the retiring room," Olivia said. "I was on my way there when I...uh...ran into Mr. C-Caxton. I'll join you shortly."

Phoebe looked at her with close concern. "Are you feeling quite well? Would you like me to come with you?"

"No, I thank you," Olivia said hastily. "Really, I am quite well, Phoebe. I'll join you shortly."

Phoebe hesitated, but Olivia didn't appear to be in distress. She nodded at Mr. Caxton and went off with purposeful step in search of her husband.

"What are you doing here? Who *are* you?" Olivia demanded in an undertone.

"Edward Caxton is delighted to make your acquaintance, Lady Olivia. Perhaps I may call upon Lady Granville one afternoon?"

"As a blundering fop or as a pirate?" Olivia demanded in a fierce undertone. "Mr. Caxton or the master of *Wind Dancer*?"

"Perhaps you should wait and see," he murmured, then turned from her as an equerry appeared at his shoulder.

"His Majesty will be pleased to grant you an audience now, Mr. Caxton."

Anthony bowed to Olivia, his eyes mocking. "I look forward to renewing our acquaintance, madam." Then he was gone, striding through the crowd, his hair bright under the lamplight.

Olivia glanced around, trying to look as if she had just had a perfectly ordinary conversation. Mistress Hammond hove into view. "Lady Olivia, I didn't realize you were acquainted with Mr. Caxton." Her eyes were sharp in her angular countenance.

"Indeed, I am not," Olivia returned. "There was an accident...he spilled wine on my gown. I should retire and try to sponge the stain."

"My maid will help you." The governor's lady took Olivia's elbow and steered her across to a small staircase at the rear of the hall.

"Does Mr. Caxton live on the island, madam?" Olivia inquired casually.

"He lodges in Newport but I believe his family home is in the New Forest, just across the Solent."

"He serves the king?"

Mistress Hammond stiffened. "We all serve the king, Lady Olivia."

"Yes, of c-course." Olivia looked down distressfully at her skirt. "I do hope the stain will come out. I should be most unhappy to spoil this gown, it's quite one of my favorites. Up the stairs...? Thank you, Mistress Hammond. There's no need to accompany me further." She shook off the hand at her elbow, gathered her skirts, and almost ran up the stairs.

When she emerged from the retiring room some twenty minutes later, she was once more mistress of herself. She paused at the head of the stairs from where she could view the great hall below. The king still sat in his chair surrounded by eager courtiers, but now there was no sign of Anthony. And she couldn't see Phoebe either. Her father, however, was talking with a tall dark-haired young man of swarthy complexion, dressed in a suit of puce silk with a scarlet waistcoat and sash. His hair curled to his shoulders, glistening with pomade, and as he talked his hand rested on the hilt of his sword. They seemed deep in conversation.

Where was Phoebe? Olivia felt suddenly rather bereft and out of place, as if everyone had forgotten her and no one was interested in her. Then she saw Phoebe tucked into a window embrasure at the far side of the throng. She was talking with great animation to a small, rather fat man of rubicund countenance and jovial appearance. He was an unlikely looking poet, but seemed to be holding Phoebe's attention.

Olivia headed towards them.

"I'M WONDERING why you haven't given your impressions to Colonel Hammond, Lord Channing?" Cato was asking.

Godfrey's tongue touched his lips in a nervous gesture. "I mean no disrespect to the governor, my lord, but he's more interested in hard facts than impressions and opinions. And I thought that you might be more open to my impressions of the king's manner."

Cato nodded slowly. There was truth in this. "You say the king has appeared distracted."

"Yes...and his mood fluctuates wildly. One day he seems depressed, the next he's full of optimism," Godfrey explained eagerly. "I am convinced that he's receiving some information that we're not aware of. When the Scots crossed the Border, he was in particularly good spirits, and I know that he was not informed of the troop movement by Colonel Hammond."

"Mmm." Cato nodded again. He had long suspected that the king had access to information about Royalist supporters on the mainland. "I'll inform Colonel Hammond of your impressions." He glanced at the young man, wondering what it was about him that he disliked. His eyes were perhaps too close together. But one could hardly fault a man for that.

"The king seems to favor me," Godfrey said. "If I can be much by his side, then perhaps I can discover more concrete information. If perhaps you suggested to the colonel that my duties should be more concentrated upon the king..." He looked a question.

"You think you'd make a good spy?" Cato inquired.

"I think I'd make an excellent spy, my lord," Godfrey said with conviction. Brian Morse had told him that Lord Granville had no time for shilly-shallying. He liked people to come to the point and speak and act with decision, and he had no time for false modesty.

"I'll discuss this with Colonel Hammond," Cato said briskly. "In the meantime, keep your eyes and ears open."

"Indeed I will, my lord." Godfrey hesitated, a tentative smile on his lips. "I was wondering, my lord, if..."

"If what?"

"If I might be introduced to Lady Olivia," Godfrey said in a rush. "I would very much like to make her acquaintance, sir."

Cato stroked his chin. "It seems a modest request," he observed. He looked around the hall. "Ah, I see her over there with Lady Granville." He moved off, Godfrey in his wake.

Godfrey had been watching Olivia all evening. Brian Morse had been correct. She was indeed a tasty piece. Notwithstanding the Granville nose. Such an heiress in his bed would do a great deal more than solve his financial problems. He had made a good impression on Granville, and with Brian's help would continue to provide him with little tidbits of information that would win the marquis's confidence. He had only to conquer the daughter. That shouldn't be too difficult. Godfrey knew he was considered charming and debonair, well dressed and passably good-looking. The Granville heiress was apparently not otherwise engaged. It should be a simple campaign. He followed the marquis with brisk step.

Phoebe didn't notice their approach. She was very content with her poet. Although he had a preference for flowery, sentimental verse, he could talk about the complexities of rhyme and meter with the best, and she had been starved of such conversation in recent weeks. During their earlier sojourn at Hampton Court, when the king had been in residence there at the pleasure of Parliament, many of the finest poets in the land had frequented the palace, but Carisbrooke was a little short on such delicacies.

Olivia merely hovered on the outskirts of the conversation, happy simply to have found an inconspicuous place where she was not obliged to make small talk with strangers. Her eye roved the hall, half dreading, half longing to see Anthony reappear. It was so dangerous for him to be here. What game was he playing? Was Caxton a real name or some alias? Was Anthony his name, or was it Edward? Did he truly have a family estate on the mainland? He'd talked of an aunt...an aunt who embroidered his nightshirts. It sounded so absurd, so unlikely.

"Olivia, my dear..."

Olivia jumped as her father's voice broke into her musing.

He smiled. "Did I startle you?"

"Oh, I was miles away," she said, her eyes going to Cato's companion.

"Allow me to present Godfrey, Lord Channing," Cato said.

Godfrey bowed low over Olivia's hand.

"Lady Olivia, it is an honor." He raised his eyes and smiled winningly.

Olivia felt the first deep shudder of revulsion. She pulled her hand loose even as she curtsied and murmured the correct responses. *What was it about him?* There was something...some echo...that filled her with terror. It was his eyes. So cold and green, even though he was smiling. Cold and calculating. She'd seen those eyes before, not the eyes but the expression. And his mouth, that thin flicker. It was a cruel mouth. And she knew it of old.

"I have been hoping to make your acquaintance all evening, Lady Olivia," Godfrey was saying, still smiling. "I trust I may call upon you and Lady Granville one afternoon."

"Yes...I mean, you should address that question to my stepmother." Olivia gestured to Phoebe, who had turned from her poet at her husband's appearance.

"Lord Channing, is it?" Phoebe said with her ready smile. She glanced at Olivia and was immediately concerned. Olivia was paler than ever. "We don't lead a very social life at Chale," Phoebe said a little hesitantly.

"Oh, I won't expect entertainment, madam," Godfrey assured her. "I should be happy just to sit with you."

Phoebe looked in some surprise at her husband, who offered a half shrug. "Well, of course we should be delighted to welcome you, sir," she said politely.

"Until later. Lady Olivia, Lady Granville,

175

my lord…" Godfrey bowed to the company in general and strolled off well satisfied with his first steps.

Brian. He reminded her of Brian. The room seemed to spin and Olivia put a hand to her throat.

"Cato, we should leave," Phoebe said swiftly. "Olivia's been up too long today."

"Yes, of course. I'll summon the carriage."

"What is it?" Phoebe asked as her husband disappeared. "You look as if you've seen a ghost."

It was as if she had, Olivia thought. Brian Morse was dead, killed by Lord Granville's sword. Phoebe had seen it happen. Godfrey Channing couldn't help that slight similarity. But anyone with eyes and a mouth like that had an evil in him.

Olivia drew a deep, steadying breath. It was ridiculous, fanciful to think like that. She would not have made such an association before her night with Anthony had released the long-buried nightmare. She must put it back again, otherwise the poison would seep into everything. It had wreaked sufficient damage already.

"The carriage is ready." Cato reappeared. "Are you feeling any better, Olivia?"

"Yes, much better. It was just a moment of weakness," Olivia said, taking his free arm.

"Why was Lord Channing so anxious to make our acquaintance?" Phoebe asked from Cato's other side. "He's not a suitor for Olivia's hand, is he?"

"He may have some such plan in mind," Cato said as they reached the carriage in the court- yard.

"No!" Olivia cried in alarm. "I don't want any such suitor." She turned to look up at her father as he handed her into the carriage, her dark eyes intense in the torchlight.

"Then you must simply tell him so," Cato said calmly. "You're at the age now, my dear, when suitors are going to come thick and fast. You must decide for yourself how to deal with them."

"I'll help you," Phoebe said, laying a hand on Olivia's arm. "There's nothing to worry about."

"No, indeed not," Cato agreed, mounting his horse to ride beside the carriage. "It's natural enough that you should have suitors, Olivia."

Olivia slumped back against the leather squabs. She was being irrational, of course she could dismiss Lord Channing's suit, if indeed it was what he had in mind. But it certainly added another skein to an already impossibly tangled knot.

Nine

BRIAN MORSE LEANED BACK against the wall in his customary place in the inglenook of the Anchor's taproom. He rubbed his thigh and as he moved his arm the thick scar beneath his ribs seemed to stretch and throb. The pain was always with him. The pain and the knowledge of defeat. It was there in the deep lines of his face, in his limp, in the constant dragging pain. No one had expected him to survive after Cato's sword had brought him down, and he hadn't wanted to during those months of agony. But somehow he had done so. After many months his body had somehow healed, not straight, not clean, but healed nevertheless.

He raised his tankard to his lips, glancing towards the door. He was expecting Godfrey Channing with a progress report. Channing married to Olivia was a pleasing prospect. A man with a vast ambition and no morality whatsoever. Thus a very dangerous man. A man clever enough to conceal his true colors to achieve his purpose. But he would show them eventually. When it was too late for the Granvilles to do anything about it. And then, oh, then, Olivia would pay the price and Cato Granville's pride and arrogance would turn to dust. It was a wonderfully subtle revenge.

The door opened and Godfrey came in. He'd changed his earlier puce and scarlet finery for riding dress and had the air of a man well satisfied with himself. He spotted Brian immediately through the blue smoke of half a dozen clay pipes and strode across to him through the clotted sawdust on the floor.

Brian indicated the pitcher of ale on the table in front of him, and with a nod of thanks Godfrey raised the jug to his lips and drank deeply.

"The evening went according to plan?" Brian inquired over the rim of his tankard.

"I believe so." Godfrey set down the pitcher and sat on a stool. "Granville was interested in what I had to say and wants me to spy on the king."

Brian nodded. "I'll give you bits and pieces of information about the progress of the Royalist uprisings and the Scots march that you can pass on to the king in some secret fashion. Then you simply tell Granville what the king knows. He'll think he's finding you very useful. And if you're useful to Granville, he'll welcome you into the bosom of his family with open arms." His mouth twitched in a sardonic smile. "And what of my little rabbit?"

"Little rabbit?" Godfrey looked puzzled.

"Olivia, my little sister. It was a pet name I had for her when she was a child. Such an endearing little rabbit she was. Particularly when she ran." The smile flickered again.

"I think she's rather appealing," Godfrey said.

"I won't have to keep my eyes closed in bed."
He gave a coarse laugh and drank from the
pitcher again.

"I haven't seen her for several years," Brian
mused. "She must be all grown up now. Does
she still stammer?"

"I didn't notice. She didn't say very much.
But my interest in her mouth has little to do
with what might come out of it." He laughed
again.

"You'd better not let her know that. I told
you, she has a brain."

"Oh, she'll soon learn there are other things
more important than books," Godfrey said carelessly. "I'll keep her far too busy to bother her
head with such nonsense." He drank from
the pitcher again and glanced at the watch in
the shape of a skull that hung from his belt.
"Well, I'd best be on my way. I've an appointment at midnight."

"Your customer?"

"Aye." Godfrey looked a little startled.
"What d'you know of him?"

Brian shook his head. "Nothing. I merely
overheard your conversation about a potential customer for your culling with George
here...just before you and I began our association. And an appointment at midnight..."
He shrugged.

Godfrey remembered. "Aye, well, you're
right. And once we've struck this deal, I'll be
a lot plumper in the pocket."

"Come to my lodgings in Ventnor in two
days' time. I'll have some more information

for you." Brian leaned back against the wall again, half closing his eyes.

"I'll be visiting the lady Olivia tomorrow," Godfrey said over his shoulder as he turned to the door.

"Ah, yes, my learned little rabbit." Brian smiled to himself. "You'd better do some scholarly reading first. Just so that you have something to talk about."

Godfrey grimaced as he left, but he was willing to listen to a man who was so clearly intimate with the habits and predispositions of the Granvilles.

PRECISELY AT MIDNIGHT, Anthony descended the narrow cliff path to Puckaster Cove for his rendezvous with Godfrey Channing. Gone were the elegant bronze silk, the lace ruffles, the black pearl, the onyx signet ring. He was dressed once more in the fisherman's garb, a limp mustache framing artistically blackened teeth, his face painted as before. The knit cap was pulled down low over his forehead. The sword at his hip was the pirate's plain, serviceable blade.

He left two men behind him on the undercliff, assigned to watch his back. As the pirate's footsteps faded on the sandy path, Sam muttered to his companion, "There's times when I reckon the master's off 'is 'ead. What's all this, then, about sendin' Mike to the lass's 'ouse, tellin' 'im to make a plan of the 'ouse?"

"Mike's good at scoutin', though," the

other replied, sucking on a blade of grass. "Best man to send, I reckon."

"Aye, but why'd he 'ave to send any bloke, that's what I want to know." Sam peered down at the cove through the screen of scrub that concealed them. The master had reached the beach and was standing, hands thrust deep into his pockets, looking out to sea, his posture as casual as if he were taking a moonlight stroll.

"It's not like the master to let a woman get under 'is skin," Sam's companion observed. "Easy come, easy go, is 'is way."

"Aye," Sam agreed, then he inched forward. "Reckon this is the bloke now. Seems t' be alone. You take a look along the path, while I keep watch 'ere."

The other man eased away down the path, and Sam took his cutlass from his belt and watched the beach.

Anthony didn't turn as Godfrey approached across the sand. He continued to look out to sea, whistling softly between his teeth. Only those who knew him very well would recognize in the set of his shoulders, the tilt of his head, that every muscle was taut, every inch of his tall frame ready for trouble.

Godfrey coughed loudly. Without turning, the fisherman observed easily, "Beautiful night, ain't it, sir?"

"I care not," Godfrey said. "Are you alone?"

A murdering popinjay who cared nothing for beauty. Anthony's lip curled but he said only, "As alone as you."

Godfrey glanced around. The beach under full moonlight was deserted. "We have to climb."

"Then lead the way." Anthony turned then and offered his black-toothed smile. "Let's see what ye've got fer me."

"You have the money? I'd see it before I show you anything."

"Not very trustin', are ye, sir?" Anthony dug into the pocket of his filthy britches and drew out a leather pouch. "There's five 'undred guineas in there. Ye'll get the rest on delivery."

Godfrey's eyes gleamed as he hefted the pouch on his palm. He untied the leather drawstring and peered inside. Gold glittered. "You'll have to move the goods yourself," he said.

Anthony reached over and took back the pouch. " 'Tis understood. But let's be seein' what you 'ave, fine sir."

Godfrey turned back to the cliff path. Anthony followed. He could barely contain his contempt. After the evening at Carisbrooke he now knew whom he was dealing with. People were always willing to retail gossip, particularly if the gossip was malicious. He knew much more about Lord Channing's affairs than that gentleman would ever wish to be revealed. He knew that the lordling's greed was fueled by necessity. He was deeply in debt. A man who aspired to power and influence needed wealth to smooth the path, and the Channings, while noble, were poor, their estates laid to waste by generations of greed and stupidity.

The present Lord Channing had a certain cunning to aid the greed. He seemed to plan well and carefully. He employed men to take the biggest risks for him. But the cunning went hand in hand with a complete absence of respect for human life...unless, of course, it was his own. He took where he could and from whom he could.

Anthony lived his life beyond the law, but this man was vermin in his eyes.

Godfrey turned to the right when they reached the undercliff. The uneven path was rocky, more of a goat trail than a path. He picked his way carefully, while Anthony strolled along as if walking on greensward.

Sam and his fellow watcher kept their distance, moving like wraiths in the shadow of the cliff.

Godfrey stopped in the middle of the path and waited for Anthony to come up beside him. "Disarm yourself. I'm not such a fool as to show you the goods when you're carrying a sword."

Anthony shrugged and unbuckled his sword-belt, laying it on the ground.

"What else are you carrying?"

Anthony bent and drew a knife from his boot. This he laid beside the sword. Then he extended his hands with another shrug.

Godfrey nodded. "This way." He turned to the cliff face and pushed through a cascade of weeds and vines. Anthony followed.

They entered a cave, black as pitch. Godfrey felt around at the entrance. Flint scraped on tinder and a small light glowed from a lantern. Godfrey held the lantern high to show the bales and crates piled up against the walls.

"Take a look." He put his free hand to his sword hilt and drew the blade an inch or two from its sheath.

Anthony's smile was not a pleasant one as he heard the sound, but his back was to Godfrey and the other man didn't see his expression.

Anthony examined the wares. They were in good condition for the most part and would sell well at auction in Portsmouth. He loathed wreckers, but was too pragmatic to look a gift horse in the mouth. Later, when Godfrey Channing was no longer useful, the pirate would impress upon him the error of his ways. For the moment, he would use him. And the king's cause would be the beneficiary.

He took a piece of chalk from his pocket and moved among the goods, marking his choices with a cross. "I'll take these four chests, the figured silks, the two bales of velvet, the Brussels lace, the case of delftware and the other of Venetian crystal. The rest is dross."

A crispness sharpened the fisherman's drawl. Godfrey didn't notice the slight change in the vowel sounds. He knew only that this was a man who would do business.

"A thousand guineas," he said. "We agreed on a thousand guineas."

"Only if I took the whole. I'll pay eight hundred for what I've named. Not a penny more."

Eight hundred was eight hundred. "Done." Godfrey rubbed his hands together. "How will you take delivery?"

"Leave it to me, young sir." Once again it was the fisherman who spoke. "They'll be gone from 'ere by mornin'."

"And payment?"

For answer, Anthony tossed the pouch across to him. Godfrey, caught by surprise, grabbed for it and missed. It fell to the ground with a heavy clink. He bent and picked it up, unaware of the fisherman's curled lip and contemptuous eye.

"The rest will be delivered to the Anchor at midday tomorrow. I reckon George'll be wantin' his share. Seein' as 'ow your ship's not come in." The fisherman laughed and it was not a kind laugh.

Godfrey's hand tightened on his sword hilt. There was nothing he would have liked better than to have spitted the man on his blade. He demanded angrily, "What time will you take delivery? I'll be here."

"Soon after dawn, I reckon," the fisherman drawled. "No need for ye to be 'ere, though. My men know what to do."

It must now be around one o'clock, Godfrey calculated. Dawn was but four hours away. He'd get no sleep tonight. "I'll be here," he stated. Did the man think he was fool enough to let him take delivery unsupervised?

"Please yerself." The fisherman shrugged and turned to the concealed entrance of the cave. "Stand watch if it pleases ye. My men'll not lay down their arms, though, I give ye fair warnin'. They move fast and quiet and will be out of 'ere by six. They'll not take kindly to bein' followed, either. An' their manners aren't as gentle as mine. So keep out of their way."

And he was gone, leaving Godfrey alone in the cave with his rage and his five hundred golden guineas.

Anthony retrieved his weapons and strode back along the trail. Sam and his fellow materialized from the shadows of the cliff some hundred feet from the cave.

"You can find it again?"

"Aye, sir."

"At dawn, then. You'll need ten men, probably three boats. The goods are marked with a chalk cross."

"Should us expect trouble?"

"I don't think so. The little man's too greedy to risk this sale. But be on the watch anyway."

"Aye, sir. You goin' back to the ship?"

Anthony smiled then and lightly clapped Sam on the shoulder. "No, not yet, my friend. And there's no need to be anxious. I have my wits about me."

"I 'ope so," Sam muttered. "Mike'll be waitin' at the top fer ye, I suppose."

"I certainly hope so." Anthony laughed and loped off down the path.

Mike was waiting at the head of the path. Two ponies grazed placidly on the springy grass of the clifftop.

"Success, Mike?" Anthony unbuckled his swordbelt.

"Aye, sir. I've drawn ye a rough plan. Miss has 'er chamber at the side of the 'ouse." Mike unfurled a sheet of paper. "See 'ere, sir." The drawing of Lord Granville's house in Chale was a competent piece of draftsmanship, every door and window clearly marked. "There's this 'ere tree, see. Magnolia." He pointed to the tree beside the window in question.

"How very convenient," the pirate murmured, peeling off his mustache with a wince. "You're positive that's her chamber? I'd hate to barge in on my lord Granville and his lady." He thrust the ratty mustache into the pocket of his britches and took out a handkerchief and a twist of paper that contained salt.

"I 'ad it from Milly, sir. She's a maid there. I've known 'er since she was a babby, an' she was 'appy enough to offer me a pot of ale in the kitchen an' chat, like."

"What about dogs?" Anthony's voice was muffled as he scrubbed his blackened teeth with the salt.

"A couple of hounds, but they're kept in the kitchen at night. They'll rouse the house if'n they 'ear ye, though."

Anthony thrust the handkerchief back into his pocket and examined the map. "The kitchen's at the back of the house?"

"Aye, sir. There." Mike pointed.

"Then they won't hear me." He folded the

map and reached into his pocket again. He drew out a slim volume, weighing it for a moment on the palm of his hand, a half smile on his face. Then he tucked the map inside its front cover and pushed the book into his pocket with the handkerchief.

He took the reins of one of the ponies. "Keep hold of my sword and I'll be back here before dawn."

"Shouldn't I come with ye, sir? Watch yer back, like?"

Anthony shook his head and swung himself astride the pony. "This is a frolic of my own, Mike. I'll watch my own back. Be here at dawn to take the pony." He grinned, raised a hand in farewell, and nudged the horse into a canter.

He left his mount at the gates to Lord Granville's house, hobbling him so he wouldn't stray, then stood back in the lane to survey the obstacles to clandestine entrance. The gates were locked; the red brick wall was high but presented no problem to a man accustomed to climbing the rigging of a frigate.

He was up and over the wall in a moment, landing in the soft earth of Lord Granville's garden. It was very dark and quiet in the shadow of the wall, the silence of the night broken only by a blackbird's trill and the rustling of small animals in the undergrowth beneath the trees.

Anthony approached the sleeping house through the trees. There were no lights visible; only a curl of smoke from the kitchen chimney gave evidence of habitation. Keeping to the grass, he walked soundlessly around the side of the house.

The magnolia was a venerable tree massed with thick, glossy leaves. A sturdy branch reached almost to Olivia's window. And the window was most conveniently ajar.

Anthony swung himself into the branches of the magnolia and climbed swiftly. In a few minutes he was sitting on the window ledge of Olivia's chamber. The room was faintly lit by the moon, and the curtains around the bed were drawn back to allow the cool night air to reach the sleeper. Even so, Olivia had kicked aside the covers. She lay with her back to the window; her nightgown was twisted and caught up around her waist, leaving her lower body naked in the moonlight.

Anthony's smile deepened. He took the book from his pocket and withdrew the map. The reverse side of the paper was blank. He dug into his other pocket for the lead pencil he always carried and looked again at the bed. Frowning slightly, he sketched the sleeping girl; a few sharply drawn lines committed the image to paper. The flow of her hair, the curve of her spine, the turned flank and the flare of her backside, the long, entwined legs, her slender feet with their rosy heels.

He examined his work with a critical air, comparing it with its subject, then folded the drawing. Taking the book from the window ledge beside him, he tucked the sketch between its leaves.

He took off his boots as he sat on the window ledge, then slipped into the chamber, his stockinged feet making no sound as he went to the door and turned the key.

A small table stood in the middle of the room, with a book open upon it beside a sheaf of papers. Olivia had been translating a passage from Ovid before she'd gone to bed. Curious, he read the translation. There was nothing of the amateur about it. Every word was carefully and cleverly chosen to reflect the meaning of the original. Olivia Granville was a formidable scholar.

Soundlessly Anthony approached the bed. He placed the book with the sketch on the bedside table and sat down on the edge of the bed. Olivia stirred and mumbled in her sleep. Lightly he caressed her bare skin, little flickering brushes of his fingertips. She wriggled as if irritated by a bothersome fly. He smiled and continued to touch her.

Olivia stirred, straightened her legs, turned onto her back. Then she sat bolt upright, her eyes wide, sightless, her mouth opened on a scream.

Swiftly Anthony placed his hand over her mouth. "Hush, my flower. It's me."

She fought him, pushing him from her, her body twisting in terror as she struggled to escape the loathsome secret touches that had invaded her sleep.

"No, no, no," Anthony said into her hair, holding her tightly the more she fought him, holding her face buried against his chest, afraid that she would scream and bring the house upon them. "Forgive me, I didn't know I would frighten you so much. Hush, love, hush."

And slowly his words penetrated the fog of nightmare. Slowly Olivia realized that this was Anthony, not Brian. The touches had been loving, sensuous, gentle. They bore no relation to the rough, contemptuous cruelty of the past.

The terror died slowly from her eyes, and her body stilled in his arms. Anthony loosened his grip, feeling her surrender, and smiled ruefully into her bewildered countenance.

Olivia simply looked at him, her eyes still wide, a lingering terror remaining in their dark depths.

"I didn't mean to frighten you so," he said, reaching to brush a lock of hair from her brow. "You must have been so deeply asleep. I wished only to bring you pleasure."

Instinctively Olivia grabbed the sheet and pulled it up to her waist. She crossed her arms over her breast, shivering slightly. "I thought...I thought..."

"What did you think?" He caressed the curve of her cheek.

She shook her head. "It was just a nightmare. But it seemed to be really happening."

Gently he took her hands, drawing them away from her body. "How mortifying to be the subject of someone's nightmare." He was still smiling ruefully, but there was a question in his eyes.

Olivia averted her gaze. There was an instant's silence, then she said, "What on earth are you doing here? My father's in the house."

"He's not going to know I'm here." Anthony caught her chin, turning her to face him. "Kiss me and then you'll know I'm no figment of a nightmare."

"No!" Olivia jerked her chin free of his hold. "You c-can't just c-come in here...come through my window like...like Romeo...and expect me to turn into Juliet."

"I thought Romeo didn't get further than the balcony," Anthony observed. But he sat back from her now, his hands resting easily on his knees.

"You certainly don't look like Romeo," Olivia said. "Why are you dressed like that? Is that paint on your face?"

"I had business to do. I didn't have time to take it off."

"Just *what* are you?" she demanded.

"A pirate...a smuggler..." He laughed slightly.

"And a man who frequents the king's presence chamber pretending to be a dandified half-wit. And now look at you..." She flung out a hand at him. "What are you supposed to be now?"

"A fisherman."

"A fisherman?" Olivia stared at him, momentarily defeated. "How many people are you, Anthony...or is it Edward?"

"Hard as it may seem to believe, just the one,"

he said simply. "And Anthony will do for you. Right now, though, I've a mind to play physician." He reached forward and twitched aside the covers. "Turn over and let me have a look at your thigh."

"It's all healed up," she said, grabbing for the sheet again. "Phoebe looked at it."

"Nevertheless, I prefer to judge the progress of my handiwork myself." His eyes darkened and he placed his hands, cool and strong, over hers as they clutched the sheet. "Why would you be so shy with me now, Olivia, after all that we shared?"

She didn't answer him, repeating instead softly, "Why did you c-come?"

"To look at your wound and to return this." He took his hands from hers and there was no disguising the disappointment, the flash of frustration in his eyes. He reached to the bedside table and gave her the book he had brought.

"You left your Aeschylus behind on the ship."

"Oh." It was the book she had been reading when she'd fallen off the cliff. She opened it and the folded sheet fell to the covers, the map uppermost. "Who drew this?"

"Mike. I wanted to be sure I found the right window."

Idly Olivia turned the map over in her hands. She stared at the sketch. "This is me! You drew me, while I was asleep! How c-could you!"

"Because it was irresistible," he said. "And you know my passion for anatomy."

"You are despicable!" Olivia declared. "Spying and c-creeping up on people. *Despicable!*"

Anthony contented himself with a raised eyebrow. He rose from the bed and began to wander around the chamber, whistling softly between his teeth. Head on one side, he examined the pictures on the walls; he ran a finger over the spines of the books in the shelf; he picked up her ivory-backed brushes and the little pearl-studded hand mirror.

"Good God, I'd forgotten for a minute I was still covered in paint. You don't mind if I use your washcloth?"

He didn't wait for an answer but proceeded to make free with soap, washcloth, and water, scrubbing the rouge from his cheeks. "There, much more presentable, don't you think?" He laid the mirror down and turned back to her with a smile that demanded approval.

Olivia told herself she would not laugh. She had been watching his careless peregrinations in an incredulous silence, wondering why it was so impossible to shame him. And now he was looking at her like a hopeful wolfhound.

Anthony grinned, reading her mind as he had so often before. His eye fell on the chessboard on its inlaid table beside the empty hearth.

"Shall we play chess?" he asked casually.

"Shall we do *what*?"

"Chess," he said. "An unexceptionable activity, I would have thought, since we will be safely separated by a board." He picked a black pawn and a white one from the table and came over to the bed, holding them behind his back. "Choose." He extended his closed fists to her.

Wordlessly, Olivia tapped his right hand. He uncurled his fingers and revealed the white pawn.

"White opens," he said.

"And white will win," Olivia declared, pushing aside the covers. A game of chess in the middle of the night! It was insane, but it also excited her. And on some strange level it felt perfectly natural to do such a thing with the pirate.

She went over to the chess table, noticing how smooth and cool the wooden floor was beneath her bare feet. She replaced the white pawn on its square.

Anthony lit the candles on a two-branched candlestick that sat on a little shelf to the side of the chess table.

"Before we start, can you still feel that wound?"

Olivia hesitated. "It throbs sometimes. It feels tight, a bit stretched if I walk fast."

He sat down and beckoned her. "Physician's hat, I promise you. There's no need to be shy."

"I'm not shy," Olivia said with perfect truth.

"Well then...?"

Olivia thought of the sketch he'd made of her. It was all too absurd. She went over to him and turned around, raising her nightgown. His fingers were cool as they brushed over the wound.

"It's healing nicely," he said dispassionately, letting his hands drop.

Olivia shook down her nightgown. "I already told you that. Phoebe looked at it."

He laughed. "She has some skill, does she?"

"As a herbalist, as much as you, I daresay," Olivia retorted. "Except that she's not a surgeon."

"I must discuss such things with her at some point."

Olivia spun around on him. "And just *how* do you propose doing that?"

He laughed again. "With a little ingenuity. Have faith, my flower."

"What kind of flower?" she asked involuntarily.

"Oh, I don't know." He smiled lazily. "Sometimes an orchid. Tonight at the castle you were an exotic orchid in that flaming gown with your midnight hair. But at other times, you're more like a daisy or a marigold, wild and slightly raggedy."

Olivia thought it was a compliment, but when he was smiling in that secret way he had, it was hard to tell.

"Let's play chess." She sat down at the table opposite him.

"By all means," he agreed cheerfully. "A nice safe thing for us to do."

Olivia looked at him suspiciously but his expression seemed quite serene. She moved pawn to queen four.

Anthony shot her a quick amused glance from beneath raised eyebrows. It was an unusual opening.

He imitated the move.

"Pawn to queen's bishop four," Olivia said, suiting action to words. She sat back and watched his reaction.

Anthony knew the gambit she was playing. If he didn't stop it, he would find himself entangled and slowly squeezed to death.

"White will win," Olivia stated again.

"Oh?" He moved his pawn to king three.

Olivia without pause for thought moved her knight to king's bishop three. "White has the advantage, but I never lose," she said. "Even if I'm playing black."

"What a cocky young thing you are," he said, making his responding move.

After that they played in silence.

Until Olivia said quietly, "Check," as she moved her rook. "And mate in three. Unless you want to play it out."

Anthony examined the board. He examined it for a very long time. He'd sensed his defeat coming several moves back and had done, he thought, everything he could to circumvent it. But she had him. There was no denying it. And much to his surprise the loss piqued him.

His long, slim forefinger tipped over his king. He sat back in his chair and regarded her.

"Still say I'm cocky?" Olivia asked, unable to hide a rather smug smile.

"I think you have to give me the return match," he said, a smile flickering in his eyes now. There was something quite endearing about her smugness.

"Best of three," Olivia said instantly. She began to replace the pieces on the board.

Anthony glanced at the window. The night darkness was lightening. It would soon be dawn. "No more now," he said, rising from his chair. "I need to be away."

Olivia followed his eyes to the window. "Oh, yes, I suppose you do." She sounded disappointed. "I know I would win playing black."

"We shall see about that, my flower." He tilted her chin on a fingertip, then in one swift graceful movement bent and kissed her mouth.

He drew back immediately before she could react, before her eyes could cloud over in the way they had when he'd touched her before.

Olivia stood very still. Her heart was beating rather fast, and although the kiss had been so swift and so light, she could still feel the imprint of his mouth on hers. And she felt only pleasure.

"The next match will be on *my* home ground," he decreed, going to the window. He straddled the sill. "Mike will contact you. Just do as he says." He touched his fingers to his lips and blew her a kiss, then he swung himself over the ledge and was gone.

Olivia went to the window and gazed down.

She thought she saw him disappear into the trees, but he moved so swiftly and silently it was hard to be certain.

Just how did he think she could drop everything and come running when he summoned her? Did he think his own plans were more important than hers?

But of course he did. Whatever those damned plans were. They were as dangerous as they were outside the law, that at least was a safe bet.

She went back to the bed where the sketch he had made lay amid the rumpled covers. The fine hairs on her nape lifted as she looked at it. It was so sensual. It was as if every stroke of his pencil was a caress over the body he was sketching. She remembered how his hands had felt on her body when they'd made love.

She tucked the paper back between the pages of Aeschylus and climbed into bed. Her hand slipped beneath her pillow, her fingers closing over his kerchief. She fell asleep with it balled in her hand as she had done every night since she'd returned from her dream on *Wind Dancer*.

Ten

"WAKE UP, LAZY. It's not like you to sleep betimes." Phoebe bounced into Olivia's bedchamber an hour or so after the pirate's departure. She carried the baby on her hip and held her elder son by the hand. "I have splendid news."

Olivia dragged herself up from sleep. It seemed that this night was destined to be broken. She blinked at Phoebe, for a confused moment wondering where she'd come from.

But gradually now the world reasserted itself. The early sunshine, the sound of birdsong, the fresh scents of the grass as the night's dew burned off. Phoebe's bright engaging smile and the baby's soft cooing.

Olivia yawned. "What news?"

Phoebe grinned mysteriously. "I'll give you three guesses." Little Earl Grafton pulled free of her hold and tottered towards the dresser, where he knew he'd find shiny enticing objects from Olivia's jewel box. Phoebe deftly removed scissors and a pincushion before his dimpled fingers could light upon them. Then her eye fell on the washstand.

She said in astonishment, "What's that all over the washcloth? It's all red. Have you cut yourself?" She picked up the cloth by a corner.

"Oh, I was experimenting with rouge," Olivia said. "I thought I looked so pale when we went out last night. But I didn't like it."

Phoebe cast her an appraising glance. "Where did you get it?"

"From a peddler."

"Well, where is it? Can I see it?"

"I threw it away."

"*Olivia!*"

Olivia looked rueful. She really was not very adept at deception. At least not with those who knew her almost as well as she knew herself. "Anthony was here. Disguised as some kind of a drunken fisherman. It's his paint."

Phoebe absorbed the implications of this in wide-eyed silence. Then she said in some awe, "The pirate? He came *here*? Into your chamber at dead of night? With Cato asleep two doors away?"

Olivia nodded. "Up the magnolia tree and through the window."

"Dear God!" Phoebe exclaimed. "What for?"

"We played chess."

Phoebe looked at her as if one or both of them had lost their minds. "Did you say chess?" Her startled gaze shot to the chessboard. The black king was toppled; neat rows of taken pieces lay beside the inlaid board. Somebody had been playing.

"I thought you said it was over."

"It is," Olivia said, her fingers knitting the coverlet. "He brought back my book...the one I was reading when I slipped. I left it on his ship by mistake."

Phoebe sat down on the chest at the foot of the bed, settling the baby on her lap. "Let me understand this. This...this pirate, whom you never expected to see again, out of the blue climbs through your window at dead of night in order to give you back a book and play a game of chess?"

"It does sound unlikely," Olivia agreed. "But he's a rather unlikely kind of a person."

"Is there something you're not telling me?" Phoebe's gaze was sharp. "You can't pretend to me, Olivia. You know you can't. We've known each other far too long."

Olivia knew she was not going to tell Phoebe about how the pirate and a dandified jackass called Mr. Caxton were one and the same. If Anthony was playing a game that put him in opposition to Cato, then Phoebe would not want to know it.

"I'm just trying to put things together, Phoebe," she said slowly. "It was such a shock. I never expected to see him again. I told you how I felt that it had just been a dream while I was on the ship, and that now I'd woken up."

She pushed aside the covers impatiently and sat on the edge of the bed, searching for words. "But when I saw him again, it felt just as strange...just as dreamlike. Can you imagine playing chess in the middle of the night

203

with a man who..." She gave a helpless little shrug.

"Playing chess with an outlaw under your father's roof in the middle of the night sounds like the product of a disordered mind to me," Phoebe said tartly. She regarded Olivia with a frown. "Was that really all you did?"

"Yes," Olivia said. "That was all." *Apart from those touches, the light brushing kiss.* Her eye went to the book that contained the sketch. She didn't think she would show that to Phoebe.

"Well, I don't like it. It seems stupidly reckless to me," Phoebe said roundly.

"You're sounding so elder-sisterly and prudish," Olivia complained. "You used not to be. You used to do reckless things yourself, if you recall. Who was it who rode off after my father and hid on his ship without his knowing?"

Phoebe brushed a loose lock of hair from her eyes. "I suppose if you put it like that...I don't mean to be prudish, but I can't help worrying about you, Olivia. You've never done anything like this before."

"Well, that is certainly true," Olivia said with a reluctant grin. "The opportunity never arose."

"That's so flippant.... Oh, sweetheart, did you bump your head?" Without ceremony, Phoebe dumped the baby into Olivia's lap and rushed to the wailing Nicholas, who had lost his precarious balance and sat down with a thump, knocking his head against the leg of a chair.

Olivia held little Charles, playing with his

toes while she waited for the kissing and wailing to cease. "I might play chess with him again," she said consideringly, when Phoebe had once more given her her full attention.

Phoebe shook her head. "I don't mean to be prim and proper, really I don't. But it's crazy, Olivia. What if Cato finds out?"

"He won't," Olivia said with a confidence she didn't quite feel. "Not if you don't tell him."

"Of course I won't," Phoebe said indignantly, taking Charles from Olivia.

Olivia offered a placatory smile. "Anyway, what was this splendid news?"

Phoebe looked as if she was unwilling to be distracted, then she sighed. "Guess."

Olivia felt she'd had enough of games, but she thought she'd put Phoebe out enough already and it would be unkind to refuse to guess. "You're going back to London with my father and you'll see all your poets again."

"No...no," Phoebe said impatiently. "It's something to please both of us."

Olivia thought, then she smiled. "When's she c-coming?"

Phoebe's blue eyes sparkled, her customary sunny temper restored. "I knew you'd guess if you'd think for a minute. Portia's coming to stay for a few days. Rufus sent a message from London. He's been dealing with the army troubles—all the mutinies and things—and needs to have talks with Governor Hammond and Cato. So he's going to stay at the castle, but Portia wants to stay with us."

"Is she bringing all the children?"

"She never goes anywhere without them." Phoebe kissed the baby in her arms as she spoke. "One couldn't, really."

"No, I suppose not." It astonished Olivia how her two friends had become so devotedly maternal. Phoebe seemed more the type, but Portia was a mystery. A woman who was once happiest riding into battle at her husband's side, and who still wore britches most of the time with a sword at her hip, was the most fond mother, drawing no distinction between her own son and daughter, and Rufus Decatur's two illegitimate sons.

"So when's she coming?"

"Any day, Cato says. He thinks there's going to be another attempt to get the king away to France, and Rufus has some information from army sources that might throw some light on it all."

Olivia nodded, but her mind had begun to race. *Was this what Anthony was about? Engineering the king's escape to France?* An action that put him in direct opposition to the marquis of Granville, who was sworn to keep the king secure.

Dear God, she thought. Of course that was what he was doing. As she'd half suspected last night, the king, or rather his supporters, were the highest bidders for the mercenary's services. And where did that leave the marquis of Granville's daughter?

She glanced at Phoebe...Phoebe, so serene, so sure of where her loyalties lay.

The baby began to wriggle and Phoebe said, "I think Charles needs changing. But let's go for a picnic on the downs. There'll be a breeze up there and Nicholas can run around. He has so much energy."

She hurried to the door as the baby began to whimper. "Come, Nicholas." She held out her hand to the marquis's son and heir. The little earl was reluctant to abandon his play with a string of pearls, but was eventually persuaded with the promise of a piece of honeycomb to go quietly with his mother.

Olivia picked up the pearls and replaced them in her jewel box, then she went to the window that looked out over the sea. From St. Catherine's Hill, just behind the house, one could look out across the Channel and see the ships coming around the point. At the top of the hill was St. Catherine's oratory, where messages to and from *Wind Dancer* were left.

The master would presumably use that means of communication to send Mike to summon his chess partner. But by the same means, the chess partner could send her own message. Olivia Granville was not at anyone's beck and call. When she was ready to play chess, she would tell the pirate so. And she would also find out exactly what he was playing at in his games at court.

GODFREY, LORD CHANNING, rode up to the front door of Lord Granville's house in Chale at four o'clock that afternoon, the fashionable hour for visiting. He dismounted and gave his horse to the servant who had run out at the sound of hooves on the gravel sweep before the front door.

Godfrey adjusted the set of his peacock blue silk doublet and brushed an imaginary speck of dust from his lime green britches. He knew he cut a very fine figure. His wardrobe was a major expense, but he'd kept back from his culling a bolt of particularly elegant painted silk, a length of figured velvet, and a roll of Brussels lace. Worth, he reckoned, at least fifty guineas. They would replenish his wardrobe nicely.

He marched to the front door, where a stately figure awaited him.

"Lord Granville is not at home, sir."

"Lord Channing is come to call upon Lady Granville. I believe she is expecting me."

Bisset thought this unlikely. Lady Granville and Lady Olivia had returned a few minutes earlier from their picnic. They had looked as disheveled as the children.

"I believe Lady Granville is not yet returned, my lord," he said diplomatically.

"Bisset, who is at the door?" Phoebe's cheerful voice rendered the butler's discretion as nought.

"Lord Channing, my lady. I didn't know if you were receiving."

"Oh, I don't think I am," Phoebe said, coming up beside him. "Good afternoon, Lord Channing. You find us at sixes and sevens, I fear. We have been having a picnic and are not at all respectable enough for visitors." On any-one else such frankness would have been heard as discourtesy, yet somehow Phoebe managed to speak such truths without giving offense.

Godfrey bowed deeply. "Forgive me, madam. I will return at a more opportune moment." He smiled as he straightened. "I wished only to pay my respects to you and Lady Olivia."

Phoebe hesitated. It seemed churlish to send the man all the way back to Carisbrooke without so much as the offer of refreshment. She had promised that she would help Olivia deal with the suitors that Cato had warned would beat a path to her door. Better not to procrastinate with this one. "You must take us as we are, but pray come in, sir. May I offer you a glass of wine?"

Godfrey stepped with alacrity into the hall. "Thank you, Lady Granville."

"Bisset, bring wine to the parlor. This way, Lord Channing."

Godfrey followed her, noticing with a shock that the hem of her skirt had come down and she seemed to have grass in her hair.

"Olivia, look who has come to call," Phoebe said brightly as she led the way into the parlor. "Lord Channing has come to pay his promised visit."

Olivia was sitting on the window seat with Nicholas, weaving a daisy chain from the mound of limp flowers in her lap. The child leaning against her was half asleep, sucking a very grubby thumb. His mouth bore evidence of the red currant bush, and some of the juice had found its way onto Olivia's gown of pale muslin. Her hair hung loose to her shoulders and she seemed to have daisies entwined in it, Godfrey realized in astonishment. And they were dead daisies too.

"Good afternoon, Lady Olivia." He bowed from the doorway.

Olivia's breath caught in her throat as his cold green eyes fixed upon her. His thin mouth smiled at her. She could detect no warmth in him, only menace. Even as she told herself she was being ridiculous, she could hear Brian's taunting voice, see his narrowed eyes flickering over her as he looked for some new way to torment her. She had felt like a butterfly about to lose its wings when Brian had looked at her like that, and she felt exactly the same now.

She stood up, careful not to disturb the sleepy child. A shower of daisies fell from her lap. "You c-catch us unawares, I'm afraid, Lord Channing."

That was more than apparent. Godfrey saw that her feet were bare and there were grass stains on her skirts. There was something offensive about the entire scene. These two high-born women looking like peasant girls on May morning, their hair disheveled, their cheeks touched with the sun, their gowns disordered. Like milkmaids, he thought with a twinge of disgust.

But according to Brian Morse, this particular milkmaid had a dowry of some hundred thousand pounds.

"I find your dishabille charming, madam."
He smiled and bowed again. "And who is the
child?"

"Mine," Phoebe said, moving swiftly to
take up her son. "Earl Grafton...Bisset, ask
Sadie to come and take him to the nursery."

"Yes, my lady." Bisset set the tray with
wine decanter and glass on the table and left
with stately tread.

There was a moment's silence, then Olivia
forced herself to speak. "Wine...you would like
a glass of wine, sir."

"Yes, I thank you."

Olivia poured the wine, aware as she did so
that he was looking at her bare feet. She felt
as vulnerable as if she were naked. Her hand
shook slightly as she gave him the glass; his
fingers brushed hers and she was suddenly cold.

"My thanks, Lady Olivia." He smiled as he
took a sip of wine.

The arrival of the nursemaid and the handing
over of the boy gave Godfrey the opportunity
to examine his quarry more carefully. Untidy,
yes, but there was something undeniably sensual about her. The thick dark hair, the large
black eyes, the warm red mouth. A man would
certainly not need to keep his eyes shut when
he possessed Olivia Granville. He felt a plea-
surable warmth in his loins.

"Do you find life at Carisbrooke interesting, Lord Channing?" Phoebe asked, desperately searching for a topic of conversation.

"I am equerry to the governor, madam. It
is an interesting and rewarding position."

"I imagine you spend much time with the king," Phoebe said.

"Indeed I am much in His Majesty's company," he responded complacently. "But when I can, I enjoy solitude with my books."

"Oh, do you have an extensive library, sir?" Phoebe shot Olivia a slightly indignant look, wondering why she was leaving the entire conversational burden to her.

"I have some interest in the philosophers, madam."

"Greek or Roman?" Olivia inquired, correctly interpreting Phoebe's look. She had retreated to the window seat once again and was sternly telling herself not to be stupidly fanciful. What possible menace could there be in Godfrey Channing?

"I find the works of Plato most enlightening," Godfrey responded solemnly, hoping she wouldn't launch into an exhaustive conversation on the subject. He had done a little reading but not enough to satisfy a true scholar. But he doubted that a woman, whatever Brian might say, could achieve true scholarship. Olivia probably merely dabbled and considered herself very learned.

"Which works in particular?" Olivia asked. "The *Republic,* I imagine, but also—"

Much to Godfrey's relief, the question remained unspoken as the door burst open to admit a veritable whirlwind. There were children and dogs and a thin young woman with startling red hair and a mass of freckles, clad astoundingly in britches and doublet. There were cries of delight, much hugging and kissing, and one of the dogs, a large mustard-colored mongrel bitch, pranced and barked and greeted all in sight, including Lord Channing.

He kicked at the dog as she sniffed eagerly at his ankles, and she retreated with raised hackles.

"Juno, what is it?" The red-haired woman bent instantly to the bitch, smoothing her neck. The woman raised slanted green eyes to Godfrey and gave him a look of such derision he wanted to strangle her.

"Juno won't hurt you. Unless, of course, you're inclined to hurt *her*," she said coldly.

"Portia, allow me to introduce Lord Channing." Phoebe stepped forward out of the turmoil of children. "Lord Channing, Lady Decatur, Countess of Rothbury."

Portia gave him a cold nod, her hand still on the dog's head.

Godfrey's bow was sketchy. He'd never seen a woman like this one. He knew, of course, of Rufus Decatur, Earl of Rothbury. A man with a checkered past. But he was still an aristocrat. What was he doing with such a travesty of a wife?

He turned to Phoebe. "I should make my farewells, Lady Granville, and leave you to your guests."

"Oh, do you have to go so soon?" Phoebe murmured politely even as she gave him her hand.

"I have overstayed my welcome," he

213

responded, kissing her hand before bowing to Olivia. "Lady Olivia, I trust I may call upon you again?"

Olivia curtsied but made no reply. She could think of nothing to say that would prevent his return. Unless or until he made her a formal offer, she had no choice but to receive him.

Godfrey waited for her to answer him, and he waited in vain. He realized he was looking foolish, standing with his hand on the doorknob, and with a short nod he left the parlor.

"WHAT AN UNPLEASANT MAN," Portia observed.

"Yes, isn't he?" Olivia agreed readily. "He gives me the shivers."

"He seems harmless enough," Phoebe said, adding, "for a popinjay."

"My father thinks he wants to pay court to me," Olivia told Portia.

Portia went into a peal of laughter. "Then I can only commend his enterprise. He doesn't know, of course, that you're sworn to celibacy."

Celibacy but not chastity! The pirate's lightly teasing words rang in Olivia's mind, and idiotically she felt herself blush. She glanced at Phoebe, who wore her air of unwonted gravity again.

Portia caught the glance and her eyes narrowed. "I detect secrets."

"Olivia has been adventuring," Phoebe said in an undertone, mindful of the children.

"Oh, sounds interesting." Portia examined

Lady Granville's rounded, serious countenance with a quizzically raised eyebrow. "You look as if you don't approve, duckie."

She cast an eye over at Olivia and saw her confusion and distress. "I think I've arrived just in time," she observed, and turned to the children. "Luke, Toby, take Alex and Eve into the garden and give Juno a run."

The two elder boys obliged cheerfully, and the three women were left in relative peace.

"Now..." Portia sat on the arm of a chair. "Let's hear it."

RUFUS DECATUR AND CATO were walking the length of the terrace, deep in conversation. The children, Juno, and the two Granville hounds exploded through the glass doors from the parlor. Rufus paused to watch with a paternal eye as they chased across the terrace and into the trees.

"Luke...Toby...don't leave the garden," he called after them. "And don't let Eve get into any trouble." He got a wave in response and laughed slightly. "She's a real tearaway, that one. Always hip deep in trouble. It seems to seek her out."

"Takes after her mother," Cato observed.

"You may have a point."

The two men glanced through the open door into the parlor. The three women were sitting in a circle, heads together, so intent on their conversation they were oblivious of their audience.

"I wonder what they're talking about," Rufus murmured.

"Oh, domestic matters probably...teething babies, difficulties with servants, complicated embroidery stitches," said Cato with a chuckle.

Rufus laughed at this absurdity. "The soldier, the poet, and the scholar. What a trio."

"An inseparable trio," Cato commented before resuming their earlier discussion. "So, there's talk off the island as well as on it about a renewed attempt to get the king away."

"Aye, the army's full of rumor, but this one seems to have some teeth."

"But no one has a name for whoever's behind it."

Rufus shook his head. "I hear only that he's well respected, well connected, and something of a brigand. He's talked about with the kind of awe people reserve for folk heroes. William Tell or Robin Hood." He shrugged. There had been a time when he too had had such a reputation.

"But he's on the island?"

"Some say yes, some say no. He's a mystery."

Cato nodded. "A mystery who can defeat even Giles Crampton's network of informants. Well, we'll just have to watch and wait. And keep the king under even closer observation. I've set a spy in place, Hammond's equerry...Godfrey Channing. Have you met him?"

Rufus shook his head. "I know the name."

"He seems to have a knack for keeping his

eyes and ears open. And he's good at interpreting the king's moods. You know how His Majesty's moods reflect what's going on. When he's cheerful and optimistic it tends to mean he's got some plan a-brewing."

"Aye," Rufus agreed. "It's not that he's stupid, just that he considers it beneath his dignity to pretend. Is he still negotiating with the Scots, d'you think?"

"I'm certain of it. And Channing said that the king knew when the Scots crossed the Border, so information's getting to him somehow. And there's money coming from somewhere too. These damned pockets of rebellion across the country are being funded from somewhere...soldiers are being paid."

"Paid soldiers fight with a damn sight more enthusiasm, and they don't much care who the paymaster is or even what they're fighting for," Rufus observed. "While Parliament's armies go unpaid and mutinous, the king's supporters are fighting with full bellies and heavy pockets."

Cato nodded. "Every time I think the end is in sight, it drifts away again."

"We've a long way to go yet," Rufus said wearily. "You'd think seven years of bloodshed would be enough, wouldn't you?"

It was a rhetorical question.

ANTHONY SURVEYED THE BOOTY from the cave, piled high in *Wind Dancer*'s hold. "What do you think Ellen would like, Adam?"

"Lace."

"If I give her lace, she'll only use it to make me more nightshirts."

"They 'ave their uses. The lass looked right pretty in 'em," Adam commented slyly.

"That's as may be," Anthony responded. "But to return to Ellen..."

"The silk's too rich fer 'er tastes. She'd like a nice bolt of kersey or some such. She's not one for folderols.... O' course, she's not agin' a drop o' cognac or a nice flagon o' that there madeira."

"Well, that's easily supplied. And a couple of bottles of burgundy too. Maybe she'd like one of the cashmere shawls. Keep the drafts out in winter."

"Aye, mebbe so. You goin' to visit now?"

"You're coming too, I'm assuming."

Adam looked pleased. "Wasn't sure I was asked."

"Oh, for God's sake, man! When would I visit Ellen without you?"

Adam merely shrugged, gathered up the gifts for Ellen, and followed Anthony out of *Wind Dancer*'s hold.

The dinghy with two sailors at the oars knocked gently against the side of the ship. Anthony jumped down into the boat, reaching up to take Adam's burdens. Adam followed with rather less agility.

The oarsmen pulled strongly towards the mouth of the chine. Beyond its mouth they hoisted the sail and kept close in to shore until they turned in to a shallow cove, running the boat up on a tiny sandy beach. The cliffs rose steeply on three sides, almost over-hanging the beach so that it would be invis-ible from the clifftop.

Anthony picked up the gifts and stepped onto the beach, reaching forward to give Adam his hand as the older man hauled himself over the side of the boat and stepped gingerly over the rivulets onto dry land.

"We'll be back 'ere tonight, master." The sailors prepared to push the dinghy back into the water.

"Aye. But don't look for us until well after nightfall."

Adam huffed and puffed up the nearly invis-ible trail to the clifftop. They passed a watchman sitting, knees drawn up, gazing out to sea. Like his fellows stationed along the undercliff path, he carried a pipe that would give warning to *Wind Dancer* of any unto-ward visitors from land or sea.

"Morning, Ben."

"Mornin', sir." The watchman offered a half salute. "Mike's at the top wi' the ponies."

Anthony nodded and continued the climb. They would ride across the island to Yarmouth and from there sail across the Solent, past Hurst Castle on its spit of sand, and up the Keyhaven River. Ellen's cottage was in the tiny hamlet of Keyhaven, and it was there that Anthony had grown up, tumbling in and out of boats almost as soon as he could walk, absorbing the seaman's craft whenever Ellen released him from the learning that she insisted a gentleman's son, even an illegitimate gentleman's son, should acquire.

Smuggling was an active trade along the Hampshire coast as well as on the Isle of Wight, and Anthony had taken to the business as naturally as a duck to water. Within a year he had made enough money to buy his own small craft, and soon after, the men who had plied the trade for themselves in small and inefficient ways had joined forces with him, accepting his leadership. The acquisition of *Wind Dancer* had followed quickly, and the pirate had taken to the high seas in search of richer game.

As far as his father's family were concerned, he did not exist. His mother's family had never known of his birth. Anthony Caxton went his own way and took care of his own. Those who earned his friendship counted themselves fortunate indeed. And by the same token, those who earned his enmity learned to regret it.

They reached the small harbor town of Yarmouth after an hour's ride. The castle stood sentinel at the head of the River Yar facing Hurst Castle on the mainland spit, both fortified edifices guarding the entrance to the Solent. It was at the tip of Hurst spit where Anthony at the height of his smuggling operations had followed local custom and landed his contraband.

They left the ponies at the King Charles tavern and went down to the quay.

A grizzled fisherman was waiting for them

in a small sailing dinghy moored at the quay. He jumped up as they approached. "Y'are in good time, sir."

"I'd not keep you waiting, Jeb, if I can help." Anthony smiled at the man who had first taught him to understand the tides and the dangers of the races for a sailor navigating the frequently treacherous waters of the Solent.

He stepped into the dinghy, shaking Jeb's hand as the other climbed out onto the quay. Adam followed Anthony and took his place on the thwart. Jeb cast them off as Anthony hauled up the two sails, then took the tiller and turned the dinghy to catch the wind as she set sail for Hurst Castle and the Keyhaven River.

Eleven

ELLEN LEYLAND WAS WORKING in her vegetable garden. She straightened from the asparagus bed she was weeding and mopped her damp brow just as the two men strolled into view around the bend in the narrow lane.

"Why, Anthony...Adam...what a lovely surprise." She hurried down the path to open the gate. "I wasn't expecting you. Do you have news, Anthony?"

"You think I only visit you when I have

news?" he chided, bending to kiss her sun-browned cheek. "Am I so undutiful?"

"Oh, get along with you," she said, giving him a little slap. "Adam, my dear, how goes it with you?"

"Well, I thankee, Ellen." Adam beamed at her. Once, many years ago, they had shared a bed, when Adam had shared with her the parenting of Edward Caxton's son.

Ellen had no time for the distinctions of social class, and in youth and robust middle age had taken both friends and lovers where she found them. But her interest in the hurly-burly of lovemaking had died in recent years, as her passion for the king's cause had absorbed all her energies, both emotional and intellectual.

"Come in," she said now, hurrying ahead of them up the path. "I've just taken a batch of bannocks out of the oven. And there's a fine chicken pie."

"And cognac, madeira, and a good burgundy to go with it," Anthony said, setting his leather flagons on the scrubbed pine table. He looked fondly around the small kitchen that had been the scene of so many of his childhood joys and troubles. As usual, it was spotless, the china plates arrayed on the Welsh dresser, the copper pots glowing on their hooks.

"I expect Adam will prefer ale. Fetch a jug from the back, will you, Anthony?"

Anthony took a jug from the dresser and went into the back scullery, where Ellen did her brewing.

Ellen busied herself putting food on the table. "Sit ye down, Adam."

Adam pulled out the bench at the table and sat down with a little sigh of relief. It had been a long sail. The wind had been against them and they'd had to tack across the Solent.

"Here you are, old man." Anthony grinned as he set the jug of ale in front of Adam. "You're getting right creaky these days."

"Now, you watch your tongue, young Anthony," Ellen scolded. "And open that burgundy."

Anthony laughed and did as he was told. They ate and drank with the companionable ease of people who had sat at table together over many years. On board *Wind Dancer*, Adam would not have considered it appropriate to eat with the master, but in this kitchen there were no social distinctions.

Ellen waited until they'd finished before broaching the subject uppermost in her mind. "So, Anthony, have you seen the king?"

"Aye, last even." He rested his forearms on the now cleared table, tapping his fingers lightly on the surface. "I managed to slip him the nitric acid so that he can cut through the window bars."

Ellen nodded. The second time the king had tried to escape, no one had thought to check whether he could squeeze through the bars on his window. The bungled attempt had been a mortifying failure. On his third attempt, he had been given nitric acid to cut the bars, but so many people were part of the plan that all its details had inevitably come to the ears of Colonel Hammond.

This fourth attempt was being organized by a master. Anthony left nothing to chance. At Ellen's behest he had been serving the king's cause since the beginning of the war. He did what he did for Ellen and not for the king, for whom he had little regard. But Ellen's loyalty to King Charles was all consuming, so for the last six years most of Anthony's profits had gone to funding the Royalist armies, and now all the formidable skills he had acquired in planning his piracy and smuggling ventures were devoted to organizing the king's escape to France.

"How did His Majesty seem?" Ellen asked anxiously. "Is he very dispirited?"

"Less than one might imagine." Anthony took a sip of wine. "He's still negotiating with the Scots through Livesay." He shrugged. "And he still seems to think those negotiations are concealed from Parliament."

"But you don't think that's so?"

"No. Forgive me, Ellen, but the king is deluded in this as in so many other areas."

Ellen's mouth tightened. "If you don't wish to do this, Anthony, I'll not blame you."

He smiled then, absently moving his cup around the table. "Yes, you would. My feelings are irrelevant, Ellen. I do this for you. I have no particular interest in the outcome of this war, except that the sooner it's over, the sooner a man will be able to resume the life that suits him."

Ellen got up and went out to the scullery, returning in a few minutes with a bowl of stewed gooseberries and a jug of thick yellow cream. "I picked these this morning."

Anthony accepted that his indifferent attitude troubled Ellen and that she had no desire to continue the conversation. He helped himself to fruit and cream. "Before we go back, I'll nail the loose door on the goat shed. The next strong wind will tear it right off."

"Thank you." Ellen pushed the bowl across to Adam, who had taken little part in the discussion. He was accustomed to being an observer rather than a participant in such matters.

Anthony finished his gooseberries and with a word of excuse took himself outside. Soon the sounds of the hammer reached the kitchen.

"He's so like his father in so many ways," Ellen said. "I don't understand how he can be so different in this one particular. Edward was full of passion and ideals, misplaced many of them, but he *believed* in so much. Anthony doesn't seem to believe strongly in anything.... Oh, nobody could be more loyal or a better friend," she added, seeing Adam's frown. "But in terms of conviction...he doesn't seem to have any."

"Reckon 'e saw what conviction did fer 'is father," Adam said. "And 'twas conviction that led the Caxtons to cast off both Sir Edward an' his son. A mere innocent babe, their own flesh and blood, cast out to die fer all they cared. A cruel thing is conviction if'n ye looks at it in a certain light."

Ellen sighed. "I suppose that's true. But sometimes when I look at him I see Edward so clearly it hurts. The same rakehell charm." She sighed again.

"Aye, well that charm's goin' to get 'im in trouble one o' these days. Shouldn't wonder if it 'asn't already done so," Adam said darkly.

Ellen's eyes sharpened. "Tell me."

Adam told her in a very few words.

"Lord Granville's daughter!" Ellen looked at him in horror. "But Granville's utterly committed to Parliament. Anthony can't possibly be involved with his daughter. She'll betray him to her father."

"Don't jump to conclusions." Adam waved a forefinger. "First off, Anthony'll never let 'er in on 'is secrets. He's far too canny an' careful." He paused, frowning, then said, "Besides, this one's not like 'is usual sport, Ellen."

"How so?"

"Spirited kind of a lass," Adam said. "I doubt she'll fall fer 'is line some'ow. One minute they're all over each other, next she's off with 'er nose in the air an' Anthony's lookin' black as a wet Monday."

"Oh dear," said Ellen helplessly. But she turned brightly at the sound of Anthony's step in the scullery. "Thank you, my dear."

"My pleasure." Anthony stood in the doorway, hands on his hips, regarding them with a quizzical gleam. "I trust you've both enjoyed your little chat. Dissected the situation thoroughly, have you?"

"Oh dear," said Ellen again. "Couldn't you...well, couldn't you find someone more suitable, Anthony?"

At that he laughed. "Suitability doesn't come into it, dearest Ellen. But don't fret, the lady's not exactly falling over herself to get into my bed." A shadow crossed his eyes as he said this, a shadow not missed by his companions.

He took his jacket off the hook where he'd hung it when they'd arrived and slung it over one shoulder. "Come, Adam, it's time we were on our way."

Ellen walked with them to the gate.

Anthony bent to kiss her and then came to the main point of this visit. "I've a considerable consignment of luxury goods to dispose of. Can you get word to our contact in Portsmouth? *Wind Dancer* will be in Portsmouth harbor the day after tomorrow and I'll hold the auction the next day."

"I'll send the message this evening. Just have a care, my dear."

Ellen watched them stroll off down the lane towards the river, then she hurried inside for her cloak and made her way to the vicarage to deliver her message.

"BEGGIN' YER PARDON, M'LORD."

Cato looked up from his breakfast the following morning at Giles Crampton's familiar portentous tones from the doorway. "What is it, Giles?"

"A letter from the colonel, m'lord." Giles came into the room, dropping his head in the gesture of a bow to the three ladies at the table. "I think summat's up," he confided.

"Sit down, break your fast." Cato waved to a chair as he took the letter.

Giles offered another nod of his head to the ladies as he took a seat at the table. He had known the three women for a long time, in Olivia's case from early childhood, and while he offered a degree of social deference, he was perfectly at home in their company.

"Ham, Giles?" Olivia pushed the wooden carving board towards him.

"Thankee, Lady Olivia." He speared ham, cut bread, helped himself to eggs, and settled into his meal.

Phoebe gestured to a servant to fill a tankard for the sergeant from the ale pitcher on the sideboard.

"Damn," Cato muttered, his eyes on the letter.

"What is it?" Phoebe asked.

"A summons to London. I'm afraid your husband is needed too, Portia." Cato glanced at his niece as he refolded the letter.

"Well, I shall stay here, if I'm welcome," Portia said with a smile.

"You and your tribe." Cato returned the smile. "We'll be away a few days, not too long." He pushed back his carved armchair.

Giles instantly set down his knife and rose too.

"No, no, Giles, finish your meal." Cato waved him back. "I've some preparations to make. I'll meet you in fifteen minutes."

Giles sat down again but it was clear to his breakfast companions that he was itching to leave and only his lord's instructions kept him at the table.

"Deviled mushrooms, Giles?" Portia inquired, passing him a bowl. They had the most enticing aroma.

His hand reached for the spoon, hovered over it, then he said, "No, I thankee, Lady Rothbury. If ye'll excuse me, Lady Granville." He set down his knife, offered them his jerky little bow, and hastened from the room, his relief to be moving after his lord very obvious.

"Ah, Giles," Portia said, remembering how he'd come to find her in Scotland after her father's death. How his bluff manner to the scrawny barmaid she had then been had convinced her of the sincerity of her uncle's offer of protection. "I wouldn't be here without him."

"I can't imagine Cato without Giles; he's somehow joined to him," Phoebe said. "It annoys me sometimes that Cato always asks Giles's opinion first on military matters, but I feel better when he has Giles riding beside him.... I remember when the king escaped from the siege of Oxford and..." She stopped, following Portia's gaze. Olivia, her expression as distanced as if she were deep in some unconstruable text, was repeatedly spreading butter on a piece of wheaten bread. The butter was now so thick it made a mountain.

"Olivia?"

"Mmm?" Olivia looked up, smoothing her butter mountain with the flat of her knife.

"We seem to have lost you, duckie." Portia reached for the ale pitcher to refill her tankard.

"I have a chess game to play," Olivia said. "With my father away, now seems the opportune moment."

"You're going to find the pirate," Phoebe declared.

"Yes. I've promised him a return match." Olivia smiled and took up her tankard. "Phoebe, don't worry. If my father's not here, you don't have to concern yourself."

"Of course I do!" Phoebe declared. "This man is...is..."

"An outlaw," Portia said gently.

Phoebe said nothing. It wasn't the man's activities that troubled her so much as the knowledge that there could be no future for Olivia in such a relationship. Phoebe could see only hurt ahead. She gave Portia a slight shrug and saw from the swift flash in Portia's eyes that she understood.

Portia said, "So, why d'you want to go and play chess with this pirate, duckie?"

"Because I owe him a game," Olivia said. "And I can play it safely, because my father is away."

"You really think you can play it safely?" Portia leaned her elbows on the table and looked closely at Olivia, her meaning clear.

Olivia met her gaze. "I think I have to decide that for myself."

There was a short silence that Olivia broke. "*You* both decided it for yourselves."

"I think the third member of our little circle has found her wings," Portia observed. "Come, Phoebe, don't look so glum."

"It worries me," Phoebe said simply.

Olivia pushed back her chair. "I don't mean to worry you." She stood with her hand on the back of her chair, and some of her confidence had evaporated. "But I don't want to go without some...some understanding."

There was a moment's silence, then Phoebe reached into her pocket and laid a ring of braided hair, faded now, upon the table.

Portia slipped fingers inside her shirt and brought out her own. She laid it beside the other.

Olivia took her own from her pocket. She placed it on the table. "Thank you," she said.

Nothing else was said as they each took back their rings. Olivia tucked hers back into her pocket. She gave them both a half smile and left the room.

"You have to let go of Olivia," Portia said as Phoebe looked down at her own ring that she now held on the palm of her hand. "She has to make her own decisions."

"I know. But she's always been the little one. The one we have to protect, take care of."

"I think she can do that for herself now." Portia slipped her own ring inside her shirt.

"But she's Cato's daughter. I feel responsible."

Portia shook her head. "She's *our* friend, Phoebe. First and foremost."

Olivia wrote her message to the pirate. It was succinct.

If you wish for a return match, I will be available either this evening or tomorrow evening. I will look for you outside the front gate at precisely six o'clock.

She sanded the ink to dry it and smiled to herself. It struck the right decisive, uncompromising note. It was time Anthony learned that his opponent in this tournament had a mind of her own. She could imagine his shock when he discovered she knew how to contact him. He was also about to discover that she had a few pointed questions to ask him and she wouldn't be satisfied with his usual evasive answers.

Throwing a shawl around her shoulders, Olivia left her chamber and hurried out of the house. It was a steep climb up St. Catherine's Hill, but the wind was behind her, coming off the sea. At the top of the hill she turned and looked out across the glittering expanse. Was *Wind Dancer* out there at the moment? Would someone be looking out for a sign from the island?

She turned to the oratory, little more than a small, loosely formed pillar of stones that crowned the summit. She could see why the master had chosen it as a contact point. It was a very prominent spot that would be visible for miles around, both on the island and from the sea.

Olivia knelt to examine the stones. There was a small space between the two bottom layers. It formed a square box, almost like a cupboard. She slipped her hand in and found a white flag closely furled on a stick. She took it out, slid her message into the space in its place, and stuck the flag at the top of the oratory, pushing the stick hard down into the stones.

The white flag flew out jauntily in the brisk breeze. Now all that was needed was a watcher.

Olivia nodded to herself and set off back down the steep hill against the wind to await developments.

ANTHONY WAS SITTING with his back to the mast, sketching a pair of gulls squabbling over a fish head, when Mike rowed his dinghy into the chine and came alongside *Wind Dancer* later that afternoon.

Mike climbed up the rope ladder and swung himself over the side of the ship. "There's a message, master...at the oratory. I can't read the writin'. It's joined up." He handed the folded paper to Anthony with a worried frown.

Anthony opened it. He whistled softly. "How the *hell*...?" He looked up at Mike, eyebrows arched in question.

"The flag was flyin', master. I thought you wanted me. Thought maybe we was puttin' to sea or summat. But when I saw the writin', like, I knew it wasn't from you." He pulled anxiously at his earlobe. "You know what it's about, sir?"

"Oh, yes," Anthony said softly, "I know exactly what it's about. What I don't know is how the hell she learned about the oratory." He leaned his head back against the mast, closing his eyes to the sun's rays as it shone directly overhead into the cool green depths of the chine. "Somebody let something slip, Mike."

Mike tugged even more fiercely on his earlobe. "Weren't me, master."

"No, I didn't imagine it was." Anthony's eyes opened and his gray gaze was uncomfortably penetrating. "But someone did." He stood up in one easy, graceful movement. "So I have some preparations to make. And I have a task for you, Mike."

"BRITCHES," OLIVIA SAID. "I would like to borrow a pair of your britches, Portia. Skirts blow about in the wind and get tangled up in things."

"Anything you like, duckie," Portia said obligingly. "I'll go and fetch a pair. You'll need a doublet too." She left Olivia's bedchamber with her usual quick stride.

"How long will you be?" Phoebe asked. "You'll be back by morning, won't you?"

Olivia stepped out of her petticoat before answering. "I imagine so...but things could delay me," she responded in a somewhat vague, musing tone. "Wind and tide for instance."

"I suppose, if you don't get back by morning, I can just tell Mistress Bisset that you're staying in bed, or studying, and don't wish to be disturbed," Phoebe said reluctantly. She was still not resigned to this plan of Olivia's, but since she had no choice but to acquiesce, she might as well do what she could to facilitate matters.

Olivia kissed her. "Don't worry, Phoebe. Everything will be perfectly all right. My father's not here, so you don't have to make up lies for his benefit. If I'm not back, just say that I'm staying in bed to work on a particularly difficult text and I don't wish to be disturbed. Everyone will believe you."

"I suppose so," Phoebe said, returning the kiss. "It wouldn't be the first time."

"I wonder what your pirate will think of his lady in britches," Portia remarked as she came back into the chamber, laying a pair of serviceable dark gray woolen britches and a doublet on the bed.

"I don't suppose he'll think anything of it." Olivia pulled on the britches and tucked her chemise into the waistband. "Not that his opinion is of much importance," she added a shade tartly. She put on the jacket and buttoned it. "These do feel strange."

"They may *feel* strange." Portia examined her critically. "But they certainly do suit you."

"It's because of her long legs," Phoebe said

somewhat gloomily. Her own shortcomings in this area were a frequent source of grievance. "You've both got such long ones. I could never wear britches. My legs are just stumpy little things."

"But you don't need to wear them," Olivia pointed out. "My father would have a fit."

Olivia pirouetted in front of the long glass. Portia was thinner than she was, but the britches were still a comfortable fit. She tugged at the bottom of the doublet. It reached her hips but did nothing to disguise their curves. Anthony would probably reach for pencil and paper, she thought, her eyes darting involuntarily to the book on the bedside table.

"What should I do about my hair? Should I wear a cap?"

"You're not pretending to be a man, so I wouldn't worry," Portia said. "Just braid it and twist it up."

Olivia followed the suggestion, pinning the two thick braids into a coronet on top of her head. The effect was rather austere and she decided she liked it.

"How are you going to leave the house in those clothes without being noticed?" Phoebe asked.

"Same way Anthony c-came in. Through the window and down the magnolia."

"Oh, you'll make a soldier yet." Portia applauded.

"A sailor," Olivia corrected. "I'll leave the soldiering to you. I find navigation much more to my taste."

"I suppose the mathematics appeal."

"Exactly so." She went to the window and surveyed the magnolia somewhat doubtfully. "Of course, if it's not to be tonight, I'll have to c-climb back this way. It might be more difficult."

"Stay out until dark and I'll make sure the side door is left open tonight. Even if you do go, if you get back before dawn you can come in through the door," Phoebe said, sounding hopeful. "I mean, how long can a chess game take?"

Portia chuckled but said nothing.

Olivia glanced at the clock on the mantelpiece. "It's a quarter to six. I'm going now."

"Be safe," Phoebe said.

"Good luck," Portia said.

Olivia gave them a quick smile, then took a deep breath and launched herself into the topmost branches of the magnolia.

She had to jump from the bottom branch, but the ground was soft and her landing was concealed by the overarching branches. She slipped across the lawn, darting from bush to bush, thinking with some astonishment that for someone who'd never had to practice concealment before, she was really rather adept at it.

Anthony had come and gone in darkness, but the early summer evening was still sun-bright and Olivia nearly ran into two gardeners watering the flowerbeds. She ducked behind the thick trunk of a copper beech and waited until her heart had slowed and the men had moved a little further away. They had their backs to her now, and with crossed fingers she darted across the small patch of open ground and into the concealment of a box hedge. From there it was easy. She was out of sight of the house now, and the driveway was lined with oak trees.

Keeping behind the trees, she raced for the gate. It was still open; the gatekeeper wouldn't close it until nightfall. She could hear the gatekeeper's children playing in the garden at the back of his cottage, but could see no one although the front door stood open to the evening air.

She was out in the lane in a heartbeat and then stood, hugging the wall, looking up and down. *Would someone be there?*

She didn't hear the low whistle at first. It mingled with the whistling songs of the birds getting ready to roost. Then she heard it, low and yet penetrating, coming from behind the high hedgerow on the far side of the lane.

Olivia ran across and pushed through a gap in the hedge.

Mike was holding the bridles of two ponies. His reaction to her costume was limited to a muttered "Lord love a duck!"

Olivia greeted him with a smile. "So we're to ride."

"Aye, miss, just to the cove. The boat's waitin' on us." He boosted her into the saddle of the smaller of the two horses and mounted the other himself.

When they reached the clifftop, Olivia saw

the narrow trail snaking down to the beach far below them. She thought it was the same path she had climbed up that miserable night when she'd left *Wind Dancer*. How different she felt this evening.

Mike tethered the ponies and led the way down the trail. It was steep and twice Olivia's foot slipped, sending a shower of sand and pebbles skittering down to the undercliff. The little sailboat was drawn up on the sand, two men sitting beside it. They jumped up as Mike and Olivia reached the beach, and pushed the boat into the shallow water.

"Beggin' yer pardon, miss, but the master says we 'ave to cover yer eyes again."

Olivia looked at Mike in disbelief. He was holding a strip of linen between his hands. "Why?" she demanded indignantly.

" 'Tis the master's orders, miss." Mike twisted the linen between his hands. He hesitated, remembering what he'd been told. The master had had a distinctly militant gleam in his eye. "He said that if'n ye didn't like it, I was to say it's the price to pay for bein' so inquisitive, like."

So he'd upped the stakes, had he? A case of two can play at that game? Should she concede this one for the moment or drop the whole business? Leave the beach and the damned master of *Wind Dancer* to play *all* his games solo?

"Give me the blindfold." She took the linen from Mike. "I'll tie it in the boat."

Mike's relief was palpable. "If you'd let

me carry you a few paces, miss, ye'll not get yer feet wet." He lifted her easily and deposited her in the boat, where the two men prepared to hoist sail. They nodded amiably to Olivia.

Mike pushed the boat further off the beach and jumped in himself. He looked expectantly at Olivia, who with a grimace tied the linen over her eyes.

She sat quietly in the darkness, listening to the soft plash of water against the bow. One of the men began to hum, and the others joined in, a soft musical undertone to the gentle skipping motion of the dinghy. Curiously she found her blindness rather sensuous...she seemed to be experiencing smells and sounds and motion much more acutely.

As before, it was hard to tell how long they sailed. It had seemed a long time that other night, and it certainly seemed no shorter this time. They must be going west, because she could feel the rays of the setting sun on her face. And then she felt the change in direction and the sun was gone. The air was close and warm and she guessed that they had entered the chine. Now they were using oars and the sound was almost muffled.

Then one of her companions produced the low hoot of an owl, and immediately there was an answering whistle, soft as rain.

"We made good time," Mike said, receiving a grunt of agreement in response. "It'd be all right for ye to take off the blindfold now, I reckon, miss."

Olivia reached up to untie the strip of linen.

Despite the softness of the light, she was dazzled for a minute. Then she made out the elegant shape of *Wind Dancer* just ahead, rocking gently at anchor in the middle of the narrow, cliff-lined chine. Of course, there must be a deep channel in the middle. Deep enough for the frigate's draft. The anchorage was utterly secluded, the cliffs rising to either side, just a sliver of sky visible at the top. The chine continued beyond the ship, but growing ever narrower.

The oarsmen brought the boat up against the ship's side, and Mike tied her up at a ring in the stern. Olivia looked up and saw Anthony leaning over the rail at the head of the rope ladder. He called down, "Stay where you are, Olivia."

"I'm coming up," she returned. Holding the blindfold, she accepted Mike's proffered hand onto the ladder and clambered up. It swung out alarmingly from the side of the ship as she climbed, and she had to remind herself that she'd once jumped across a boarding net with the open sea yawning many feet below her. The britches made the climb easier, though.

Anthony offered her his hand but she scorned his assistance and swung herself over the rail, followed by Mike and the oarsmen. With a gesture of disdain, she flicked the linen blindfold at him. It snapped against his cheek.

Anthony twitched it out of her hands. "Annoyed you, did it?" He sounded somewhat satisfied.

"Tit for tat?" she demanded.

"Precisely." His eyes gleamed.

"Are we going to play chess?"

"Why else did you go to such trouble to get me a message?" he mocked. "If you'd like to return to the dinghy, we'll be on our way."

"On our way where?" Olivia to her annoyance was startled and heard herself express it.

"Wait and see, my flower." He regarded her still with that gleam in his eye.

Without a word, Olivia swung herself back over the rail, climbed down the ladder, and deposited herself in the boat.

"I'd tread cautious if I was you," Adam muttered as Anthony leaned over the rail beside him.

Anthony regarded the boat's occupant rather in the manner of one assessing the temper of an unpredictable feline. "You may have a point. But I think I'm a match."

"Are you coming or not?" Olivia shouted up at him.

Anthony shot Adam a grin. "Then again, maybe not." He swung himself over the rail and climbed down to the dinghy.

Whistling softly, he reached up and loosed the painter from its ring. He sat down and took up the oars, using one to push the boat away from the side of the ship. He pulled strongly, still whistling, heading further down the chine.

"Where are we going?" Olivia stared over his shoulder as he rowed. It seemed as if they were going to disappear into the cliffs at the narrowest point.

"Wait and see" was the infuriating response.

At the moment when it really seemed they were about to run up against the wall of cliff at the furthest point of the chine, Anthony rested on his oars, regarding Olivia thoughtfully.

"So, how did you discover the secret of the oratory?"

"A question for a question," she said, folding her hands in her lap.

"Go on."

"Are you intending to rescue the king?"

He said nothing immediately, whistling between his teeth in customary fashion, frowning at the anchored ship behind her.

"And if I am?" he asked eventually.

Olivia shrugged. "Nothing," she said. "But I'm not a fool, and I won't be taken for one."

"Oh, believe me, I have never done that," he said definitely.

"So *are* you? Is that why you're pretending to be a nitwit hanger-on at the court, so no one will take any notice of you? So no one will ever think you're capable of planning so much as a walk along the clifftop?"

Anthony laughed softly. "I trust no one else can see through my little game."

"Well, of course they won't. I can see through it because I know you."

"Do you?" He leaned on his oars, watching her closely in the dim light of the chine.

"I know what you are...or at least, I know what you are not," she corrected.

"So, how did you discover about the oratory?"

243

"You haven't answered my question."

"I think I have."

She supposed that in the absence of a denial, she had an affirmative. "A little boy was so excited about his toy ship that he let some things slip while he was playing."

"Ah, one of the Barker brood." He took up his oars again. "An inherent risk, but one I consider reasonable." He frowned at her. "So, how does Lord Granville's daughter view this matter?"

"I don't know," Olivia said. "I haven't asked her."

Anthony's crooked smile flashed.

Twelve

Anthony turned the boat in the narrow passage. "Can you swim?"

Olivia shook her head. "No. I grew up in Yorkshire. No one swims in Yorkshire. I'd never even seen the sea until we came here."

"Then it's time you learned."

"I thought we were going to play chess."

"That too."

Then Olivia saw the gap in the cliff. It was a very narrow arch. The boat shot through it with one pull on the oars, and suddenly they were in a small sandy cove, open to the sea, but protected on three sides by the overhang of the undercliff.

Olivia gazed at the great red ball of the setting sun dipping into the sea just beyond the jagged rocks of the Needles. After the confines of the chine it was like being on open sea once more.

Anthony smiled at her rapt pleasure and pulled into the beach. "In those clothes, you can manage to scramble ashore unaided," he commented.

"Do you like them?" She stood up and the boat rocked alarmingly.

"They have their advantages," he said judiciously. "But on the whole I prefer you naked. As you know, in general I like to use nude models."

Olivia began to feel as if things were slipping away from her again. She had thought she had been so much in control of this encounter, but now she wasn't so sure. "I have no intention of sitting for you," she stated. "Nude or otherwise."

"Take your shoes and stockings off before you paddle ashore," he instructed as if he hadn't heard her.

Olivia did as he said but found that her fingers were clumsy.

"You should roll up the britches too."

Sucking in her lower lip, Olivia rolled the britches to her knees. The pirate gave her his hand and she jumped into the shallow water. It was delightfully warm and the ridged sand was both hard and soft against her unaccustomed soles. She paddled to shore while Anthony hauled the boat up onto the sand.

"What is all this?" Olivia gestured in amazement to the collection of objects on the beach.

"A chessboard," he pointed out. "Then supper. I trust you like roast chicken. And blankets and pillows for a night under the stars."

The chicken looked utterly inedible by anything other than a fox, although it did seem to be plucked. "You're going to c-cook that?"

"I'm an expert," he assured her. "You'll find driftwood along the tideline. Pick smaller pieces as well for kindling."

Olivia hesitated. She looked across at the setting sun; she felt its rays on her face, the sand beneath her feet. And slowly, inexorably, the skeins of the dream wrapped themselves around her once more.

She set off up the small beach in her rolled-up britches, scrunching her toes into the sand. She gathered pieces of wood with all the care another woman might have given to the selection of embroidery silks, and returned triumphant.

"See, I have little pieces here and bigger ones for later." She dropped her armful onto the sand.

Anthony had constructed a fireplace of flat stones and had threaded the chicken on a long stick that would serve as a spit. He laid the fire, struck flint on tinder, and within minutes the fire glowed and the chicken was in place across the stones.

"So, now we play chess." He set the board on another flat stone and sat cross-legged in front of white's pieces. "You, I believe, have the disadvantage this game."

"Hah!" Olivia said, dropping to the sand. "I never lose, even when I play black."

"This time you will," he said with confidence. "And then I shall teach you to swim. In exchange, you will sit for me. I shall draw you, sitting just as you are on the sand, with your hair up like that...but without the clothes."

Olivia glanced at him, her face touched by the fire's light. "If I win, I shall say whether you may or may not."

"You always have that right," he said quietly, his eyes now grave as they met hers. "*Always,* Olivia."

And she knew that she did. With this man, she had the rights to her body, to her responses. It was for her to decide.

"Make your move," she said.

Anthony moved pawn to king four.

"Oh, how conventional," Olivia crowed as she made the standard response.

"I save my surprises for later," he murmured.

And then an hour later, as the sun sank into the sea, he said almost to himself, "You are the very devil, Olivia. I could have sworn I had you two moves back."

"I'll offer you a draw," she said, grinning. "Take it while you can."

"You have no choice but to agree to a draw," he pointed out with perfect truth.

"There's no way you can win any more than I can."

"Oh, I was hoping you wouldn't realize that."

"Don't add insult to injury," Anthony said, leaning sideways to turn the chicken. "And don't forget we have one more game to play."

"Why would you want to endure another crushing defeat?" Olivia asked in mock astonishment.

"You are *so* cocky!" he exclaimed. "I think it's time for some cold water." He bent and took her hands, pulling her to her feet. "Get your clothes off, I'm going to teach you to swim." He began to discard his clothes.

Olivia watched him for a second, then slowly she shrugged out of her doublet and unbuttoned her chemise.

"Let me help you." Naked he came over to her and slipped the chemise from her shoulders. The cool air brushed her breasts and her nipples peaked. He looked down at her, a question in his eyes. His hands went to the buttons of her britches, but slowly, giving her time.

Olivia touched his mouth with her thumb.

He pushed the britches over her hips and down, his hands lightly brushing her skin. She stepped out of them and stood naked on the sand, every inch of her skin exquisitely sensitized, anticipation trembling in her belly, tightening her thighs.

Anthony drew her against him. His hands moved down her back without urgency, again giving her time to draw back.

But Olivia no longer needed time. She slipped a hand down his belly. The muscles of his abdomen contracted and his sex sprang alive under her touch. She leaned into him, loving the warmth of his skin, the hardness of his body, the little breeze that came off the water to make her even more conscious of her own nakedness.

"Perhaps swimming should wait," she murmured, licking the little hollow of his throat, tasting the salt and the sea.

"There is a way to combine both," he whispered against her cheek, as he moved his lips to the corner of her mouth. Then his tongue darted into her ear, making her squirm with delight.

"Come." He took her hand and led her into the water. He led her out until the little waves broke against her calves, and then he drew her into a hard embrace, holding her immobile against his length as his tongue drove deep within her mouth and she moaned softly against his lips. Now there was an urgency to his hands on her body, a fierceness to his caresses.

Olivia shivered as the coolness of the evening air bathed her heated skin. Her toes scrunched into the soft wet sand, and her nipples rose against his chest. He held her buttocks and they tightened against his palms as he pressed her to him so that his penis moved against her thigh.

She shifted, parting her legs to give him entrance, her guiding hand leading him within.

"Put your arms around my neck."

Olivia obeyed eagerly and he caught her behind the knees, lifting her off the sand as he slid within her. His hold moved to her bottom, supporting her on the shelf of his palms. Fleetingly Olivia wondered if anyone could see them, two naked lovers in the surf, joined in flagrant lust, then she couldn't have cared if they were exposed on the public stage. She sucked on his lower lip as if it were a ripe plum, then nibbled, little teasing tugs of her teeth as she rode his hips. He kept very still, unmoving inside her, filling her, becoming part of her.

And long long before she was ready, he loosened his hold and she slid down his length with a little sigh of disappointment.

He laughed gently at her expression as she looked up at him in startled discontent. "Don't worry, my flower. The best is yet to come."

Taking her hand again, he led her deeper into the water. When the water reached the top of her thighs, he drew her close against him again, an arm encircling her waist as he pushed up her chin with his free hand and for a long minute gazed down into her face. Her tongue lightly touched her lips, her dark eyes held his gaze, and he read his own passion reflected in their velvet depths.

Was this passion what his father had felt for Elizabeth of Bohemia?

His father had thrown consequences to the devil when he'd pursued that passion. And the innocent had suffered those consequences.

Anthony closed his mind to a reflection

that only ever brought bitterness. He had Olivia here. She was no part of his past, bore no blame for his father's impulses. And whatever devils had been pursuing her after their last loving, it was clear from the desire in her eyes, the hunger of her responses, that they were, for this moment at least, vanquished.

He kissed her and her eyes closed. His hand moved from her chin to trace the outline of her breasts rising clear of the water that cooled and stroked her lower body. Gently, he rolled her hardening nipples between thumb and forefinger, increasing the pressure until she moaned and shivered, the throbbing heat of her body in sharp contrast to the cool, lapping sea.

He bent her backwards over his encircling arm as his free hand slid downward over her smooth white belly. His fingers twined in the soft dark triangle at the apex of her thighs. His knee nudged her legs apart to receive the cold caress of the sea even as his fingers followed the water, probing deeply, insistently, until her moans became little sobbing cries of delight. The sea became as much an instrument of her pleasure as his hand, and he used it, drawing her backwards into deeper water still, where she floated against his arm, her body opened, abandoned to the dual caresses.

She drifted, her eyes closed, now only a mindless sensate being at one with the water that held her and explored her with intimate searching fingers indivisible from her lover's.

She was barely aware as Anthony cradled her

against him, carrying her back to the water's edge. He laid her down in the shallow, creaming surf. The sand shifted beneath her under the rhythmic progression and retreat of the little waves. She reached up for him, lifting her hips as he drove fiercely within her, to possess her so utterly that she had no sense of her self existing outside the body that filled and took her as she lay caught between it and the shifting sand and sea, helplessly abandoned to the wild coursing joy of completion.

And slowly the waves of delight receded, leaving only the sucking sounds of the surf, and Olivia shivered in Anthony's arms as he gathered her against him. "That was a most unusual swimming lesson," she murmured.

He laughed softly and stood up, pulling her up with him. "Come, quickly now." She stood, disoriented, still caught in the half-world of her dissolution. Anthony grabbed her hand and pulled her back into the water, swiftly washing the sand off her back, intimately but without lingering, cleansing the nooks and crannies of her body.

"Run in," he instructed. "There are towels beside the fire. I'm going to swim." He turned her to the beach, giving her a playful smack of encouragement, and Olivia returned to her self.

She ran for the beach, leaping over the little waves, her teeth chattering, her skin prickled with goose bumps. The wonderful rich smell of roasting chicken rising on the air, the crackle of crisping flesh, the hiss as fat dripped into the fire, made her hungrier than she would have thought possible. A magnificent hunger, a glorious feeling, as the lethargy of afterglow fought with the physical stimulation of cold water and the evening air on her bare wet skin.

There were towels, as Anthony had said. She grabbed one and rubbed herself dry, watching the sea, watching the swimmer cleaving the water with powerful strokes.

She waited for the black cloud of revulsion to envelop her. But the residual glories of loving were untarnished.

She stepped closer to the fire, warming the backs of her legs as Anthony rose from the waves and came running up the beach, water streaming from his hair.

Olivia gazed at him, loving every line of his body, the little buttons of his nipples, the hard, flat planes of his belly, the soft, quiescent sex in its nest of gold curls, dark now with water, the long, muscular length of his thighs.

"Stop that!" he said, laughing as he reached for a towel and rubbed himself dry briskly if somewhat perfunctorily. "It's enough to embarrass a man."

"Oh, pah!" Olivia scoffed. "I thought you were the one who adored the human body, fat, thin, stooped, straight. All the most wondrous creations. Isn't that what you said?"

"And it's true enough," he said, snatching the wet towel from her. His eyes touched her body, lingering over every inch.

Olivia shivered and he bent to pick up another towel.

"You'll catch your death!" Roughly now he rubbed her all over, turning and twisting her as if she were a rag doll, bending her over his forearm to dry her back and buttocks and down the length of her thighs.

When he was satisfied, he tossed aside the towel and picked up a blanket, wrapping it securely around her. "There now. You're all ready for bed."

"I thought you were going to draw me." Olivia huddled closer into the rough wool of the blanket.

"In the morning, when the sun will warm you." He threw more wood on the fire. The chicken skin hissed and crackled. "This'll be ready soon."

"Oh, good. I'm famished." She sat down beside the fire, wrapped in the blanket.

Anthony opened a basket and took out a loaf of bread, cheese, a flagon of wine, and two pewter goblets. He poured the wine, a pale creamy canary, and broke bread. "We eat with our fingers tonight."

"How else." Olivia took the goblet and the crusty hunk of bread. It smelled as if it had just come out of the oven. "Aren't you going to wear a blanket too?"

"I don't find it cold," he returned with one of his secret little smiles.

"Then you c-can't object if I feast my eyes upon you," she mumbled through a mouthful of bread and cheese.

Anthony merely laughed and squatted beside the fire, using the tip of his dagger to test the chicken. The firelight danced over his deeply tanned skin, illuminated the knobbly curve of his spine, sent a finger of light into the dark secret shadows of his loins.

Olivia, curled up in her blanket, drank wine and gazed at him with unabashed lust. She thought suddenly of Godfrey Channing, of what he would think if he could see her thus. And she thought of Brian, probing the thought as if it were an aching tooth, waiting for the nerve to blossom with pain.

Anthony levered a leg away from the body of the bird, watching the color of the juices. "Are you cold?" He didn't look up as he spoke and yet somehow he'd felt the change in her, and he dreaded looking at her, seeing the revulsion, the withdrawal once again in her eyes.

"No," she said, resting her chin on her drawn-up knees. "No, not in the least." Her voice was firm.

Only as he felt the relief seep into him did Anthony realize how much he had been afraid. He began to pull the roasted chicken apart with his fingers, slicing the breast with his dagger, piling the richly fragrant meat on two large flat pebbles.

They ate and drank in the firelight as the moon rose high, sending a silver river of light across the sea.

Later, Olivia lay in the circle of his arm between the blankets. She was sleepy and yet her eyes refused to close. The star-filled night was too beautiful. After their loving, she was filled with such peace and contentment that not even the certainty of its ephemeral quality could spoil her languid joy. It was as if her wounds had been closed. This was the memory she would carry with her. Many years from now she would still remember how it felt to lie here under this rough blanket in the glow of the fire, listening to the lullaby of the waves breaking on the shore, with Anthony's body against hers, her head in the hollow of his shoulder, his legs twined around hers. Many women...most women...never knew such piercing joy, however long they lived.

This one intense passion would last her lifetime, and it *must* be better than years of the bland and ordinary unenlivened by even a glimpse of the glory that could be between a man and a woman.

Olivia closed her eyes at last and was surprised to find that tears squeezed from beneath the lids. She hadn't realized she was crying soundlessly as she talked herself into acceptance of a future reality where this passion could not possibly exist. Lord Granville's daughter and Anthony Caxton could not enjoy each other in the real world, only in the dream that they had spun for themselves.

It was just before dawn when she awoke, and she was alone under the blanket. She sat up in the gray light, holding the blanket to her. There was a definite chill in the early morning air. Off to the east, the as yet invisible sun drew a thin red line on the horizon. As she watched, the line spread and the sky glowed red and orange, and then the great ball of the sun peeped above the horizon. It rose rapidly until it was all there, casting a brilliant red light upon the flat surface of the sea.

"Beautiful, isn't it?"

She turned at Anthony's voice behind her. He was dressed now and held two fish dangling from their hooks. "Breakfast," he said, bending to kiss her upturned face.

"I have to…"

"There are rocks behind you and the sea in front," he said, tossing the fish to the sand and squatting to rekindle the fire from the faint glow of the embers.

Olivia stood up, dropping the blanket. She stretched luxuriously, watching his deft, competent hands at their task. The fire flared and he took up the fish again and carried them to the water to clean them.

Olivia watched him for a minute, then, remembering her need, made her way to the seclusion of an outcrop of rocks. When she came back, he already had the fish on flat stones cooking over the fire.

She dressed and it felt strange to be clothed once more.

"There's water in that other flagon, if you're thirsty." Anthony gestured to the basket.

Olivia drank deep of the fresh springwater. It tasted wonderful. Every sense seemed so much sharper, every experience so much more intense out here on this tiny beach under the ruddy dawn sky.

"As soon as we get back to the ship, Mike will sail you home," Anthony said, taking the water as she held it out to him.

Olivia gazed out over his shoulder to the sea. They didn't have to waken from the dream just yet. Her father would not be back for several days. Phoebe and Portia would find a way to satisfy the household about Olivia's seclusion behind the bedcurtains. It would be wasteful to pass up this gift of time.

"I don't have to go back today."

Anthony took the water bottle from his lips. "What about your father?"

"He's not at home. He won't be back for several days."

"And his wife?"

"I'll just need to send a message so she and Portia don't worry if I'm away a little longer than they expected."

Anthony made no response for a minute. "What exactly do they know?"

"They know I'm playing chess with the pirate who kidnapped me," she said with a little laugh. "And Phoebe doesn't approve of my playing chess or anything else with such an unsavory character. Portia is more sympathetic, but then, she knows all about passion with unsavory strangers."

Anthony tipped the water flask to his lips. *Was that all Olivia had told her closest friends and confidantes? The wives of the enemy? Had she said nothing about Edward Caxton?*

He handed her back the water flask. "I have to sail *Wind Dancer* to Portsmouth on the

258

morning tide. We can be back tomorrow night." He turned the fish on the stone.

"Am I invited?" She had the feeling that he had become suddenly tense.

He looked up with a smile of such promise that all sense of tension dissipated. "Mike will take a message to your friends."

"What are you doing in Portsmouth?"

"I have a little business."

Olivia knelt on the sand, sniffing hungrily. "What business?"

"I have goods to sell." He handed Olivia one of the two fishes.

She broke it apart with her fingers and ate. Fish had never tasted this good before. A pirate would always have goods to sell. And presumably, since they'd only been back from sea a few days, Anthony still had everything he'd taken from the *Doña Elena*.

"JUST THIS, MISS?" Mike looked at the little ring of braided hair that Olivia had given him once they'd returned to *Wind Dancer*.

"Just that," Olivia said. "But you must make sure you give it either to Lady Granville or to Lady Rothbury." If she sent a written message, it might fall into Bisset's hands. The ring would mean nothing to him. Villagers were often sending strange items to Lady Granville, either in thanks for her services or as herbalists' suggestions for a new medicine. Bisset would think nothing of a local villager delivering something of that peculiar nature to his mistress.

"Put the flag up, Mike, so that we know the message was delivered safely and there was no trouble," Anthony said, without looking up from the charts he was plotting. "We'll be standing out in the channel by ten o'clock. If the flag's not flying, we'll still be close enough in to put Lady Olivia into the sailing dinghy and get her to shore."

"Right y'are, master." Mike tucked the fragile ring into the breast pocket of his doublet. "I'll be off, then."

"Thank you," Olivia said.

Mike bobbed his head and left the cabin.

THE CHANNEL WAS TOO NARROW to turn *Wind Dancer,* and she was warped backwards out of her anchorage. The sailors sang in rhythm with each sweep of the oars as they pulled her along the narrow channel. Olivia stood on the quarterdeck as the chine widened and the first glimpse of the sea appeared. And then they emerged from the cleft in the cliff and the oarsmen pulled the frigate out into the main channel.

Anthony stood at the wheel, calling orders, his voice crisp and clear. Olivia looked back at the cliff, trying to make out the entrance to the chine. Try as she would, she couldn't detect the break in the cliff. There were tiny rocky coves, one presumably where she and the pirate had passed the night, but it seemed as if the chine had closed over as they'd left it.

"Flag, master!" a voice yelled down from the mizzenmast.

Anthony raised the telescope. A white flag fluttered from the top of St. Catherine's Hill. He handed the glass to Olivia.

"It seems we have some time," she said, watching the jaunty message from her friends.

"So it does." He gave the order for the oarsmen to climb aboard. The longboats were winched after them, even as the sails were unfurled and caught the wind. The ship heeled over as Anthony swung her onto the port tack, then she straightened and began to dance across the swelling waves.

Olivia sat down on the deck, warmed by the sun, and closed her eyes, letting her body flow with the rhythm of the ship. The wonderful smell of frying bacon rose on the air and something else, a strange, bitter scent. Adam came up to the quarterdeck carrying a tray that he set down on the deck beside her. There was bread and bacon, two tiny china cups, and a small copper pot of some strongly aromatic black liquid.

"What's that, Adam?"

"Coffee...comes from Turkey. We was there a few months back an' the master took a fancy to it." The elderly man's nose wrinkled. "Powerful strong stuff, it is. Can't abide it meself."

"Are you maligning my coffee, Adam?" Anthony had handed the helm to Jethro and now came over to them.

"Each to 'is own, I say," Adam declared, and went off.

Anthony sat down beside Olivia. He poured a little of the thick black stuff into each cup and handed one to her. "Try it."

She took a sip. It was bitter and yet sweet. "I don't think I like it."

"It's an acquired taste," he said, piling bacon onto bread with his fingers. He leaned back against the rail and took a healthy bite.

Olivia followed suit. "How long to Portsmouth?"

"We should be there by late afternoon. Once we round the Needles, I'll be able to leave the quarterdeck."

Olivia turned to look at the approaching ridge of jagged rocks. "They look very dangerous."

"They are."

"More so than St. Catherine's Point?"

"It depends on the conditions. St. Catherine's rocks are smaller and as a result perhaps more vicious. It's probably easier on a dark night to run afoul of them than the Needles." He said it carelessly, helping himself to more bacon.

Olivia looked out at the rocks and the boiling sea at their base. She shivered.

PORTSMOUTH HARBOR WAS FILLED with the navy's ships. The quay was alive with sailors. Longboats ferrying officers and supplies moved constantly among the great ships, accompanied by the twitter of pipes and the roll of drums.

Olivia stood in a secluded corner of the quarterdeck as Anthony brought *Wind Dancer* to anchor in the roads between another frigate and a ship of the line. She knew less than nothing of sailing, but knowledge wasn't needed to appreciate the delicacy of the maneuver. They dropped anchor with a great rattle of chains, and the ship rocked gently on the swell.

"What happens now?" Olivia asked.

"What do you wish to happen?" He traced the curve of her cheek with a forefinger.

Olivia glanced around at the lively harbor. "I look like a boy. What will people think if they see you doing that?"

"That I practice the English vice," he responded with a grin. "It's not uncommon among sailors.... They spend so much time at sea, you understand."

"I didn't know it was an English vice," Olivia said seriously. "The Greeks and Romans, of course, but...Oh, you're laughing at me!"

"Only a very little." He leaned against the rail, idly watching the scene. "If you like, we could spend the evening in the town."

"But I have no c-clothes...only these."

"Oh, I suspect we might be able to find something suitable from among the treasures in the hold. Come, let us go and look." He moved off with his leisurely stride.

She followed him down into the waist of the ship, where he collected an oil lamp. He lit it and led the way down into the dark hold that smelled of sea and the pitch that caulked the timbers.

Chests, barrels, bales, were stacked to the

ceiling. "Now, which of those chests...Ah, this one, I believe." He went unerringly to an ironbound chest. "Hold the lamp."

She took it and held it high as he knelt and opened the chest.

"What do you fancy? Muslin...cambric... silk...even velvet we have here." He rifled through the pile of material. "There are some gowns made up at the bottom, as I recall. How about this?" He drew out a gown of dark green muslin.

"It's very pretty," Olivia said, examining it in the light. "Will it fit?"

He rose with the gown and held it up against her. "It looks perfect to me. Adam'll be able to make any adjustments. Now you need stockings and slippers and a shawl."

He returned to the chests, lifting lids at random, until he had assembled the necessary garments. "There, you'll be as fine as fivepence."

Olivia exchanged the lamp for the bundle of clothes. "Shall we eat supper in the town?"

"At the Pelican, madam. It has a very fine table."

In her borrowed finery, Olivia sat in the stern of the small boat as they were rowed to the quay. Anthony had dressed for the occasion in doublet and britches of a gray silk, so dark it was almost black. Olivia knew she was living a dream. She was part of a play of which she didn't know the words. She didn't know how the next scene would play. It was a thrilling, entrancing world that bore no relation to the real one. But they had bought the time and she allowed the dream to catch her up, sweep her along, unfold before her.

It was late when they returned to the ship, and Olivia was aware that she had perhaps drunk too much burgundy for wisdom. She felt as if she were floating on froth...a delightful feeling that she tried to describe to Anthony, but without much success. She caught the grins of the two sailors who were rowing them back, and wondered vaguely but without much concern whether her words sounded different from the way they sounded in her head.

When they were tied up at the ship's side, Anthony looked up at the rope ladder and then assessingly at Olivia. "You know, I don't think I want to risk it."

"Risk what?" A little hiccup escaped her.

"Never mind. Come." He drew her to her feet. The little boat rocked alarmingly. He bent to put his shoulder against her belly and hitched her up and over, holding her securely behind the knees.

Olivia found her gaze focusing on the points of his shoulder blades through the gray silk. She would have liked to kiss them, but she couldn't quite reach them. So she gave up the attempt and instead gazed down dreamily through the black veil of her hair at the dark green water washing against the white sides of the frigate. Hands leaned over the rail to take her and lift her clear onto the deck. Anthony jumped down beside her and stood laughing down at her.

"I'm very much afraid you're not going to have a happy morning," he said, brushing her tumbled hair away from her face.

"I'm very happy now," Olivia assured him.

"Yes, my flower, I can see that."

A little ripple of amusement went around the deck, and Olivia smiled sunnily at these friendly men, whose faces were now so familiar.

"Can you walk to the cabin? Or should I carry you?"

"Oh, I think you should c-carry me," she said with another little hiccup. "It's strange but my legs don't seem to belong to me."

"Over you go, then." He hoisted her up over his shoulder and went down to the cabin with his prize.

She swayed on the floor and smiled delightfully at him. "You'll have to undress me. My hands don't seem to belong to me either."

"Well, that is always a pleasure."

Olivia regarded her borrowed garments with an air of inquiry as they slid from her body. "Did these c-come from the *Doña Elena*? They don't seem very Spanish."

"No, they came from a wreck," he said, drawing her chemise over her head.

Pirate. Smuggler. Wrecker.

She could hear his voice saying so carelessly how easy it was for a ship to run afoul of the rocks off St. Catherine's Point. Just like the wreck that had been driven to its doom the night before she'd fallen into the air just above the point.

And the morning after, she had fallen at the

feet of *Wind Dancer*'s watchman, just a short way down the coast from the point. So easy to have lured the ship onto the rocks and then to have transported the spoils to the safety of the chine. So very easy.

Piracy. Smuggling. Those were beyond the law. Olivia knew that they were dirty and dangerous, and men were killed in their pursuit. And she knew too that for most smugglers, wrecking was a mere sideline. She knew that, it was island lore, but she couldn't grasp it. Not with Anthony. Anthony could not...

She felt sick. A great unstoppable wave of nausea. She pushed past him blindly, desperate for the commode.

Anthony moved to hold her head as she retched miserably, but she shook him off with such desperation that he left her. He remembered too well the miseries of his own first overindulgence, and he wouldn't add to her mortification.

He went up on deck thinking of the morning's auction. At dawn they would come, the merchants and shopkeepers, the tavern keepers and the private buyers. They would come in their small boats to examine his wares, and they would bid well for them. He would pay his crew, pay the pensions and bonuses to the men who worked for him, men who were his friends, and he would put aside what he needed to live as he chose. And the rest would go to Ellen to be disbursed to the Royalist insurgents where she and her vicar saw fit.

And on the next night of the new moon, *Wind*

Dancer would take the king of England to France.

Anthony yawned, stretched, and took himself below. Olivia was curled in the far corner of the bed. He undressed by the dimmest of candlelight and slipped in beside her. He reached to roll her into his embrace, but she seemed surrounded by an invisible thorn hedge. Assuming that in her nausea she needed to be left utterly alone, he turned away from her. But he was unable to fall asleep until he had gently moved his back against hers.

Thirteen

ANTHONY ROSE BEFORE DAWN, leaving Olivia asleep. He dressed and went on deck, where Adam had soap and hot water waiting for him.

" 'Ow's the lass?" Adam handed him the razor.

"Asleep. I hope she'll sleep it off." He bent to the small mirror Adam held up. "I suppose I should have stopped her. But she's not a child. It's a lesson we all learn sometime."

"Not Lord Granville's daughter, I reckon," Adam stated, and there was no disguising the hint of disapproval in his voice.

Anthony carefully shaved above his top lip, then he set down the razor and took the towel Adam handed him. "She knows what she's doing as much as I do, Adam."

"Aye, as little; that's what's bothersome," the other said. "Ye've missed a bit, jest under yer chin."

Anthony dipped the razor in the hot water again and applied himself anew. He knew from his earliest years that there was no point entering into an argument with Adam.

The buyers came as the sun rose. They gathered in the hold, all aware that they were buying contraband, no one interested in its provenance.

Olivia could hear the bustle as she lay dry-mouthed with pounding head, desperate to return to a sleep that would not come. She heard the scrape of the boats against the ship's side, the feet on the deck, the voices, the comings and goings down the companionway. She couldn't hear what was happening in the hold, but she could guess.

A wrecker.

He had said so, as casually as if it were the most natural thing in the world, as if, of course, she would know it anyway. She knew he was a smuggler and a pirate, what more natural than that he should turn his hand to a bit of wrecking now and again?

If she turned her head, she could see the gown, the slippers, the stockings that she had worn during the enchanted hours of last evening. To whom had they belonged? What women, dashed to their deaths on St. Catherine's Point, had treasured that green gown, those silk stockings, those satin slippers?

Nausea rose anew and Olivia struggled over the high sides of the bed and stumbled across the cabin to hang uselessly over the commode. She had never felt so ill, so achingly aware of every pulse and joint in her body. And she felt so bereft of hope, of happiness, of even the ordinary expectations of the little satisfactions of everyday life. She had swung high on the pendulum of entrancement. Its downward swing brought misery in exact proportion to the joy.

But she had felt this way before. Many times before. Throughout her childhood. One minute she had been happy, contented, deep in her books or her play, and then it would happen. This great black cloud would come out of nowhere, and there was no more happiness, no more contentment. She hadn't known then where it came from, hadn't connected it with those dreadful moments at Brian's hands, but she knew it now. And this time the black cloud was of Anthony's making.

She crawled back into bed and pulled the covers over her head. Her misery was her own fault. After Brian had touched her, she had always felt that she was somehow to blame; now she felt that same unfocused guilt. She had been a naive fool, allowed herself to be entranced by Anthony, invited him to entrance her, just as she had once believed that she had invited Brian's violations. Believed that if she'd done something, said something different, they wouldn't have happened.

IT WAS MID-MORNING when Anthony came down to the cabin. He came in quietly, glancing towards the still figure in the bed. He hesitated, wondering whether to see if she was awake, but then, slipping into the habit he had acquired when Olivia had slept through the draft he had given her, he sat down at his table to work through the figures of the auction. It had been a very successful operation. He had paid Godfrey Channing eight hundred, but he had made seventeen hundred. Enough to please Ellen. Whether it was enough to sweeten the taste in his mouth from his dealings with the lordling was another matter.

Olivia felt rather than heard Anthony in the cabin. Her back still held the memory of his. His particular fragrance was in the air. Her curled and unhappy body still responded on a deep instinctual level to the knowledge of its partner so close.

Somehow she had to face him. Had to get off the ship and go home. And yet she didn't know how to wake up. How to show herself. She didn't think she could bear to look at him.

"Drink this, Olivia."

He had come to the side of the bed with a cup in his hand. Olivia turned over, holding an arm over her eyes.

"It *will* help."

271

"I'm not sure anything could," she muttered even as she dragged herself up onto an elbow, keeping her eyes closed, afraid of what they would reveal if he looked into them. "When will we get back to the island?"

"By nightfall." Anthony held the cup to her lips. "My poor sweet, does the light hurt that badly?"

"Terribly," she murmured, thankful now for the excuse of her bodily ills.

"Never mind, you'll be in your bed by midnight."

"What is this?" Olivia sniffed the acrid contents of the cup.

"A hangover cure."

She drank it. There were some ills he could ameliorate.

THERE WAS A SOFT LIGHT in her bedchamber. Someone had left a candle burning. Olivia stood at the foot of the magnolia calculating her climb. As she'd expected, it was going to be more difficult than the descent, but she'd climbed rope ladders onto frigates, jumped across boarding nets. She could do this. Phoebe had said she would leave the side door open, but this would be a safer way into the house. There would be no chance at all of running into anyone.

She jumped for the lowest branch, caught it with her arms, swung her legs against the trunk, and hauled herself up so that she hung over the branch. It was hard against her belly...just as Anthony's shoulder had been as he'd carried her up over the side of *Wind Dancer*.

She threw out her legs, swung sideways, and straddled the branch. The rest was easy.

"So there you are, duckie." Portia came to the window as Olivia emerged from the magnolia. "Did you have a delicious time?"

"Delicious." Olivia jumped down. Her face was in shadow as she bent to acknowledge Juno's exuberant greeting. "Is all well?"

"Cato and Rufus aren't back yet. Phoebe and I have disposed of the food Mistress Bisset sent up and sat vigil around the bedcurtains. No one's asked any awkward questions." Portia struck flint on tinder and lit candles.

She lit the two-branched candlestick that Anthony had used for the chess game. Olivia moved into the shadows as Portia raised the candlestick.

"What's wrong, Olivia?" Portia's voice sharpened.

"I drank too much wine last night." Olivia laughed slightly, keeping her face averted from the light.

"That's all?" Portia set the candlestick on the mantelshelf. Her green-eyed gaze was uncomfortably penetrating.

Olivia turned to the bed, drawing aside the curtains. The soft white solitude offered by her deep feather bed was the only thing she desired. Bigger, deeper, more comforting than any passion.

"There's no future to it, Portia."

"Ah." Portia understood. "No," she said. "How could there be? Lord Granville's daughter and a pirate in some cozy domestic setting? *Impossible.* That's why Phoebe's so troubled. It's not so much your pirate's somewhat unsavory means of earning a living. She doesn't want you to be hurt.... Oh, neither do I, of course...but it's easier for me to see that you must decide for yourself." She put her arm around Olivia's shoulders.

"You do understand," Olivia said quietly.

"How could I not?" Portia squeezed her shoulders.

Could she tell Portia about the wrecking? No, she couldn't. It was too shaming. That she had allowed herself to be lost with desire for a man she didn't understand at all...a man who could do such a thing.

"Will you see him again?"

"I don't know," Olivia replied.

Portia regarded her in silence for a minute, her eyes concerned. "It might be better to make a clean break now," she suggested.

"Yes," Olivia agreed.

Portia waited for her to go on, and when she didn't, she said, "I can see you need your bed. I'll leave you to it." She kissed her and went to the door. "Oh, by the bye, Lord Channing came a-calling. In saffron silk." She raised an ironic eyebrow. "With a gold plume to his hat. Quite the dandy, he is. He seemed quite put out when we said you were busy with your books and not receiving visitors."

A shiver went down Olivia's spine.

"Someone walk over your grave?" Portia inquired, her hand on the door.

"Does he remind you of Brian?"

Portia considered, her head to one side. "In what way?"

"His eyes. They're so small and cold and hard. When he smiles it's not really a smile at all. Just like Brian."

"I don't know. I'll have to look at him more closely next time. I can't say I like him, though. He kicks dogs. Sleep well, now." Portia went out, Juno on her heels.

Olivia sat down on the bed. Her head ached fiercely and she felt beset on all sides.

Anthony himself had sailed her to the cove just below Chale. He had walked with her to the boundary of the estate and left her to skirt the orchard and go in through the gate in the kitchen garden. To her relief he had seemed to accept her silence and had not questioned her mood. Olivia guessed he had put it down to the ill effects of her unwise evening.

He'd kissed her good night and said with one of his quiet smiles that she should look for him at Carisbrooke the next evening if she chose to attend the king's presence.

Olivia didn't know whether she would or not. She didn't know whether she could bear to see him again. The black cloud enveloped her. He seemed to have a hand in everything that was unsavory, unlawful, immoral. What had once seemed amusing, exciting about his lifestyle and his view of the world now struck her as tawdry, as *wrong*. Everything about him was in direct opposition to her father, his beliefs, his honor, the way he lived his life. The way hitherto she had lived her own. And Anthony was going to try to rescue the king. She knew this and she had to keep this knowledge from her father. By keeping silent, she was colluding in a wrecker's plot to outwit him.

CATO AND RUFUS RETURNED the next morning. "You're looking well, Olivia," Cato observed as he passed her in the hall, noticing how her glowing complexion had a golden tinge to it. "Have you been out in the sun?"

"We've been taking the children for picnics," she said.

"Ah, that would explain it." He smiled. "I was just talking to Phoebe and Portia. They are attending the audience at Carisbrooke this evening. Will you accompany them?"

Olivia hesitated. Maybe her father could help her with one of her problems. "I would come willingly, but Lord Channing troubles me."

"In what way?" Cato frowned.

"I don't like him, sir," she said simply. "And I don't want him for a suitor, but I don't know how to tell him that when he hasn't actually declared himself. I was wondering if you might put him off for me."

"It's hard to put him off if he hasn't declared himself."

"I know, but maybe if you told him in

passing that I intend never to marry, he'll take the hint," she suggested.

Cato shook his head in some amusement. "You'll have to forgive me, Olivia, if I don't take that too seriously. At some point you'll change your mind. But you may rest assured I'll make no attempt to press you to do so."

He thought how like her mother she was. The same thick creamy complexion and black hair. Olivia had his own dark eyes, but they took their velvety quality from her mother. She had inherited from her father the long Granville nose and a certain determination to her mouth and chin. Additions that added distinction and character to her otherwise conventional beauty.

"I foresee an endless procession of prospective suitors," he went on, still smiling. "You're of age to marry and you have much to recommend you." This last was said in a teasing voice, and Olivia couldn't help responding with her own somewhat rueful smile.

"I shall reject them all, sir," she declared. "But please c-could you try to reject this one for me? I really c-can't endure to be in his presence."

Cato knew the stammer only escaped her under pressure. "What has he done?" The question was sharp with concern.

Olivia shrugged helplessly. "Nothing...it's just a feeling."

Cato looked relieved. "I'll see what I can discreetly do," he offered, beginning to move away, his thoughts once more returning to the issue uppermost in his mind. Someone, somewhere on the island, had information about a plan for the king's escape. Ordinarily the king's affairs were known to his jailers almost before Charles was aware of them himself. It made the present impenetrable secrecy all the more puzzling.

It was this issue that had summoned him to London. Cromwell had suggested strongly that they move the king to some other, more secure prison. Cato had been reluctant to make the king's life even more restricted than it was when they had nothing definite to go on, and it had been left that he would make what decisions he considered necessary as circumstances developed. If the king *did* escape, Lord Granville would be held solely responsible. It was an uncomfortable burden.

Olivia made her way to the parlor, where Phoebe and Portia were to be found in the noisy midst of their children.

"You came back just in time," Phoebe said bluntly. "Cato returned at dawn."

"And I was safely asleep in my bed," Olivia said. "Thank you for...for, well, you know what I mean."

"The ring was a clever idea...once we'd decided it wasn't a cry for help," Phoebe said, reaching into her pocket for Olivia's braided ring.

Olivia took it. "Surely you didn't think..."

"No, of course we didn't," Portia said, looking up with a quick smile from the toy soldier whose broken leg she was mending for her impatiently waiting son. "Phoebe's only teasing."

Olivia managed a half smile. "My father says you're going to the c-castle this evening."

"Yes, I'm missing my husband," Portia said with a grin.

"Are you coming too, Olivia?" Phoebe asked.

Was she going to go? And yet even as she asked herself the question, she heard herself say, "Yes, I might as well, I suppose."

Phoebe's blue eyes glowed in ready sympathy. "It might take your mind off things, love. I don't mean to pry but you seem so sad. Did things not go well after all?"

"They went very well. I'm just facing reality, that's all." Olivia picked up her small half brother. "So, my lord Grafton, how are you this fine morning?"

The child regarded her solemnly from eyes as dark as her own. Then he threw back his head and shrieked with laughter as if she had said something hilariously funny.

"He has such a wonderful sense of humor," Phoebe said proudly, diverted for a moment from her concern for Olivia.

Olivia couldn't help laughing as she relinquished the ecstatic child to his doting mother. "I wish he'd share the joke." She was aware of Portia's sharp scrutiny and bent hastily to stroke Juno.

"Do you play bowls, Mr. Caxton?" King Charles turned from the casement in the chamber above the great hall and regarded his visitor from beneath heavy-lidded eyes.

"Indifferently, Sire." Anthony stood beside the empty fireplace, one silk-clad arm resting along the carved mantelpiece. There were perhaps ten men in attendance on the king. Colonel Hammond stood beside the door, his stance watchful, his gaze roaming the chamber as if he expected the king to disappear suddenly into thin air.

"Hammond, my friend, you seem perturbed," the king remarked gently. "These last days I've found you most unsettled. Is something troubling you?"

The governor controlled his irritation with difficulty. If plans *were* afoot to rescue the king, then His Sovereign Majesty was well aware of what was disturbing his jailer.

"I am aware of no perturbation, Your Majesty."

"I am so glad to hear it," the king responded sweetly. "But now I have a mind to bowl. Mr. Caxton, you shall show your skill."

Anthony bowed low and Godfrey Channing jumped to open the door. The little group followed their sovereign down the stairs and out into the courtyard.

"Walk with me, Mr. Caxton." The king beckoned Anthony to his side and took his arm. "Tell me something of your family estates. I have always had a fondness for the New Forest."

Anthony talked glibly as they crossed the courtyard, went through the postern gate and into the outer bailey, which the governor had turned into a bowling green for his royal prisoner's entertainment.

The round bowls were piled at the far side of the green, and the group strolled across under the afternoon sun, the king's arm still resting on Anthony's. No one saw as Anthony slipped a tiny fold of paper into the deep cuff of His Majesty's coat.

"You shall roll first, Mr. Caxton." The king gestured to where a soldier stood holding the first bowl.

Anthony demurred politely but allowed himself to be persuaded. Laughingly he protested his lack of skill and made a great play of hefting the bowl before rolling it across the smooth green lawn. It was a pathetic roll and drew laughter from the assembled courtiers. No one noticed the king retrieve the slip of paper and put it in his pocket.

They were still playing when Mistress Hammond with the Granville party approached through the postern gate.

"Your Majesty is winning as usual," she observed.

"I fear I'm unable to give His Majesty a good game, Mistress Hammond," Anthony said with a little titter. "Lady Granville...Lady Olivia." He bowed with a flourish of his plumed hat.

"Lady Rothbury, allow me to present Mr. Edward Caxton." The governor offered Portia a gallant bow as he gestured to Anthony.

"I'm delighted to make your acquaintance,

madam. Such a pleasure, I do declare." Anthony bowed over her hand, brushing it lightly with his lips, before acknowledging the men who had accompanied the ladies.

"Lord Granville...Lord Rothbury. Such a pleasure, my lords. Such an honor to have your notice." They were the enemy, formidable individually, together an almost insuperable force. Outwitting them would be no easy task and Anthony harbored no illusions, but his expression showed only a hopeful eagerness to please.

They acknowledged his greeting with polite nods that nevertheless conveyed a degree of contemptuous indifference that reassured Anthony that he was playing his part well.

He stepped aside as the king with a brief nod deigned to acknowledge the new arrivals.

"Lady Olivia, how delightful to see you. I was *so* disappointed to miss you yesterday." Godfrey Channing swept her a flourishing bow. "I trust you'll indulge me with a little private speech anon."

Olivia could see nothing but his thin lips and the cold calculation in his eyes. Involuntarily her gaze darted to Anthony, who gave her a vague smile.

"What's this...what's this?" the king inquired with a burst of joviality. "D'ye have an eye for the lady Olivia, my lord Channing?"

Olivia flushed to the tips of her ears and turned to Cato with a gesture of appeal, but before he could intervene Godfrey had bowed to the king and was answering him.

"A man could not call himself a man, Sire, if he failed to see the lady's beauty. What man would not aspire to the lady's hand if given a word of encouragement?"

"Well, I've always enjoyed a wedding," the king declared as jovially as before. "I trust you would give my lord a word of encouragement, madam?"

Olivia was struck dumb. Desperately she sought for an answer. Channing had come out in the open now, in the most public way imaginable, and the king had signaled his approval of his subject's suit. In fact he'd all but ordered her compliance.

"Sire, my daughter is but newly entered this society," Cato said quietly. "I would give her time to find her feet before she's swept off them."

The king frowned. In the past such jocular attention as he'd bestowed upon the marquis's daughter would have been seen as the greatest sign of royal favor. His countenance took on a petulant air.

"Well, be that as it may," he said, turning his shoulder to Lord Granville. "Hammond, I have done with bowls for today. Mr. Caxton, give me your arm again."

Anthony obeyed. *That greedy, dangerous, cowardly fool was intending to court Olivia.* His expression gave away nothing as he strolled with the king back to the postern gate, maintaining an even flow of flattering responses to his sovereign's lethargic conversation.

Once back in the great hall, where supper

was laid at the long banqueting table, Anthony accepted his dismissal and left the king's side.

The guests were taking their places on the long benches at the table, and Godfrey Channing was making his way purposefully to Olivia and her two friends. Rufus and Cato were nowhere in view. Anthony crossed the room, his one thought to forestall Godfrey Channing.

"Lady Olivia, may I escort you to the table?"

She turned and for a moment her expression was unguarded. Her eyes, filled with a riot of trouble and question, flew to Anthony's face.

"There's no need to be afeard," he murmured, instinctively feeling her terror and confusion.

She wanted to believe him. Wanted to believe that he would protect her from Godfrey Channing, wanted to believe he would protect her from himself, from *her*self. But how could he protect her from this tangled skein of dreams and deception when it was a skein of his own tangling? If only he was a different man, a man who didn't do the things he did. But what good was a different man when this was the one she wanted?

Her hand fluttered towards him, then fell to her side. "I'm not afeard," she said, and turned back to her friends.

Anthony moved away immediately, wondering why she'd refused his escort. Sometimes he didn't understand her at all. He told himself that she was merely playing his game, keeping away from him because it was safer.

He told himself that, but it didn't somehow ring true. There had been such trouble in her eyes. Perhaps it had something to do with Channing's declared suit.

Anthony's mouth hardened. He would have to put a stop to that, but how to do it without breaking his own cover?

Godfrey Channing approached the three women as they reached the table. "My ladies, allow me to escort you to the top of the table." He spoke to all three of them, but his eyes were on Olivia and it was Olivia to whom he offered his silk-clad arm.

"Why, you may escort us with pleasure, sir," Portia said, taking the proffered arm before Olivia could move. "Our husbands appear to have deserted us."

"Lady Olivia..." Godfrey offered her his free arm.

"Olivia can take my arm and you may escort Lady Granville," Portia said firmly. "We are very strict about rank, and married ladies take precedence."

Phoebe controlled her laughter at this absurdity and took up her cue. Godfrey had no choice but to accept the fait accompli.

Cato and Rufus awaited their wives at the head of the board. Cato saw the strain in Olivia's eyes as she approached, clinging to Phoebe's arm. "Come and sit beside me, Olivia," he said, taking her hand and drawing her down to the bench beside him.

"If Lady Olivia will permit me..." Godfrey smiled and took his place on her other side.

Olivia sat rigid. Her eyes darted down the table to where Anthony was sitting idly toying with his wine goblet. He looked at her just once, then turned to his neighbor.

Godfrey placed a slice of roast swan on Olivia's platter. "Pray allow me to serve you, my lady...in all ways. I am always and entirely at your service." His thin mouth smiled meaningfully; his cold eyes regarded her hungrily.

Olivia said in an undertone, "You must forgive me, Lord Channing, but I have no interest in marriage. My father is aware of this. I am a scholar, and have no time for marrying."

"I trust your feelings are not already engaged," he said, his voice suddenly sharp, his fingers tightening around his goblet.

Olivia shook her head. "No."

"Then I may hope," he returned, smiling again. He touched her hand as she picked up her knife. "I have been reading the poetry of Catullus. There was a stanza I found somewhat confusing. I wonder if you would enlighten me."

"Catullus is not one of my favorites," Olivia lied, her voice dull. "You'll have to forgive me."

Godfrey cast about for another topic of conversation as Olivia sat still as stone beside him, the food cooling on her plate. He moved his thigh closer to hers, and she jumped as if burned.

This was not going to be as easy as Brian Morse had implied. But he would have her in the end. He glanced sideways at her. She was beautiful. A man would be proud to own such

a wife. Such a wealthy wife. If gentle persuasion didn't work, then there were other ways.
He would have her.

Godfrey turned his attention to the conversation between Lord Rothbury and Lord
Granville. There at least Brian's tactics had
succeeded. Lord Granville had complimented
him several times on his astute observations.

Cato, anxious to take the pressure off his
daughter, whose strained silence was as loud
as a thunderclap, leaned across her and
inquired, "Channing, what do you know of this
Caxton fellow? He's a relatively new acolyte
at the king's altar. My men found little of
interest when they checked him out. He lodges
in Newport, I believe."

Rufus speared venison on the tip of his
knife. "I gather he's well known on the island."

"He's a hanger-on," Godfrey said, eager to
impart what he knew. "A man who likes to brag
that he dines at the king's table. He has some
fortune, I believe, but comes from an undis-
tinguished family on the mainland."

Olivia listened. Anthony's game was clearly
succeeding. He appeared so insignificant, no
one would give him the time of day in this
heavily suspicious atmosphere. But how, she
wondered, could anyone be truly fooled if
they looked at him? Everything about him
radiated authority and competence. How
could anyone not see the wicked gleam of
amusement in his eye? Not be aware of the
razor-sharp mind behind the foolish, vacant
exterior?

"The king seems to favor him," Cato said thoughtfully.

"Sometimes it pleases His Majesty to play favorites," Godfrey said. "I've noticed how, particularly if he's out of sorts with Colonel Hammond, he'll deliberately take up with some nobody, almost as if he would slight the governor." He nodded authoritatively as he spoke, and glanced down the table at the man in question. Caxton had turned his head towards his neighbor. Godfrey's hand stilled as he raised his goblet to his lips. There was something about his profile...something so familiar...

Godfrey stared. But the reference eluded him. He'd seen Caxton before at Carisbrooke. The king was notorious for choosing to favor insignificant outsiders. He did it to pique his noble jailers. Governor Hammond understood this, as did his staff. They put up with the king's little game, because, after all, how few power games remained to him?

And yet there was something about this lowly esquire that didn't sit right. Godfrey watched him. He was doing nothing out of the ordinary, had his usual vapid smile on his lips.

So what in the devil's name was it about the man?

The king set down his silver chalice. He was bored with his supper, bored with his company, and had something better to do. "I will retire, Hammond."

The company set down their utensils. Most

288

hadn't finished their first course, but they rose awkwardly at the benches as the governor moved to the king's chair.

His Majesty cast a glance down the table, offering the favor of a nod to no one, then he stepped away from the board. The governor escorted him to the barred and guarded chamber in the north curtain wall.

"I bid you good night, Sire." Colonel Hammond bowed in the doorway.

"The nightingale in his cage, Hammond." The king gave a short laugh as he looked around his comfortable prison. "But I must thank you for taking such good care of me."

"I will take such care of Your Majesty as conscience and duty dictate, Sire." The words were carefully chosen, designed to let the king know that this newest escape plan was a secret only in its proposed execution.

"Good night, Hammond."

"Sire." The governor bowed himself from the chamber. The two guards moved into place. They would not turn the key on His Sovereign Majesty, but only a spirit could pass unnoticed through the door.

"Pour hot water, Dirk. I would wash my hands."

The valet turned to the washstand and hurriedly Charles took the folded slip of paper from his pocket. He slid it beneath his pillow, then stretched and yawned.

"Your Majesty is fatigued." The valet held a basin of hot water, a towel draped over his arm.

"Aye. But 'tis the fatigue of the spirit, Dirk. Not that of bodily exertion." The king washed his hands, dried them. "You may go now. I'll put myself to bed."

"Your nightshirt, Sire." The valet was uncomfortable with the command and lifted the snowy garment from the end of the bed. "I should take Your Majesty's suit for brushing."

"Leave me, man!" There was an unusually rough note in the king's tone.

The valet bowed himself out.

The king waited until the soft conversation between the valet, a servant of the governor's, and the guards had ceased before he took Edward Caxton's slip of paper from beneath his pillow.

The message had no seigneurial courtesies.

Be prepared for the night of the new moon. You will be alerted of the exact time on the day itself. Burn through the bars and lower yourself with the cord over the curtain wall. We will be waiting for you.

Charles read the message several times. Curiously its lack of adornment gave him confidence. He'd been let down too many times by those with more heart than sense. He held the paper over the candle flame and watched it curl and disintegrate. Then he swept the embers into his palm and tossed them through the bars of his window. A window that looked out over the downs towards the sea.

Caxton would free him. The king knew that Caxton didn't belong in the ranks of all the passionate men who had thrown their lives into the scale on their sovereign's side. Caxton was a mercenary, one who would as soon see the king lose this war as win it. But one could trust a mercenary not to let his heart rule his head. The passionate would be paying Caxton, and the mercenary would execute the plan. King Charles of England trusted this arrangement.

Fourteen

"*WIND DANCER* WILL stand out from Puckaster Cove with Jethro in command. I'll take the dinghy into the cove myself. Mike will meet me with horses and come with me to bring away the king. We'll need three horses, Mike." Anthony laid out his plan to the group assembled in his cabin.

"We're lookin' fer the night of the new moon, sir?"

"Yes, and we'll pray for a dark one."

Anthony bent over the chart table. "The tide will be with us at midnight on that night. We'll create the diversion at eleven. The king will make his escape then, and with fast horses we should be back at the cove within thirty minutes. With a fair wind for the dinghy, we'll be on board again in time to catch the tide. Adam, you'll have this cabin prepared for the king."

"What kind of diversion?" Adam inquired.

Anthony smiled. "One of our friends in the castle will set off a series of small gunpowder explosions on the battlements. I hope it'll distract the guard on the ramparts long enough for the king to lower himself from his window."

Adam nodded. The Isle of Wight was strongly Royalist. There were friends of the king among the colonel's troops at Carisbrooke, just as there were in all the local garrisons on the island. Anthony knew them all.

"So, are your positions clear?" Anthony looked around at his men.

"Reckon so. But, 'ow are we to talk to the king?"

The puzzled question made Anthony laugh. "I doubt you'll have the chance to speak to him at all, Jethro. But if you do, a bow and a murmured 'Your Majesty' will probably suffice."

"Lord, never thought to sail wi' a king," Sam muttered.

"Well, if there are no more questions, that's all for now, gentlemen."

The men left with the exception of Adam, who began to tidy the cabin.

Anthony cast off the finery he'd worn to the castle. He dressed swiftly in britches and shirt, fastening his dagger at his hip.

"You goin' to the girl *now*?" Adam demanded,

regarding these preparations with some dismay.

"Any objections, old man?" The pirate raised a teasing quizzical eyebrow as he pulled on his boots.

"Ye've barely three hours before dawn."

"It's sufficient." Anthony winked and Adam tutted.

An hour later he was riding through the night-dark village of Chale. Olivia wouldn't be expecting him and he knew it was reckless to go so late, but he couldn't rid himself of the image of her troubled eyes, of the way she'd turned from him, almost as if there was something she would say to him but couldn't. And he wanted her. Wanted her now with a precipitate urgency that astonished him. He could explain it only by the knowledge that time was running out for them. Once the king was safely in France, Granville would have no reason to stay on the island. And where he went, Olivia went. Anthony's life was here. When he'd rescued the king, he would return to the life he knew, because what else was there for him? And so now while he could, he would take whatever opportunity offered to love Olivia.

Olivia was sitting on the window seat in her bedchamber when Anthony glided stealthily across the dark garden. She had been sitting there since they had returned from the castle. She was too unhappy to sleep and the nameless dread that hung over her seemed heavier than ever.

She had no sense of Anthony's approach until

she heard a soft scrape on the bark of the magnolia tree. She knew instantly who it was and despite everything her heart jumped with gladness.

"Anthony?"

"Shhh." His golden head emerged from the glossy leaves, and his gray eyes laughed across the distance that separated them. He put a finger to his lips, then swung himself from the branch onto the window ledge.

"You're mad to come so late," she whispered, looking at him in helpless turmoil. "The dogs will be out by six."

"It's barely five." He reached for her. For a moment she held back, confusion, distress, anger twisting in her heart and her head. He smiled at her, a little questioning smile, and without volition she went into his arms. It was as if she had no will. She clung to him, quivering with longing, aware of the urgency of her need, of the little time they had together. The first birdsong of the predawn chorus came through the window as he dropped to the floor with her.

"Kneel up, sweet." He turned her with his hands at her waist so she had her back to him. He pushed her shift to her waist, caressed her flanks, slid a flat palm between her thighs, stroking deeply in the hot wet furrow of her body. She groaned, fell forward with her hands on the floor, her back dipping as, shamelessly wanton, she pushed backward, opening herself to his caresses.

With one hand he continued to play with her

as he tore open his britches, releasing the aching shaft of flesh. Then he held her hips and slid within her slick and welcoming body with the sigh of a man who has come home.

She rose with him on the tide of ecstasy, her bottom pressed into his belly, reveling in the bruising grip of his fingers on her hips. Little sobs of delight broke from her lips and he moved one hand to grasp the back of her neck, his fingers pushing up into the tumbled fall of her hair. And then her knees gave way and she slipped to the floor beneath his weight, her face pressed to the rug, as the waves broke over her. She tightened her thighs around him, holding him within her, reveling in the deep throb of his flesh, and then he withdrew and she felt the hot stickiness of his seed bathing her bottom and thighs.

Anthony rolled sideways until he was lying beside her on the rug. He reached out to stroke the curve of her cheek, lifting a lock of damp hair from her forehead. "I don't know what you do to me, my flower. But when I'm with you I'm as uncontrolled as a virgin lad with his first whore."

Olivia chuckled weakly. "I don't know quite how to take that."

"No, perhaps it didn't come out quite right." He propped himself on an elbow and lightly stroked her shoulder, her upper arm, feather-light brushes of his fingertips.

Olivia rolled onto her side facing him.

Did it matter what he was?

Surely she could manage to separate this

glory, the wonder of this loving, from the wrong that he had done. Piracy, smuggling, they excited her, she embraced them as part of her lover. Why should the other thing be any different?

"Why so serious all of a sudden?" He touched her mouth.

"It's near dawn." She struggled to her feet, shaking her shift down.

Anthony rose, fastening his britches. "Something more than the dawn is troubling you, Olivia."

"Why do you say that?"

He caught the long black cascade of her hair and twisted it around his hand, drawing her to him. "Do you think, after what we've shared, that I am not aware of every change in your mood, every shadow in your eyes? Something is troubling you. I knew it at the castle."

Olivia regarded him without speaking for a minute, then she said, "Your little game seems to be working. They were discussing you at supper. Rufus, my father, and Channing..." She shuddered. "You really have them all fooled. They dismissed you as a nonentity."

"Good," Anthony said, frowning at the bitterness of her voice that seemed to have come out of nowhere.

"You're going to try to outwit my father, and what for? I know you're not doing it because you believe it's the right thing to do. You're just doing it because it's amusing and I suppose someone's paying you. You are a mercenary, after all."

And a wrecker! She turned aside with a gesture of unmistakable disgust.

Anthony's eyes hardened, and when finally he spoke, it was with a rough edge to his voice. "You don't appear to know me as well as you thought. As it happens, no one is paying me. Indeed, it's costing me a small fortune. I am not totally without loyalties, my dear Olivia, whatever you might think. Someone very close to me wishes me to do this. I would not disoblige her."

Olivia looked at him. "Who? A wife?"

"I am many things, Olivia, but not a betrayer of women." His voice was icy and Olivia understood that she had touched some deep wound.

She looked out at the faint gray light beyond the window, uncertain what to say or do next. It seemed he had an honorable motive for what he was doing for the king. Loyalty to friends or family. But what difference did that really make to her? In colluding with him, she was betraying her father. Betraying her father for a wrecker.

"What *do* you believe in?" she asked softly.

"This. You. Now," he replied.

She turned then to face him. "It's not enough, Anthony. How is it that I can feel what I do for you when everything about you is so wrong!" It was an anguished cry, her great dark eyes gazed at him, desperately seeking an answer to her question.

But he gave her none. He looked at her for a moment, his eyes now distant. When finally he spoke, his voice was even, neutral almost. "I will ask only that you keep what you know of me to yourself."

She nodded. There was nothing further to say.

"Thank you."

And he was gone.

Olivia stood in the empty chamber, her fingers pressed to her mouth, her eyes tight shut as if she could somehow banish the pain, control the wretched confusion of her emotions. Then, shivering, she crept into bed.

"So, LORD CHANNING, how goes your pursuit of Lady Olivia?" The king spoke idly from his carved chair, where he leaned back at his ease, ankles crossed, one beringed hand dangling from the chair arm, the finger and thumb of his other stroking his neat pointed beard. His eyes held a slightly malicious glitter. He was bored and in search of amusement.

"I thought she looked most uncomfortable in your company last evening," he continued. "Could it be that she's proving a difficult conquest?"

Godfrey flushed. It was never pleasant to be the butt of the king's wit. When the king laughed, others laughed with him. He caught a couple of surreptitious smiles, a few behind-the-hand whispers. Everyone was watching him, waiting for his response.

He gave an unconvincing laugh. "The lady was not feeling too well last evening, Sire. I believe like so many young ladies she is inclined to the megrims. Her mood will be altogether changed when next I see her, I assure you."

His gaze fell upon Edward Caxton and once again he was troubled by the sense of familiarity. Caxton's smooth countenance gave him no clues, however. Indeed, if anything, it seemed even more vacuous than usual, as if its owner were absent from the present proceedings.

"A changeable maid, is she?" the king mused, still with that glitter in his eye. "Have a care, Channing. A wife with the megrims can plague a man to death, isn't that so, Hammond?"

"I'm fortunate not to know, Sire," the governor said, drawing a laugh from the assembled company. "But Lady Olivia is as rich as she's beautiful. Compensations, eh, Channing?"

Everyone was laughing now and Godfrey had no choice but to laugh with them. "Wives can be trained," he said, and was disconcerted when the king threw his head back and roared with laughter as if Godfrey had made the most exquisite jest.

The others joined in and Godfrey was left wondering what on earth was so funny about such a truth.

"No, no, Channing. It's husbands who are trained," the king said, wiping his eyes. "You will learn, dear boy."

Godfrey smiled awkwardly, concealing his fury. To be mocked in this fashion was insupportable.

Behind the bland exterior, Anthony was watching Channing carefully. He understood as did no one else in the king's presence chamber that the lordling was a bad man to make a fool of. He read the chagrin, followed quickly by fury, in Godfrey's eyes. He saw the white shade around his thin mouth, the little twitch of a muscle in his cheek, even as with an unconvincing bray he joined in the laughter at his expense.

Anthony had decided he would move against Channing in some secret fashion as soon as he could. He had to be kept away from Olivia certainly, but he was also a wrecker and he had to be stopped. An accident or an abduction would be simple to arrange. They could spirit the man away on a French smuggling vessel. Although such a fate was probably too good for him.

Anthony's lip curled as he contained his impatience. He had no wish to be here playing the pointless game of fawning courtier. His plans were well laid; the king was ready. His Majesty knew what to do when the time came. They waited only for the new moon. But Anthony knew that if he suddenly ceased his sycophantic attendance on the king, it would be noticed. Those responsible for keeping the king's person secure were alert to the slightest sign of anything unusual.

So far he had played his part well. He knew he'd been investigated. As part of his cover he rented lodgings from a couple called Yarrow in Newport. He had known them for many years, their son had sailed with him several times, and he knew they would have given nothing away. They certainly wouldn't tell anyone that their so-called lodger had never yet laid his head on the pillow in the chamber abovestairs. The chamber itself would reveal nothing beyond the obvious possessions of a country squire whose conceit was fed by the illusion of being the king's confidant. There were plenty like him, fawning upon the king in his imprisonment, ignoring the fact that if His Majesty were at liberty, holding court in his palaces, they would never be admitted within the gates.

The king refused to have the windows opened around him, and the heat in the room was growing intense. A fly droned. Anthony swallowed a yawn. He'd had no sleep the previous night. By the time he'd left Olivia, day was all but broken. He'd just managed to get over the wall before the dogs were released. They had caught his scent and followed it to the wall, where they'd jumped and barked uselessly as Anthony rode off.

He had thought to catch a nap for an hour or two in the morning, but sleep had eluded him. He understood Olivia's difficulty with divided loyalties, but he didn't understand the depths of the bitterness that had fueled her attack. She had been accusing him of something else, something more than simply being her father's opponent. She had said everything about him was so *wrong*.

It was such a denial of what he had believed

they shared. Such an abrupt turnabout from the idyllic day and night they had spent on the beach and at Portsmouth.

Once before, she'd withdrawn from him without explanation, and he still had none, although he'd pushed it to the back of his mind with the resumption of their loving. But this attack he was not going to suffer in silence. There had been no time last night, and he'd been too taken aback, to probe. But he was not going to leave it there.

"I would have music, Hammond," the king declared with a yawn. "Gentlemen, leave me. I would soothe my soul with music."

The assembled company bowed and filed from the chamber as the musicians entered. The governor took a seat on the opposite side of the chamber from His Majesty and rubbed his eyes wearily as the three players tuned their instruments.

"Guarding your sovereign is proving somewhat tiring, I see, Hammond," the king observed with that same slightly malicious glint.

"It is my duty to my sovereign, to the Parliament, and to the kingdom to use the utmost of my endeavors to preserve your person, Sire," Hammond returned, sitting up straight in his chair.

"But a sadly wearisome duty it is," the king said, and this time Hammond made no demur.

GODFREY STRODE down the staircase into the great hall. He wiped the sweat from his brow with the back of his hand. It had been hot as hell in the upstairs chamber, and the mockery he'd had to endure had set up a fire in his belly that raged like a furnace.

He left the great hall and bellowed to a soldier to bring his horse to the gatehouse. He was going to visit Lady Olivia. He was going to prove to the laughing court that he was not easily scorned. If the lady was surrounded by her friends, their children, all the vigorous defenses of domesticity, then he would insist on a private interview. He had publicly declared his suit; her explanation for why she wouldn't entertain it had been no explanation. It was perfectly reasonable for him to ask for more.

He rode fast, goading his horse with spur and whip as he vented his frustration. He rode up to the front door of Lord Granville's house, dismounted, and ran up the steps. He was about to bang with his whip on the door and controlled himself with some difficulty. He couldn't afford to give the wrong impression. He was a calm, courteous suitor come to inquire after the lady. He should have brought something. A token of courtship. He glanced around. A rosebush bloomed along the driveway. He could see no one around on this hot afternoon.

Godfrey ran back, hastily plucked three of

the finest blooms, and returned to the door. He knocked firmly but without urgency.

Bisset opened the door. He recognized the visitor and bowed. "Good afternoon, Lord Channing. Lady Granville is from home."

"I had hoped to see Lady Olivia." Godfrey smiled, glanced meaningfully at his little bouquet.

Bisset had no reason to deny his lordship. He had been received by Lady Granville and must therefore have the marquis's permission to call.

"Lady Olivia is in the orchard, I believe, sir." He stepped outside and gestured to the side of the house. "Just beyond the lake, behind the stand of poplars."

"Thank you. It's Bisset, isn't it?"

"Yes, my lord." Bisset bowed again.

"Could you ask someone to water my horse while I'm with Lady Olivia."

"Certainly, my lord."

Godfrey slipped a golden guinea into the butler's hand and ran boyishly down the steps with his roses.

OLIVIA RESTED HER BACK against the apple tree that spread its shade above her. She could hear the soft plash of the fountain in the ornamental lake on the main lawn, but the orchard was cool and fragrant, the sunless grass lush.

Phoebe had gone into the village on a pastoral errand. She was often in demand with her stillroom skills, her open purse, and her ready compassion that extended as easily to helping out in the stable or cowshed as it did to lending a sympathetic ear at the kitchen table.

Portia had gone riding with the children, and Olivia was glad of the solitude. Her abstraction since she'd returned from her adventure troubled her friends, and she hadn't the energy to dissemble, not yet. They assumed it was because she was facing the fact that her time with the pirate was by its very nature ephemeral. And that was a part of her unhappiness, certainly, but only a very little part now.

She glanced at the book in her lap. Usually Plutarch's *Lives* had the power to take her away from everything, but this afternoon the usual magic was absent. She should have brought a text that challenged her. Plato perhaps—

"Ah, I find my lady alone, communing with nature." A shadow fell across her, blocking out the light filtered through the leaves of the apple tree.

Olivia knew the voice. "Lord Channing. How...how..." She looked up. His swarthy, slightly soft, courtier's face smiled down at her. It was the smile that terrified her. There was no warmth, no genuine feeling. His close-set eyes seemed to have a strange light behind them. A predatory light that brought back a host of evil memories.

She rose to her feet, her book falling to the grass. She could hear two gardeners talking as they weeded the beds at the edge of the orchard. She had only to call and they would come at once. She was not alone but the unreasoning fear swamped her. He wouldn't hurt her. Of course he wouldn't. He had no reason to do so. He wasn't Brian. But Brian had had no reason to hurt her either.

"Roses, my lady." He presented his bouquet. "A rose for a rose."

Automatically Olivia took the proffered flowers. She looked down at them as if she didn't know what they were. She murmured, "Thank you. But you must forgive me, Lord Channing, I have to return to the house."

"Not yet. You must do me the courtesy of hearing me out." He laid a restraining hand on her arm.

Olivia shook her arm free. "No," she said. "I explained last night that I cannot accept your suit. You must let me go, sir." She turned, gathering up her skirts to hurry from him.

He caught her wrist, saying softly, teasingly, "Don't run from me, little rabbit."

Olivia stared at him, for the moment unable to move. The flowers fell from her fingers. The significance of what he'd said wouldn't penetrate her brain. He was smiling, his fingers uncomfortably tight on her wrist. He moved a hand to catch her chin, tilting her face towards him.

"A kiss," he said. "You won't deny me that. A chaste kiss, my little rabbit." He bent down and his mouth filled her vision, distorted and huge.

"Brian!" she whispered. Panic swamped her. Olivia raked his face with the nails of her free hand as she twisted away from him. He

gave a cry of outrage and released her chin. She wrenched her wrist free and ran, her breath sobbing in her chest. She didn't slow her pace even though she sensed he wasn't following her, and burst through the trees into the bright sunlight of the driveway almost under the hooves of an approaching horse.

"Olivia!" Anthony hauled back on the reins, and his alarmed mount came to a halt inches from where Olivia stood, staring up at him through the tumbled mass of her hair, her eyes wild with panic.

"What's happened?" He dismounted, glancing quickly around. They were out of sight of the house around a bend in the drive.

"Brian," she gasped. "It's Brian."

"What's Brian? Who's Brian?" Frightened at her pallor, at the wildness in her eyes, he moved swiftly to gather her into his arms.

"He's not dead," she said. "He c-can't be dead. He sent that...that c-c-creature....He c called me 'little rabbit.' Only Brian c-called me that...." The words flooded without sense from her lips as she clung to Anthony's rock solid body. His arms were tight around her, he stroked her hair, not knowing what else to do.

It was hard at first to make sense of what she was saying, but slowly he began to grasp the nightmare. Such a dark and dreadful nightmare revealed under the hot sun and brilliant blue sky of this summer afternoon. She wept into his shirt as he held her, stroked her, soothed her with little murmurs, kissed her tear-drenched eyes when the words no longer came and she shivered in his arms, silent at last.

"Why didn't you tell me before?"

"I c-couldn't. I c-couldn't bear to remember it. That first time, on the ship, in the morning it all c-came back to me."

"Dear God!" he said softly, finally understanding what had driven her from him.

"But he's not dead," she said, raising her head from his chest. "Don't you see that? He must be here somewhere."

"It could have been just coincidence, Channing using those words."

"No!" she cried, shaking her head violently. "No, it isn't, I know it isn't. Channing even looks like him. It's as if he's c-come back in Channing's body."

"Now you're being foolish," he chided gently, rubbing her back as she trembled like a sapling in a gale.

Godfrey Channing stood in the trees and watched in cold jealous rage. Only a lover would hold a woman like that. She was clinging to Edward Caxton with all the intimacy of a woman who'd just climbed out of his bed. She was no virgin, she was a whore who'd given herself to a nobody, a mere country squire, a foppish nitwit with neither fortune nor lineage. He took an involuntary step forward out of the shelter of the trees.

As if sensing the movement, Caxton raised his eyes, looked over Olivia's head towards the trees. Godfrey stepped back hastily but not before their eyes had met. It was a brief contact but it was enough. Channing now knew what was familiar about the man. He'd seen those eyes before, been subjected before to that hard, sharp, contemptuous look.

This man who called himself Edward Caxton was the man who'd bought his culling. Just as the foul fisherman had not been what he had seemed, so Edward Caxton was not the insipid, fawning hanger-on in the king's presence chamber that he seemed. And he'd taken his prize from him.

Olivia took a deep sobbing breath as she felt Anthony's sudden alertness. "Is he there? Did he see us?"

"Don't worry about him."

"But if he saw us, he'll tell people."

"I'll take care of Godfrey Channing," Anthony said grimly. "Did he hurt you?"

"He tried to kiss me." She shuddered again, scrubbing her hand across her mouth. "I'm so frightened of him. He must know Brian. He *must*. How else would he know to call me that? Brian must have told him what he did to me; they must have talked about me. And now he'll tell everyone that he saw us together." Her voice was rising alarmingly and Anthony hushed her gently.

"I'll take care of it," he repeated.

"How?" She looked helplessly at him.

"Just trust me." He paused, then said deliberately, "In this at least you can trust me to do something without the promise of financial reward." Both eyes and voice challenged her for an explanation.

The warmth of a minute earlier vanished, leaving Olivia cold and empty again.

She answered the challenge with one of her own. "Why did you c-come here? Won't you draw attention to yourself? If my father was home, he'd ask questions. I thought you needed to avoid that."

"I happen to know he's not here."

"Yes, I suppose you would know that. You must have spies."

"Yes, I do." He looked at her in frustration, controlling his anger at her arid tone. It seemed he'd solved one puzzle, only to be faced with another. "Is that part of what makes me so *wrong* for you, Olivia?"

"You said yourself you're no gentleman. You don't act by the rules of honor," Olivia said slowly.

"Is that what this is about?" he demanded. "It never seemed to trouble you before."

"In the dream, such a thing as acting honorably didn't seem to matter," she said. "But now I'm awake I find that it does."

Honor! His father had dishonored his mother. Their child had been born in dishonor. His father's family under the shield and buckler of honor had rejected the dishonored infant, abandoned him without a qualm to survive or not.

Anthony said bitterly, "Honor is a luxury not everyone can afford, my dear Olivia. And when I see how much dishonor is perpetrated in the name of honor, I'm glad it's beyond my reach."

"My father is honorable," she said in a low voice. "He would not do a dishonorable act."

Anthony looked at her bleakly. There seemed nothing to say to this unspoken comparison.

"I will leave you here," he said, his voice without expression. "I will take care of Channing and see what I can discover about this Brian character. Spies have their uses," he added with an ironic smile. He turned and mounted his horse, riding off down the driveway without a backward glance.

Olivia went slowly back to the house. She had accused Anthony of dishonor. But what other word was there for a wrecker? The most despicable, cowardly act of thievery. Piracy and smuggling—they were swashbuckling, daring. Piracy certainly was thievery; smuggling was not considered such. Smugglers merely deprived the loathed revenuers of their equally loathed taxes. Even her father took delivery of smuggled cognac.

She thought of the taking of the *Doña Elena*. That had been stealing, no question. But he had stolen from barbarians. He had freed the slaves, given them the ship. It had seemed at the time like a fair fight, a legitimate cause.

She sat on the window seat, looking out through the open window at the sea. She felt emptied of all emotion; even her fear of Brian had faded somehow. Nothing seemed to matter anymore. The day was sunlit and yet it seemed gray. The sea sparkled and yet it seemed dull. Everything was lifeless and pointless.

Fifteen

BRIAN MORSE SET DOWN his wine cup as someone banged on the door of his chamber in the Gull at Ventnor. "Who is it?"

"Channing."

"Come in, dear boy, come in." He didn't rise from his chair as Godfrey entered. An eyebrow lifted as he took in his visitor's appearance. Lord Channing looked less than immaculate for once. Dust coated his boots and coat; his stock was twisted; the plume on his hat was seriously windswept. He had blood on his cheek.

"You look as if you're in something of a hurry," Brian observed, leaning forward to pour wine for his visitor.

Godfrey drained the cup and then refilled it before saying, "I rode hell for leather. Something's happened."

"Oh?" Brian's eyes sharpened. "Your pursuit of the fair Olivia has met a snag?"

"She's a whore," Godfrey spat out.

"Oh, no, dear boy. You must be mistaken. Pure as the driven snow, I'd swear it."

"Then you'd be forsworn! She has a lover."

"You begin to interest me," Brian said. "Tell me all."

He listened, meditatively rubbing his aching

thigh, as Godfrey poured out his tale, repeating when he'd finished, "She ran from me. Ran straight into the bastard's arms."

"Why did she run from you? Did you frighten her? I told you to tread carefully with her."

"You also told me she was a virgin!"

"Mmm. I'm surprised, I must confess. She was always such a timid creature."

"She said your name," Godfrey remembered. "Just before she ran, she said your name."

Brian's expression lost its air of mild amusement. "Why would she do that? What did you say to her? Did you tell her I was here?"

"No, of course not. I'm no fool." Godfrey shook his head. "I was trying to soften her up, tease her a little. You told me she had a pet name as a child. I called her 'little rabbit' to make her feel at ease."

"You did *what*?" Brian got to his feet, wincing as his leg took his weight. His face was suffused with rage. "You idiot! I didn't tell you to say that. *Did I?*"

Godfrey had a temper of his own and it was running high already, but instinctively he backed away from Brian Morse, who had his stick in his hand and looked as if he was about to use it. "What harm could it do?" he muttered sullenly.

"What harm? It was a private name. One only I used," Brian said furiously.

"She could have forgotten. It was a long time ago."

"She wouldn't have forgotten *that*," Brian

said with grim conviction. "You've ruined everything with your blabbing tongue."

He sat down again, staring into the empty fireplace, trying to work out if he could salvage anything of his master plan. "If we get rid of Caxton—"

"That's easily done," Godfrey said eagerly. "I came to you first but as soon as I return to Carisbrooke I'll have Caxton arrested."

Brian turned skeptical eyes upon him. "How so?"

"Because he's not what he seems. He's the man who bought my culling. And Granville is going to be very interested to know that Edward Caxton is playing a part," Godfrey said. "He's the man they're after, the one who's plotting to rescue the king. He has to be. When I tell them what I know of him, they'll throw him into Winchester jail. They'll break him, force the truth from him, and then, if there's anything left to hang, they'll hang him."

"I can see that might appeal," Brian observed. "But don't forget that Caxton knows a few things about you that won't bear the light of day." He raised an ironic eyebrow.

Godfrey shook his head. "I'll spin a tale that explains how I know about him. I'm trusted, well respected—"

"Thanks to me," Brian interjected gently.

Godfrey ignored this. "They won't take Caxton's word over mine. He can scream 'wrecker' till he's blue, they won't believe him, I'll make certain of it."

Brian nodded. "So we get rid of the rival, but you still have to win the lady."

"I don't know that I want a whore," Godfrey said savagely.

"So she's secondhand. Why should that worry you? She's still wealthy and she's still tasty. A little bit of experience can be an advantage in a man's bed."

Godfrey said nothing. To take another man's leavings would hurt his pride, but then, it would be an even greater revenge on Caxton.

"If Cato could somehow learn that his daughter is damaged goods, seduced by a traitor, then he might be quite eager to accept an impeccable offer for her," Brian mused. "You find a way to tell him, then you present yourself as the rescuer of his daughter's reputation. You love her, have loved her from afar. You'll take her as she is."

He picked up his cup again and drank. "It might work. But you'll have to tread carefully. Cato won't easily accept tales against his daughter. Maybe you can get that truth forced out of Caxton, so that Cato hears it from his own lips."

"During the interrogation." Godfrey's eyes gleamed. "I could spring it on him during the interrogation. Granville will attend. He'll have to."

Brian gazed moodily into the grate. If Olivia suspected he was alive, then he had his own problems. Cato hadn't made sure he was dead after the duel in Rotterdam; he'd certainly be most interested to know that he was still alive.

He looked across at Godfrey with savage contempt. "You are a babbling dolt."

Godfrey flushed, his hands curled into fists. "I'll have no more of your insults."

Brian gave a harsh crack of laughter. "You'll take what I dish out, my friend. You forget that I too know a few things about you that would see you at the end of the hangman's rope."

Godfrey whitened. He advanced on Brian and then found himself staring into the muzzle of a pistol.

"Be very careful," Brian said softly.

Godfrey stood for a minute, then turned on his heel and banged from the chamber.

Brian laid the pistol on the table. He limped to the window and watched Godfrey Channing ride off on his lathered horse. The man was proving an unreliable tool, but he was all Brian had.

GODFREY RODE BACK to the castle still seething with anger at Brian's insults. But the man had found a way to salvage his hopes. He needed Olivia's dowry and Cato would pay handsomely to dispose of his unvirgin daughter. And secondhand though she was, she would still be a pleasure in his bed. And if he chose to make her pay for the way she'd insulted him, then he could think of many most satisfying ways to do so.

He rode under the gatehouse, calling to the guards, "Is Lord Granville in the castle? Or Lord Rothbury?"

"Aye, sir. Both of 'em. They been 'ere all day. Closeted wi' Colonel Hammond, I'd guess."

Godfrey left his horse and strode into the castle. The guard looked at the animal's heaving flanks, foaming mouth, and sweating hide, gouged by spurs. "Right vicious bastard, 'e is," the guard muttered. "Wouldn't want to meet 'im on a dark night." He took the bridle and led the exhausted animal away.

"I DON'T KNOW what else we can do," Cato was saying wearily in Colonel Hammond's privy chamber. "It's impossible to police every tiny cove and chine on the island. We're watching the harbors at Yarmouth and Newport. We have guards at every sizable cove around the island. If he's to leave by ship—and how can he do otherwise?—then he'll have to be rowed out from a beach somewhere. A good-sized ship will have to stand out from shore."

"Someone has to know something," Rufus stated, turning from the window where he'd been looking down at the courtyard.

"Of course. But the islanders are as close-mouthed as clams. They're staunch Royalists to a man, and if the mastermind we're looking for is indeed some kind of folk hero to them, then such a combination will ensure the silence of the grave. Giles can't pry a thing loose, not with bribes, not with menaces. All his usual sources are dry as an old well."

"I've doubled the guard on the king's chamber," Hammond said. "He never walks alone in the castle. The only time he's alone is at night. And I can't bring myself to post a guard within his chamber. He's no criminal."

"That depends on your perspective," Rufus said grimly. "There are some who say the king has sacrificed the peace of his kingdom, has spilled the blood of his subjects for his own ends. There are those who call him traitor."

Hammond sighed. "I've heard the arguments, Rothbury...." He turned at the knock on the door. "Enter. Oh, it's you, Channing."

"Yes, Governor." Godfrey bowed and came straight to the point. "Lord Granville, Lord Rothbury. I believe I have found the man behind the plan to contrive the king's escape," he declared solemnly.

There was a moment of astounded silence.

"Go on," Cato prompted.

"I've suspected the man for some time," Godfrey continued. "There was something amiss with him, but it took me until today to realize what it was."

"Get to the point, man," the governor demanded. "We need a name."

"Edward Caxton." Godfrey looked at them in open triumph. "I have suspected him these many days," he reiterated in case the message got lost. He and he alone had succeeded, had followed his hunches and uncovered the plot.

"Caxton?" The governor frowned. "But he's a nobody."

"Or likes to appear so," Cato said slowly. "You had better begin at the beginning, Channing."

"He's a smuggler and, I believe, a wrecker," Godfrey said, noticing how as one they grimaced at the latter accusation. "I believe he was responsible for the wreck off St. Catherine's Point the other week." *How sweet this was.*

"I wished to take a delivery of cognac for my personal use." He shrugged boyishly at this admission. It was not a peccadillo anyone would hold against him.

"I knew of a contact in the Anchor in Niton. The innkeeper there. A villain called George. He put me in touch with a fisherman. Or that's what he said he was. But that fisherman is Edward Caxton."

"How do you know they are one and the same?" Cato asked, watching him closely. There was something not quite right about Godfrey Channing. An odd brittle wildness.

Godfrey's voice quavered with exultation as he wove his story. It was coming to him as he spoke, all the details, utterly convincing.

"I recognized him. Last night, at the king's table. I was watching him and I knew. It was a look he had. I knew it immediately. I went to the Anchor this afternoon to see if I could learn anything. He was in the back room with George. I heard his voice as clearly as I hear yours. It was Caxton's voice, not the island accents he put on when he was playing the smuggler."

"As I recall, you said your men had checked Caxton's background." Rufus looked at Cato.

"Aye. He and everyone else who hangs around the king. As I said, they could find nothing amiss. He lodges in Newport when he's on the island."

"Perhaps he merits further investigation," Rufus suggested aridly.

Cato nodded. "I'll put Giles himself onto it. He'll run the truth to earth if anyone can. The Newport landlady is probably as much a conspirator as the rest of the island."

"But what of Caxton?" Godfrey leaned forward in his chair. "You'll arrest him now?"

"Not yet," Cato answered. "Let's find out some more about him before we jump."

Godfrey didn't like the sound of that, but he was obliged to be satisfied. "Is there anything further I can do, my lords?"

"Just keep your eyes and ears open as you have been doing," Cato said, giving him a nod of approval.

Godfrey bowed and withdrew.

OLIVIA LISTENED to the sounds of the children returning from their ride with Portia. It was the usual Decatur babble. They all seemed to talk at once and yet they all seemed to understand each other perfectly. She leaned her head against the chair back and tried to summon the energy to go downstairs, to be her usual self. It seemed impossible.

Would Godfrey Channing have reported

what he'd seen on the driveway? Would her father have questions about Anthony? She couldn't say anything about Brian without revealing what she could not bear to reveal, although if he was on the island her father would want to know it. It was so complicated, all such a muddle. What had started with a dream of entrancement had become a web of half-truths, outright lies, and a swamp of impossible feelings.

If only she had never slipped from the cliff. Never met the pirate. And yet Olivia knew that she could never wish for that.

Wearily she got to her feet. It was close to six and suppertime, and she could hear her father's voice in the hall, talking with Rufus. She couldn't cower in her chamber all evening even if she wanted to. She needed to discover if Godfrey had said anything to her father.

Olivia left her chamber. She heard the voices in the hall more clearly now and reflected on another sign of changing times. Rufus Decatur would eat at Cato Granville's table. He would not lay his head beneath his roof, although he was happy for his family to do so, but he would break bread with him. Seven years ago he would have killed Granville as readily as Cato would have served him the same. They had made common cause in this war, and their wives had forced them to acknowledge the good in each other. They were not friends exactly, but they respected each other.

Giles Crampton and Portia were in the hall with Cato and Rufus when Olivia came slowly downstairs.

"I would start with the Newport landlady, Giles," Cato was saying. "See if you can frighten something from her. She must know something. The entire goddamned island knows something that we don't. Let's try for a roundup of conspirators. Get as many into the net as you can, and don't worry too much how good your evidence is. If our man sees his friends threatened, he might make a premature move. Then we can—" He broke off when he saw Olivia on the stairs.

"Ah, there you are. Do you know where Phoebe is?"

Olivia took a second to answer. There was nothing significant in her father's greeting, but there was an air of grim satisfaction about the three men, a sense of purpose that she knew had eluded them during the last weeks. Unease prickled her spine.

"Do you know where Phoebe is?" Cato repeated. "Portia doesn't."

"She went to the village. Isn't she returned yet?"

"Not according to Bisset." He frowned. It was growing late and he didn't want Phoebe roaming the lanes at dusk.

"Giles, before you go to Newport, go into the village and escort Lady Granville home."

"Aye, sir." Giles turned to the open front door. "Oh, 'ere she is now, sir."

Phoebe came hurrying in. "Have I kept

322

supper waiting? I do beg your pardon." She beamed. "I was helping to deliver a baby. A fine healthy girl. Shall we go in to supper?"

"I think it can wait a few more minutes," Cato said gently. "Just while you wash your face and hands and tidy your hair perhaps."

Phoebe's beam didn't waver. "Oh, do I still look like a midwife? You go in to supper. I'll be but a minute." She hastened up the stairs.

"Shall we?" Cato gestured to the dining room. They took their places at the long table and waited for Phoebe, who reappeared looking only moderately tidy a few minutes later. She helped herself to a dish of cod and peas in a cream sauce and launched into a detailed description of the birth she had attended.

"Phoebe, must we have all the gruesome details?" Portia asked.

"Oh, are they gruesome?" Phoebe looked surprised. "It was all very natural and really quite quick."

"But not perhaps supper table conversation," Cato murmured. He took a chicken pasty from a dish and resolutely turned the topic. "What do you think of Mr. Caxton, Olivia? You seem to have had some conversation with him, as I recall."

Olivia's heart jumped and plunged. Was this a prelude to a discussion of what had happened that afternoon? She coughed as if a piece of chicken had gone down the wrong way, and took up her wine cup. Cato waited courteously until the spasm seemed to have passed.

"Why do you ask, sir?"

Cato shrugged. "I saw you talking to him at the castle one evening. I wondered if you had formed an impression."

So Godfrey had held his tongue, at least for the moment. "I don't think anything of him, sir," she said calmly. "His c-conversation has little merit, I believe."

"By which you mean he has no obvious scholarship," Cato observed with a slight smile.

"He's such a ninnyhammer," Phoebe observed. "Why are you interested in him?"

"It's possible he's not quite the ninny-hammer he seems," Cato said.

Olivia's fingers quivered on her fork and she put the utensil down. "How do you mean?"

"He may have an ulterior motive for hanging around the king," Rufus said. "There are those who think so."

"Oh," Olivia said, taking up her fork again. Was this behind that conversation in the hall? "You mean he might want to rescue the king?"

"If it's true that he's not what he seems, it's not an unlikely deduction," Rufus said.

"What makes you suspect him?" Portia took a forkful of dressed crab. "These island crabs are delicious."

"A whisper," Cato replied. "Just a whisper."

Who? Olivia pushed a piece of fish around her plate, trying to appear as if this information was of little interest. *Who could have let slip a whisper?* How much did they know? Did

Anthony know he'd fallen under suspicion?

"I was thinking it might be pleasant to go up to the castle this evening," she said casually, reaching for her wine goblet, adding, "If you're returning there yourself, sir."

"I had thought to do so. There are preparations to be made." He sounded surprised at his daughter's suggestion.

He wasn't the only one. Olivia was aware of her friends' sudden scrutiny. It was most unlike Olivia to suggest voluntarily subjecting herself to a castle soiree. She met their gaze steadily, her eyes shooting her appeal for their support.

"In that case, we'll come with you," Portia said.

"Yes, maybe Mr. Johnson will be there," Phoebe put in.

"I had intended you should accompany me to the castle tonight, anyway, Portia," Rufus said casually.

"Oh, are you borrowing me for the whole night?" his wife inquired with an air of innocence completely at odds with the gleam in her eyes.

"That was my intention." He raised a pointed eyebrow. Portia grinned.

"In that case we had better change our dress," Phoebe said, pushing back her chair.

"Yes, riding britches probably won't do," Portia agreed cheerfully. "Come, Olivia."

Olivia followed them from the room. By mutual consent nothing was said until they'd reached Olivia's bedchamber.

Portia closed the door quietly and came to the point. "What's going on, duckie?"

Olivia looked between them. Blue eyes and green held only concern.

"You might as well know," she said. "It can't do any harm now. Edward Caxton is my pirate."

"*What?*" They stared at her.

"I should have guessed," Phoebe said after a minute. "That first night, when you were talking to him, I felt something was strange. But your pirate's called *Anthony*...oh, of course. He'd hardly use his own name." She pulled at a loose piece of skin around her thumb, cross with herself for such a stupid question.

"And your pirate is intending to rescue the king," Portia stated, a deep frown drawing her sandy eyebrows together. "What a pretty pickle. No wonder you've been so glum."

"And you want to warn him tonight, if he's at the castle," Phoebe said slowly.

"*If* he's there," Olivia stated. "But I needed you to come with me, otherwise it would look very strange."

"But if you warn him, then you'll foil Cato's plan. By helping you to warn him, then I'm deceiving my husband," Phoebe said in distress.

"But my father is only interested in preventing the king's escape," Olivia said swiftly. "If Anthony calls off the attempt, everyone will be happy. It's not necessary to capture him and hang him, is it?"

Phoebe shook her head. "No, I suppose not. Can you persuade him to call off his plan?"

"I'm going to try," Olivia said. She looked at her friends. "I know you won't betray me...him?" It was part statement, part question.

There was a short silence, then Portia answered the question in her own way. "Do you ever think about when we first met?"

"In the boathouse at Diana's wedding." Olivia shook her head. "It was only seven years ago and the world's changed out of all recognition. Everything's upside down. So many lives lost...so much blood. When will it be over?"

"Rufus thinks they will put the king on trial," Portia said. "It all began with the execution of the earl of Strafford. It will end with the king's."

"They would *kill* the king?" Olivia stared at her.

"There are those who would," Phoebe said gravely. "But not Cato."

"Nor Rufus," Portia said. They were all so used to a world at war, it was hard to imagine their lives in a land at peace. But the killing of a king would not bring peace. Only the deluded or the fanatical believed that.

"It's hard to think of you as you were," Olivia said. She knew this reminiscence was answer to her question. It was a reminder of the depths of their friendship. "Straight up and down like a ruler. Determined never to marry. And children...heaven forbid!"

"Well, I wanted to be a soldier and I am," Portia said.

"And I wanted to be a poet and I am," Phoebe said.

"And I wanted to be a scholar," Olivia said.

"As you are."

"Yes," she said flatly.

"So we had better get changed and try to sort out this muddle," Portia said briskly. She was a doer, a fixer, always ready to apply herself to solutions. She looked at Phoebe.

"Yes," Phoebe agreed. "Of course." But her eyes were troubled.

"Thank you," Olivia said simply. "I won't make it difficult for you again."

Phoebe nodded.

They left Olivia to change her own gown. She knew that humanity and friendship had allowed Phoebe to make this one small gesture. But from there on, her loyalty to her husband and his cause was absolute. Portia, much less emotional, much more pragmatic, would spend little energy on debating competing loyalties.

For herself, nothing was clear. Nothing was simple. Except that she couldn't bear Anthony's death. She had chosen never to love him again, but she could not endure to think of the world without him.

Sixteen

"PRUE, THEM SOLDIERS IS BACK." Goodman Yarrow called to his wife as he entered the tiny cottage on Holyrood Street. "They was just passin' St. Thomas's."

"Well, what's that to us?" Prue asked, taking another iron from the fire. She spat on it and nodded at the satisfactory sizzle before applying the flatiron to the shirt spread out on the table.

"They're comin' 'ere next," her husband said. "They be goin' 'ouse to 'ouse from the church. Askin' questions."

"They can ask away," Prue said, folding the shirt deftly. "We got nothin' to 'ide."

"They'll be askin' about the master." The goodman sat heavily at the other end of the table that took up most of the square kitchen.

"An' we show 'em 'is chamber jest like afore." Prue picked up another shirt and exchanged the cold iron for the one heating on the range. "Don't get all agitated, man. Jest stick to the story, that's all we 'ave to do."

"But 'e 'asn't been around 'ere fer a month." The goodman was clearly unable to take his wife's advice.

"That's none of our business," she said

placidly. "We jest rents 'im the chamber. It's nothin' to us when 'e comes or when 'e goes. That's all we 'ave to say. You jest leave the talkin' to me."

The goodman heaved himself to his feet and fetched down a jug of ale from a shelf above the range. He drank directly from the jug as tramping feet sounded from the narrow street beyond the open door.

Giles Crampton loomed in the doorway. "Good even, goodwife."

Prue set down her iron. The man wore a sergeant's insignia. Their previous visitor had been a mere private. "Come ye in, sir. Ye'll take a drink of ale?"

"No, I thankee. Not today." Giles entered the kitchen. Behind him in the street ranged a phalanx of soldiers, armed with pikes and muskets. Doors closed up and down the street, a series of hasty little bangs, and curious faces appeared at upper windows.

Prue's hand trembled infinitesimally as she smoothed the garment she'd been ironing. "What can we do fer ye, Sergeant?"

"Well, it's like this, see." Giles came closer, his voice confidential, friendly. "We've 'eard some things about this lodger of your'n. He still lodge 'ere?"

"No," the goodman said. "He's left 'ere."

Prue laughed. "That's what my man likes t' think," she said. "Doesn't 'ave much time fer 'im, but 'e pays well, I say. That's all that matters. Us 'asn't seen him in a few days, but 'is things is still 'ere." She gestured with her head to the narrow staircase at the rear of the kitchen. "Go on up if ye like, Sergeant."

Giles clumped up the stairs. The small chamber under the eaves was neat, the quilt and pillow on the cot smooth and clean. He poked around. There was an ironbound chest at the foot of the bed. It was unlocked and he raised the lid. It showed him nothing of interest. Just small clothes, neckerchiefs, a spare pair of boots, a handsome leather belt, a saddle, and spurs. All perfectly innocent. All perfectly appropriate for a country squire trying to make a place for himself at court.

But something was amiss. He stood and sniffed like a bloodhound. It was not that there was a smell in the chamber so much as the total absence of such. This place was not used by Edward Caxton or anyone else, Giles decided. He supposed he couldn't blame the man he'd sent before for failing to notice this indefinable clue. He'd had no reason to suspect Caxton. It had been merely a routine check.

So why would a man pay rent, keep clothes and these few possessions, in a place where he didn't live?

He went downstairs again. He caught the flicker of a glance between the goodman and his wife. An anxious glance. The goodman lifted the ale jug to his lips again and drank noisily. When he set it down again, there was a tremor to his fingers.

"Well, now," said Giles comfortably. "Let's talk about Mr. Caxton, shall we?"

"We know nothin' about 'im," the goodman

blustered. "We jest takes 'is money an' he comes an' goes as 'e pleases."

"Which is not very often," Giles observed, leaning his shoulders against the wall, hands driven deep into the pockets of his britches. "So, when he's not 'ere, where is he?"

"How should us know?" Prue wiped her hands on her apron. "As my man says, we're glad o' the money. We don't pry."

"Well, mebbe you could think a little," Giles suggested, raising a beckoning finger towards his men at the door. They moved forward, the shadow of their presence falling across the door, blocking out the last vestiges of evening light.

"I'm sure there's summat you know that I'd find 'elpful," Giles continued, his voice cajoling. "His friends? Visitors when he's 'ere? Where 'e goes when he's not 'ere?"

Prue shook her head. "We told ye, Sergeant. We don't know nothin'."

Giles sighed heavily. He said regretfully, "Well, you see, I don't believe you, goodwife. I think you know a lot about this 'ere Mr. Caxton. An' it's my business to find out what. So we'll go somewhere a bit quiet, like, an' 'ave another little chat."

He pointed to his men and they surged into the little cottage. "Ye can't take us away!" Goodman Yarrow protested, panic in his voice. "We're good law-abidin' folk." His face twisted in fear as the men laid hold of him.

"My man 'as the right of it," Prue declared,

her voice much steadier than her husband's. "Ye've a warrant or some such?"

"The governor's writ, goodwife," Giles said. "If ye've done nothin', ye've nothin' to fear."

Prue snorted with disbelief, but unlike her husband, she made no further protest as she was bundled out of the cottage.

"You want us to lock up, goodman?" Giles inquired solicitously. "Or shall we leave it open in case yer lodger comes 'ome?"

"Turn the key," Prue said with something of a snarl. "It's on the hook be'ind the door."

Giles obliged and then followed the procession down Holyrood Street to the quay. They would take the goodman and his wife by boat to Yarmouth Castle, where they could be questioned in privacy.

He was aware of the eyes following them, of the hastily closed doors as they passed, and he was satisfied that his little raid had had the right effect. The removal of citizens from their homes was a sound intimidation tactic. A few more such raids would weaken the loyalty these folk had to Mr. Edward Caxton, if he was indeed the man they were looking for.

The Yarrows would provide him with the answer to that. The goodman would break first, Giles reckoned. It was strange how women, the so-called weaker sex, should be so much harder to intimidate. But it was a fact he'd noticed before.

Maybe the pains of childbirth hardened them, he thought, watching as his prisoners were hustled into the boat at the quay. He watched the boat heading up the Medina River, then turned for his horse. He would return to Carisbrooke with the news of his success and then meet his prisoners when they were disembarked at Yarmouth.

MIKE WAS WAITING on the beach of the small cove as Anthony turned the dinghy into the shore. "Looks like it's goin' to turn foul later," Mike observed as he bent to pull the small boat onto the sand.

Anthony stepped onto the wet sand, carrying his stockings and his elegant tooled-leather boots. He sniffed the wind. "I came to that conclusion myself. A good night for a wreck, I would have said."

Mike heard the musing tone and waited for more. When the master spoke in that voice, it meant he was about to divulge a carefully considered plan.

"I've been thinking it's time we had a hand in things, Mike. We'll stage a little surprise for anyone who might be considering some dirty work later on."

"Off the point?"

"Aye. A group from *Wind Dancer* are already set to reach the beach by midnight. Can you round up a few good men to set up on the clifftop?"

Mike grinned. "Easy," he said. "Pa'll be one o' the first, and three of me brothers. We'll watch for 'em lighting the beacon. We'll give 'em a right thumpin'."

"Exactly so." Anthony sat down on a rock away from the water's edge, brushed the sand off the soles of his feet, and pulled on his stockings and boots. "I'll not stay long at the castle tonight. Just long enough to pass the message to the king that we move tomorrow. I just hope to God he doesn't give anything away. He's not the best conspirator."

Anthony grimaced. The king found it difficult to dissemble. Mainly because he considered it beneath his dignity. If he knew his departure from prison was imminent, there was a chance that something in his manner would alert the ever watchful governor. It had happened that way before. But it was an inherent risk. If Anthony was to keep his promise to Ellen, he had to take it.

"I'll join you on the beach when I'm finished at the castle."

Mike touched his forelock and loped off up the steep path. Anthony followed at a steady pace. He could smell the coming storm. It would be the first since the night of the last wreck. Would it bring out Channing and his men? It would be the perfect opportunity to snatch Godfrey Channing and kill two birds with one stone. Stop the wrecking, or at least until some other evil brain took over, and get the lordling well away from Olivia before he could do any further damage. That would leave Anthony with only one small problem to take care of before he took the king. This mysterious and vile Brian Morse.

Anthony was most interested in meeting

the man who had abused the child Olivia. Channing could help him there too.

He entered the great hall at Carisbrooke, his step casual, his smile of greeting easy and friendly. The king was playing cards at the fireside, but there was no sign of Granville, Rothbury, or Hammond. With his usual pleasantly vacuous expression, Anthony greeted Mistress Hammond and bestowed his devastating smile on the ladies around her. They fluttered their fans and smiled upon him, and Mistress Hammond chided him with her gap-toothed smile for being a shocking flirt to throw her ladies into such disarray.

He was saved from a response by an equerry bidding him join His Majesty at cards. Anthony smiled, bowed to the ladies, kissed a few hands, and strolled indolently across the hall to obey the king's summons.

"I'm an indifferent whist player, Sire," Anthony demurred with his annoying little titter as he bowed to his sovereign. "I'm sure my fellow players will grow impatient."

"Oh, never mind that. I daresay Lord Daubney will be happy to partner you. You couldn't be worse than his present partner."

"I had not the cards, Sire," the gentleman in question murmured unhappily as he rose from his seat at the table and gave his place to Edward Caxton.

Anthony sat down. His eyes were alert beneath lazily drooping lids. He held his cards in one hand, but as always his other rested on the jeweled hilt of his sword. He was in the midst of the enemy. If anything went wrong, he would have no chance to fight his way out of the hall, let alone out of the castle, but he would have a damned good try.

"Has Your Majesty walked the battlements this evening?" he inquired casually, laying down his cards for his partner's play.

"No, I find the night humors irritate my lungs," the king responded, casting a heavy-lidded look across the table.

Anthony didn't meet the look. The king, alerted by the mention of the battlements, knew now that Caxton had a message for him. He would find a way to receive it.

Five minutes later the king stretched to pick up the hand he had just won, and the edge of his wide velvet sleeve caught his wine goblet. It fell to the table, the ruby contents splattering over the cards.

Anthony had his handkerchief in his hand and bent to catch the spill before it ran over into the king's lap.

"My thanks, Caxton. You move quickly," the king said, letting his hand fall into his lap as he thrust his chair back from the table. "I fear I'm more than usually clumsy this evening."

"Oh, indeed not...my fault I'm certain...how could Your Majesty ever be clumsy? It was my fault, most certainly my fault!" Anthony exclaimed. The men around the table exchanged contemptuous smiles. Servants busied themselves cleaning the table, fetching new cards, refilling the king's goblet.

The king thrust his hand negligently into his

pocket and leaned back while the cleanup was completed. Then he leaned forward for the new pack, breaking it deftly.

"Shall we resume, gentlemen?" He cut to his opponents.

Anthony felt Olivia's arrival before he saw her. It was as if there had been a change in the air.

No other woman had had this effect on him...and no other woman had accused him of dishonor. No other woman was so damned fickle, he thought savagely. Loving with such warmth and passion one minute, and the next prating about moral failings and pushing him away as if he were some loathsome beetle.

"Your bid, Mr. Caxton," the king prompted.

Anthony forced his attention back to the cards in his hand. "Two spades, gentlemen." He took up his wine goblet and glanced with seeming idleness around the hall.

She was wearing the orange gown again, and again he thought she looked like some flaming orchid with her pale coloring and her glossy dark hair massed at her nape against the brilliant glow of the gown.

She looked directly at him as she stood between Lady Granville and Lady Rothbury. There was no mistaking the message in those velvet eyes. It was a penetrating demand for his attention. There was nothing sensual about the look, none of the luminous promise, the flickering embers of desire, the wicked mischief that her eyes so often revealed.

He gave an infinitesimal nod and turned back to his cards.

Olivia was satisfied. He would come to her.

She turned to Mistress Hammond with a demure inquiry about one of the tapestries on the walls of the great hall. Mistress Hammond launched instantly into an elaborate description that reduced her audience to glassy-eyed boredom but gave Olivia at least the opportunity to prepare her message to Anthony. She would have little time to pass it on. It would have to be succinct.

Anthony played his card, neatly destroying his game, and endured the angrily derisive complaints of his partner, who had lost five guineas on Caxton's poor play.

"So sorry...so sorry...of course, I yield my place." Anthony fluttered his hands in distress. "I fear my lord Daubney has had ill luck with his partners this evening. But I am such a poor cardplayer. Mr. Taunton, perhaps you can compensate for me?" He gestured to the gentleman who was standing at the king's elbow.

"Yes, yes, if you wish it," the man said eagerly. "I own I have long wished for the honor of playing with His Majesty."

Charles smiled faintly. Candlelight set the rings on his white hand sparkling as he indicated that this other esquire hungry for royal notice should take Anthony's seat.

Anthony bowed to his sovereign and melted into the throng. Olivia was still in the knot of people around Mistress Hammond. She was clearly restless, shifting from foot to foot, opening and closing her fan, but he noticed with a touch of bitterness that she had learned from their clandestine love enough of conspiracy to keep her eyes from wandering, seeking him out, now that she'd signaled her message.

"Lady Granville...Lady Rothbury. How delightful to see you here. I hardly dared hope that I would have the honor of meeting with you again." He simpered as he bowed to the two married women.

"The honor, Mr. Caxton, is all ours," Portia said with a distinctly ironic flash of her green eyes.

Anthony caught the flash, but he turned to greet Olivia. "Lady Olivia. I am so happy to see that your gown suffered no ill effects from my clumsiness."

"We were fortunate, Mr. Caxton." She curtsied, her eyes demurely lowered. "But if you would make recompense..."

"Anything, dear madam. Anything I can do to make you think well of me again." He raised her hand to his lips. As he did so, he caught the faintest glimmer of appreciative amusement on Lady Rothbury's countenance, another flash of those green eyes. He glanced at Lady Granville and she averted her gaze with that slight touch of hauteur he'd noticed before.

So Olivia had confided in her friends.

"My shawl," Olivia said. "I find myself a little chilly and I wonder if you would escort me to the carriage so that I may retrieve it."

"It will be my pleasure, Lady Olivia." His tone was noncommittal as he gave her his arm.

Olivia laid a hand on his arm and felt the muscles beneath the dark blue silk immediately harden beneath her fingers. Just touching him in this way brought a wave of heat flooding her skin, setting her head spinning. Her grip tightened, her fingers involuntarily biting into his arm, as he led her from the hall.

The courtyard was bustling with soldiers as the watch was changed on the battlements. "What is it?" Anthony demanded quietly. "I assume you're not seeking a lovers' tryst."

He sounded so cold, so hard.

"May we walk in the privy garden?" Olivia whispered. His bitterness was only to be expected—she had caused it—but it hurt most dreadfully. She wanted to scream at him that it was as hard for her as for him. Demand that he understand how she felt. But if ever there had been a moment for that kind of revelation, it had passed.

Anthony without comment directed their steps across the courtyard to the chapel and the garden beyond it.

There were a few couples taking the evening air in the walled garden, and no one looked curiously at the new arrivals.

"So, what is it you wish to say to me?" His voice was low but curt.

Olivia kept her eyes on the gravel path. "You have fallen under suspicion," she murmured. "I wanted to warn you. They are saying you're not what you seem."

She felt the muscle in his arm jump beneath her hand, but his step didn't falter. He glanced around once, quickly, as if assessing the situation, then said, "So you let something slip."

"*No!*" she exclaimed. "Of course I didn't. I said I wouldn't. I wouldn't break a promise."

"Hush," he commanded. "Don't draw attention to yourself. Tell me what you know."

In soft, rushed tones Olivia related the supper table conversation. "My father said it was just a whisper."

"And where did the whisper come from? If not from you, then from one of the friends in whom you confided my secrets?" His tone was harsh.

"No," Olivia repeated firmly, but her hurt was clear in her voice despite its strength. "I needed their help to get here tonight without causing comment. They knew of nothing until now...when it didn't matter anymore. You're already under suspicion. No one I know has betrayed you. My friends would not betray a friend of mine. Friends don't betray friends."

He glanced down at her. She met his gaze steadily, although he could read the pain in her eyes at his accusation.

"I came to warn you," she repeated.

Slowly he nodded. "In friendship?"

No, in love. Olivia hesitated, then she said, "If you like."

He gave a short laugh. "Well, I thank you for your friendship, my flower. I'm sure it's more than a dishonorable man deserves. Now I must go before they set the dogs on me. I will leave you at the hall. If I leave you here alone, it will draw attention." He strode with her across the courtyard, then moved his arm from beneath her hand.

He looked down into her pale face in bleak silence for a minute, then as if he couldn't help himself he slowly raised a hand and cupped the curve of her cheek before saying with quiet finality, "Goodbye, Olivia." He turned on his heel and strode towards the gatehouse.

Olivia stood in the light from the open doorway. She struggled to compose her expression. She could not go back inside, into that noisy oblivious throng, with tears clogging her throat, pricking behind her eyes. She felt as if she had lost all touch with herself, her knowledge of who and what she was. She would never see him again. He would be gone from the island before they caught him, and she would never see him again. It was what had to be and yet her heart wept in protest.

But go back into the hall she must. She must do nothing to draw attention to Anthony's abrupt departure. She took a step towards the light, then a familiar voice in the courtyard gave her pause.

"My lord?" It was Giles Crampton, hurrying across the courtyard from the gatehouse.

"Giles, what news?" Cato appeared out of the shadows of the barbican wall.

Olivia guessed he had been making his way to the hall. He had not seen her as yet. She trod soundlessly back down the stairs. There was a niche in the wall, untouched by the light of the pitch torches around the courtyard. She pressed herself into the tiny dark space and listened.

"We took the Yarrows, sir. I'll swear Caxton never lays his 'ead in that room of theirs. It 'as his things in it, but he's not been there in months, if ever."

"Are they talking?"

Olivia held her breath. She seemed now to inhabit some cold, clear space where her mind was lucid, emptied of all emotional turbulence. The Yarrows must be the people in Newport, where he was supposed to lodge.

"They're about to be disembarked at Yarmouth, sir. I'll go along an' welcome 'em. Just thought to let ye know where we're at."

"Good. Bring me any information as soon as you have it." Cato turned to mount the steps to the hall, then he paused, saying over his shoulder, "Don't do anything you don't have to do, Giles. No need for…for *heroic* measures." His tone was ironic.

"Goodman Yarrow'll tell all 'e knows an' the 'istory of the universe into the bargain afore ye can get close enough to say 'boo,' " Giles said scornfully.

"Then see that no one says more than 'boo,' Giles." Cato disappeared into the hall. He had little stomach for torture. There were occasions when it was necessary. It was a fact of ordinary life, let alone war. But a civilized man moderated its use.

Olivia waited until her father would be well into the hall, engulfed in the throng, before she slipped back up the steps.

Suddenly Portia was there beside her. "Take my arm," she whispered in Olivia's ear as she stood for a minute almost paralyzed in the light. "Just remember that we've been walking outside. You were feeling faint with the heat."

"Yes," Olivia said, taking the arm. "So I was."

Seventeen

TOMORROW NIGHT. *At eleven, at the change of the third watch.*

In the quiet of his prison chamber, the king touched the scrap of paper with the candle flame and watched it disintegrate. At last it was to happen.

He went to the barred window and examined the bars. The nitric acid he'd been given would burn through the two middle bars. He kept it on his person at all times. The governor conducted regular searches of his prisoner's chamber but had not yet had the effrontery to search the royal person. The rope that would take him over the wall was cleverly concealed within the bedropes that formed the frame of his bed.

He had become aware of increased security in the last several weeks, and this evening, when Hammond had escorted him to his chamber and bidden him good night, the king had sensed a new watchfulness. Did they know something? Or just suspect?

This would be his last chance, the king knew. One more failed attempt and they would move him from the relative comfort of his island prison to somewhere as secure as the Tower. The Scots were ready to cross the Border in his support. If only he could reach France, then the movement to return him to his throne would produce a groundswell that would topple Cromwell and his Parliament like sheaves of corn before the scythe.

What was Edward Caxton? This man on whom the future of a country's sovereignty rested. A mercenary. An actor. Not a pleasant man, at least not in the king's estimation. He found Caxton's twisted smile disconcerting, and the cool gray eyes seemed to see so much more than his mere surroundings. And the indolent, foppish manner concealed a power, a cynicism that chilled the king. He couldn't understand how other people didn't notice it, but then, they didn't know Caxton was to be the king's savior. They weren't looking for something beyond the surface the fawning courtier chose to present.

But was this cynical, cold side to the man the real Caxton? Sometimes the king had glimpsed something else. A flash of genuine humor, a merriness in the deep-set eyes, a lightness to his step. He was a warm and attractive man then.

Not that it mattered what kind of man he was. It mattered only that he should succeed. The king sat down beneath his barred window and listened to the wind of freedom, the shriek of the gulls circling the battlements. The clock in the chapel tower struck one.

In just twenty-two hours he would make his bid for freedom.

GOODMAN YARROW AND HIS WIFE stood in the base court of Yarmouth Castle. It was full dark and they'd been left there unattended for hours it seemed, ignored by the soldiers who hurried up and down the stone steps leading to the earthen gun platform above. They could hear the sea crashing against the walls, and Prue shivered in the dampness of this cold, gray, square fortification.

A soldier appeared from the gateway. He shouldered his pike as he marched across the courtyard, and his step slowed as he passed them. He spoke out of the corner of his mouth. "Keep a good 'eart." Then he continued his march to the gun platform.

"What's 'e say?" the goodman demanded, cupping his ear.

"Told us to keep a good 'eart," Prue whispered. "Reckon he's one of us. Fer the king, like."

The goodman clapped his arms around his chest. "Much good that does us."

" 'Tis a comfort," Prue said grimly. "You jest keep a still tongue in yer 'ead, man. Don't say nothin' at all. You may not think summat's important, but it could be. I fer one'll be silent as the grave."

There was a bustle at the gatehouse and Giles Crampton strode into the base court. "Sea's pickin' up. Reckon it's goin' to storm," he observed as he came over to them. " 'Ope it wasn't too rough for ye."

Goodman Yarrow spat his disgust at such an implication; Prue merely regarded Giles with disdain.

"Island folk, o' course," Giles said easily. "Well, why don't ye come inside in the warm." He gestured to the door to the master gunner's house. "There's a fire in the range." He swept them ahead of him into the house.

Prue looked around in disbelief. She'd expected a dungeon, not an ordinary domestic kitchen.

"Mary, 'ow about a cup of elderflower tea fer the goodwife," Giles called cheerfully to a plump woman tending a bread oven.

"Right y'are, Sergeant." In a minute she bustled over with a tin cup and set it on the table.

Prue drank gratefully, but the kindness did nothing to lull her suspicions, which came to full fruition when Giles said, "Ye'd prefer a pot of ale, goodman, I'll be bound," and led her eager husband into the pantry at the rear of the kitchen.

Her man would babble everything under the

influence of ale, she thought despairingly. The sergeant had read his prisoners correctly, and he knew where to put the pressure and what incentive to use.

"That was a right good drop o' tea, mistress. I thankee kindly," she said. "Ye want some 'elp wi' the bakin'?"

"Oh, aye, if'n ye've a mind," Mary said. "I'd count it a kindness. Can't 'ardly keep pace wi' the men's bellies these days."

In the scullery Giles chatted gently to Goodman Yarrow about the man Giles knew as Edward Caxton. Emboldened by the ale, relieved by the absence of threat, the goodman roamed far and wide over his limited knowledge of the man the islanders called the master. But he was slyly aware as he talked of how unimportant was the information he was providing.

"Master of what?" Giles refilled his tankard.

"A frigate," the goodman said proudly. "Pretty a ship as ye've seen."

"And where's her anchorage?"

The goodman shook his head mournfully. "That I don't know, sir. I'm tellin' ye the truth. There's few folk on the island what knows that."

"Tell me who might know." Giles regarded him steadily over the rim of his own tankard.

The goodman looked uncomfortable. " 'Tis 'ard to say, like. Those what 'elps the master only knows a few of t'others. An' Prue an' me, like, we don't know nothin' very much. The master, 'e jest comes and goes."

He could see that the sergeant was not very impressed, and hit upon a name. "There's George at the Anchor in Niton. 'E might know summat."

Godfrey Channing had already put them on to George. Giles had sent men to have a word with the landlord some time ago.

"So what does this *master* do wi' his frigate?"

The goodman buried his nose in his tankard. This he did know. And it was information that could condemn the master.

"Come on, man, out wi' it!" Giles leaned forward across the table and now there was menace in his eyes. "Go easy on yerself," he said softly.

Goodman Yarrow glanced around the pantry. It was an unthreatening place, but he could hear the slosh of the moat washing against the south wall under the rising wind. This was a fortress. A moat on two sides, the sea on the remaining two. He could die in its dungeons and no one know.

Goodman Yarrow was not a brave man.

"Smugglin', an' a bit o' piracy, I 'eard tell," he muttered.

"Piracy, eh?" Giles nodded. "An' what is it that he smuggles? Goods...or summat a little more interesting, maybe?" His eyes narrowed as he watched his prey wriggle like a worm on the end of a hook.

"I dunno. I dunno." There was desperation in the goodman's voice. He knew nothing, but there were rumors.

"For the king, is he?"

The goodman lowered his head. But it was enough for Giles. He had his confirmation. Caxton was a smuggler and a pirate. A mercenary with Royalist sympathies. A man who could blend into the king's court, but who also knew how to slip in and out of secret anchorages, to plot a course to France, to evade and outdistance pursuit. They had their man.

"This frigate, she 'ave a name?"

Goodman Yarrow shrugged helplessly. "*Wind Dancer,* I'm told, sir."

Giles nodded, observing, "Pretty name." So far he was doing well with Goodman Yarrow, but maybe there was still more he could get out of him, some little nugget of information, something that the goodman didn't even know was important.

"Y'are an island man. Where would you find deep channel anchorage fer a frigate?" He refilled their tankards once again.

The goodman seized his eagerly and took a deep draft before saying, "In a chine, o' course."

"Which side o' the island?"

Goodman Yarrow shrugged again. "Them's all down the coast from Yarmouth to Shanklin. Some deep, some not."

"Give me a name, man. Somewhere to start lookin'."

"Why you so interested in the master, anyways? There's smugglers aplenty along these coasts." The goodman, emboldened by ale, felt the first stirrings of rebellion.

Giles pushed back his stool with a scrape on

the flagstones. " 'Tis up to you," he said carelessly, rising to his feet. Then he bellowed with shocking suddenness, *"Men!"* The hurried tramp of booted feet resounded from the courtyard beyond the scullery door.

"Puckaster Cove," Yarrow blurted as the door burst open. "Somewheres around there, I've 'eard tell."

Giles sent the men away with a flick of his fingers. "Well, thankee, goodman." He strolled to the courtyard door that still stood open. "We'll 'ave to keep ye and the goodwife fer a spell, but ye'll not be too uncomfortable, I trust."

Soldiers came in soon after the sergeant's departure and escorted the Yarrows to a small barred chamber beneath the gun platform.

"Well?" Prue demanded. "What did ye tell 'em?"

" 'Twas man's talk, so keep a still tongue in yer 'ead, woman!" the goodman snarled.

So you told him what he wanted to hear. Prue took the thin blanket from the straw pallet and drew it around her shoulders. She sat on the cold stone floor, her back against the frigid damp wall.

"If'n ye betrayed the master, there's those on the island who'll not forget it."

"What was I supposed t' do? After gettin' the thumbscrews, 'e was," he muttered, flinging himself on the pallet.

"There's those on the island what wouldn't 'ave told whatever 'appened," Prue said softly.

GILES RODE BACK to Carisbrooke, but when he arrived it was late, the king had retired, and Lord Granville had returned to Chale with his wife and daughter. The men Giles had sent to question the landlord of the Anchor had little to report. George knew of no Edward Caxton. He referred familiarly to a man he called "our friend," and was coaxed into admitting that the same character was also known as the master. He could always be relied upon to supply contraband, and when he made contact he was always in fisherman's guise. Other than that, no one asked questions and no one volunteered information.

Giles rode to Chale and was informed that Lord Granville too had retired. If the sergeant had truly urgent information, they were to wake his lordship, otherwise the sergeant should report to him at dawn.

Giles debated whether his information warranted dragging his lord from his wife's bed. He could hear the wind getting up, great swirling eddies as it whipped off the sea and across the cliffs. No sane man would attempt to rescue the king on such a night.

He took himself to his own bed and lay visualizing the island's coastline. Puckaster Cove lay just below Niton. Niton was where George and the Anchor had their being. There had to be a connection.

OLIVIA LAY LISTENING to the wildness of the night. She could hear the waves breaking on the shore of Chale Bay some two miles distant. A fork of lightning illuminated her window, and the crash of thunder followed within seconds.

It was a wrecker's night.

But Anthony had other fish to fry at present. He had to leave the island, get himself to safety. Surely he wouldn't risk his freedom for the wealth of a wreck?

But she couldn't second-guess him. Despite everything they'd shared, she understood only that he was a mercenary, that he loved danger. She understood nothing about his real motives.

The branch of the magnolia tree whipped against the diamond windowpanes. Sleep was impossible. Olivia got up and went to the window. She pressed her forehead against the glass and stared out across the dark garden where the shapes of the trees swaying in the wind took on a strange and ethereal life.

What ships were out there on the black foam-tipped water? In her mind's eye, she could see the jagged black rocks of St. Catherine's Point, the sea turbulent around them even on a balmy day. What would they be like now?

And the compulsion to go and see grew until it could not be denied. It was madness to go out on such a night, to walk the cliff path. And yet she seemed to have no choice.

She still had the britches and jacket she'd borrowed from Portia, and almost without conscious intent Olivia dressed herself. She took her thickest cloak and crept downstairs.

The house was in darkness, the hall black as pitch as she crossed it on tiptoe. The dogs raised their heads and growled warningly as she slipped into the kitchen, but they recognized her and dropped their heads to their forepaws again with breathy sighs.

The back door from the scullery opened into the kitchen courtyard. As Olivia raised the latch the wind snatched the door from her hand and it crashed against the wall of the house. The dogs barked and she leaped through the door, slamming it behind her.

The wind howled, the trees swayed, the rain beat down. No one would have noticed the banging of the door amid nature's own racket.

Olivia let herself out through the small gate at the rear of the kitchen garden, skirted the orchard, and emerged into the lane some distance from the locked and bolted main gates.

The wind tore at her cloak and she was drenched within minutes. It was cold and her thin shirt was plastered to her skin, but she kept on up the lane until she reached the narrow path that led to the clifftop. And here on the exposed cliff she could barely keep her feet. She could hear the waves crashing against the cliffs below her, and the wind screamed in her ears. She battled against the wind, keeping her head down, barely noticing how far she had gone. Now there was something exhilarating about being out in this elemental force, pitting her puny strength against the battering of the storm.

In a momentary lull she raised her head and looked towards the point of cliff ahead of her. A lone figure stood outlined against the black sky. His black cloak swirled around him like Lucifer's wings. As she watched she saw a spark of flint on tinder, and then the bright flare of the beacon.

She began to run, gasping for each breath that was snatched from her on the wind. And then suddenly men came out of nowhere, shapes elongated in the beacon's light. The man at the beacon was engulfed as they surged on him. For a few seconds the beacon flared strongly into the night, and then it was doused.

A sheet of lightning lit up the sea, showing Olivia the boiling rocks, then thunder cracked and it was as if the heavens themselves had been split open.

Faintly from far below came shouts, the sound of steel on steel. Fighting.

She fell to the grass, inching forward on her belly until she could look down over the cliff edge.

Men were swaying in strange embraces; some were lying still on the ground. It was dark as pitch now under the relentless rain, and she couldn't distinguish a familiar figure anywhere in the melee. But they had to be

Anthony's men. Who were they fighting? Had they been caught by the watch? Was Anthony even now on his way to the dungeons of Yarmouth Castle, and the gibbet? She needed to know, to see for herself what was happening.

She could just make out a snaky path that seemed to drop sheer to the beach below. Behind her a curious silence seemed to have fallen. She stood up carefully, glancing over her shoulder. The men at the doused beacon were standing in a circle, their backs to her. She scrambled over the edge of the cliff and onto the path. It was steep and she slipped and slithered on the wet sand, but she managed to keep her feet. Now she could hear the waves on the rocks ever more clearly and the sounds of the fighting on the beach, barely audible over the noise of the storm.

She reached the beach and stood with her back to the cliff. As she watched the battle she recognized some of the men from her days on *Wind Dancer*. A curious cold detachment came over her. There were a few shapes lying still on the sand, but she couldn't seem to see them as human bodies. It was as if she were divorced from reality. When men began to run past her towards the path she'd just descended, fleeing muskets fired in the air behind them, she made no attempt to conceal herself. They ran shouting and screaming into the wind, leaving the pirate's men in possession of the beach. Of Anthony there was no sign.

Vaguely she realized she was shivering, her

teeth chattering, yet she didn't really feel cold. She felt nothing. She gazed out at the black water. There were two boats, just this side of the rocks, and their oarsmen seemed to be racing against each other. Then there was a crash as they met and a confused crescendo of shouts. Men rose, flourishing oars as weapons while the sea boiled around them, then as she watched one of the boats seemed to topple sideways. Its crew just slid into the sea, vanishing below the white-topped surf.

And then she heard the loud melancholy sound of the bell buoy carried on the wind. And the victorious rowboat struggled back to the beach.

The man who jumped ashore first was Anthony.

Olivia gazed at the tall, slender figure; his hair, torn from its ribbon, whipped in the wind around his face; his shirt and britches were plastered to his body. He was barefoot.

And he was the most beautiful sight.

She came to herself as if waking from a deep sleep. She ran across the beach towards him, calling his name.

Anthony spun around. He stared in disbelief as she hurtled against him, her arms flying around his neck, her soaked body pressed to his. *"Olivia?"* He spoke her name as if it were a question, even as he held her against him. "Olivia? What are you doing here?"

He held her against him, his bare feet braced in the sand, his hands splayed across her back as he looked down into her face. His sodden hair clung to his cheek and forehead, and his eyes glittered with the lingering ferocity of the battle he had just fought.

The wonderful sound of the bell clanged its warning across the waves. "I love you," Olivia said. "I came to tell you I love you."

"Dear God!" He continued to look at her in utter disbelief. Would he ever understand this mercurial woman? "Why now? Why here?"

"I'm so happy. I c-can't tell you how happy I am." Olivia smiled up at him, her eyes radiant through the sheeting rain.

Anthony shook his hair away from his face. "This is all very sudden, my flower, gratifying I grant you, but very sudden. I am totally confused as to—"

He broke off as Mike and Jethro came down the path from the clifftop, driving in front of them the man Olivia had seen light the beacon.

It was Godfrey Channing, and Mike held a pistol against his back.

Anthony glanced down once at Olivia. "You shall explain later," he said. He stepped away from her and took a small dagger from the sheath at his hip. He walked over to where Channing stood on the sand.

"Well, well, if it isn't Lord Channing at his merry work again," Anthony said.

Godfrey stared at him, hatred in his eyes. He saw Olivia as she approached across the sand, and with a vile oath he lunged at Anthony, a knife in his hand.

Anthony's dagger slashed across Godfrey's wrist, and the knife fell to the sand. "You might have disarmed him, Mike," the pirate murmured, kicking the knife away.

Abashed, Mike apologized. "I thought I had, master."

"I expect he had it up his sleeve," Anthony observed.

Godfrey held his bleeding wrist and a stream of obscenities poured from his lips.

"Olivia, you'd better block your ears," Anthony said over his shoulder. "Our friend has no respect for a lady's finer sensibilities."

"*Whore!*" Godfrey spat at Olivia as she drew closer. "Trollop!"

Anthony hit him in the mouth with his closed fist. "You will speak only when spoken to, my friend," he said almost pleasantly.

"He was at the beacon," Olivia said in bewilderment. "He lit the beacon."

"Precisely so."

"He's a wrecker?"

"Precisely so." Anthony smiled and it was a most unpleasant smile. "Olivia, why don't you make yourself useful, since you're here."

"Doing what?" Olivia couldn't tear her fascinated, horrified gaze from Channing. He had no power to frighten her now, but he horrified her. His eyes were as cold and hateful as ever, even though she could tell that he was himself frightened. He reminded her of a cornered snake, scared but dangerous.

"Help my men tidy up the beach. There are some wounded; they need to be disarmed. You are, as I recall, rather adept at disarming villains." A very different smile flickered across his mouth, and his eyes were suddenly warm as they rested on her face.

"What are you going to do?"

"Have a little talk with Lord Channing. There's something he needs to tell me. I would prefer you were not here. Besides, a little work will warm you up."

Olivia hesitated. Anthony said quietly, "Go, Olivia."

"I want to know what he knows about Brian," she said, standing her ground.

"So do I."

She looked once again at Godfrey, demanding with soft ferocity, "Is Brian here, on the island?"

Godfrey made no answer. He spat blood onto the sand.

"Olivia, would you go, please? I want to get this over with."

"No, I want to stay," she said. "I want to hear what he has to say. I need to hear it."

"Very well," Anthony said shortly. He turned back to Godfrey and his eyes were pure agate. He wiped his dagger on his britches and said softly, "So, where will I find Brian Morse?"

Godfrey stared back at him in silence. Anthony nodded to Mike, who seized Godfrey's wrists, dragging them behind his back. Jethro roped them together. Anthony placed the tip of his knife against Godfrey's ear. "I wonder whether simply slitting your ears would be sufficient penalty for a wrecker. Maybe I should just remove both of them, and then slit your nose? Mark you indelibly as a felon." He drew the tip of the dagger behind Godfrey's ear, leaving a thin red line.

Godfrey was sweating and Olivia realized that Anthony had known her better than she'd known herself. Much as she loathed Channing, she couldn't watch this. She turned and ran off down the beach towards the men dealing with the wounded. A scream shivered through the rain behind her.

It seemed a very long time before Anthony walked back along the beach. Olivia was on her knees beside one of the wounded men. She didn't look up as Anthony stood beside her. She noticed how long his bare sandy feet were, the big toes slightly knobbly, and she wondered why she'd never noticed them before. "Did he tell you?"

"Yes."

"Is Brian on the island?"

"Yes."

Olivia looked up at him then. "Where?" she whispered. Her eyes were suddenly haunted, her earlier elation vanquished by the thought of Brian's proximity.

"In Ventnor, apparently."

"He came back to hurt me...or my father," she said with conviction. "He must have some plan, some—"

"It seemed he had the idea that you would make the perfect wife for Channing. The perfect *rich* wife. His idea, if I understood our friend aright, was that he would share in the financial windfall." He shook his head in mock amazement. "The ideas people come up with."

"It would be more than that," Olivia said. "Not just the money. He'd want to hurt us in some other way."

"And what better than seeing you married to a man like Godfrey Channing? I doubt the Granville pride could stand the truth."

"Vile man. You hurt him, didn't you?"

"As much as was necessary," Anthony responded calmly. "And he is now walking to Yarmouth, tied to Mike's stirrup, where he will take ship to the Sublime Porte. I think he might find it quite difficult to find his way home from there."

"The Turks will probably sell him into slavery," Olivia said in awe. "Isn't that what they do with foreigners?"

"Quite possibly. It seems a well-deserved fate. I was thinking he and Mr. Morse might care to make the journey together."

"But...but how could that happen?"

"With a little ingenuity, my flower." He laughed at her astounded expression. This was the Anthony she had first known. A man with rakehell amusement in his eyes, a merry quirk to his mouth; a man exhilarated by whatever life had to offer, certain of his utter competence to deal with whatever twist and turn fate presented him. This was the Anthony from the early dream days of entrancement, and her spirit rose to join his as it had done then.

He pushed her soaked hair from her face and

said, "I shall need your help to enhance my ingenuity."

"How?"

"Nothing too difficult. I'll explain all in good time."

He bent over the wounded man, examined the wound in his shoulder. "You'll live long enough for the hangman," he said dismissively. "You and the rest of your murdering friends."

He stood up, took Olivia's hand, and pulled her to her feet. "Adam?"

"Aye?" Adam came over to them.

"What's the damage?"

"Tim 'as a scratch, 'an it looks as if Colin's broke a finger."

"That's it?"

Adam nodded. "Sam's gone fer the watch. They'll pick up this lot."

"Good, then let's get dry. Tell the men to find berths in the village. We'll not get back to *Wind Dancer* in this."

Adam glanced at Olivia. "Like a bad penny, you are," he said. "What in 'ell's teeth are you doin' out 'ere?"

"It certainly is a puzzle," Anthony said. "A distinctly puzzling volte-face. But I'm about to find the answer." His fingers closed tightly over her hand that he still held.

He said almost as an afterthought, "Adam, I want three men in Ventnor, in the taproom of the Gull at dawn."

"More mischief, I suppose," Adam grumbled.

"Of the most necessary kind," Anthony said with an edge to his voice, an edge that Adam knew boded ill for someone.

"Come, Olivia," Anthony said quietly.

Olivia found herself half running to keep up with his lengthy stride. "Where are we going?"

"Somewhere where we can dry out and you can tell me what brought you out here in the middle of a gale."

Olivia's spirits sank abruptly. She knew she would have to tell him the truth, and she dreaded having to make such a confession. Would he understand how she had come to make such a mistake? Would he understand how much of it was his fault? He had told her nothing about himself, nothing about why he did what he did. Nothing about his family, except for the embroidering aunt. A man who believed in nothing, followed no rules, had no scruples. She had had ample excuse for her mistake. But would Anthony see it that way?

Eighteen

ANTHONY STRODE up the snaky path to the clifftop. He held Olivia's hand tightly. When she stubbed her toe on a rock and stumbled, he caught her up against him. "You're so cold and wet," he said in almost chiding tones, trying for a minute to warm her shivering body against his own icy wetness. "What madness could have brought you out on such a night?"

"I knew...I just knew there was going to be a wreck. I thought maybe I could stop it. It was c-crazy, I know, but I couldn't seem to help myself." It was the best she could do for the moment.

"It took twenty men to stop it," Anthony pointed out. "And why would Lord Granville's daughter have any interest in wrecking? It's a vile and vicious thing. Not to mention dangerous. If we hadn't been there, or if the battle had gone the other way, and you'd been spotted by the wreckers, they would have killed you as soon as look at you. Surely you understood that?"

Olivia made no answer. Her teeth chattered.

Anthony shook his head and began to walk fast again. They were striding along the under-cliff path, and the wind and rain were less fierce under the overhang. He stopped suddenly and Olivia almost ran into him.

"Where are we?"

"A safe place," he said. He pushed his rain-darkened hair out of his eyes. "It's not the most comfortable spot, but at least it's quiet and dry."

He turned aside from the path and seemed to walk into the cliff, Olivia's hand firmly in his. And they were in a dark place, suddenly silent, as the storm raged outside. It was cold and Olivia's teeth were chattering like castanets. The hood of her cloak had long since blown off, and water dripped from her hair down her neck.

"This way." He drew her with him across a floor where the sand scrunched beneath her boots. Her eyes grew slowly accustomed to the darkness, and she could see that they were in a large cave. Then they were in a passage, narrow and dark, and she clung to his hand, the flat dry warmth of his palm comforting her. The passage opened out into a smaller space than the first.

Anthony dropped her hand and she stood still in a darkness that was more profound than it had been before. She heard him moving around, then flint scraped on tinder and light glowed from a lantern.

Olivia looked around in amazement at the rudimentary furnishings of this inner cave.

Anthony pulled blankets off a straw palliasse. "Get your clothes off while I light the fire." Urgency made his tone brusque. He tossed a blanket across to her, then busied himself at a round stone hearth in the center of the cave.

"Won't we be smoked out?" Olivia shrugged out of her cloak and doublet and stood shivering.

"There's a natural flue in the roof." He looked up from the hearth. "Hurry up, Olivia! Get out of those clothes. Don't just stand there!"

His gaze rested on her breasts, pink and round beneath the sodden white chemise. Her nipples were hard dark points against the pink.

"Dear God," he said softly. "What is it that you do to me?"

"What you do to me," she responded as softly.

The comforting crackle of catching wood filled the cave. He straightened. His gaze held hers and this time her shiver was not due to cold and wet. "Take your clothes off, Olivia!"

He watched her through narrowed eyes as she flung aside her wet clothes. Naked she drew close to the fire. On some distant plane she realized that she was warm again. She could feel the fire against her side. She looked up at him and saw her own face in the dark irises.

He put his hands on her shoulders, cupping the curve where they met her upper arms. He ran his hands down her arms and the fine hairs prickled. He took her hands, turned them palm up. They were filthy, encrusted with sand and dirt. He held each hand in turn and lightly smacked the grime from each palm.

There was an edge to his caresses. An edge that Olivia sensed had to do with the battle he'd fought with the wreckers. A lingering residue of the savage intensity that had defeated the enemy. Something in herself responded. She tugged her hands free and undid the buttons on his shirt with rough haste, heedless when one flew off into the far corner of the cave. She unfastened his belt buckle, slowly, making of each movement a deliberate act. She slithered the belt through its loops and unfastened the buttons of his britches.

Her nails raked his flanks as she pushed his britches over his hips. She heard his quick indrawn breath. Then he kicked his feet free of the britches and caught her face between his hands.

His mouth was hard, relentless, offering no quarter. And Olivia asked for none. She pushed her hands up inside his opened shirt, over his ribs, up to his shoulders. She thrust the garment from him until he stood as naked as she.

His hands went to her bottom, pulling her hard against him. She caught his lower lip between her teeth, drove her tongue within his mouth on her own exploration. She would not be dominated by his urgency; her own met and matched his in a competition that escalated with each breath. Her hands were everywhere, following their own instincts. She gripped his buttocks, sliding a finger into the deep, narrow cleft between them. She ran her flat palm over his belly, dipped a finger into his navel, slid down to clasp his penis, moved back between his thighs to cup the hot swelling globes. She was on tiptoe now, pressing herself against him, giving herself to his hungry hands, feeling the heat of her own arousal, the flowing juices, the absolute desperation of their shared need.

They slid to the floor beside the fire. Olivia was unaware of the hard sand-covered rock beneath her. Her hips rose to meet his penetration and he gathered her up, lifting her off the hard floor, holding her, his hands flattened on her back, protecting her, as they rose and fell together in a silence that sang with all the sweetness of a cathedral choir.

And when it was over, when he held her tightly against him, rocking her in the aftershocks of passion, she pressed her lips to the fast-beating pulse at the base of his throat and thought that if she never experienced such joy again, she would die content.

But when the world reasserted itself, she understood the stupidity and the futility of such a belief.

As the glow of lovemaking faded she moved from his embrace, and he let her go without protest, reaching for the blanket that lay discarded on the sandy floor. He put it around her shoulders, then rose to throw more wood on the fire.

Olivia drew the blanket tight around her as she stood up too. She was tense now as she watched him dress again. She couldn't help the unworthy hope that their lovemaking had driven all questions about her presence on the beach from his mind...that she would be spared her confession.

"So you thought to stop a wreck single-handed, my flower?" He raised his eyebrows, his gray eyes suddenly uncomfortably penetrating.

She clutched the blanket at her throat with one hand and stepped closer to the fire, the sand soft as silk beneath her feet.

"I have to confess something," she said, keeping her head lowered, her eyes on the fire.

Anthony was suddenly very still. She could feel his stillness, hear the soft in and out of his breath. "Go on," he said.

"I think it was probably unforgivable," she said. "I know you're going to be very angry and you have every right. But I hope you'll understand why it happened."

"You're alarming me." He clasped the back of her bent neck, his hand warm and somehow reassuring. It gave her the courage to speak.

"I thought it was you," she said.

"I don't understand you."

"The wreckers," she said simply. "I thought...and then I think I thought that maybe I could persuade you to stop."

Her words hung in the cave's dank and stuffy air. For an eternity there was no sound but the crackle of the fire. Slowly Anthony's hand dropped from her neck. It left a cold place where before it had been warm.

When at last he spoke it was in a tone of utter disbelief. "You thought *I* was one of those filthy vermin? You thought *I* could do such a thing?"

Olivia turned to face him. She forced herself to meet his eyes, where incredulity mingled with a deep anger. "You said...you said in Portsmouth when you gave me the c-clothes that they'd c-come from a wreck." She tried to control the stammer but her agitation was out of hand.

"I didn't say I had caused the wreck." Anthony's voice was now very cold and soft, and it was impossible to imagine the way they had loved a few short minutes ago.

"I thought you did. It's what I *heard* you say. You sounded so c-casual, as if it was quite natural.... You're a smuggler, a pirate. Everyone knows that smugglers are often wreckers. You were on the island the night of the last wreck, and the goods from the wreck were in *Wind Dancer*'s hold."

She extended one hand in a gesture of appeal. "What was I supposed to think? I didn't know anything really about you. I still don't," she added. "I don't know why you are as you are...why you do what you do."

There was a challenge in her voice now, but Anthony didn't answer it. He stood with his hands on his hips, feet braced on the sandy floor. His icy regard never left her countenance.

After a second, Olivia continued in the face of his silence, "We'd been living a dream, an idyll on the beach and on the ship. It wasn't real. And then I saw everything with new eyes, as if the dream was shattered and I was seeing the real world again. And in the real world, piracy, smuggling, and wrecking go hand in hand. I'd seen you c-capture the *Doña Elena*. I saw you steal her c-cargo. I heard you tell me the c-clothes c-came from a wreck!"

And at last he spoke. "I don't understand how, when we had loved together in the way that we did, that you could imagine I could do anything that vile," he declared with soft savagery. "Was that why you threw dishonor in my face?"

She nodded dismally. "Only for that."

"Not piracy, nor smuggling, nor the fact that I am an enemy of your most honorable father? Not the fact that I will do everything I can to outwit him, regardless of honor?" he asked with bitter irony.

Olivia winced. "No, none of those things."

"Isn't that somewhat illogical?"

"What we have together has never been logical," she answered with desperate truth.

"But believing that I was a wrecker destroyed what you felt for me...what we had together?"

"No." She shook her head. "But it made it impossible for me to lose myself in the dream anymore."

Anthony bent and threw more sticks on the fire. The flames threw his shadow huge against the wall of the cave. "Trust," he said with the same bitter irony. "You said you loved me, Olivia, out there on the beach. There can be no love without trust. Lust, certainly. But not love. It seems to me, Olivia, that you are confusing love with lust."

"I do trust you," she said in a low voice.

He straightened. "You haven't trusted me, Olivia, since the day we met. How long did it take you to tell me about Brian Morse? Would you ever have told me if you'd continued to believe him dead?"

"I c-couldn't tell anyone that," she said painfully, searching for the words that would convince him, would banish the cold angry hurt from his eyes and voice. "I felt it was my fault, you see. When I was little I thought that perhaps, perhaps I had made him do it."

Anthony looked at her in dawning horror. He saw reflected in her dark eyes the child she had been, violated, terrified, guilt-ridden, driven into a silence as deep as the grave. "Oh, no!" he exclaimed softly. He reached for her, holding her tightly, stroking her wet hair, his bitterness falling from him. In the face of what Olivia had suffered, her mistake, hurtful though it was, became irrelevant.

"I know now it was stupid of me to believe such a thing of you. But I started to feel that men were never what they seemed and I had allowed myself to be blinded by…by passion, by desire…. And I had brought this whole wretchedness upon myself. If I could have asked you…but I couldn't bring myself to talk of it. Just as I couldn't talk about Brian."

She looked up at him, her cheek resting on his chest. "I am so sorry. Can you ever forgive me?"

He gazed down at her, a rueful expression in his eyes. "It's true that I am not always what I seem," he said. "And it's true that you know very little about me."

"But I should have known what you couldn't do, couldn't be," she said insistently, perversely feeling that by accepting her excuse so readily, Anthony had failed to realize the magnitude of her error.

"I would like to think that you should have known," he agreed with a faint smile. "But perhaps I didn't make it easy for you."

"You can't blame yourself!" Olivia exclaimed. "Of course I should have known."

"Well, let us agree that of course you should have known. That you did me a grave injustice, but there were extenuating circumstances," he said solemnly. "Now, must you expiate your crime further or can we put it to rest now?"

"You really do forgive me?" She searched his face.

"Yes," he said. He was remembering her radiance as she'd run to him across the beach. Her bubbling declaration of love. "Do you love me, Olivia?"

"Yes," she said simply. "And I think you love me."

"Yes," he agreed, rubbing his knuckles along the line of her jaw. "And I don't know what the devil we're going to do about it, my flower."

"There's nothing much we can do really. Things being as they are. You being who you are, me being who I am."

He cupped the curve of her cheek in the way he had and said only, "Get dressed now. We must go."

Olivia wanted to cling to this moment. Once they left the cave, went out into the cold night, it would be finished. The dream finally broken. "Couldn't we stay here by the fire just a little longer?"

Regretfully, Anthony shook his head. "It will soon be dawn and we have work to do."

"Yes." Olivia relinquished the dream. She

scrambled into her clothes. They were still very damp and felt wretched against her warmed skin. Her chilled fingers had difficulty with the buttons of her chemise, and Anthony moved her fingers aside to button it himself. His palm lightly cupped each breast.

Fleetingly she put her hands over his. "I meant to tell you. After you'd left last night, Giles was talking to my father about some people called the Yarrows. He said they were being taken to Yarmouth Castle."

His face in the faint light of the dying fire paled beneath the sun's bronzing. "Bastards!" he said softly, his hands falling from her breasts.

"Giles said he thought the goodman would tell everything he knew without much persuasion," she said, her eyes anxious. There was no softness in the cave now. Only harsh reality.

"Aye, I'm sure he has that much sense," Anthony said grimly. "Not that he knows very much."

She said hesitantly, "My father told Giles not to hurt them."

Anthony regarded her with a frown in his eyes. "Am I supposed to believe that?"

"Why would I lie?" she asked quietly. "I love you, remember."

"You might wish to put your father in a good light," he suggested, watching her closely.

"I don't need to do that," she stated. "I don't need to defend him to *anyone*." She added softly, "Any more than I need to defend *you*."

Some of the grimness left his expression, and

a tiny smile warmed his gaze. "I'm probably a little harder to defend. Poor Olivia, divided loyalties are the very devil."

Olivia said nothing.

He reached out and tipped her chin. He kissed the corner of her mouth, repeating softly, "Poor Olivia."

"I'm not 'poor Olivia,' " she said with a touch of indignation. "What are you going to do about the Yarrows?"

"Get them out of there," he responded. Suddenly he laughed; his teeth flashed in a crooked grin and the reckless gleam was once more in his eyes. "I foresee a very busy day."

Olivia regarded him warily. She knew of old that this exuberant amusement accompanied his most dangerous exploits.

He turned and stamped out the embers of the fire, then blew out the lantern. The darkness was complete. Olivia stood still as stone.

"Give me your hand." His own closed firmly over hers. "Follow me."

She stuck closer than his shadow, if he could have had one in the darkness, back down the narrow passage and into the outer cave. The sound of the wind and the waves was much diminished now as they stepped out onto the narrow path. The rain had stopped and there was only the melancholy steady dripping from the bushes and scrawny trees clinging to the cliffside.

Olivia shivered in her damp clothes. "God, it's cold."

"Run, it'll warm you up." Holding her

hand, he began to run with her along the undercliff away from St. Catherine's Point.

"Where are we going?"

"To Ventnor. We have a rendezvous at dawn, if you recall. We'll borrow a horse at Gowan's farm, just around the next corner."

"Brian," Olivia said, her voice curiously flat.

"Exactly so." His fingers tightened over hers as he turned to climb up another path to the top of the cliff. "Ah, good. Gowan's left his ponies in the field. Now, which one do you think would be strong enough for the two of us?" Whistling between his teeth, he surveyed the three horses standing sheltering under a giant oak in the middle of the field. "The chestnut, I think. He has a nice broad back."

He sounded as carefree as if they were embarking on a midsummer picnic instead of standing in wet clothes in a sodden field at daybreak after a sleepless night.

"Why do you need me?" Olivia asked suddenly.

"Because, my flower, I need to do this as expeditiously and as quietly as possible. I need bait for the trap, and you are going to be that bait." Still whistling, Anthony set off towards the horses.

"I don't want to see him," Olivia said when he came back leading the chestnut.

Anthony looked at her for a minute, and his expression was no longer carefree or amused. "I want you to know once and for all that it's over. That he's gone and won't ever trouble you again. If you see him go, you'll know for sure."

Olivia crossed her arms over her breast in a convulsive hug. "I don't know if I'm brave enough, Anthony."

He put his hands on her shoulders and gave her a slight reassuring shake. He smiled down at her. "Yes, you are. You're a pirate; you jumped over a boarding net to disarm a galleon full of Spanish soldiers without turning a hair. This is nothing. You'll go up and knock on his door. Call out to him so that he'll come to the door. We'll be right behind you. When he unlocks the door, we'll barge in. We get him out of the inn with no one being any the wiser, and on the noon tide he and his friend Channing will be on their way to another life."

"You make it sound so easy."

"It is. Trust me."

"I do," she said. "But I'm still frightened of him."

She had thought she'd overcome her fear of Brian after Portia had shown her how to make a fool of him all those years ago in Castle Granville. Portia had drawn the monster's teeth, and when Olivia had seen him again in Oxford, she'd been able to deal with her revulsion. But she hadn't then remembered why it was that she loathed him, why she was so frightened of him. Now that she had remembered, it was as if she was back in that hideous time, dreading the sound of his voice, his step, expecting them every waking minute.

"Trust me, Olivia."

Olivia gave a little shrug of surrender.

Anthony lifted her easily onto the back of the chestnut and swung up behind her. He circled her waist with one arm and twisted his fingers securely into the animal's mane. "Hold tight, we're a little later than I intended."

Olivia clung to the mane as the horse galloped flat out across the field, along the clifftop, over St. Boniface Down.

Just above the little village of Ventnor atop Horseshoe Bay, Anthony eased the chestnut to a halt. He dismounted and lifted Olivia down.

"Won't the farmer wonder what happened to his horse?"

"No, he'll know I have him. I left him a sign." Anthony led the pony into a field where a herd of cows lying on the wet grass raised their heads and gazed with bovine lack of interest at the new arrival. Anthony sent the horse off to pasture with a slap on the flank.

"A sign? What kind of sign?" Olivia couldn't help being intrigued despite her anxiety.

Anthony laughed. "Crossed sticks, if you must know. Sometimes it's necessary for me to make free with an islander's possessions or hospitality. If they know it's me, they don't fret."

"Do you think of yourself as an islander?" She followed him back to the path, the wet grass swishing around her ankles.

"No. You have to be born and bred for that. I was born many miles from here."

"Where?"

He glanced over his shoulder at her. "Bohemia."

"*Bohemia!*"

"Strange birthplace, don't you think?"

And now Olivia could detect a tension in his voice, a threshold that she was fast approaching. She pressed nevertheless. "You grew up there?"

"No. I grew up just across the Solent," he replied in a dismissive tone. "The Gull's on the main village street. My men should be in the taproom already." He was walking a little ahead of her, and Olivia knew she'd gone as far as she could with her questions. And, indeed, as she drew close to Brian, she could concentrate only on mastering her anxiety.

The village street was deserted. The fishermen would be checking their crab pots in the bay, but the rest of the world was barely awake. The front door of the Gull stood open, however.

"Stay here, it's best if you're not seen for the moment. You don't look too much like one of my crew." Anthony clasped the dark cascade of Olivia's hair at the nape of her neck in explanation.

"If I did, I would hardly be bait for Brian," Olivia observed, tossing her head.

Anthony threw her a grin over his shoulder as he went into the inn, and it was all the response she needed.

She stood back on the street and looked up at the shuttered windows of the inn. Behind one of those slept Brian Morse. He had tried to kill her father. Phoebe had been there in Rotterdam, when Brian had ambushed Cato. Phoebe had probably saved her husband's life. Cato had believed that he had killed Brian in the duel, but he had refused to make certain. Cold-blooded killing was not his way. And Brian Morse had come back to life. Back to torment his stepsister as he'd tormented her in childhood.

Not anymore, Olivia resolved, digging her hands deep into her britches' pockets. *Not anymore.*

THREE OF *Wind Dancer's* crew sat with Adam on stools at the bar counter. Anthony nodded to them and they nodded back. A wizened old man filled ale tankards, muttering under his breath.

"So, old friend, did we drag you from your bed betimes?" Anthony said cheerfully, tossing a handful of coins onto the counter.

The man's face cracked into the semblance of a smile as he scooped the coins into his palm. "Aye, master, but it wouldn't be the first time."

"And it won't be the last, I daresay." Anthony hitched himself onto a stool. "You've a guest, I hear."

"Aye." The man's expression soured. " 'E's a regular tightfist."

"He lodge above?" Anthony gestured with his head to the stairs.

"Best chamber in the 'ouse. At the 'ead of the stairs," the man said. "Up an' down them stairs I goes, at 'is beck an' call. An' never a sign o' thanks."

Anthony tutted sympathetically. "Fetch me a pint of porter, Bert."

The man pulled the pint and set it on the counter.

"And if you could see your way to getting a bite of breakfast for my friends and me, we'd be more than grateful."

"Been busy this night, then?" The man looked curious.

"Aye, we been stoppin' a wreck," Adam responded. "An' mighty sharp set we be."

"Damned wreckers!" Bert spat into the sawdust behind him. "There's some blood puddin' an' a few suet dumplin's from last night."

"If ye can heat 'em, we can eat 'em," Adam said definitely.

Bert shuffled off to the kitchen.

"So now what?" Adam demanded of Anthony.

"Olivia is going to get our man to unlock his chamber door. As soon as he does so, we grab him. Derek, we'll use your cloak to swaddle him. There's rope behind the counter there, around the beer barrel. We'll use that to bind him. Once he's bound and gagged, you get him out of the village. Then I have something to send him to sleep." Anthony patted his pocket.

"So who is this bloke?" Adam inquired.

Anthony's face was suddenly bleak. "I may tell you one day."

"An' mebbe I don't want to know," Adam muttered. "So best get on wi' it." He gestured significantly towards the kitchen, where Bert could be heard banging pots.

Anthony nodded and went out to Olivia. "He's in the chamber at the top of the stairs. Run up and knock on the door. Call out to him, so he knows it's you. We'll be right behind you."

Olivia glanced up again at the shuttered windows, a considering frown drawing her thick black brows together. "D'you know which window is his?"

"I think the one in the center, from what I know of the inn."

"Then I have a better idea," she said firmly. "I'll throw stones at the shutters until he wakes up. He's bound to come to the window to see what's going on. When he sees me, I'll beckon him and he'll come downstairs. He's bound to."

"If you think that's a better plan," Anthony said.

"I do. It keeps me out here for a start." Olivia bent to pick up a large round stone. She hurled it at Brian's shuttered window with such force that the wood splintered.

Anthony raised an eyebrow and strode back into the inn. "Ready, gentlemen?"

Soft-footed they mounted the stairs and pressed themselves against the wall on either side of Brian Morse's door.

Outside, Olivia hurled stones merrily at the shutters. Her aim was amazingly true, she discovered. It took four crashes before the shutters were flung open and Brian Morse stood there in his nightshirt. The man she saw bore little resemblance to the Brian she remembered. This man had white hair and a face creased with suffering. But his eyes were the same, his mouth was the same, and the power of his malevolence jumped out at her.

"What in hell's teeth is going on down there?" he demanded angrily. "You wretched urchin! What do you think you're doing?"

"Trying to wake you up, Brian," Olivia called sweetly, softly. "I have a message for you from Lord Channing."

Brian stared at her, recognition slowly dawning. *"Olivia!"*

"The very same." She dropped him a mock curtsy made ludicrous by her britches. To her astonishment she was enjoying herself. It was just the way she had felt when she'd put powdered senna in his ale and condemned him to hours of purging on the close-stool.

"Come up here!" he commanded.

Olivia shook her head and laughed at him. "I'm not such a fool, Brian. I'll see you in the open street. I have a most urgent message from Lord Channing."

Brian retreated from the window, and Olivia went into the dim cool of the inn's hallway. She stood listening, her heart thumping. He would come down. He wouldn't be able to resist.

Everything happened very quickly. She heard a muffled cry, then footsteps on the stairs. Heavy footsteps. Three men went past her, carrying a wrapped shape. They disappeared into the street.

Anthony and Adam came slowly down the stairs.

"All right?" Anthony touched her cheek.

"Yes."

"You want breakfast or not?" a plaintive voice called from the taproom.

"Yes, but we're only three now, I'm afraid," Anthony responded cheerfully. He put an arm around Olivia's shoulders and urged her ahead of him into the taproom.

Bert looked at the tumbled black hair, the female figure outlined in the tight-fitting britches and jerkin, and thumped three laden plates on the counter without a word.

Nineteen

ON THE BATTLEMENTS of Carisbrooke Castle, Colonel Hammond stood and watched the dawn. Behind him two sentries marched their route, back and forth with monotonous rhythm.

"You're up and about early, Hammond."

The governor turned at the pleasant tone. "As are you, Lord Granville."

Cato nodded and came to stand beside him.

"There was quite a fracas out at St. Catherine's Point last night," the governor observed. "Those damnable wreckers were about their business but someone stopped them. We got a message from someone not willing to give his name to go and pick up the pieces. We found the beacon and a neat parcel of wounded men waiting for us on the beach."

"I wonder if Caxton had a hand in it," Cato mused. "I've just had my sergeant's report on the couple he took into Yarmouth Castle last night. There seems little doubt that Caxton *is* our man. Turns out he's both a pirate and a smuggler...has a frigate which he keeps in some secret chine. He knows this coast and the French like the back of his hand."

"Then we had best pick him up," Hammond said. He looked around in some annoyance. "I sent for Channing half an hour ago. It's not like him to delay answering a summons."

"Perhaps he's a heavy sleeper," Cato suggested. "We do face a small problem in picking up Caxton."

"Oh?"

"We don't know where to find him," Cato pointed out gently.

The governor only grunted at this reminder.

"Yarrow mentioned a cove, Puckaster Cove, that he thinks might have some relevance to Caxton's ship. Rothbury's gone with some men to take a look. They'll throw a net over the area and see if they catch anything."

"If he doesn't know we suspect him, he

387

might turn up here. He did last night...played whist with the king."

"I think we need to move the king," Cato said decisively. "Move him in secret to Newport."

Hammond looked worried. "I don't have orders from Parliament," he pointed out.

"You may consider that you have," Cato said aridly. "I'm representing Parliament in this matter."

"You will take responsibility?"

"Haven't I just said so?"

Hammond bowed his head in acknowledgment. "It might be difficult to move him secretly."

"We do it now while the island's still half asleep. Have you visited His Majesty this morning?"

"Not as yet. I don't usually go in to him until after seven."

"Well, let us pay him a visit now. Have a closed carriage ready and waiting in the courtyard. We'll both accompany the king to the barracks in Newport. You'd best send a messenger ahead to have his lodging prepared." Cato was already moving briskly back along the battlements as he spoke.

The governor hurried after him. "Channing can take the message, but where the devil is the man? You there..." He beckoned a servant, who came running. "Go to Lord Channing's chamber again. This time make sure he's awake before you leave. Make sure he answers you."

The man ran off.

The sentry outside the king's chamber in the north curtain wall saluted.

"Has His Majesty sent for his valet as yet?"

"Aye, Colonel. He's with him now."

Cato knocked imperatively on the door and it was opened by the valet.

"His Majesty is not yet attired to receive visitors, my lord."

"His Majesty will excuse our intrusion," Cato said brusquely. He stepped around the valet and bowed to his sovereign. "I give you good morning, Sire."

The king was in the process of being shaved. He looked at his visitors in some indignation. "What is this?"

"Your Majesty is to be moved to Newport," Cato said.

The king paled. He wiped soap from his face with a towel and stood up. "I beg your pardon?"

"Parliament's orders, Sire." Hammond stepped forward and bowed. "You are to be moved immediately."

The king's eyes burned in his white face. It was the end, then. They had been discovered. Within hours of his rescue. His disappointment was so profound he made no attempt to conceal it. He knew it had been his last chance.

"May I ask why?" he demanded when he had mastered himself sufficiently to speak.

"I believe Your Majesty knows why," Cato said quietly. "You will leave within the hour."

"I have not yet broken my fast."

"It is but two miles to Newport, Sire. A meal will await you there."

The adamant tone was laced with courtesy, but it didn't disguise the fact that the marquis had given his sovereign an order.

"Granville, you were once loyal," the king said sadly. "A most loyal friend."

"I am loyal to my country, Sire, and I would continue to stand your friend," Cato said in the same quiet voice. "I will leave you to your preparations." He bowed low and stepped out of the chamber.

Colonel Hammond made his own obeisance and followed. The servant he had sent for Godfrey Channing was waiting in the corridor.

"Lord Channing, sir, he wasn't in 'is chamber. His man said his bed 'asn't been slept in."

"Good God!" Hammond exclaimed. "How could that be?"

"It seems unlike the man," Cato observed. "He's always been most assiduous about his duties. However, it seems we must do without him for the moment. Who else can you send to Newport?"

"Latham. He can keep a still tongue in his head." The colonel sent the messenger for his other equerry. "D'ye care to break your fast, Granville, while we wait for the king to complete his toilette?"

BRIAN MORSE GAZED up into the face of a man he'd never seen before. A man he felt sure he would never wish to see again.

The man knelt beside Brian as he lay bound, swaddled tightly in the thick, heavy folds of a cloak, under a dripping hedge some half mile from the village of Ventnor. Brian had been carried to this spot, his mouth stopped with the folds of the cloak. Three men had carried him as easily as if he were a baby.

Anthony surveyed him in silence. His face was expressionless except for his eyes, and what Brian read in those eyes filled him with a cold dread.

"So you like to play with little girls," Anthony said softly. "Tell me about it, Mr. Morse." He jerked the folds of material from Brian's mouth. "Do explain the fascination for me."

Brian spat pieces of lint from his mouth. "So my little sister has been telling tales to her lover, has she? I never thought she'd turn whore. She always swore she'd never have anything to do with a man." Somehow he managed to sneer even through his fear.

Anthony's hands closed around Brian's throat. The long, slim fingers squeezed. Hands that could hold a ship steady into the wind in the teeth of a gale. Brian gasped like a gaffed fish. His chest was so tight he knew it was going to burst. Spots danced before his eyes. He could feel them bulging. The hands squeezed tighter. And then the black wave swamped him.

Anthony took his hands from Brian's throat. He flexed his fingers, then massaged his palms with his thumbs.

"You have killed him." Olivia stepped forward, her voice flat. "You killed him."

Anthony shook his head. "I have never yet managed to kill in cold blood, however great the temptation," he said. "Besides, I would rather condemn this piece of vileness to a living hell."

He reached into his pocket and took out a small vial. "Hold his head, Adam."

Adam put an arm behind the unconscious man's neck and lifted his head on his wrist. Brian's mouth fell open as his head fell back. His neck was livid with the marks of Anthony's fingers.

Anthony tipped the contents of the vial down the opened throat, and the unconscious man swallowed convulsively. "That will keep him out for twelve hours."

He stood up and addressed the three men who stood beside the limp figure. "Put him on a cart and carry him to Yarmouth. *Seamew* is waiting with her other passenger for the noon tide. Give this to her master." He dug into his pocket again and took out a leather pouch. It clinked as he passed it over.

Olivia's gaze was riveted by the immobile bundle that was Brian. Now, looking at him, it was hard to imagine how he had terrified her. He looked so old and yellow and lifeless.

Anthony glanced up at the full-risen sun and turned back to Olivia. "You will be missed, I fear."

Olivia dragged her eyes from Brian. "I'll find an explanation," she said absently. She was thinking how it didn't much matter now. Anthony would be gone from the island in a matter of hours.

"I'll be off to Yarmouth, then, see about the Yarrows," Adam said. "I'll find a fishin' boat in Ventnor to sail me round."

"How are you going to get into the castle?"

"Crab pots," Adam said laconically. "Powerful fond of crabs, is the cook. An' she'll tell me a thing or two. Quite gabby, she is." He sounded faintly disapproving of Mary's useful vice.

"See who's on duty. Pete will—"

"Aye, there's no need to teach yer grandmother to suck eggs," Adam interrupted. "I'll 'ave 'em out of there, don't you worry."

Anthony laughed. "I don't, old man, I don't. But I need you back on *Wind Dancer* by early afternoon. You need to tell the crew that there's been a change of plan. I'll not return to the ship until I have the king. Warp her out of the chine on the ebb tide and take her into the Channel. Jethro should sail her for Puckaster Cove at nine tonight. He should be in position by ten. But before that, Sam should sail the dinghy and beach her in the cove, so she's ready and waiting for us."

Adam nodded and set off back to Ventnor to find a boat to take him to Yarmouth.

Olivia had listened to this exchange in slowly dawning horror. "Anthony, you can't still mean to rescue the king!" she exclaimed. "Not now that they know." She looked at him as if he was out of his mind.

"My flower, I have a promise to keep," he said, taking her hand and walking with her back to the field where they had left Gowan's horse.

"Don't be ridiculous! Whoever this woman is, she wouldn't expect you to do this *now*. No woman in her senses would."

Anthony's response was instant and unthinking. "This is *my* business, Olivia. My commitments are *my* affair, not yours."

She pulled her hand out of his, stopping dead on the lane. "What are you saying?" Her eyes were bewildered. How when they had talked of love could he dismiss her concern so curtly?

He read her confusion and her anger in her eyes and moderated his tone as he tried to explain. "I'm the master of a ship, Olivia. Men rely on my decisions. I must make those decisions alone and take their consequences myself. It's always been like that for me, and, believe me, I learned the lessons the hard way."

"So you never listen to advice?" she demanded in disbelief. "You never change your mind?"

"Of course I do," he said with a touch of impatience. "But the final decisions are mine."

Her father would have said the same, Olivia reflected. She frowned, thinking of what

Anthony had just said. "You learned the hard way. As a child, you mean? From your parents?"

"You could say that."

Olivia lost all patience. "Damn you, Anthony!" she cried. "Isn't it time you explained some things to me? Don't you owe me something?"

Anthony gazed across her head, over the hedge to the sea, but he saw little of the scenery. How to explain what it was like to be an outsider, to belong nowhere? How to explain that to Olivia, whose own place in the world was so firmly entrenched? How could she understand?

"My mother and father were killed on the night of my birth. Ellen and Adam took care of me," he said distantly.

"Is Ellen the one who would have you rescue the king?"

"A woman of a most powerful conviction," Anthony said. "And since I owe her more than I could ever repay, I will do whatever she asks of me."

"How were your parents killed?"

"They were murdered."

"In Bohemia?"

"Yes.... Does that satisfy you, Olivia? I don't wish to discuss this further."

She struggled to understand what that night must have been like. That night of violent death and birth. So much blood, she thought. There must have been so much blood.

"But...but what of your grandparents, of other family?"

"I have no other family," he said flatly. "Ellen and Adam are my friends and all the family I need."

She heard the bitter finality in his voice.

"I don't believe Ellen would ask this of you if she knew the danger you were in now," Olivia stated shrewdly. She saw from the quick flicker of his eyes that she had hit truth.

He began walking again briskly as he spoke. "Be that as it may, I keep my promises. And I don't like to give up a plan halfway through."

"That's foolhardy." She was half running now to keep up with his rangy stride.

"No. Dangerous maybe. But as you know, the most dangerous enterprises are the most satisfying...and," he added, "more often than not, the ones most likely to succeed." He turned in to the field where the chestnut was grazing peacefully among the cows. "I have made certain changes to the original plan," he conceded. "In light of changed circumstances."

Olivia waited until he'd caught the chestnut and brought him back to the gate. "They'll ambush you."

"Maybe. But I'll take precautions. They can't know exactly when I'm going to make the attempt. Only the men of *Wind Dancer* know that. And they can't know how I plan to do it, because only those same people know that.... Up you get, now." He took her by the waist and lifted her onto the horse.

"Please don't do this," she said as he mounted behind her. "I am so afraid for you."

"O ye of little faith," he mocked, reaching

around her to grab the mane. "I was going to create one diversion on the battlements, but now I intend to stage a performance that will have every soldier and officer in the castle utterly occupied for the few minutes it will take the king to make his move."

He laughed softly at the thought and Olivia knew she had lost this battle. If he believed he could do it, then he would do it. And he would succeed. She had to believe that.

"And when you have the king, when you've taken him safely to France, will you c-come back?" Her voice sounded thick.

"I come and go," he said obliquely. "But this is where my ship has her anchorage. Where my friends are, where my crew have their families."

"And if the king isn't here, then my father will leave," she said, gazing straight ahead as the chestnut cantered across the clifftop. The sea was very blue, sparkling with the morning sun, and the Dorset coast stood out so clearly it was almost as if one could reach across the dazzling water and touch it.

"Yes," he agreed. "It is as it is." Softly he quoted her earlier words, "Things being as they are. You being who you are, me being who I am."

"What would you say if I said I would come with you?"

Anthony was silent for a minute, then he said, "I would be afraid that once the dream faded, as it must, you would not be happy."

"And I would hamper you, constrict you,"

she stated, her eyes still on the sea. The blue seemed fuzzy and she realized it was filtered through tears.

"I would worry that you were regretting the life you'd left. Your family, your loyalties, your place. Those are not mine and they mean nothing to me."

He fell silent. Olivia stared ahead, feeling his hard body at her back. *Was he right?* Were passion, *love*, not strong enough to overcome such odds? But they had lived a dream, it had never been more than that. And one woke up from dreams.

"If we stayed on the island," she said. "If we stayed on the island, then whenever you came back we could live the dream again."

"But you cannot stay."

"Would you wish to dream again?"

For a minute he didn't answer her, then he said, making his voice flat and distant, "There was never a future to this. We both understood that. Be happy with what we've had. Carry the memories, as I shall."

It took half an hour before they reached the boundary of Lord Granville's property. A half hour in which their thoughts hung heavy and unspoken. As they approached the orchard, Olivia said, "Stop here."

Anthony drew the chestnut to a halt and dismounted. He lifted Olivia down and held her hands. "I know of no other answer," he said. "I would not be responsible for your unhappiness."

"And I would not be responsible for yours,"

she returned. Slowly she drew her hands from his. "Say goodbye. Say it now."

He cupped her face and kissed her gently. "Farewell, Olivia."

"Farewell." She brushed his mouth with her fingertips, lingering as if to imprint forever the feel of his mouth on her skin.

Then she turned and ran from him. If he succeeded this night, the Granvilles would leave the island. She couldn't bear to think then of *Wind Dancer* slipping into her chine in the darkness, when she herself was not asleep or wakeful in her bed in the house in Chale. Waiting for his return. She couldn't bear to think of *Wind Dancer* on the open sea, with her master at the wheel and the deck beneath his feet, his hair blown back from his face, his strong throat bared to the wind as he looked up at the sails.

She couldn't bear to think of him sailing away from her.

But she must bear it, because one couldn't live entranced forever.

ANTHONY STOOD for a long time in the lane after she had disappeared into the trees. Had he been right? But he knew that he had. First would have come disillusion that would usher in contempt and then bitter dislike. They would have learned to hate each other as they pulled in different directions. There was no place for Olivia in his life, and he could not live hers. But he thought as he turned to go that his heart would break.

OLIVIA DARTED through the orchard, heading for the garden and the back stairs, hoping, although it seemed a forlorn hope, that she wouldn't be seen in her strange garb by any of the servants.

She was so absorbed in her unhappiness that she nearly stepped into the path of her father and Rufus before the sound of their voices alerted her to their presence in the orchard. She froze, her heart banging against her ribs. Cato was talking to Rufus above little Evie's importunate demand that her father carry her. They were so close, a mere row of fruit trees away.

Olivia almost without thinking scrambled into the branches of a crab apple tree whose massed foliage provided a perfect screen. The two men turned into the aisle and strolled towards Olivia's tree, deep in conversation.

"How did the king take his removal?" Rufus asked, swinging his small daughter onto his shoulders.

"With dignity, as always," Cato replied. "Newport barracks is rather more primitive than Carisbrooke, but he affected not to notice."

"We found nothing at Puckaster Cove, or anywhere close to it," Rufus said, adjusting his hold on Eve's ankles as she bounced to grab a crab apple from the tree.

Evie pulled at the apple, bending its branch low.

Olivia shrank back against the tree trunk, holding her breath. Then the branch bounced back again as the men passed beneath the tree, and she breathed again.

She leaned forward to catch the continued conversation as it drifted back to her. The men were walking slowly and she could hear their words clearly.

Rufus was saying, "We combed the area; although we didn't find anything it still looks a likely spot. A deep cove, deep channel at the mouth, sheltered by two headlands. Shall we set a watch over it? Could you take that crab apple away from Eve? It'll give her the belly-ache and I'll never hear the last of it from Portia."

"I'd like to catch the man," Cato said, reaching up to take the crab apple from Eve's small fist. "Even though the king's out of his reach, I'd still like to catch him; he sounds a nasty piece of work whichever way you look at it. Since he won't know that we've moved the king, he still might make his attempt and we might grab him in the act. Here, Evie, this is a nice ripe pear." He plucked the fruit and gave it to the child, who accepted the replacement with serene good humor.

"Then we'll give it a try. I suggest we station cannon on each headland. They'll be positioned to blow the ship out of the water if she comes into the channel. And for the next couple of nights, we'll put men in ambush on the clifftop. If he comes out, we'll catch him."

"I suppose Godfrey Channing didn't join your expedition?" Cato inquired.

"No. Hammond asked me the same question. He seems to have disappeared off the face of the earth."

"Very odd. We'd best send out search parties. It seems likely he's met with an accident."

Not the kind of accident they'd ever imagine, Olivia thought fleetingly as she craned from her perch to watch them break out onto the lawn.

Now she climbed down slowly, trying to make sense of what she had just heard. They had moved the king. Tonight Anthony was going to go to Carisbrooke to rescue the king, but the king wasn't there anymore, he was in Newport. And *Wind Dancer* would sail all unknowing into Puckaster Cove and be smashed to pieces by Parliament's cannon.

She was exhausted; her sleepless night and the aching misery of their final parting seemed to overwhelm her. But she could not give in. Somehow she had to get this information to Anthony. But how in the name of God was she to do it? She had no idea where he was going after he'd left her. Since he'd changed his plans, he would presumably have extra preparations to make. He wasn't going back to his ship, so where would he be?

She tiptoed through the trees to the edge of the lawn, where a screen of bushes marked the boundary of the orchard. From this concealment she looked out at the scene on the lawn. Phoebe and Portia were sitting in the shade of an oak tree while the children splashed in the ornamental lake, running under the fountain with shrieks of glee as Juno chased them, waving her unruly feathery tail. Cato and Rufus had joined the women and stood talking to them under the tree.

Olivia wondered if they were asking where she was. Her absence would have been remarked upon. She hadn't thought it would matter once Anthony was safe. But he wasn't. She forced her tired mind to think clearly. If only she was wearing proper clothes, she could saunter out from the trees and say she'd been for a long walk and had fallen asleep in the sun...anything would do. But she had to change her clothes. And then she could decide what to do next.

Juno began to run round and around, chasing her tail with exuberant enthusiasm. Olivia picked up a stick and threw it towards the dog.

Juno was immediately distracted. She picked up the stick and raced for the orchard, wagging her tail, eager for whatever game awaited her.

She dropped the stick at Olivia's feet and looked up at her expectantly. "Fetch Portia," Olivia said, bending to pat the dog. "Go fetch Portia."

Juno's bright eyes looked intelligently at her, but she didn't move, merely picked up the stick and dropped it again in invitation.

"Stupid dog!" Olivia muttered. "You know what *Go fetch* means, and you know who Portia is."

Juno gave a short hopeful bark.

Olivia put a hand on the dog's collar. Juno tried to pull free. Olivia tightened her hold and Juno began to bark, short, frenzied little yapping barks that meant she didn't like what was happening.

Olivia held on and prayed that Portia would come to see what was the matter with her beloved Juno. She prayed that it was Portia who would come, not one of the children or worst of all, Rufus.

She watched the party under the tree, holding Juno, who was now struggling for release, her barks more in earnest. Portia looked around, frowning, then she got to her feet and came across the grass.

"Juno? Juno? What's the matter?"

"I'm holding her," Olivia whispered through the bushes. "Come into the orchard."

Portia pushed through the bushes as Olivia released Juno. The dog flung herself on her mistress as if she'd hadn't seen her in a year.

"Good God, Olivia! Where have you been?" Portia stared at her incredulously. "We've been at our wits' end trying to cover up your absence. What have you been doing? You look dreadful."

"I feel dreadful. I can't tell you all the details now. But I can't come out looking like this. Can you bring me some clothes? I can just reappear then and say I got up very early and went for a long walk."

"What exactly is going on?"

"I can't tell you. But *please* get me some clothes so I can come out of here."

"I assume this is pirate business," Portia said. "Should I expect you to tell me?"

"No," Olivia responded. She met her friend's gaze steadily.

Portia nodded and she hurried away, Juno gamboling at her heels.

Olivia waited impatiently behind the bushes. To her relief, Cato and Rufus soon went back to the house, dodging wet children, leaving Phoebe alone. Portia reappeared in a very few minutes from the side door of the house. She paused by Phoebe, and Olivia saw Phoebe's startled glance towards the bushes. Portia came over to the orchard, her step nonchalant. She carried a basket on her arm.

"This should get you into the house, duckie." She handed Olivia the basket. "But you look such a mess; your hair's like a bird's nest and you're filthy. You can't be seen properly until you've done something to yourself."

"I was out in the storm last night," Olivia said, stripping off her doublet and britches. "I got soaked and then I was in a sandy cave..." Her blood surged with the memory. It was so vivid, she could almost smell and taste and feel his body on hers. Hastily she dragged over her head the simple print gown Portia had brought her. By the time she'd pulled it down and buttoned it up, she was mistress of herself once again.

"Did you bring shoes?"

"No, I forgot. Your boots are pretty well hidden by your skirt. You only have to get into the house."

"Thank you." Olivia bundled the britches and doublet into the basket. "I'll join you on the lawn later." She hurried away with the basket of memories, exchanging a glance with Phoebe as she passed. She slipped into the house by the side door, keeping her head lowered when she passed a maid on the stairs, and reached the haven of her bedchamber.

She looked at herself in the small mirror. She really did look a fright. Her hair was impossibly matted, and when she tried to brush it a shower of sand fell onto the dresser.

Now that she'd reached safety, her exhaustion overwhelmed her. Just the effort to raise her arms to brush her hair was too much. She sank down on the bed to pull off her boots, kicked them free of her feet, and then without volition simply fell backwards. She would just lie here for a few minutes in peace and quiet and think about her next move.

She fell asleep with her legs dangling over the edge of the bed, her head on the quilt.

Olivia awoke with a start, unsure how long she had slept. She glanced to the window and saw with a shock that the sun was now low. She could still hear the voices of the children from the lawn below the window.

She sat up. Her eyes felt gritty, her limbs heavy as if she'd been drugged. How much time had she wasted in sleep?

She struggled off the bed and went to the

window. The scene on the lawn didn't seem to have changed much, although the shadows were now long. The children were still playing in the water; Phoebe and Portia were still sitting beneath the tree. There was no sign of either Cato or Rufus.

Olivia splashed cold water on her face and renewed her attack on her hair. She managed to get the sand out and braid the tangled mess. She dug the grit out from beneath her fingernails and washed her filthy feet. Then, feeling relatively respectable, she took up a book in an effort to appear to be behaving quite normally and went downstairs and out onto the lawn.

"Woken up at last." Phoebe assessed her with an experienced glance as she gathered a blue-lipped Nicholas into a towel. "You were so deeply asleep we didn't want to wake you. You slept through dinner."

"We told Cato that you'd been working at your books until late last night and were really tired," Portia said.

"Thank you," Olivia said. "Did he mind?"

"He didn't seem to. It's not as if he's not used to it."

"No," Olivia agreed.

"I won't ask what's going on," Phoebe said.

"What the eye don't see, the 'eart don't grieve over," Portia observed with a half smile.

"Precisely," Olivia said, sitting down on the grass beside them.

She opened her book. Her head was clear

now, the mists of sleep dissipated. It was perhaps an hour to sunset. Anthony was not going to make his move until after ten. He'd told Adam to make sure that the frigate was in the cove by ten.

A company of soldiers, and cannon to dismast *Wind Dancer*. While Anthony was on a fruitless rescue mission, he would lose his ship. He would go back to the beach and run into an ambush.

Olivia's eyes remained on her book and she turned the pages at regular intervals although she read not a word as her mind raced, examining and discarding possibilities. The Barkers would know if it was possible to stop *Wind Dancer* from sailing into the trap. The flag at the oratory, if it could be seen at night, would bring someone from the ship, but they needed a much more urgent means of communication. There was no time for the leisurely progress of the sailing dinghy to and from the chine. But there must be some other kind of signal. If Mike was there, he would know.

Her mind filled with rioting images of soldiers with pikes and muskets, of the sound of cannon and the crash of a fallen mast.

She closed her eyes and was back with Anthony in his little boat as he ran it up on the beach. She knew the maneuvers so well now. She could almost feel the grab of the sand beneath the boat. She could see him as he jumped over the side, barefoot, the knee buckles of his britches catching the light as he hauled the boat higher on the sand. He was laughing, his crooked teeth flashing in the brown face. A lock of hair the color of golden guineas flopped over his eyes as he bent to his task, and he brushed it aside with a swift careless movement of his long, strong hand.

She could see him. She could smell him. The memory image was so vivid, so powerful, her senses swam.

"Olivia? *Olivia!*"

Portia's imperative tone shattered the dream memory into shards of longing.

"Forgive me. I was daydreaming."

"That was fairly obvious, duckie. In fact, I thought you were asleep. It's time for supper."

Olivia became aware of nursemaids retrieving their charges and wondered how she hadn't noticed either the summons that had brought them or their arrival. Childish protests rose on the air as the little ones were borne away.

"We're going to the kitchen for *our* supper," Luke announced. "We don't eat in the nursery."

"No, of course you don't," Portia agreed readily. "But whatever you do, don't annoy Mistress Bisset. Our own supper depends on her good temper."

"We don't annoy her. She *loves* us," Toby declared extravagantly. "She wishes we belonged to her. She said so." The boys ran off, tackling each other, rolling in the grass and leaping up again in one continuous blur of movement.

"It's true, she does," Phoebe said, dusting grass off her skirt.

"Everyone loves them. They're Rufus's." Portia sounded more than a little smug.

"I think I'd better change my dress before supper. It seems to have acquired bits of Nicholas's sucked gingerbread." Phoebe peered at an unbecoming smear on her skirt. She shot Olivia a quick glance.

Olivia closed her book and jumped to her feet. "Is my father in the house?"

"No, he and Rufus returned to the castle after dinner."

"Then I'm going out now," Olivia said. "I have something to do."

Portia and Phoebe exchanged a glance. "You need to eat something," Phoebe said practically.

It had been a long time since breakfast in the Gull in Ventnor, Olivia realized. "I'll take some bread and cheese from the supper table. But I have to go."

"Will you be back by the morning?"

Olivia looked at them bleakly. She would do what she had to for the pirate tonight, and then one way or another he would be gone from her. "I expect so," she said.

Twenty

OLIVIA TOOK BREAD, cheese, and cold beef from the supper table, together with an apple, and left the house through the side door.

Eating her makeshift supper, she strolled into the stable yard, ducked casually into the tack room, and took a rope halter from the row hanging on the wall. She held it against her skirts and as casually as before left the stable yard, again drawing little attention from a pair of grooms who were playing knucklebones on an upturned water butt.

She made her way to the pasture where the ponies had been put to graze during the warm summer nights. Her own pony, a dappled mare, was placidly cropping the grass under the hedge a few feet from her.

"Grayling," Olivia called softly, holding out the apple.

The pony looked up and then walked over to her. Olivia held out the apple on the palm of her hand, and Grayling lifted it off delicately between her thick velvety lips. Olivia slipped the halter around her neck and led her to a tree stump.

Grayling showed no objection to being ridden bareback. Olivia tucked her muslin skirts securely beneath her to protect herself from the pony's coarse hair and clicked her tongue, guiding the mare to the gate onto the lane.

She hoped she remembered the way to the Barkers' farm. She hadn't been concentrating too well the previous time; there had been too many things on her mind. However, she found she recognized a crossroads and knew to take the right-hand lane. It led her through the small hamlet that she remembered as being about ten minutes away from the cattle track that led to the Barkers' farm.

It was dusk as she rode into the farmyard. It was quiet, no children tumbling on the straw-strewn cobbles, the chickens, ducks, and geese shut away from the fox for the night. But the farmhouse door stood open to let in the evening breeze.

Olivia dismounted and looped Grayling's halter over a fence post, then she approached the door. She knocked and peered into the kitchen. It was deserted and her heart sank. Were they all abed already?

She knocked louder and then called softly, "Anyone home?" To her relief came the clatter of booted feet from the ladder staircase at the back of the kitchen.

"Who the 'ell's callin' at this time o' night?" A man Olivia didn't recognize came into the kitchen, tucking his shirt into the waist of his britches.

She got a good look as he came closer, and saw Mike's features in the older face.

"Goodman Barker?"

"Aye, an' who wants 'im?" He peered at her in the half-light.

"Olivia Granville. Lord Granville's daughter," she added when he seemed at a loss. "Is Mike here? I have to speak to him."

The goodman regarded her suspiciously and just then his wife's voice called imperatively, "Who is it, Barker?"

"The Granville miss," he called over his shoulder. "Wants our Mike."

Goodwife Barker came down the ladder backwards. She wore a voluminous nightgown; her hair was tucked into a cap. "What's it you want, miss?" she demanded.

Olivia took a deep breath. "Goodwife, they've moved the king to Newport. Anthony doesn't know it and I know he's going to Carisbrooke tonight to try to rescue the king."

The Barkers looked at her in bewilderment as if trying to comprehend what she was saying.

Olivia continued urgently, "*Wind Dancer* is in danger. They have cannons on the headland to sink her when she sails into Puckaster Cove." She had the feeling that if she paused for a second, the woman would cut her off and send her packing. "Mike must know how to send a message to the ship so she won't drop anchor.

"We have to warn the ship!" she repeated, hoping at last to see some light of understanding in the goodwife's suspicious stare. "And we have to stop Anthony from going to the beach. If someone from here can send the signal to the ship, I'll go to the castle and warn Anthony."

Goodwife Barker said, " 'Ow d'ye know this, miss?"

"I overheard my father, Lord Granville, talking about it." She tried for patience, but it deserted her and she exclaimed, "For God's sake, woman, is Mike here?"

Goodman Barker answered her. "He's wi' the master."

Olivia used a barnyard oath that she'd picked up from Portia. "Do *you* know how to warn the ship?"

Both Barkers shook their heads. "Our Mike's the only one 'ere what knows the signals," the goodwife said.

"An' he's wi' the master," the goodman repeated, still shaking his head.

Maybe it was too late for the ship, but she could still keep Anthony from walking into an ambush. "I have to go to the castle to warn Anthony." She was calculating times and distances as she spoke. "Tell me which road to take from here. I only know the way from Chale. There must be a way to get to the castle without going back through Chale. Across the downs...some other route."

"Our Billy 'ad better go wi' you. Over Bleak Down and across the Medina. 'Tis the quickest way." The goodman spoke up with what Olivia thought was probably uncharacteristic authority. He turned to his wife and demanded sharply, "Fetch Billy, woman!"

The goodman went past Olivia to the door.

He looked up at the sky. " 'Tis close on ten. Ye'd best get a move on. It'll take ye an hour at least."

His wife was already at the foot of the ladder. "Billy! Our Billy, get down 'ere quick!"

"Eh, Ma, what's up?" A sleepy Billy stumbled down the steps in his nightshirt. His eye fell on Olivia still standing by the door. "Lor'! 'Tis Miss!"

"Ye've to show Miss the way to the castle, across Bleak Down." His mother thrust a pair of boots at him.

"I needs me britches," Billy protested, turning back to the steps.

"Jest be quick about it."

He was down again in a minute and sat on the bottom step to pull on his boots.

"Aye. Now fetch an 'orse. Get goin'!" His mother gave him a shove to the door.

"All right, all right, I'm goin'!" He ran off, the untucked tail of his shirt flapping behind him.

Olivia's heart was beating too fast; anxiety coursed through her veins as she waited for Billy to reappear with his horse. She stepped out into the farmyard, her arms crossed over her breast. There was a new moon, a crescent sliver hanging low on the horizon.

Billy on a round cob trotted into the yard, and Olivia ran for her horse. She unlooped the halter and Goodman Barker gave her a leg up. "God go wi' ye, miss."

Goodwife Barker hurried over to them, her face creased with anxiety. "Now, our Billy, y'are not to go to the castle. 'Tis bad enough our Mike's there, puttin' himself in danger and all for nowt. Jest get Miss across the down and over the river."

Billy looked a trifle disgusted but he shrugged in half acceptance. "Come on, then, miss." He kicked the cob's round flanks and the animal broke into a lumbering trot. Grayling followed with a prancing step.

Olivia brought Grayling up beside Billy's cob as they left the cart track at the end of the farm and turned onto the lane. "Your father said it would take us an hour to get there, Billy?"

"Oh, Pa's not much of a rider," Billy said scornfully. "It might take 'im an hour, but I reckon we can do better than that, miss. We goes this a-way." He turned his horse to push through a hedge and they were in an open stretch of land where the trees were scrawny and bent by the wind's frequent onslaughts.

" 'Tis called Bleak Down," Billy told Olivia. "There's no villages around 'ere, the wind is powerful fierce in the winter."

By mutual consent they put their horses to the gallop and rode neck and neck. The wind whistled past Olivia's ears, caught her thick black hair, pulling it loose from its ribbon so it flew out like a raven's wing behind her. Her heart seemed to race in rhythm with Grayling's beating hooves across the rough turf.

Was it already too late for Anthony to get a message to *Wind Dancer*? He had told Adam that the ship must be in position by ten. She would already be sailing into the mouth of the cove, under the cannon. Anthony must have some way of signaling her to leave. But there would be soldiers stationed on the clifftop, waiting...

There would be a way...a way...a way... The refrain filled her head, blocking out all other thought as she clung to the pony's mane, keeping low on Grayling's neck to encourage her speed. A narrow ribbon of dark water loomed suddenly in front of her.

"We 'ave to ford the river," Billy shouted, not drawing rein. " 'Tis low at this time o' year. Jest follow me."

Grayling followed the cob into the water. They didn't slacken speed and Olivia's skirts were soaked as the cob kicked up water ahead of her and Grayling leaped through the spray. But there ahead of them now loomed the great mass of Carisbrooke Castle up on the hill, the giant keep on its high motte towering from the northwest corner.

Olivia thought rapidly. The king's chamber was, *had been*, in the north curtain wall. Anthony and Mike would be waiting with their horses somewhere close to there, somewhere right under the battlements. It was madness! she thought with a surge of fury. Other people had tried to rescue the king and failed miserably.

But then, Anthony was not other people. If it could have been done, he would have succeeded. If the king were there, ready to do his part, he would be away to France within the hour.

"Leave me here, Billy," she instructed crisply. "I'll go the rest of the way alone."

"Eh, I could 'elp a bit, miss," he said hopefully.

"Your mother wants you back. So go. I don't have time to waste."

"Ma's jest a worrier," he said.

"With good reason. Now *go!*"

Her voice was fierce enough to send even the reluctant Billy back the way he had come.

Olivia headed for a line of trees that marched along the spine of the down. The moon was obscured by clouds for the moment, but the trees would conceal her approach if the moon suddenly shone clear.

Just where would Anthony be? The gatehouse was very close to the southern end of the north wall. There would be soldiers patrolling the ramparts. She could see the flicker of torches on the battlements. Her heart pounded so fiercely she thought she would be sick. And yet her head was clear and cold, her thinking sharp and bright as an icicle.

As she guided Grayling at a walk under the line of trees, she heard the whicker of a horse. Immediately she drew rein. Grayling lifted his nose and gave a curious snort at the presence of his own kind.

"Where are they?" she murmured, her ears straining to catch a sound. Faintly she heard the muffled shuffle of hooves, and then the faintest chink of a bridle. They were coming from a group of trees that stood very close to the battlements.

Olivia dismounted and led Grayling towards the trees. She had no idea what she would find. It could as easily be a party of Lord Granville's troopers as Anthony and Mike.

There were three horses tethered in the copse, placidly cropping the mossy grass. Three horses, positioned for a quick getaway.

Olivia tethered Grayling close to them and then crept on tiptoe out of the copse. The moon came out as she emerged under the grass-covered curtain wall beneath the north battlements. She could see the king's barred window high up beneath the rampart. There was no light in the window. Torches still flickered on the battlements above.

If she hugged the wall, she would be concealed from a watcher on the ramparts. She moved at a crouch, making herself as small as possible, towards the wall beneath the king's window.

The clock in the castle chapel struck eleven, its gong chiming out across a still night. Olivia's heart jumped.

And then the night exploded. There was a crash of a cannon; sparks flew into the air, a shower of orange and red. Muskets fired in rapid succession and then there was a whoosh of orange flame from the battlements. It looked as if the entire castle was on fire.

And then Olivia saw them. The two black shapes pressed as she was against the wall. They were immediately below the king's window. Anthony's tall, dark-clad figure was unmistakable. He wore a black cap pulled down over his bright head, and he seemed to blend into the night, a shadowy part of the night and the wall itself.

Now it sounded as if a pitched battle was being fought within the walls overhead. Men were shouting, torches wavered, flames rose, crackling and smoky in the night. Anthony had said he would create a diversion, but this was a full-scale war.

Olivia raced towards Anthony. She called his name, confident that in the chaos above, her own small voice would not reach the battlements.

Anthony spun around. A knife was in his raised hand. Then the hand dropped as he saw who it was. Olivia stopped, bent double as she tried to catch her breath. Anthony made no attempt to press her to explain herself, and his steady quiet, the aura of calm, had its effect. When she spoke, she spoke clearly and to the point.

"He's not here...the king...he's not here." Olivia pointed upward to the window. "They moved him this morning."

Anthony asked no questions. He seized her hand and ran with her, crouching low to the ground, into the shelter of the trees. Mike raced soundlessly beside them.

"Well, that was a waste of some splendid fireworks," Anthony declared coolly as they reached cover. "Gordon and his men did a magnificent job."

"Aye," Mike agreed. "We could 'ave got five kings away under that cover."

"Your ship," Olivia gasped. *Wind Dancer...*"

"What of her?" Anthony demanded, his calm suddenly banished. Then almost immediately he was in command of himself. He said quietly, "Take a breath, Olivia. Tell me what you know."

"They have stationed cannon on the headlands above Puckaster Cove, in case your ship comes into the channel."

"Yarrow," Mike said disgustedly.

Anthony shook his head. "You can't blame him, Mike. I'd rather he told what he knew than risk hurt."

"Prue wouldn't 'ave spoken, whatever they did," Mike stated with the same disgust.

"That's as may be." Anthony was brusquely dismissive. "What else, Olivia?"

"Soldiers. In ambush on the clifftop in case you come ashore."

"Or leave the shore," he said with a short laugh. "On the clifftop? Are you certain?"

Olivia nodded. "That's what they said. Anthony, what are you—"

But he had turned from them and walked away through the trees. The king's cause was lost.

But his ship! His men! Adam, Jethro, Sam...they were his lifeblood, his family. He owed them everything he had. *Wind Dancer,* precious though she was, was nothing compared to his friends. And yet, to save his friends, he had to save his ship. He turned back. His expression was calm, his eyes cool and gray as a still, dawn sea.

"Sam will have left the dinghy in the cove. I can evade the ambush by taking the path from Binnel Point. It'll bring me to the beach without going near the cliff above the cove," he said crisply. "I'll have a few minutes to get the dinghy into the water before they realize I'm there."

"They'll fire on you," Olivia said. "When they see you pushing the dinghy out, they'll fire on you."

"Once he's hoisted sail, the master can outmaneuver anyone," Mike said. "He did summat like it afore. In Tangier. They was after 'im fer..." He stopped and coughed. "Can't quite remember what."

Anthony gave him an ironical smile. "How discreet you are, Mike."

"Oh, I don't care if you'd invaded the sultan's harem," Olivia exclaimed. "I only want to know if it worked."

"I am here." Anthony bowed, his eyes gleaming with that reckless light that she now knew so well. "Here and...uh...intact, as I'm sure you can vouch for."

"So it *was* the sultan's...oh, why must you joke at such a time?"

"Because, my flower, there is always time to laugh. And laughter calms the nerves." He touched her cheek in habitual fashion and in habitual fashion she leaned her face into his palm. His eyes grazed hers.

"What of *Wind Dancer*?" she said urgently. "Once they see you, they'll certainly fire the cannon at her, if they haven't already destroyed her."

The light disappeared from his eyes. "I learned long ago not to anticipate disaster; it's a waste of energy. Jethro will know what to do until I can take command." Anthony turned for his horse. "Mike, escort Olivia home and then go home yourself. *Wind Dancer* will make sail for France as soon as I'm aboard her. We'll return to the chine in a month or so and—"

"Beggin' yer pardon, master, but I'm not goin' to leave you. Ye'll need 'elp pushin' the dinghy off. Besides, I go where *Wind Dancer* goes."

Anthony hesitated beside his horse, one hand on the pommel, the other holding the reins. He spoke to Olivia, who had gone to Grayling. "Can you find your own way home?"

"That's a stupid, if not an insulting, question. I found my own way here, of course I could find my way home. But I'm not going home."

Anthony had mounted his horse. "What do you mean?"

Olivia spoke slowly and clearly. "I mean that if my father's men are in ambush above the beach, and I am down on the beach with you, pushing you and your boat out, they are not going to shoot."

"They'll recognize Miss on the beach," Mike said as he took the point.

"Exactly. If my father's not there, the men are bound to be under Giles Crampton's command. He'll recognize me immediately." She grabbed Grayling's mane, jumped, and hauled herself across the mare's back, scrambling herself astride, scrunching her skirts beneath her.

"And just how are you intending to explain *that* to your father?" Anthony demanded.

"That's my problem," she said. "Like you, I make my own decisions, and I accept their consequences." She flung his own words back at him with a certain satisfaction. "My commitments are *my* affair, Mr. Caxton."

It was dark among the trees but she could see his eyes flare, his fine mouth harden. "Don't you dare follow me, Olivia," he said with a low-voiced ferocity that she had never heard from him before. "Come, Mike." He turned and galloped his horse out onto the downs.

Mike gave her a little shrug of resignation and followed.

Twenty-one

OLIVIA KICKED GRAYLING'S FLANKS and pursued them. The castle was still in an uproar, fires hurling flames into the darkness, gunpowder exploding in rhythmic succession.

Olivia kept the men in view but stayed well back. She didn't know if Anthony was aware that she was following, but she didn't care.

Everything seemed very clear to her now. At some point in this wild night, the emotional turmoil of the last weeks had smoothed out, the maelstrom had become a millpond. She didn't question herself or what she was about to do. And she wasn't going to waste time and mental energy on discussing her epiphany with Anthony.

It was half an hour later when Anthony and Mike drew rein on the clifftop. It was a place unfamiliar to Olivia. And it was deserted, the only sound the occasional mew of a gull. The crescent moon shone on the quiet sea and there was the sense that the world held its breath. Anthony and Mike dismounted and Olivia brought Grayling up to them.

Anthony looked at her. *"Why?"* The single word cracked like a pistol shot.

"Because you need my help," Olivia said simply, swinging down from her horse. Her legs quivered after her two long rides, and she had to stiffen her knees when she stood on the ground. "Where are we?"

It was Mike who answered her. "Binnel Point, miss." He went to the very edge of the cliff and, kneeling, pulled aside a thick patch of undergrowth. Olivia saw a pale trail, barely thicker than a hand's span, creeping downward through the undergrowth. It reminded her of the path she had taken to the wrecker's beach. Such a short time ago, and yet it felt like someone else's lifetime.

"We takes the path, miss. It winds a good bit along the cliff afore goin' through an 'ole in the cliff just above the beach at Puckaster Cove."

"So we avoid the ambush on the clifftop."

"That is certainly the hope," Anthony said dryly. He took her shoulders in a hard grip. "I do not need you, Olivia, do you understand that?"

"Well, you see, I think you do," she responded. She reached up and put her hands over his. "Should we not go now? Every minute we wait, the ship is in danger."

"I do not need you to remind me of that," he declared, his frustration obvious in eyes and voice.

"Then let us go." She broke free of his grasp and headed for the cliff path where Mike stood. She felt a powerful burst of exhilaration, the same she had felt whenever she and the pirate went adventuring.

Anthony overtook her. "Stay behind Mike," he instructed her. "When we get to the beach, you will stay on the path. You can see everything, but you will not be seen. Understand that, Olivia. You will *not* show yourself. I have no need of your help, and you will only hinder me. I'm not going to lose my ship for some childish impulse of yours."

It was harsh but Olivia said nothing. She took her place on the path behind Mike. After two steps, she turned and went down backwards; it was far too steep for a head-on descent. Soon she had no time or inclination for exhilaration. The path seemed to wind sideways and down forever. But the men didn't stop and she wasn't going to show weakness herself by pausing to catch her breath. Once she turned carefully to look out over her shoulder at the smooth waters of the Channel, where the sea lay silver under the starlight. *Wind Dancer* rocked gently at anchor at the mouth of the cove.

She was still safe. Olivia almost cried out with relief. The men's pace increased and she scrambled down after them, slipping and sliding, heedless of grazes and scratches. A jut of cliff seemed to block the path, but then she saw there was a small gap and Anthony and Mike disappeared through it. She edged through after them and found herself standing above a gently undulating cove at whose entrance rocked the pirate's ship.

Anthony and Mike jumped lightly to the beach and Olivia, in a shower of pebbles, sand, and gravel, landed beside them. Sweat trickled into her eyes despite the cool breeze from the sea. She listened for a sound, any sound that would tell her her father's men were gathered in ambush. But she could hear nothing, not a snapping twig, not a breath.

UP ON THE CLIFF, Cato gazed out at the elegant ship at anchor.

"Should we give the signal to fire on 'er, my lord?" Giles as always sounded impatient for action.

"She's not doing anything illegal or harmful out there," Cato pointed out. "I don't see the justification for damaging her when she's just sitting there. What d'you think, Rothbury?"

Rufus was meditatively chewing on a piece of grass. "We don't even know for sure that she is this *Wind Dancer*. We're too far to read her name."

"Of course it is, m'lord," Giles said. "She's waitin' fer someone, or something."

"Let's signal them to send a warning shot across her bows," Rufus suggested. "See how she reacts."

Giles was already issuing orders to his men to light their flares.

"WHAT THE HELL'S THAT?" Anthony looked up at the clifftop as a pattern of lights began to dance across the sea. He had his answer almost immediately. A cannon boomed from the headland and water rose in a great spume of foam just astern of the frigate.

Olivia drew a sharp breath. Anthony turned to her. "They're on the clifftop. Stay here out of sight until it's all over, then go home." He still sounded harsh and angry. He seemed to hesitate, then, as if against his will, he grasped her upper arms and bent and kissed her hard on the mouth. He released her immediately. "Let's make a dash for the dinghy, Mike." They ran across the sand, dark figures in the shadows of the cliff.

Olivia now saw the dinghy, pulled up on the sand and concealed from the clifftop by an outcrop of rocks. The first shot came from the

428

clifftop as they reached the rocks. Her heart jumped into her mouth, but they had dodged and ducked and were dragging the dinghy down the beach, keeping low against its side so it served as a shield. But when they had to push it in the water, they would be exposed.

Olivia raced into the middle of the beach. She faced the cliff, waving her arms, leaping in a mad dance of distraction.

Cato stared down in disbelief. The sea breeze pressed her pale gown against her body; her loosened black hair swung around her, obscuring her face. But he knew his daughter.

"Hold your fire!" he bellowed.

"Should we rush the beach, sir?" Giles Crampton was utterly bewildered at what he was seeing. "Get Lady Olivia out of 'arm's way?"

"What the hell's she doing down there?" Rufus demanded.

"God only knows!" Cato hesitated for an instant. The two men had the dinghy in the shallows. Its sail was loosely bundled around the boom. It would take only a few moments to unfurl and hoist.

"Charge the beach!" he ordered. "But there's to be no firing while Olivia's there. She's not to be put at risk."

Anthony and Mike pushed the dinghy, desperate to get it into water deep enough for them to lower the centerboard and run up the sail.

"Lord love a duck," Mike muttered. "Whatever's Miss doin'?"

"Proving that she makes her own choices," Anthony said grimly. He shoved with his shoulder and the little dinghy was suddenly properly afloat. The cannon boomed again but he didn't waste time looking up to see if his ship had been hit. One shot would not sink *Wind Dancer*. But she needed her master at the wheel.

Now Olivia heard the sound of feet. Feet on the regular path from the clifftop, the one they hadn't taken coming down to the beach themselves. She ran towards the shore where Mike, up to his waist in water, was pushing the dinghy into the deeper channel, turning it into the wind, as Anthony, already aboard, unfurled the sail from the boom.

The thunder of feet behind her was suddenly so loud it filled her head. Yelling voices, the ominous click of muskets. She spun around, instinctively extending her arms as if to make herself a human shield while Anthony hauled on the sheets to raise the sail.

Silence fell. Olivia turned back to the dinghy. She could feel behind her the presence of the armed troop in a collective breath, a collective shift of feet on the sand.

Anthony seized the tiller. Olivia stood in the surf and slowly turned once again to face the beach, defying her father's men to rush the boat before she was under sail. She knew she had to wait for just the right moment, to make her move at the only possible moment when it would succeed. When the dinghy was free and under sail, but before she was out of reach.

Anthony stood holding the tiller, then he

swung it and the sail caught the wind. He was still standing, looking back at the mass of men on the beach. Their muskets were aimed but Olivia was in the way.

The marquis of Granville stood a few feet in front of his men.

"Olivia?" he said quietly, questioningly.

She looked at him, feeling where she couldn't see the dinghy moving away from the beach. She felt it as if her skin was being flayed inch by inch.

And she knew that she had no more time.

She held out her hands, palm up in a gesture of helplessness. "Forgive me," she said simply. "I have no time to explain, but it must be this way."

Then she turned and plunged into the lapping waves. The dinghy was reaching deeper water. "Anthony!" she yelled as the water reached her waist. "Anthony, damn you! Wait for me. You know I can't swim!"

Behind her now came Cato's men, surging through the surf. She was just ahead of them, floundering as the waves swelled against her body and her skirt caught in her legs, hampering her movements.

Anthony brought the boat head to wind. He reached over the stern and lifted her bodily out of the water. Olivia tumbled into the dinghy onto her knees. Anthony moved the tiller and the sail caught the wind again.

"Hold your fire!" Cato bellowed again as his men still plunged through the water in a last-ditch attempt to seize the dinghy.

Olivia had her hand at her throat. "Will they catch us?"

"No, we're over the shelf now. They'll have to swim, and we can sail faster than they can swim."

As if in confirmation the pursuit suddenly stopped. Men stood in the water at the point where the sandy bottom shelved steeply, and watched as their quarry sped from them.

Olivia stared at the scene on the beach. She could see her father standing where she had left him. What she had done was irrevocable. Phoebe and Portia would explain, but would he ever forgive her? Would she ever see him again?

Another boom from the cannon banished all but the present from her mind. "They're going to blow *Wind Dancer* out of the water!"

"They seem to be firing across her stern for the present," Anthony said calmly. "Once I get on board there'll be nothing to worry about."

Olivia looked and saw that the frigate now had her mainsail raised. She saw too that they'd dropped the rope ladder over the side, ready for their approach. She could hear on the still night air the strong rhythmic singing as the men turned the winch to haul up the anchor. There was a sense of purpose, but not of alarm. Both here in the dinghy and on *Wind Dancer*. There seemed little point worrying herself when no one else was.

The wind was much brisker as they approached the mouth of the cove. She shivered. "Why is it that I always get soaked when I'm with you?"

"For some reason I find you exceptionally appealing when you're wet," Anthony said solemnly. "It must play to my mermaid fantasies."

"Mermaid fantasies!" Olivia exclaimed. "You never said anything about them before."

"Perhaps because I've only just realized I have them," he responded with a grin. "That dress is clinging to you in the most seductive fashion."

Olivia glanced down at herself. The pale muslin seemed to have become transparent. "How can I go on board looking like this? It's as if I'm wearing nothing at all." She became abruptly conscious of Mike's presence. His ears were rather red and he looked as if he wished he were anywhere but within earshot of this conversation.

Anthony merely laughed and unbuttoned his shirt with one hand, shrugging out of it, exchanging hands on the tiller as he did so. "Here, this'll make you decent until you can change into one of my nightshirts. You know where I keep them."

Olivia slipped on the shirt. It was warmed from his skin and carried his own special fragrance of salt and sea. She sat in the bow as they came alongside *Wind Dancer* and Anthony dropped the single sail. He secured the dinghy and steadied the rope ladder for Olivia.

She scrambled up and willing hands helped her over the side. No one seemed surprised to see her, and she assumed that they had been watching events on the beach through the spyglass.

"We gettin' out of 'ere, master?" Jethro stood at the wheel.

"Yes, it's getting a little too hot for comfort." Anthony jumped the steps to the quarterdeck. Jethro stepped aside and Anthony took the wheel. "Go below, Olivia, and change out of those wet clothes," he called.

"I can do that later." She came up beside him. "What are you going to do? If they dismast you..."

"They won't. Fortunately cannon have a poor aim if they're not right up against you." He looked down at her and his eyes were sparkling with exhilaration. This was an adventure worthy of a pirate.

There was a loud report, a whine as a cannonball crossed the ship, missing the rigging by a hair. It splashed into the sea just beyond the bow. Anthony laughed and turned the wheel. "A little too close, that one. They seem to be getting serious. Hoist the topsail."

Men swarmed up the rigging just as another ball crashed into the sea from the other headland. If Anthony hadn't adjusted the wheel when he did, it would have smashed into the ship's side.

"That would have been on target," Olivia observed, astonished at her own objectivity.

"True.... Wear ship," Anthony called without any indication of haste or dismay. The frigate turned onto the starboard tack and seemed to Olivia's astounded eyes to be on a direct path to the right-hand cliff. It took them well clear of the range of the cannon on the left headland, but it seemed to be taking them directly into the line of fire of the other one.

"What are you doing?"

"Coming in under the gun," he told her, his voice exultant, his deep-set eyes afire. "You see, they can't hit us if we're beneath them any more than they can if we're out of range. We'll sail against the cliff, under the headland, below the one and out of range of the other."

"But the rocks! Won't you run aground?" Even as she asked the question, she knew it was absurd. Anthony wouldn't run aground in these waters with his eyes shut.

"Not if I pick my way," he responded.

Olivia fell silent. Anthony was whistling softly between his teeth as he sailed his ship almost into the cliff and brought her about the instant Olivia was certain they would drive into the cliff face. Above them, the cannon boomed, balls falling harmlessly across their bows, sending up fountains of spume.

Hugging the cliff, *Wind Dancer* rounded the headland, and open sea lay glinting silver before them. The crew cheered and threw their caps in the air as the cannons acknowledged defeat and fell silent.

Olivia looked back at the island as the ship picked up speed in the freshening wind.

She glanced up at her pirate, who was still whistling to himself, his eyes on the big sail.

Sensing her glance, he looked down at her. "No regrets?"

"No," she said definitely. "Have you?"

He shook his head and smiled his wonderful smile, and Olivia knew that she had seized her only chance of happiness. She would never love like this again. Only one man could bring her such deep, deep joy. To throw away the promise of such happiness would be to spit in the face of the gods.

"Go below," he said softly. "Get dry. I will come to you when we're clear of the island."

Olivia looked again across the water to the receding hump of the Isle of Wight. "Will we come back?"

"You will need to make peace with your father."

"Yes," she said, and went below.

"So, you decided to run away to sea?" He gazed down into her face, holding himself above her as dawn fingered the sky and a soft ray of pink light fell through the open window across the bed.

"So it would seem," she agreed, caressing the hard, taut cheeks of his buttocks. "We shall go adventuring and never be ordinary."

"Of course not," he agreed gravely. He withdrew to the very edge of her body, and her dark eyes took on a luminous glow.

"Not at all ordinary," she repeated.

"Not in the slightest degree." He eased

himself into her again, delicately, fraction by fraction.

She bit her lower lip on a little exhalation of delight. Her finger probed wickedly and he threw his head back with a moan. "How did you learn to do that?"

"Instinct," she said with a chuckle. "I'm a pirate's doxy now. I know such tricks." She was fighting to hold herself back from a climax that would bring to an end this wonderful loving.

Anthony watched her face, searching her eyes. When he saw she was about to give up the fight, he withdrew again, waiting for her urgency to subside a little before sinking himself within her again.

"I don't want this ever to stop," she said, stroking his inner thighs, loving the stretched power of his muscles against her hand.

"This is but the beginning, my love," he whispered, bending to take her mouth with his own. She tasted his sweetness as his tongue moved within her mouth and he moved within her body, hard and fast now until she thought she would explode. And yet still she hung on the edge in ever astounding bliss, meeting and matching his thrusts with her own, her tongue engaged with his in a savage dance of delight.

Her fingers raked his back, bit deep into his buttocks, pulling him against her as if she could make them one. And then the world flew apart and she clung to him like a drowning woman to a spar as the torrent took her, tossed her and tumbled her, and she cried out his name with wild abandon.

The sun rose out of the sea, flooding the sky with orange. He gathered her to him as he fell to the bed, smoothing her damp hair from her cheek. "How is it possible to love so much?" he whispered. "It terrifies me. I couldn't bear to lose you."

"You won't," she returned, turning her lips into the hollow of his throat where the pulse beat fast against his sweat-slick skin. "We are meant for each other. We will live and die together, my love."

He took her head in both hands and kissed the corners of her mouth, the tip of her nose, the tip of her chin.

"But we won't marry," Olivia declared, her tongue darting to lick the tip of his nose in turn. "Wives don't make good pirates."

"I'm not the marrying kind myself," Anthony said lazily. "I'd rather have a doxy any day."

Twenty-two

THE EARLY SEPTEMBER AIR was soft as *Wind Dancer* slipped into her chine and the cliff face seemed to close around her. The deep channel at the end of the chine awaited her, quiet

438

and undisturbed in the two months of the ship's absence.

Olivia stood on the deck, watching the cliff walls slide past, thinking of the first time she had been aboard the ship, when *Wind Dancer* had returned to her safe anchorage so that her passenger could be escorted back to the real world, to the life she knew and understood.

She looked up at the quarterdeck where Anthony was bringing his ship home. He handed the wheel to Jethro and came down to her. He stood at the rail beside her, an arm resting lightly over her shoulders.

"Are you ready?"

"Yes." She reached up to touch his face.

The rattle of the anchor chain disturbed the evening quiet, and *Wind Dancer* came to rest. The small boat was lowered and Olivia hopped over the side with all the agility of newfound experience.

Anthony jumped down beside her and took up the oars. He pulled strongly out of the chine and then hoisted the single sail. They sailed along the coast in a silence that reflected their mood. They were both tense and anxious.

"Maybe they've already left the island," Olivia said as the little boat entered the small cove just below the village of Chale. She bit off a loose fingernail, deep frown lines forming between her brows. Anything could have happened in two months.

Anthony reached over and gently moved her hand from her mouth. "The king is still here. Your father will be too."

"I suppose so."

The boat came to rest in the shallows, and Anthony jumped over the side. "It's only a short walk into the village from the cliff. You go left along the lane," he said as he pulled the boat up onto the sand.

"I know. I've done it before," she reminded him, hearing his anxiety in the unnecessary directions. She took his outstretched hand and jumped barefoot to the beach, holding her shoes in her other hand.

She sat on a rock to put on her shoes. "You'll wait here for me?"

Anthony looked down at her, rubbing his mouth with his fingertips. "I'll forgive such a stupid question...but just this once, mind."

She smiled, a smile as taut as his. She stood up. "It's just that I don't know how long I'll be."

"I'll wait for as long as it takes." He caught her chin, tilting her face for his kiss. "Now go and do what you have to do. And then come back to me."

"Always," she whispered, then turned, gathering her skirts into her hand as she ran across the beach and up the path to the clifftop.

Anthony tried to master his anxiety. He knew it was unfounded. Olivia had made her choice. She would come back to him, when she had made her peace. Of course she would. He took a writing case from the dinghy and sat down on a rock. He took up a lead pencil and began to draw. He drew what filled his mind. *Olivia*.

Olivia skirted the orchard and slipped through the gate into the kitchen garden. There were a few lamps still lit in the house, and as she made her way around the house, keeping to the shadows, she saw with a little jolt of mingled apprehension and relief that Lord Granville's study window was illuminated. He was at home and she would not have to go to the front door, be exclaimed over by the Bissets. She didn't want to talk to anyone, even Phoebe, before she had had her accounting with her father.

She crept up to the long window to Cato's study, treading softly across the gravel path, and looked in. Her father was sitting at his desk working on a stack of papers.

Olivia's heart beat fast. She hesitated. It would be so much easier to see Phoebe first, have her smooth the path. But she despised the thought and put it from her. This was something that lay between herself and her father. She raised her hand and knocked on the window.

Cato looked up. He stared at the window and then jumped to his feet. He flung open the window and leaned on the sill, looking down at her in patent disbelief. "Olivia?"

"Yes," she said simply. "May I come in?" When he didn't respond, she jumped sideways onto the low sill and swung her legs into the room. He stepped aside as she jumped down.

"Have you come home?" His voice was quiet, his eyes grave, but they were taking in everything about her. The glow of her skin, the luminous light in her eye, the confident grace of someone who has found herself and her place in the world.

"No, I c-cannot."

"Then why are you here?"

Olivia heard the uncompromising note. "I c-came to explain, to ask your forgiveness."

"I don't want your explanations, I had sufficient from Phoebe," Cato said in the same icy tone. "Of course you have my forgiveness. You are my daughter and always will be."

"I love you." She held out her sun-browned hand in a gesture of appeal, desperate now to break through this cold exterior. She had expected anger, hurt, maybe even a threat to prevent her returning to the life she had chosen, but this quiet, frigid response to her appeal was much worse than anything she had imagined.

Cato did not take her hand. He looked at her in silence. In the two months of her disappearance, he had been so angry, so confused, so crazed with worry for her that to see her standing here, so obviously well, so clearly happy, was like an unbearable insult.

"You don't forgive me," she stated, her hand falling to her side. "I had wanted your blessing."

"You wanted *what*?" His anger broke free of its reins. "You run off with a damned pirate. The bastard son of an ideological fool who—"

"How do you know about that?" Olivia interrupted.

"Do you think I couldn't find out?" he said

furiously. "You think you can run off without a word of explanation, betray my cause to the enemy, ensure the escape of an illegitimate ruffian who should by rights be hanging from a gibbet, and I'm just going to shrug and accept it?"

"You don't know him," she said in a low voice. "You have no right to speak of him in those terms. I love him. I can only be happy with him. I felt I owed you an explanation. But now I don't think I did." She turned from him with a tiny resigned shrug that conveyed the depths of her bitterness and disappointment, and went back to the still-open window.

"*Olivia!*" It was a cry of anguish.

She spun around. Tears stood out in his eyes. He held out his arms to her.

She ran into his embrace, her own tears flowing fast and free now. Cato held her close, stroking her hair. "I have been out of my mind with worry," he said. "What kind of life can you lead with such a man?"

"The life I want." She raised her tear-drenched eyes to his face. "It is the life that suits me. We read together, play chess together, laugh...oh, laugh so much together. And love so much. He makes me whole. Without him I am not whole."

He sighed, stroking her cheek. "Must I accept this, my daughter?"

"If you would make me truly happy."

"Then I suppose I must." He sighed again. "Your mother was such a docile, respectable woman. How did she produce *you*, I wonder?"

Olivia smiled hesitantly. "I never knew her. But maybe it comes from your side of the family. Think of Portia. Her father was your brother."

"That had not occurred to me." He shook his head. "Portia and Phoebe sprung their surprises: I should have been ready for you."

"*I* wasn't ready for it," Olivia said. "It c-came out of the blue."

Cato understood all too well love's inconvenient manner of arrival. "There are things I should discuss with your...your..."

"My pirate," she supplied. "Anthony's not interested in dowries and things, sir."

"Then he's to be commended," Cato said dryly. "It's a rare man who doesn't consider such things."

"He *is* a rare man, and he's well able to provide for me."

"From his ill-gotten gains, I suppose." The note of exasperation returned to his voice. "For God's sake, Olivia, there must be some way he could be persuaded to live a decent, law-abiding life."

"He's not like other people," she said softly. "If he were, I wouldn't love him. And if I tried to change him, he wouldn't be able to love me."

Cato exhaled in frustration. He stood in frowning silence for a moment, still holding her, then said, "I will not have my daughter dependent on any man's whims or the vicissitudes of his fortune. I will set up a trust for you."

"It isn't necessary, but I thank you for it," she said.

"The king is to be returned soon to London. I will give you an address in the city where you can send me news."

He moved his arms from her and turned back to the table. "I will require frequent news," he said, writing rapidly on a sheet of parchment.

"I will write whenever I can."

"And when your pirate can spare you for a few days...?" He raised an eyebrow as he sanded the sheet.

"It's a very uncertain life, piracy," she said, taking the paper from him.

"Yes, so I can imagine." He sighed again. "Is there really no way you could...?"

"No," she said simply.

"And you're not going to regularize this union?" He glanced pointedly at her ringless hand.

Olivia shook her head.

"Dear God!" he muttered. "Well, at least you'll have your own money if worst comes to worst."

"It won't," she said firmly. "You must have faith in Anthony. As I do."

"I am not in love with him," he pointed out aridly. "And you are my daughter."

Olivia had no answer and after a second he said, "Go to Phoebe now. And don't leave us anxious for news." He drew her towards him and kissed her brow. "What about your books? Where should they be sent?"

Olivia's eyes glowed. "May I truly have them?"

"Dear girl, they're yours. No one else in this household is going to find a use for Plato and Livy and Ovid and all the rest of 'em."

"Then I'll ask Mike to c-come tomorrow morning with the cart to collect them." She reached up to kiss his cheek. "I love you."

"I love you too. You have chosen this man. Love him well and be happy."

The tears in her eyes mirrored his as she held his hand, then he released his hold and turned away, dashing a hand across his eyes. Weeping without restraint, Olivia went to find Phoebe.

Why were there always choices to be made when it came to happiness? Why couldn't one have all the people one loved close by? she thought sadly, opening the parlor door.

Phoebe's cry of delight was loud enough to wake the dead.

An hour later Olivia tiptoed over the sand to where Anthony sat sketching on his rock, his back to the cliff. He was completely absorbed and around him sheets of discarded paper fluttered gently under the sea breeze. He must have been drawing ever since she had left.

She stopped on the sand and gazed at him, delighting in him, feeling almost as if she was stealing something from him by watching him when he was so unaware of her presence. Would the intensity of this love ever diminish? Sometimes it was so piercing it was as close to pain as joy.

"Come closer," he said softly without turning or raising his head. "I want to look at something."

"How did you know I was here?"

"I always know when you're near." He looked up now as she reached him. "You've been crying."

"Yes, a lot."

"Kneel down." He gestured to the sand at his feet.

Olivia knelt and he reached forward and touched the hollow of her throat.

"This is what's been eluding me. This little pointy bit of your collarbone."

He went back to his drawing and she picked up the scattered papers. The sketches that covered them were all of her. Of her face caught in a dozen different expressions. She stayed kneeling in front of him, waiting for him to be finished.

"Are you very unhappy?" he asked.

"A little sad, but also happy. He understands. He doesn't like it, but he accepts it. Did you want a dowry?"

"Doxies don't come with dowries."

"No, I suppose they don't." She leaned forward, resting her forearms on his knee. "Kiss me."

"All in good time."

Olivia smiled and leaned in to brush the tip of her tongue over his mouth. "I am not in the mood to play second fiddle to a mere image of me." She began to kiss his face, dry little baby kisses on his eyebrows, his eyelids, his cheeks, his chin.

Pen and paper fell to the sand as he drew her between his knees. "Now you belong only to me," he stated with a soft finality that sent a shiver down her spine. "Body and soul, only to me."

"As you belong to me," she responded, drawing her head back to look deep into his eyes. "We are in thrall, you and I. Each to the other."

The incoming tide sent wavelets creeping up the beach, but they were oblivious of all but the connection that bound them, the certainty of their union, sealed within their own circle of entrancement.

Epilogue

LONDON, JANUARY 30, 1649

"CHARLES STUART, for levying war against the present Parliament and people therein represented, shall be put to death by beheading, as a tyrant, traitor, murderer, and public enemy of the good people of this land."

From the steps of the scaffold erected before the banqueting-house at the palace of Whitehall, the herald's voice rang out across the heads of the crowd. Thousands upon thousands gathered before Whitehall Gate to witness this judicial punishment of a sovereign.

The king mounted the scaffold. A dreadful expectant silence fell over the huge mass of people. Some stood on tiptoe to see over the serried ranks of soldiers surrounding the scaffold.

The king was bareheaded, his hair tied at his nape. He handed his coat to an attendant and himself removed his cravat and loosened his shirt collar. He turned to address the crowd but his voice could not carry across the deep ranks of soldiers.

In the front of the crowd, Anthony stood with his arm around Ellen Leyland. When the king knelt before the block, she turned her head into his shoulder, her body shaken with sobs.

Olivia put a hand on Ellen's arm, offering her own silent comfort, but she could not take her eyes away from the scaffold. She watched, numbed, as the executioner raised his axe. The hush was profound. Thousands of people stood immobile, barely breathing.

The axe fell.

At the same moment, a great groan went up from the crowd, a collective moan of horror and grief.

Olivia saw her father and Rufus, standing motionless and bareheaded at the foot of the scaffold. Their names had not been among the fifty-nine signatures on the king's death warrant. But they stood there now, stony-faced, Parliamentary witnesses to the death of Charles Stuart.

"Is it over?" Ellen whispered, unable to raise her eyes.

"Aye, 'tis over," Anthony said softly. He followed Olivia's gaze to where Lords Granville and Rothbury stood grim and immobile. He put his free arm around Olivia.

She leaned into him for a moment. So at last it was over. What had begun on a summer's day eight years earlier had come full circle. Eight years of war. Eight years of bloodshed. What had begun with an execution had ended with one. She could still hear in her head the persistent raucous screams of the mob on that May afternoon in 1641 as the earl of Strafford lost his head on Tower Hill. There were no such triumphant cries today, only this somber grief-filled silence.

And what of the future?

She looked up at Anthony. Whatever happened in England now, her future and his were bound together with the indissoluble chains of love. Portia and Rufus, Cato and Phoebe, herself and Anthony. Love bound them all, and only love would direct the future.